Everyone Loves The Smoky Mountain Series

"Lin Stepp creates a heart-warming tale of love and redemption, family and faith. ... Readers will fall in love with not only her charming characters but the picturesque setting ... The Smoky Mountain series is sure to garner fans across genre offering a plot filled with romance and suspense, set amidst the backdrop of the breathtaking Smoky Mountains."

- Christy Tillery French, MIDWEST REVIEW

"Well, I've finally come across someone that believes in all the things that I do ... love, family, faith, intrigue, mystery, loyalty, romance, and a great love for our beloved Smoky Mountains. Dr. Lin Stepp, I salute you."

- Dolly Parton, award-winning country music entertainer

"Dr. Lin Stepp ... has reason to smile these days with ... acceptance for publication of her planned 12-book Smoky Mountain series ... a glowing review from Dolly Parton ... and positive comments about the first book in the series."

- THE GREENEVILLE SUN Newspaper

"Lin Stepp paints a charming portrait of the Smokies, their people, and a wonderful way of life. *The Foster Girls* will make readers eager for more of Lin Stepp's endearing stories. A richly satisfying novel of love, family and friendship."

- Deborah Smith, New York Times best-selling author

"The settings for all 12 of Dr. Lin Stepp's books are tucked away against the backdrop of the Great Smoky Mountains National Park ... modern day romance books ... based in the hollows, hills and ridges ... with plenty of suspense and conflict."

-Melanie Tucker, THE MARYVILLE DAILY TIMES

"Lin Stepp's story packs intriguing surprises. The back cover condenses the plot into a line or two, which does no justice to Stepp's lovingly crafted descriptions, strongly lined characters, and well-paced action."

- Schuyler Kaufman, CAROLINA MC

<u>Also by Lin Stepp</u>
THE FOSTER GIRLS

Tell Me About Orchard Hollow

Second Novel in the
Smoky Mountain Series

LIN STEPP

Canterbury House Publishing

www.canterburyhousepublishing.com
Vilas, North Carolina

Canterbury House Publishing

225 Ira Harmon Road
Vilas, NC 28692
www.canterburyhousepublishing.com

AUTHOR'S NOTE:
This is a work of fiction. Although there are numerous elements of historical and geographic accuracy in this and other novels in the Smoky Mountain series, specific environs, place names and incidents are entirely the product of the author's imagination. In addition, all characters are fictitious and any resemblance to actual persons, living or dead, is entirely coincidental.

Book design by Tracy Arendt

Library of Congress Cataloging-in-Publication Data

Stepp, Lin.
  Tell Me About Orchard Hollow / by Lin Stepp.
     p. cm. -- (The Smoky Mountain series ; bk. 2)
  ISBN 978-0-9825396-1-3
  1.   Young women--Fiction. 2.   Life change events--Fiction. 3. Mountain life--Great Smoky Mountains Region (N.C. and Tenn.)--Fiction. 4. Great Smoky Mountains Region (N.C. and Tenn.)--Fiction. I. Title.
  PS3619.T47695T45 2010
  813'.6--dc22

                                        2009049447

February 2010

Dedication & Acknowledgements

This book is dedicated to my daughter, Katherine, my ever-enthusiastic champion – who encourages and cheers me, maintains my website, and eagerly reads and helps copyedit every book I write. Thanks, Kate.

THANKS also goes to ….

My husband, and on-going, tireless business manager and friend, J.L. – who shares my writing journey.

My wonderful publishing team – who believe in me and support me in all I do …

Wendy Dingwall – President and Publisher of Canterbury House Publishing, Ltd.

Carolyn Sakowski – President and CEO of Distributor, John F. Blair Publishing, Inc.

And my fine editor, Sandy Horton.

Cover Art

The beautiful work of art, featured on the front cover of this book, was painted by the well-known regional artist Jim Gray. It is entitled *Mountain Memories.*

Jim Gray is a nationally recognized artist who has been painting Smoky Mountain scenes and southern landscapes for over thirty years. In 1966, Gray and his family moved to East Tennessee so that Jim could explore and paint the beauty of the countryside surrounding the Smoky Mountains. Today, Jim Gray has three galleries in East Tennessee and one in Alabama. He has sold over 2000 paintings and 125,000 prints to collectors in the United States and abroad. Jim is listed in Who's Who in American Art and has been featured in many publications, including National Geographic and Southern Living.

Prints of *Mountain Memories,* or other fine works of art, can be purchased in Jim Gray galleries or ordered through Jim Gray's website at: http://www.jimgraygallery.com

Jim Gray's business address is:

GREENBRIAR INCORPORATED
P. O. Box 735, Gatlinburg, TN 37738
Business Phone: (865) 573-0579

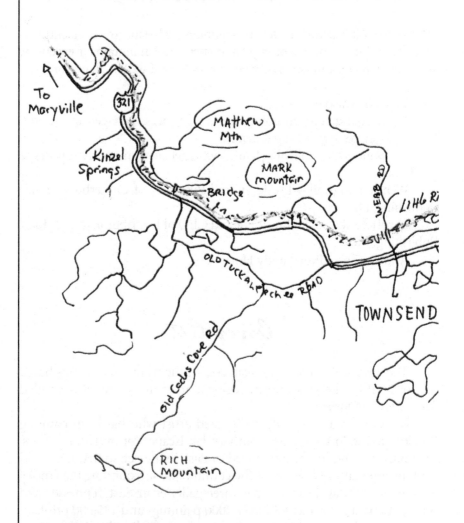

Map for Townsend area in
TELL ME ABOUT
ORCHARD HOLLOW

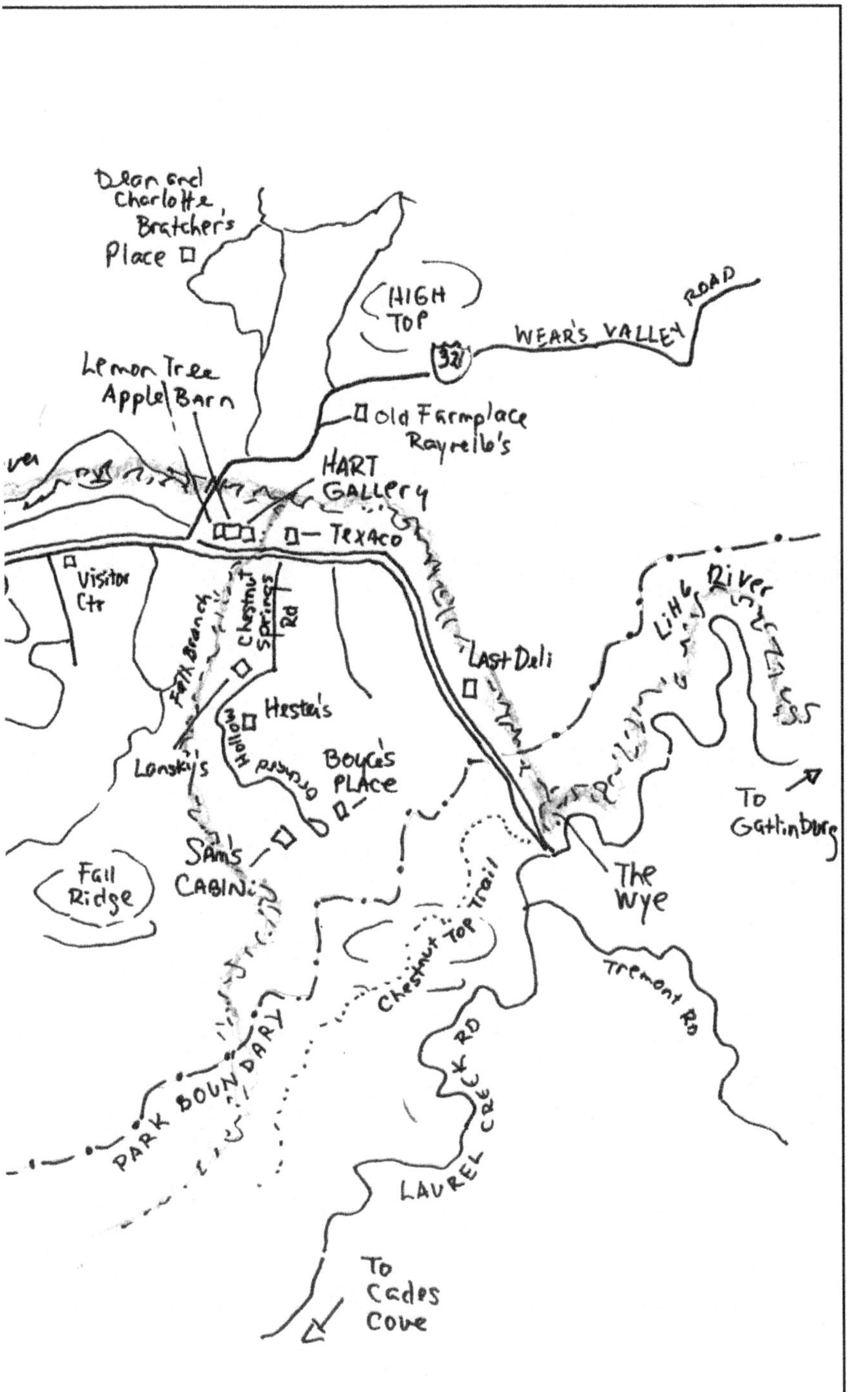
Dean and Charlotte Bratcher's Place
HIGH TOP
321
WEAR'S VALLEY ROAD
Lemon Tree
Apple Barn
Old Farmplace
HART GALLERY
Texaco
Visitor Ctr
Fall Branch
Chestnut Springs Rd
Last Deli
Little River
Hester's
Hollow
Orchard
Boyce's PLACE
Lansky's
Sam's CABIN
Fall Ridge
Chestnut Top Trail
The Wye
To Gatlinburg
Tremont Rd
LAUREL CREEK RD
PARK BOUNDARY
To Cades Cove

Chapter 1

Out of the corner of her eye, Jenna saw daffodils in a shop window. Daffodils through a haze of misting snow. Enchanted, she stopped abruptly to stare – a big mistake at lunch hour on Park Avenue, one of New York's busiest downtown streets. Two men, heads bent against the wind and focused intently on their own thoughts, nearly plowed into her.

"Sorry," she muttered to their mumbled cursing as they pushed past.

Jenna worked her way closer to the florist window, angling between the crush of people – all hurrying to get to lunch or rushing to get back to the office.

"Always hurrying," Jenna said softly to herself. "And look what they're missing."

She stopped in front of the small florist to gaze at the display with delight. Pots of dazzling yellow daffodils filled the window around a colorful display of bright gardening pots and watering cans.

Jenna sighed with pleasure, taking in the happy sight. Here in late March, daffodils were only an alluring dream in New York. The temperature, even at noon today, was only in the thirties and a bitter wind roared like an angry demon down the tunnel between Manhattan's tall buildings.

A young executive paused as he pushed open the door of the florist, sizing Jenna up from head to toe. He raised an eyebrow and gave her a nod of approval before buttoning his coat against the wind.

"Pretty woman," he said as he merged into the crowd.

Jenna looked at herself thoughtfully in the florist window. "Am I pretty?" She bit her lip as she studied her reflection. Dark brown eyes in a soft oval face looked back at her. Her sleek, dark hair was pulled back neatly in a French braid and tucked into the collar of her new tan coat.

She frowned at the coat. She had wanted the red coat – a gorgeous claret red one with a swirling skirt - but Elliott insisted she get the tan.

"It's much more sophisticated." He gave her that look across his glasses which let her know the matter was settled.

Jenna straightened her shoulders and offered a carefully practiced smile to the girl in the window as she remembered the scene.

She could still see Elliott dismissing the red coat with a quick flick of his hand. "You're Mrs. Elliott Howell, Jenna. Always keep that in mind. Image is important."

The floral assistant came to nod at Jenna through the window.

A quick flush rose up her neck. She'd stood there too long and drawn attention to herself. Elliott would hate that.

Jenna looked around with a sense of dread, almost expecting to see him. So little she did pleased him these days.

Offering a small smile to the florist, Jenna turned away to head back into the street, resisting the urge to order a pot of daffodils sent to her apartment.

"You need to grow up and stop all these childish impulses," her mother told her last week when she'd given her scarf to a street woman on a cold day. "Elliott tells your father and me that you indulge entirely too much in romantic dreaming."

Jenna blew out a quiet breath. She often felt like a patchwork quilt of what everyone else thought she should be and not a real person at all.

Picking up her pace to better match that of the noon crowd hurrying down the street, Jenna looked for the restaurant where she was meeting her best friend Carla for a birthday celebration.

Spotting the red awnings of DaVinci's ahead on the corner, Jenna gratefully slipped into the Italian restaurant and out of the cold. Carla waved to her from a table by the front window.

"Happy twenty-second birthday!" Carla got up and wrapped Jenna in a warm hug. Her flyaway red curls stood out in their usual disarray and her blue eyes twinkled with fun.

Jenna smiled at Carla with affection. Their friendship threaded from early private school days through four years of college and after. Both were tall young women, but there, all resemblance stopped. In contrast to Jenna's dark looks, Carla was light and fair, her eyes a brilliant blue, and her hair a tumble of strawberry blond waves.

Carla scooted into the booth with an enthusiastic flounce. "I'm so glad you picked DaVinci's for our birthday place. I haven't been here to eat since the restaurant opened three months ago, and I hear the food is fabulous."

"Well, it's wonderful John could cover at the bookstore so we could have our annual birthday lunch." Jenna removed her coat, shaking off the snow before hanging it up, and then settled into the seat across from Carla.

"Oh, well, that was no problem." Carla waved a hand dismissively. "John has a lover's view."

She grinned at Jenna. "He's still besotted with me even after a year of marriage."

Even while Jenna laughed and agreed, she envied it. John and Carla enjoyed an easy and fun loving relationship – their mutual affection obvious. Jenna loved watching the way John looked at Carla, the way he found ways to lean against her, to touch her hair, to make contact with her. And the look Carla always gave back to him.

"You know, I still remember the day you two met, Carla. John had just come home to manage the family bookstore after college. We went in Tate's to shop and some chemistry clicked immediately between the two of you from the minute you walked in the door. I saw it happen – and it's one of my favorite memories."

"Mine, too." Carla smiled as she handed Jenna one of the menus the waiter left.

Jenna sighed while she studied the options. She knew Elliott felt uncomfortable around John and Carla's relationship. Her own marriage with Elliott had always been formal.

"It's not natural for a man and woman to get along that well in a work relationship," Elliott said once, frowning. "I think a marital relationship should be practical and traditional. I'm glad we both know our place in our marriage."

Still, Jenna secretly wished her marriage was more like Carla and John's, light and fun. She sighed inwardly. She hated herself sometimes for feeling dissatisfied with her marriage. Her courtship with Elliott had been sweet but after they married, she saw less and less of him. Elliott worked so hard and many nights his ad projects continued late into the night. It was that way in the advertising field, especially in New York, Elliott told her.

Checking her thoughts, Jenna eyed the gift bag sitting on the table. "Can I open your present, Carla?"

Carla put down her menu and pulled the gift bag back playfully. "Not until dessert. I'm keeping you in suspense."

They giggled, stifling their laughter as the waiter arrived with beverages Carla had ordered earlier.

Stirring cream into her coffee, Carla looked across at Jenna. "What is

Elliott giving you for your birthday?"

Jenna bit her lip. "I hope a trip to Paris with him. I've hinted often enough. On Sunday, he's leaving for six weeks to help set up the new Abercrombie branch there."

Carla pushed a flyaway clump of curls behind her ear. "Well, he should take you. With the company paying for the accommodations, it wouldn't cost much more for you to go." She sipped her hot coffee tentatively. "Besides, we all know Elliott makes more than enough money to take you with him."

Jenna chewed on her lip considering this. "I have a little of my own money saved up, too, from the greeting card work I do for Park Press."

"So quit hinting and just tell him you want to go," insisted Carla in her usual direct way.

"Well, Elliott and I are having dinner out tonight for my birthday. He's taking me to Davenport's on the harbor." She hesitated. "Maybe he'll tell me about it then. He said he had a special surprise for me for my birthday."

"Good." Carla's voice sounded pleased. "Elliott owes you. He is gone so much with his work. He neglects you, Jen. You spend too much time on your own. Anyway, I hope he gets home tonight to take you out for this special dinner you're looking forward to."

"He promised he would." Jenna's voice tightened. "We're going to spend the whole evening together."

Carla nodded absently, her eyes now on her menu.

Jenna's mind drifted ahead. She would pick something tasteful and elegant to wear tonight and make a special effort to look calm, serene, and sophisticated for Elliott. That's what he liked. Maybe they would have a real chance to just sit and talk, too.

Realizing she was daydreaming, Jenna scanned the bill of fare quickly, deciding what she wanted to order. Then she reached for her purse. "Carla, I need to use the restroom. If the waiter comes before I get back, tell him I want the cannelloni." She pointed at the menu item as she scooted out of the booth.

Jenna threaded her way to the back of the crowded restaurant. Coming out of the ladies room, she found the main aisle blocked by a dessert cart. Starting up a side aisle in detour, her eyes widened in astonishment as she saw a man slip his hand right up the inside of a woman's skirt in the corner booth. The woman's eyes were half shut, her lips parted –her expression almost orgasmic.

"Good heavens, I'll have to tell Carla about this one." The amusement on Jenna's face vanished as she looked more closely. She recognized the brown hair, squared shoulders, and the Harvard ring on the hand that reached out to draw the woman's face toward his. It was Elliott Howell, her own husband. He leaned across the booth now to French-kiss the woman, his tongue soon half-way down her throat.

Stunned, Jenna froze in place, feeling sick. The woman was a plush, svelte blond with a dress cut down to China in the front. Jenna didn't know her, but Elliott obviously did. His hand drifted caressingly across the top of her breasts now while he tongued her. He didn't even see Jenna standing near by.

Jenna backed out of the aisle, and pushed her way around the waiter's dessert cart to return to her seat the way she'd come before. Her legs felt like rubber.

"You're as white as a sheet." Carla's eyes widened as Jenna sat down at their table again. "What's wrong?'

Jenna didn't know what to say, so she just stared at Carla.

"Jenna, what is it?" Carla leaned forward, alarm spreading over her face.

"Go and see," Jenna finally got out. "The back booth right beside the bathroom. Go and see, but don't do anything, Carla. Just go and see and come right back."

When she returned, Jenna knew from her expression that Carla had seen all too much.

"Did he see you?" Jenna bit on her lip.

"No, he was too busy," Carla answered flatly.

They both sat in shocked silence for a minute. Carla reached across the table and gripped Jenna's hand.

"What do you want to do, Jen?"

Tears welled up in Jenna's eyes. "I want to leave, Carla. I can't stay. Oh, please, Carla, I can't stay." She felt the tears begin to trickle down her face despite her efforts to hold them back.

"Come on, we'll go to my place." Carla dropped a bill on the table and grabbed Jenna's hand along with the gift bag. She pulled Jenna out the front door and flagged down the first cab she found.

As soon as they got back to Carla's apartment, Jenna collapsed in wrenching sobs. She felt like a part of her was dying inside – and the scenes of Elliott with that woman flashed in and out of her mind like a garish neon sign. Carla provided a shoulder and cried along with her some of the time. Finally, hiccupping and heaving, Jenna stopped.

"Oh, Carla," she managed to say. "I've spoiled the birthday party. I'm so sorry."

"You spoiled nothing, silly. How can you even think about that in the midst of this mess," she raged, her face flushed with anger. "It's that jerk, Elliott, who spoiled things. I can't believe he would cheat on a wonderful, selfless person like you. I just hate him for it. I wish I'd gone and thrown something on his head or hit him now. But I was in such a shock. I just couldn't think."

"Oh, Carla." Jenna shivered. "What am I going to do?" She pulled a sofa cushion into her arms, hoping it would offer her some warmth and comfort.

"Well, Jenna, you're going to step out of your dream world and realize all those rumors about Elliott fooling around are true." Carla put her hands on her hips in anger. "I'm sorry, Jen, I should have told you a long time ago and maybe this wouldn't have happened. Maybe you wouldn't have been hurt so badly, wouldn't have had to see this. But it was all rumors, Jen. John and I didn't know if they were true or not. I mean, we heard things, but we never saw Elliott being intimate with anyone or saw him out with anyone else. Besides, we didn't know if you would believe us, anyway. You've never been able to see anything but good in Elliott. We just didn't know the right thing to do."

Stunned at the thought, Jenna could only stare. "You mean people talk about Elliott being with other women. That this might not be the first time."

"Yes, Jenna. As bad as it is, you have the right to know the truth now. It's bloody likely that all the other rumors are true. My God, I could kill him. I could just kill him. What an insufferable creep."

Carla paced around the room now, punching a throw pillow she carried. "I wish this was that jerk's head. I really do. And to think I've tried to be nice to him all this time just for you. I wish now I'd told him what I thought of him."

"You don't like Elliott?" Jenna asked, one incredible revelation following another.

She scowled. "No, Jenna, I don't, and neither does John – or anyone else who really loves you. But John and I bit our tongues and smiled through our teeth a zillion times when Elliott was a pompous ass so we wouldn't hurt your feelings. And now look what Elliott's done. I mean the man just has no limits on the asshole scale."

Carla gave Jenna a pitying look. "Oh, Jenna, I guess I didn't want to believe the worst myself. But still it's a shocker. I am so sorry."

"Yes. So am I." She sucked in a shaky breath, her head reeling now.

Somehow, Jenna got through the afternoon with Carla and found her way back home. Carla wanted to come with her, but Jenna insisted she would be all right. She needed to be alone. It didn't surprise her to find a message on the answering machine from Elliott.

"I have to work late again, Jenna. Sorry, but you know how it is. We'll have to postpone our dinner until tomorrow night." He paused, adding an afterthought. "Don't wait up; I'll be late."

"Working late." She shook her head, her eyes moving to look at herself in the mirror over the desk. "All this time, I thought he was always working late. How could I have been so stupid? It's not as though I don't read novels and see films where couples cheat. How could I have been so truly naïve?"

She sat down numbly at the desk, still babbling to her own reflection in the mirror. "I thought Elliott was going to take me to Paris for my birthday. He's going to Paris, you know. He's been talking about it, how beautiful Paris is in the spring and that he hoped I could see it one day. I thought he was laying out little hints. I'll bet he's not taking me at all."

Jenna cried some more just thinking about it, then impulsively went back to the bedroom to search through the clothes and bags Elliott had already started to lay out for his trip. In an inside pocket of his travel bag she found two airline tickets. One had Elliott's name on it. The other did not say Jenna Howell; it read Lena Morrow.

Jenna sat down on the bed and stared at the tickets, more tears trickling down her cheeks. "I thought that blond looked vaguely familiar." She wiped her face with her arm. "She was Lena Morrow, Elliott's new secretary."

It seemed like Elliott employed a new one every few months - always young and beautiful. Jenna even commented about it once.

Elliott waved the matter aside. "It's important for the company image that a front desk secretary be both competent and attractive, Jenna. Surely you can understand that."

A lump filled her throat. "Well, I certainly do now."

After indulging in another sweep of anguished tears, Jenna stormed through the house on a cleaning tear, just for something to do with her rage and frustration. But as the afternoon grew long and a longer evening loomed ahead, Jenna found herself heading across the hall to Sam's apartment.

She paused at the door, realizing how often she ran to Sam when she needed love and comfort. They had little in common. Sam Oliver wasn't a native New Yorker like Jenna and he wasn't anywhere near her own age. He was eighty-five and had been in a wheelchair for five years.

Elliott said, "Why do you hang out with that old man all the time? He's disabled and he's from some Podunk town in the mountains of Tennessee. He still speaks like a hick and dresses like one, too. It embarrasses me when you run around with him."

Jenna winced. "Elliott, that isn't fair. Sam is a well-respected author. He won the Boston Globe Award for the Overland Adventure books he writes, and he just spoke to a packed house at King's College last month. Sam's not a hick; he's a very a smart man. Everyone loves his colorful tales about the mountains."

Elliott hadn't understood and Jenna found it hard to explain the part that Sam played in her life. Not having a warm relationship with her parents, Jenna knew she substituted Sam as a loving father figure in her life. And Sam's warm stories of his earlier life in the Tennessee hills fascinated Jenna – transporting her to a softer, gentler world she loved to hear about.

Still, she hesitated at Sam's door. She hated to burden him with her problems; he had enough of his own right now. The war he'd waged with cancer these last years had taken a toll on him. And he'd lost his old setter, Dan, recently – leaving another void in his life.

She sighed. At least Sam wouldn't have divided loyalties over her situation. There was no love lost between Sam and Elliott.

Jenna rang the doorbell at last.

"How's my favorite girl?" Sam quipped as he opened the door. But after a look at Jenna's face, he stopped the jokes.

"Did Carla call you?" she asked, not wanting to explain unless she had to.

"Yes," Sam admitted honestly. "Why don't you come in and we'll talk."

"I just needed to get out of that apartment," she said, pacing around the room restlessly. "Everything there makes me think of him."

"Let's go in the kitchen." Sam turned his wheelchair in that direction. "I'm heating up some lasagna that Mary made for me. You know, I'm blessed to have that woman for a housekeeper. She's a fine cook. And I'm glad to have Henry Aiken coming in to help more now that my health is acting poorly again. He got his CNA last month, you know."

Jenna followed Sam into the kitchen, knowing he was making light conversation to keep her mind off her problems.

"Have you eaten today since all this happened?" he asked.

Jenna nodded no.

"Good, then you can eat with me." He continued. "Come help me dish things out to the table. Mary's left some salad there, too."

Jenna automatically got out plates and silverware, poured iced tea, and started helping Sam put the food out.

"I don't think I can eat anything," she said, fighting back tears.

"Well, put some food on your plate, anyway, to be companionable with me." He positioned his wheelchair closer to the table. "You know I hate to eat alone. Humor me."

She almost smiled.

"This is an awful mess, Sam. I don't know what I'm going to do." Jenna sat down and dropped her face in her hands, the tears trickling down her cheeks as she started to weep again.

"The answers will come to you. With a little time." Sam reached across the table to pat her hand. "It doesn't all have to be resolved tonight, Jenna. Elliott doesn't even know you saw him. So there won't be a confrontation when he comes home unless you start one. You can just play along the same as always and give it a little time while you think things through."

"That's true," she said, breathing out a little. "He doesn't know that I know. I don't have to deal with any more tonight." She paused, tears starting to well again. "I don't think I could deal with any more right now, Sam. I really don't."

"Well, then, that's a fortunate thing," he responded.

She blew out a breath. "I feel like I've been living in some kind of bubble, in a life I thought was real but wasn't."

"Betrayal is a hard thing to live through." Sam handed her a napkin to mop the tears.

"It might be worse than just betrayal. I think maybe Elliott never really loved me, Sam." She flinched. "That I was just another of those things it was time for him to acquire. I've seen how charming he can be when he is trying to get something he wants. It's how he is in business, too, with his clients. He can seem so sincere, and then I've heard him laugh later about how well he played those clients to get what he wanted. And they never knew. They thought his affection and interest were genuine."

Jenna sniffed and wiped away more tears. "I thought so, too, Sam."

"Talk to me about it, Jenna." Sam laid a hand over hers. "It will do you good to look back and think it through."

"Do you think so?" She lifted her eyes to his.

"I do." He nodded, encouraging her to go on.

Jenna stopped to sort through old memories. "I was only nineteen when Elliott and I first met at a spring debutante party Mother and Daddy insisted I go to. Elliott was fifteen years older than me and seemed so suave and polished. I remember he kissed my hand and told me I was beautiful. Beautiful and sweet. The next time I saw him, he said the same thing – that I was so beautiful and sweet he couldn't stop thinking about me. He seemed so sincere."

"You are beautiful and sweet, Jenna. He didn't lie about that."

She shook her head. "He courted me like a fairy tale princess all summer and into the fall after we became engaged. Elliott often came to the house and went places with Mother and Daddy and me. They both liked him and were thrilled when Elliott proposed. He came from a wealthy family, knew all the right people, and held a prestigious job."

Jenna began crying raggedly now. "We got married in December and I moved in with Elliott for our first Christmas together. His apartment sat right here on the Upper East Side where I'd always lived - not far from my parents or the college I attended. I was so happy at first. Or I thought I was happy. I continued going to Barnard from our apartment here, but things started to be different not long after we married."

She turned anguished eyes to Sam. "Elliott changed. He stopped being sweet. I kept looking for that man I fell in love with and I couldn't find him. I couldn't understand it. He found fault in me all the time. I tried so hard to please him but nothing seemed to work. The more I tried, the crosser he seemed to get. I didn't know what to do, Sam. I've been unhappy for a long time. Maybe now I understand why. It was because Elliott really didn't love me. I don't think he ever did."

Jenna put her head into her hands and started to sob. She felt sick and ached all over from the tears and strain of the day.

Sam reached across the table to hold her hand. "I'm so sorry, Jenna girl. Elliott was a great fool. And a stupid fool, too. Don't you ever think differently. It is he that has the black heart and you the one of gold. I hate that he used and hurt you so."

He paused. "Elliott's not good people, Jenna. You need to get away from him."

"Where would I go, Sam?" Jenna's voice trembled. "I can't go home. My Mother and Father think Elliott is wonderful. And Mother tells me stories all the time of the affairs of her society friends. She thinks they are amusing. One of her friends divorced her rich husband recently over a string of adulteries, and Mother called her a fool. Even years ago when Aunt Lydia, her own sister, broke her engagement to a rich banker because he kept a mistress, mother was completely unsupportive. She broke ties with Lydia over it – but not with the banker or the banker's family."

Jenna shook her head sadly. "That's the way Mother is, Sam. Money and status have always meant more to her than anything else."

Sam scratched his chin thoughtfully. "Well, then, you could probably go to Aunt Lydia's for a space, if you wish. I'd say she might understand, given that history."

He looked up with a sudden, bright smile. "Or you could go down to Orchard Hollow – to my cabin in the Smokies. You could go there to think and take a space for yourself before you decide what you want to do. It's quiet and peaceful; it always helps straighten out my thoughts when I go down there."

Jenna smiled back at Sam, despite her sorrows. "It's nice of you to offer that, Sam." She knew he deeply cherished his place in the mountains. He'd spun her countless tales about his upbringing and life there before moving to New York.

They finished their meal and talked some more. Jenna did eat a little, at last, and somehow comforted herself that she had only tonight and tomorrow to get through. Elliott left for Paris early on Sunday.

She couldn't face the idea of a scene with him with her emotions so shattered. Elliott would get angry, cut her with his words. He'd find a way to blame her - just like he always did when there were problems between them. She bit her lip anxiously. If she even tried to confront Elliott – or her parents – they would simply explain away all her concerns and make her feel foolish. They'd take over any decisions to be made. They always did. Her own opinion wouldn't matter at all.

Jenna clenched her hands just thinking about it. No. For now, she'd wait. And while Elliott was gone, she'd decide what she needed to do. By herself. She couldn't let them take over her life again. Not this time.

On Sam's glass-enclosed porch after dinner, Jenna closed her eyes and leaned back on the glider with Sam's cat Maizie curled up on her lap. The lights of the city and the shadows of the trees of Central Park spread out in a panorama before them.

Sam's comfortable voice broke the silence. "You know, when I look out over the trees of the park here, with the light just so, even on this cold March night, it makes me think of looking out over the mountains at Orchard Hollow."

"Tell me about Orchard Hollow again, Sam." Jenna heaved a deep sigh. "I want to go somewhere else in my mind right now. Tell me some of your stories. I want to see the mountains and the creek behind your cabin, and

I want to hear about the people and the places you've known there. Weave me a tale, Sam."

And so Sam spun his tales to help ease the hurt of his girl.

"Well, there's no place on earth like it." He closed his eyes, settling into his memories. "Whenever I go back, a sense of home comes over me as soon as I start out the highway past Maryville and get my first glimpse of the Smoky Mountains in the distance. Even my dog Dan used to know when we'd get close to home; he'd jump up in the front seat and start barking. Maizie even quit her wailing in the cat carrier. They both seemed to know we were getting toward home. They could already sense the peace coming toward us."

Jenna began to relax as Sam talked, the tension starting to leave her muscles. Sam's stories always comforted her.

"The mountains never look the same in the Smokies." Sam's soothing voice continued. "There are all shades of blue and purple on the far horizon, and closer up is every shade of green imaginable in the spring time. There's a sort of yellow green color at the first hint of spring that I don't think I've ever seen captured by paint accurately. You'd appreciate that as an artist, Jenna."

"I'm not an artist, Sam," Jenna interjected. "I just do some little greeting card pictures and write the verse. As Elliott says, it's only a nice little hobby."

Sam scowled. "There are all kinds of art, Jenna. You might be surprised how some folks might view your talents."

Jenna shrugged.

Picking up the threads of the Orchard Hollow story, she asked him, "What's the name of that place where you round the corner as you're coming toward Townsend?"

"Kinzel Springs," he answered.

"That's it." Jenna smiled. "A little, white country church sits on the right. And after that a bend in the road winds around and down to follow along the Little River. That's a sign you're coming into Townsend."

"You know this story as well as I do now, Jenna," Sam said, chuckling. "Maybe you should tell it to me."

"You know I like it better when you tell it to me, Sam." She patted him fondly on the knee. "But knowing parts of it ahead of time makes it nicer to hear – like I'm going back to a familiar place."

"So tell me, Jenna, how do you get to Orchard Hollow after you pass Kinzel Springs Baptist Church?" Sam asked.

"Well, you come on around that bend at Old Tuckaleechee Road, past the bridge over to River Road, and down into Townsend." She stopped then and waited for him to carry the story on.

"It's not much of a town by the standards of places like New York," Sam said. "Just a small rural community set at the base of one side of the Smoky Mountains. People call it the quiet side of the mountain because it hasn't developed as much as some of the other areas around the Smokies. There are a few stores as you go in to Townsend, a post office, a bank, another church or two, some motels, and several restaurants – like The Back Porch Restaurant, Deadbeat Pete's, and Miss Lily's Café. Because it's a tourist town, a rustic, log visitor center sits near the center of town with quaint arts and crafts shops scattered along - Mountain Sage, Nawger Knob, the dulcimer shop."

He settled back into his memories with pleasure. "After the Apple Barn on the left – you know the one my sister owns – and the Texaco station just after that, you watch for Chestnut Springs Road on the right. It's a little paved two-lane road that rolls gently uphill by the old McNally Farm's fence line.

"After you turn right on Chestnut Springs Road, you start this gradual uphill ascent into the woods. Next, you angle off to the right onto Orchard Hollow Road, a little winding road that twists up into the mountains along Fall Branch Creek to come to a dead end loop."

"And there's your place." Jenna heaved a little sigh.

Sam closed his eyes. "Yes, sir, there at the end of the loop on the right is my place, the cabin I helped to build for Frances and myself after my books started to sell." He took a deep, satisfied breath. "Down behind the house is the creek and you can hear it gurgling and rushing over the rocks when you have the windows open. It's a great sound like no other – the sound of a rushing mountain stream in the Smokies."

"It sounds wonderful," Jenna said, already calmed by the soothing tone of Sam's words.

Jenna sat up suddenly, leaning toward Sam, her eyes wide.

"You know, Sam, if you really meant it, I think I will go down to Orchard Hollow. Elliott is leaving for Paris on Sunday for six weeks. I could go down to the mountains for a visit to think things through."

The idea excited her as she began to consider it. "It might be good for me to get away for a while. I could see all the places you've talked about."

Sam looked out over Central Park, watching the snow fall and thinking about her idea. "Actually, I believe it would be good for you to have a change of scene right now."

He gave her a considering look. "You know I've always wanted you to go down to my place, Jenna. I'm not well enough to go myself right now."

Jenna felt a wrench in her heart. He was taking chemo again with the return of his cancer.

"You could check on things for me – see all my friends and family, call and tell me stories." He chuckled at his own thoughts, enjoying the idea of her going to Tennessee. "Yes, sir. I think it's a fine idea for you to go down to Orchard Hollow."

Jenna knew it would be running away to leave right now – but the idea seemed too heavenly to argue with. She offered Sam a small smile and leaned back to close her eyes. She would do it. She'd go to the mountains, and somehow, while she was there, she would figure out what she needed to do about her life.

Sam reached out a hand to pat Jenna's arm. "You could stay in the up- stairs bedroom at Orchard Hollow. You'd like that room, Jenna. There's a little painting of Frances over the chest of drawers and a big painting of mountain flowers over the bed – both by the same artist. It's Boyce Hart's work, and it's real good. Frances and I have known Boyce since he was a kid. Local boy that made good. You remember, I told you he rented my cabin a few years back while he had one built across the road from me? He watches after my old place now, and he's a fine neighbor. You'll like him, Jenna. I'm sorry you missed meeting him when he was up here last summer."

"Yes, I went down to Martha's Vineyard with my parents then."

Sam often talked about Boyce Hart, but Jenna had never met him - or Sam's sister Raynelle - or any of the other people from Orchard Hollow Sam talked about so much – except through Sam's stories.

He paused with another chuckle. "Did I ever tell you about the time I hiked up Chestnut Ridge behind the cabin and ran across that girl running naked in the woods?"

She giggled. "No, Sam, tell me that one."

Sam's comforting voice soon drifted over her again, helping to ease the hurt of the day.

Chapter 2

$\mathcal{B}$oyce Hart rang up another small sale and dropped the matted art print and a box of note cards into a Hart Gallery gift bag. The bell jangled on the front door, letting in yet another stream of customers.

He scowled. It just figured the gallery would be busier than usual the one day he worked the store by himself, Boyce thought. And dadgumit, it was only Wednesday and still a weekday. He thought it would be quiet today and that he might get a little painting done in the back room.

"Oh, there he is!" A matronly woman pointed as she entered the shop. She nudged her balding husband with her other arm. "It's Boyce Hart."

She made her way to the register where Boyce sat, relaxed on a stool.

"I just can't believe we've been lucky enough to meet you today," the woman cooed, holding out a pudgy hand, wreathed in rings.

Following her enthusiastic handshake, Boyce took the man's hand dutifully.

The woman leaned toward him with bright eyes. "We bought three of your paintings when we were down here last year and took them back to hang in our den in Ohio. I just can't tell you how many compliments we've had on them."

She gushed on, reciting the names of the paintings and reiterating the comments people made about them. Her husband added a few words, and then both launched into a discussion about their children and grandchildren.

Boyce kept a congenial, plastic smile on his face. Why did people always assume strangers wanted to hear detailed stories about the cute things their grandchildren did?

The man spoke then, pushing a "Retired and Happy" ballcap back from his forehead. "We just bought a vacation place on Davis Mountain over in Wear's Valley. We decided to decorate it in a Smokies theme, so we came in today to get some more of your paintings."

Boyce felt grateful then for his patient congeniality. For the next thirty minutes - between other customers - he helped the couple decide on six paintings for their new house. Even if they were a little annoying to deal with, Boyce was pleased they admired his work as much as they did. And they did have money to spend.

Out of the corner of his eye, he saw Raynelle Bratcher come in the gallery while he finished up business with Earle and Estalee Crabtree. By this point, they were on a first name basis with Boyce, and he knew the entire story of their lives, when they retired, what medications they took and what health problems they had, and why they'd bought a vacation home in the mountains.

Raynelle came over to give Boyce a hug when the Crabtrees left. "Lord in heaven, those two could talk." She laughed. "How come the most tedious folks seem to have the most money?"

"I never have figured out the answer to that one." Boyce grinned at her. "What brought you visiting in my store, neighbor?"

Raynelle and Vernon Bratcher owned the big country crafts store next door. Boyce always appreciated the spillover of the heavy tourist traffic from their store into his.

With the store quiet for a moment, Raynelle perched on a tall stool beside the counter. "It sure feels good to sit down," she said.

Boyce propped himself on the other store stool behind the counter.

"Sam called me last night to tell me that a neighbor of his in New York is coming down to stay in his cabin at Orchard Hollow for a few weeks." She glanced at the desk calendar on the counter. "She ought to be here about Tuesday of next week."

"She?" Boyce asked.

"It's the young girl that lives across from Sam at The Carlton. You know, the girl he talks so much about that's so good to him – Jenna Howell, I think her name is."

Boyce thought for a minute. "Socialite type that's married to some ad executive? I do remember Sam talking about her." He paused. "Is her husband coming down with her? Or any friends?"

Raynelle shook her head. "No. Just the girl. Seems she's having some sort of problems in her marriage. Needs time away to think and decide what she ought to do. Sam wants us to be nice to her."

Boyce rolled his eyes. "Great. Just what we need is some spoiled little

New Yorker type to look after."

Raynelle interrupted him. "Now, that's not nice at all, Boyce. You don't even know the girl. And you know how you hate people typing us mountain folks all in one lump. We don't know what this girl's like."

She shook a finger at Boyce. "What we do know is that she's Sam's girl. Sam loves her like a daughter and says she's been good to him. And if he's asked us to be nice and hospitable to her, we're going to be nice and hospitable to her." She gave Boyce a pointed look. "Sam's my brother, Boyce Hart, and if he cares for this girl that's good enough for me. It ought to be good enough for you, too."

Boyce winced. "You're right, Raynelle. You just caught me in a foul mood today. I'm sorry if I spouted off without thinking."

"Where's Charlotte?" Raynelle looked around.

"Still at the doctor."

Charlotte Bratcher was one of Boyce's best part-time gallery workers. Right now she was heavily pregnant and visiting the doctor to be checked.

Raynelle frowned. Charlotte was also Raynelle's niece. "I thought she was due back before now."

The door opened before Raynelle could add to that thought.

"Sorry I'm late," Charlotte said as she let herself in. She waddled over to the counter, a hand under her belly. "That doctor made me wait nearly two hours in the waiting room. He had to run over to the hospital to deliver someone's baby." She shook her head. "It was just my luck to come on a day he had a delivery."

"Babies don't give out their timetables of when they're arriving," Raynelle told her.

"That's for sure." Charlotte grinned. "If so, I could make some better plans for when this baby might show up."

She came over to drop her purse on the counter.

"Looks like you haven't been very busy, Boyce." She looked around at the empty store, tucking a hand under her big belly again, as if to help hold it up.

It made Boyce nervous having a woman as pregnant as Charlotte in the store. He'd never been very comfortable around this baby business.

Raynelle laughed. "Boyce had one of his busiest mornings today while you've been gone."

"Yeah, and I'm sure glad to see you back." He looked affectionately toward Charlotte. She ran his gallery with competence the days she worked, leaving Boyce free to paint in his studio.

Charlotte glanced over at the sales receipt still lying on the counter. The delivery address for the Crabtrees was written out in Boyce's bold scrawl across the top.

"Well, Lordy be, it looks like Earle and Estalee were in here today from Ohio." She grinned. "How's their new grandbaby?"

Boyce shook his head. That's why he loved Charlotte so much. She genuinely liked working with the customers and loved hearing all about their lives and families. She remembered every detail about people, too.

"They've bought a vacation house over in Wear's Valley," Boyce told her.

"Well, I'll be." Charlotte leaned against the counter. "I guess that means we'll see a lot more of them."

"By the way," Boyce interrupted. "When is your cousin Leeta Walker coming in to train as your replacement in the store?" He studied her stomach. "It looks to me like we ought to get her in here pretty soon."

"Well, there might be a problem there." Charlotte wrinkled her nose.

"No *might be* about it." Raynelle grinned. "Leeta ran off with a trucker to Texas this weekend. Her folks are just sick about it. They didn't even know the boy, and they didn't think Leeta knew him well enough to marry him sudden-like the way she did."

"Well, great." Boyce stood up in irritation. "Who's going to work the gallery on your regular days now, Charlotte? You'll be out at least a month to six weeks when the baby comes."

"I don't know, Boyce." She walked around the counter to snag his stool. "I've started calling around. But I haven't found anyone yet."

He paced restlessly. "I can't give two days a week right now to work in the gallery full-time. And Una goes to class on Tuesday and Thursday; she can't add any more work days. The kid that works after high school and on Saturday can't do weekday hours and we already asked Jim Graham. His accounting work takes up too much time for him to add more part-time hours here."

Charlotte smiled at him. "Don't get yourself all upset, Boyce. I'm sure we'll find someone. It's just hard to locate anyone that only wants to fill in for six weeks."

Boyce ran a hand through his hair. "I've got that big contract going with Haldeman right now. I need every day up in my studio to get my paintings done for him." He looked at Raynelle. "Maybe we can borrow one of your employees?"

Raynelle shook her head. "Not a chance with the spring tourist traffic picking up right now. Spring break is kicking in, the wildflowers are starting to bloom, and the area is filling up with tourists. Tubing will be starting on the river soon, too. I need every employee I've got."

She snapped her fingers in the air suddenly. "Hey, I'll tell you what. I called to talk to Sam's girl after I spoke to Sam last night – you know, to make her feel welcome. I told her I'd use her part-time in the store to keep her busy." Raynelle paused. "Sam told me she works volunteer in a big New York gallery. I'll bet she could do real good here in your place. She already knows about art and all."

Boyce frowned.

"I'll let her work part-time over here for you instead of me." Raynelle smiled at Boyce. "In return, you can go up and clean out Sam's cabin to get it ready for her. You still have your set of keys. The place probably needs a good airing out – and you might spray for bugs, too. We want everything to be real nice for Sam's girl."

Charlotte looked puzzled. "Who in the world are you talking about, Raynelle?"

Boyce answered her. "A neighbor of Sam's is coming down from New York to spend a month or so at his place at Orchard Hollow."

"No kidding? A real New Yorker?" Charlotte's face lit up. "Wow. What do we know about her?"

Boyce rolled his eyes.

Raynelle cut a glance his way. "Boyce, using this New York girl for your shop is a good answer unless we come up with another before the time. You go on up to your studio and paint now. Charlotte's here and she can mind the store." She waved her hand at him in dismissal. "I'll fill Charlotte in on all the details about Jenna Howell. After all, Charlotte is Sam's cousin by marriage and she'll want to know all about her."

Getting the message that the two wanted to gossip – and wanted him out of the way – Boyce left. It didn't take a rocket scientist to run his small art gallery in Townsend. He figured a New York girl could manage for a spell if she needed to. Besides, Raynelle would be next door to help her. It would be an answer if they didn't find someone else before Charlotte's time.

Driving back to his own place at Orchard Hollow, Boyce tried to remember what Sam had told him about his neighbor, Jenna Howell. Not much, actually. Just that she visited with him all the time and was good to him. He scowled. He did remember Sam had never liked her husband, Elliott Howell, very much - even if he was his nearest neighbor.

Sam's old setter, Dan, never liked Elliott much, either. That was a telling fact, since Dan had always been a good judge of character. Sam said the dog would pee on Elliott's foot given any sort of a chance. Boyce chuckled at the memory.

Pulling into the driveway of his cabin, Boyce saw Patrick, one of Dan's offspring, heading toward his car with a welcoming bark – red ears flapping. Patrick, another Irish Setter, was a pup from a litter Dan sired. He was also Boyce's roommate and best companion.

After greeting Patrick, the two made their way over to Sam's place to get it ready for the girl from New York.

Boyce walked up on the porch of the rustic mountain house. "We've got some sissy New York girl coming down here to stay for a while, Patrick. Sam says we need to be nice to her. She's going through some sort of hard time."

He let himself into the house and started opening the windows. He turned on all the fans to air out the house and sprayed for bugs.

Leaving the cabin later, he stopped to look back over the comfortable living room with its worn sofas and chairs gathered around the big, rock fireplace. Perhaps it would be nice for the old place to have someone living in it for a while. It saddened him that the house had been empty for so long.

"I sure miss Sam and Frances," Boyce told the dog. "They were fine people and good friends. Sam helped me out many times over the years."

Boyce smiled to himself, reaching down to scratch the dog's ears. "I still remember the day Sam brought you over to my door, Patrick – just a rowdy, little pup with long, floppy ears and big, brown eyes. He insisted I accept you as a gift for caring for his cabin." Boyce chuckled. "I'm grateful for that favor, too."

He closed the front door and locked it. "Don't worry, Sam. I'll be good to your girl and see that she's taken care of while she's here. I owe it to you."

Chapter 3

*S*omehow, Jenna made it through the next day by avoiding the apartment and Elliott's company as much as possible. She visited her Mother and tried to broach the subject of Elliott's indiscretions.

"Marriage is a social arrangement, darling." Her Mother studied a polished red nail abstractly. "Don't look for the happy-ever-after fairy tale. Just enjoy all the fine things you have and the good position in society you enjoy. Believe me, most women would envy and give anything for your life. Look on the positive, dear, and overlook the little negatives. Don't be so sensitive about Elliott's little foibles. Not all men are constant, dear. Just remind yourself that you're the one Elliott chose to marry. That's what matters."

Jenna came home with a heavy heart. She obviously could expect little support from her parents. Her mother's last words before giving her a breezy air kiss were, "Be smart and look the other way, dear."

When she let herself in her apartment later in the day, she found a message on the answering machine from Elliott. "Jenna, don't forget our dinner at Davenport's this evening. I'll be home to pick you up by six o'clock."

"Great," Jenna complained to herself. "The one evening I actually hoped Elliott would cancel a date and he decides to keep his promise."

She heaved a sigh. The dinner would undoubtedly be a small nightmare to get through.

Glancing at the clock with resignation, she headed for the bedroom to get ready. "At least Elliott has no idea anything is different between us," she said to herself. "He pays so little attention to my moods or emotions, he probably won't even notice anything is wrong."

A short time later, Elliott drove them to the restaurant in a new gold Cadillac convertible he proudly announced the company gave him as a bonus. They sat at a cozy table by the window where they could see the sun set over the water and watch the boats go by in the harbor. Jenna spent a lot of time looking out the window – wishing she was anywhere but with her husband.

Elliott oozed charm all evening. He gave Jenna his undivided attention, toasted her with his wine glass, and held her hand across the table. It was all Jenna could do not to snatch her hand from his in disgust, remembering a similar – but sultrier - scene with Elliott and his secretary in the restaurant only yesterday.

After dinner, Elliott handed her a red velvet box tied with lavish gold ribbon.

Jenna offered a forced smile. "What is it?" she said, taking the box.

"Open it and see," Elliott replied, smiling back.

She did, and found a key on a sparkling gold key ring shaped like a heart.

"What is this?" She looked up at him, puzzled.

"It's the key to the Cadillac we drove to Davenport's tonight." Elliott toasted her with a wineglass. "I'm giving it to you for your birthday, darling. It will be your very own car – a special present for a special girl on her twenty-second birthday."

"I thought you said the car was a bonus from the company." Jenna frowned.

Elliott flashed her a broad smile. "Well, it was in a way – the company's gold bonus for most ad sales. But I decided to give it to you rather than keep it. You don't have a car of your own, and I thought it was time you did. Besides, you can use it to take some outings down to your parents' place at the Vineyard or outside the city for a day trip while I'm in Paris. It will keep you from feeling so lonely."

"I hoped you would take me to Paris with you." Jenna studied the key ring in her hand as she spoke, not wanting Elliott to see her eyes.

"Well, darling, you know that's not possible," Elliott answered smoothly. "The company will have me busy every minute setting up the new business there, and I'll have no time for sightseeing. Besides, the firm made it clear this trip is strictly for business only, and they put the word out emphatically that there shouldn't be any thoughts about bringing someone along this time."

He lifted his hands expressively. "I hoped to take you, darling, but, I can't. Besides, you know you wouldn't like being there on your own even if I could take you, and I wouldn't want you wandering around the city without a companion or chaperone while I work. It would be dangerous.

We'll plan a trip to Paris later when we can savor the city together. Won't that be more fun? It will be something both of us can look forward to. I'll try to find us a nice place to stay while I'm there this trip. When we go to Paris together, it should be a trip for both of us to cherish and remember – not a business trip where I am working all the time and you have to see the sights by yourself."

Jenna watched Elliott's face while he talked. What a smooth liar, she thought. And he seemed so utterly charming while he lied. It was easy to believe anything he said – even when this time Jenna knew it wasn't even remotely true.

"I thought the car would help make up a little for you not being able to go," he said, reaching across the table to take her hand. "You do like it, don't you? You said the car was wonderful when we were driving to Davenport's in it."

"Yes, it is wonderful." Jenna answered honestly. It would be good to have her own car rather than borrowing Elliott's to go to Orchard Hollow.

Elliott looked thoughtful then. "I'm flying out to Paris early in the morning, you know, and am scheduled to be in Paris at least six weeks – through April and possibly into May. It may take more than six weeks to get the new Abercrombie branch up and running. I'll miss you, Jenna, being away from you for so long. We've never been apart this long before."

He smiled and picked up Jenna's fingers to kiss them gently. For a moment she wanted to believe that he would truly miss her, and then she remembered Lena Morrow would be going along with Elliott to keep him company and to keep him too occupied to be lonely for her. Lena would see all the sights Jenna had hoped to enjoy. It wasn't difficult to work up a few tears at that moment for Elliott to see.

Elliott let Jenna drive the new car back to their apartment when their dinner ended. She shivered as they walked down the hall toward their apartment door. How could she prevent Elliott from sleeping with her or being intimate with her tonight? There had to be some way. Perhaps she could feign being sick.

Luckily, he solved the problem for her.

"I have to go back to the office to get the last of my paperwork ready for the trip tomorrow, Jenna." He studied his watch as he spoke. "I didn't get finished before our dinner. I'm sorry about that. My flight leaves early at 6:00 am, you know. I think it will be best if I just finish packing and carry everything over to the office. I can work into the night, catch a little sleep, and then take a taxi to the airport from there."

He patted her cheek. "It will be easier on you, and I won't have to wake you in the middle of the night." He gave her a smile. "Besides, we've already had a special dinner for our goodbye celebration, haven't we?"

Jenna tried to force her face to smile again.

Elliott gave her a considering look. "You have had a nice birthday, haven't you Jenna?"

Jenna tried to think what to say. Her relief that he wasn't spending the night almost clouded her logic.

"I like the car," she finally said. There was nothing else she could think to offer.

"Well, good." Elliott added this distractedly, already heading for the bedroom to finish his packing.

By Monday morning, Elliott had left for Paris, and Jenna was almost packed and ready to go to Orchard Hollow in Townsend, Tennessee.

Carla stuffed a last box into the back of Jenna's new car.

"I can't believe Elliott actually gave you a car for your birthday. I have to admit that once in a while, that man's timing is actually good." She laughed at her own joke.

Jenna winced, unable to joke about the situation yet.

"Now, don't you worry." Carla took the bag from Jenna's hands and deftly packed it into a remaining corner of the trunk. "Everything is going to be okay. We've got everything covered here. Your parents and Elliott think you're going with John and me to our place in the Poconos for a vacation break, and when we come back we're going to say you decided to stay on for a few weeks longer. It's nice up there in late March and April. It's totally believable you'd want to stay on."

Carla rearranged the luggage in the trunk to work in another bag.

"Mrs. Bynam, our neighbor, will mail all your nice cards from Pennsylvania after we leave. So Elliott and your parents will get a sweet, little note every week from you telling them everything is hunkey-dorey." She shut the trunk firmly. "Back here in New York, Jake Saunders – that detective friend of Sam's you hired - will be gathering information on Elliott in case you need it. And the attorney Sam helped you locate – Maury something, I can't remember the last name - will be keeping in touch with you and Sam. Everything's all arranged."

Jenna sighed. "I hate it that Sam had to help me with all this."

"Well, if he hadn't, John or I would have helped." Carla made a face. "It's not as though you could have counted on your parents for any help with this, Jenna. And you were in no shape to take it on. Don't be so hard on yourself."

She turned to hug Jenna. "You just get away, have a nice stay at Sam's place, and try to enjoy yourself while you're deciding what to do." She pulled back to study Jenna's face. "I'm so sorry all this has happened to you, Jen. You know I will be right here anytime you want to talk."

"I know, and thanks, Carla."

Carla shoved a note into Jenna's hands. "Here are everyone's phone numbers and contact information. You call me when you get to your Aunt Lydia's tonight and then when you get to the mountains tomorrow, you hear? We'll all be anxious until we know you arrived safely."

She frowned then. "I don't much like the idea of you being out on the road when you have so much on your mind. You'll be careful, won't you, Jenna?"

"I will and everything will be fine, Carla," Jenna told her, giving her a last hug.

She waved at Carla gaily as she pulled out of the garage. But in truth, Jenna felt scared to death. She'd never taken a long car trip alone in her life and never driven more than 100 miles anywhere by herself. In addition, Jenna had never lived alone. She lived with her parents, even while going to college, and then she married and moved in with Elliott. She'd always been supervised and sheltered, and, unlike her other friends, she had done few things all by herself.

"It *will* be fine, Jenna," she told herself firmly as she headed out into the New York traffic. "It *will*. You're twenty two years old, a smart and competent woman, and you're having your first great adventure all by yourself."

Over the next two days, she gave herself this pep talk repeatedly and hoped she would eventually believe it.

On Tuesday, after stopping over at Aunt Lydia's, Jenna headed down Highway 321 outside of Maryville, Tennessee. As she swept around a turn in the highway, Jenna caught her breath. There in the distance were the mountains on the horizon, just as Sam had described them so often. Her trip was nearly over. She wasn't far from Orchard Hollow.

Shortly after, Jenna pulled the Cadillac into the parking lot at the Apple Barn. Sam said his sister Raynelle, who owned the Apple Barn, would give her the spare key to the cabin. It felt good to get out and stretch after the long trip down from Virginia. She'd driven eight hours today, and it was about three o'clock now. She could get settled before the sun went down.

The Apple Barn was a big, log craft store with a long covered porch across the front. Tourists lounged on the porch's rocking chairs, and Jenna could see there were many more visitors inside. She felt surprised to see so many people in the store on a Tuesday, but remembered Sam telling her the Smokies started getting busy in late March as the weather warmed and the early wildflowers started to bloom.

The Apple Barn proved a wonderful store, packed with handmade craft items, Appalachian giftware and collectibles, homemade candies and jellies. Jenna looked around while one of the clerks went to get Raynelle Bratcher from the back of the store.

An attractive, grey-haired lady came toward Jenna now, smiling broadly with her arms held out in welcome.

"Well, there you are, honey. We're so glad to see you arrived here safe and sound. Let me give you a hug."

Raynelle stood about five foot four, with short, curly grey hair, and a warm smile much like Sam's. She wore a loose, blue t-shirt printed with butterflies of all colors. And she talked a mile a minute, asking Jenna about her trip, wanting to know if she'd stopped to have her lunch, telling her Sam had called twice since noon to see if she'd arrived yet.

Raynelle stopped her prattle at last and stood back to look Jenna over.

"Lord, girl, you're even more beautiful than Sam told us," she said, smiling. "We sure are glad to have you with us for a space. I can't tell you how excited Sam is about you coming down here. We're all going to see that you have a real nice time while you're here."

She tucked Jenna's arm in hers. "You come on back to the office with me, I'll give you the keys to the cabin and the shed out back where you can put your car. I've got a basket full of things to help you get started in the house, plus Zita – that's Sam's other sister - and I have already gone over and cleaned the cabin, made up the beds, and put in groceries for you."

"That was really nice of you," Jenna said. "But you really shouldn't have …."

"Oh, it was nothing." Raynelle interrupted her, waving a hand to dismiss Jenna's thanks. "And Zita's left you a casserole and some other things in the refrigerator for tonight's meal. We're all wanting to have you over for dinner, but we thought you'd be tired tonight and that you'd just want to settle in and rest."

The door to the back office banged open before Raynelle could say any more, and a tall, broad-shouldered, young man filled the doorway.

"Thank God, you're here, Raynelle." His voice came out in an anxious rush. "Come quick. It's Charlotte. Her time's come, and my car's in the shop. She needs to get to the hospital right now."

Raynelle's eyes widened. "Good gracious mercy. I'd better get right over there. Come on with me for a minute, Jenna. It may just be a false alarm. My niece Charlotte's due a baby any time now. If it is her time, we'll get her husband, Dean, on his way over here."

They swept out through the store and down a side porch to a small shop next door to the Apple Barn. A swinging sign hung on the rail that said Hart Gallery. Inside the store were Smokies paintings on all the walls - mountain scenes, wildflowers, old barns. Jenna saw them in a whirl as they pushed through the storefront toward the back room of the store. There a young girl sat curled up on a small sofa, doubled over and holding her arms under a very large belly.

"Oh, Raynelle," she cried. "I'm so glad you're here. My water's done broke, and the pains are coming bad. They're real close, and I need you to get me up to the hospital in Maryville right now. Boyce's car's in the shop, and I can't find my Dean anywhere. Will said he'd gone back to the hardware store to get some more nails. They'd run out on the house they're working on." She stopped to groan and hold her stomach again. "I don't want to go in one of those ambulances, Raynelle. Besides, I don't think I can wait 'til it gets out here to get me and take me back into Maryville to the hospital."

"Where's your car, Raynelle?" Boyce's voice interrupted impatiently. "I'll go get it and bring it around to the door." He was rubbing his hands through his hair nervously.

"Vernon's got the car today," Raynelle told him with a shake of her head. "He dropped me off this morning, and he was going to pick me back up at 5:00. We'll have to figure out something else."

"Do you have a car?" Boyce turned to Jenna with his question, seeming to notice she was there for the first time.

"Boyce, this is Sam's Jenna." Raynelle frowned at him. "She's just gotten here from off the road all day. You run on over and see if one of the girls in the store will loan us a car."

"No." Jenna stepped forward. "You don't need to do that. Let's take my car. It will be quicker, and it's right outside."

She pushed her keys at Boyce. "Here are the keys. You go bring the car around to the door. It's the gold one right in front of the Apple Barn with the New York plates. I'll help Raynelle get this girl out to the car to meet you. And you can drive. You'll know where we need to go."

"Great." Boyce snatched the keys and headed out the door, obviously glad to have an assigned task to do.

"That's good of you, Jenna." Raynelle turned to Jenna gratefully. "And a good idea. Charlotte's pains are coming closer now. We need to get this girl on into the hospital right away."

Charlotte cleared her throat. "I'm Charlotte Bratcher," she said to Jenna. "No one's bothered to introduce us. And I sure do thank you for this. I'm Raynelle's niece and kin to Sam through marriage, too. I've been really looking forward to meeting you, but I wasn't hopin' to meet you like this." She giggled before another pain started to hit.

In less than ten minutes, Boyce had them on the way to the hospital in Maryville. Between her pains, Charlotte talked almost nonstop as they sped up the highway.

"I can't believe I'm going to the hospital to have my baby in a gold Cadillac convertible," Charlotte said. "This is just the most beautiful car I've ever seen in my life. I can't wait to tell Dean about this. This is going to be the most exciting story later on. And I'm just thrilled to be meeting you at last, Jenna. Look at your clothes and your hair. You sure can tell you're from New York City. It just must be the most exciting place to live. Sam's told me all about you, and you know, you and I have a lot in common. We both got married young, and we like art, and we both have birthdays in March and are the same age. Did you know that?"

Jenna shook her head. "No, I didn't."

"This is going to be my second baby." She puffed through another sweep of labor pains. "My first, Tyler Dean, just turned three and he's real excited about this new baby. I've been real pleased about how grown up he's already acting. We've got him potty-trained and sleeping in a big bed, and he's so proud of himself – keeps telling us what a big boy he is now. It's so cute. All that's going to make it a lot easier, too, when I have this new baby in the house. My friend, Twila, had two in diapers and cribs at once, and she just about went crazy."

While Charlotte was caught up in another set of labor pains, Raynelle leaned over to whisper to Jenna. "Charlotte talks a mile a minute when she gets nervous or scared. She won't always bend your ear off like this, but just let her talk right now. It helps to keep her mind off her fear and off the pains."

Boyce didn't say more than two words on the trip, but he drove steadily and fast until they got to Blount Memorial Hospital. He looked nervous and anxious. Jenna sat in the front seat with him, and she found herself studying him now and then out of the corner of her eye. Obviously, this was the Boyce Hart Sam talked about so much, the man that had lived in Sam's cabin for a while and then built his own place across the street. He was a painter, Jenna knew, and she assumed the Hart Gallery they had been in earlier was his. She wondered if the Smokies paintings on the walls were Boyce's own work or that of other local artists.

Boyce Hart looked very different from Elliott. Elliott, a tall, slim man with grey eyes and neat, slicked back, brown hair above a long distinguished face, always dressed impeccably. Boyce was tall with brown hair, too. But his hair was a lighter brown, longish and tousled, and streaked with bits of blond from the sun. He wore faded jeans and a t-shirt with a loose flannel shirt over the top. An arrowhead on a gold chain swung loosely around his neck. He was tan and his shoulders were muscular. His hands, resting lightly on the steering wheel of the car, appeared so different from Elliott's long slim ones - broad and strong, with bits of what looked like paint under the nails. In fact, dabs of paint were on his jeans and t-shirt, too.

He turned to look at her, as if aware she had been studying him. Jenna offered a casual comment to be polite and then looked away at the scenery.

At the hospital, Jenna and Raynelle helped Charlotte out of the car at the emergency room entrance while Boyce went to find a place to park. There were some anxious moments in admittance until Raynelle convinced the staff that Charlotte was very close to delivery.

By the time Charlotte was admitted and taken up to delivery, more of the Bratcher family started to arrive in the waiting area. First Charlotte's husband Dean and his daddy Will Bratcher rushed in. Boyce and Raynelle settled both of them down and told them Charlotte was fine. Then Charlotte's mother and father, the Walkers, arrived, along with Charlotte's aunt, and Raynelle's sister, Zita Walker, Dean's mother Betty Nelle, and his grandmother Etta Bratcher. Finally, Raynelle's husband Vernon Bratcher arrived. The chairs were full, and the men stood propped around the wall.

Everyone who arrived heard the story of Charlotte's trip to the hospital and thanked Jenna over and over for her help in getting Charlotte there. When the doctor came out to announce the baby's arrival, and that all was well with mother and baby, a spate of hugging, rejoicing, and back-slapping ensued. Everyone trooped down to see the baby in the nursery window and then took turns going in to see Charlotte when she got settled in a room.

Just as Jenna hoped she might get to leave, Charlotte's husband came out and shyly told Jenna that Charlotte had asked to see her. Jenna found Charlotte propped up in her hospital bed holding her new baby girl wrapped in a pink blanket.

"I wanted you to see her before you left." Charlotte leaned the baby forward for Jenna to see more clearly. "Isn't she beautiful?"

She was indeed, dark-haired with a rosebud mouth, and sleeping peacefully. Jenna felt a little clutch at her heart as she looked at her.

"She is beautiful, Charlotte, just like her mother." Jenna smiled at her.

"Well, that's real nice of you." Charlotte smiled back. "And I'll never forget you helping to get me to the hospital in time to deliver her without any problems."

"It was just loaning my car," Jenna started to say.

"No, it was more," Charlotte insisted. "It was a sign we're going to be friends. It bonded us. I've named the baby Jennie Rae – after you and Raynelle. Do you like it? I hope you don't mind. And I'm going to write up in her baby book about this day, too, so she'll never forget she rode to the hospital with her New York namesake in a brand new gold Cadillac."

"I'm touched and flattered, Charlotte, that you would name your daughter after me. And I think Jennie Rae is a fine name." Jenna found she had tears in her eyes as she finished saying these words to Charlotte.

More of the family came back in the room now. And Raynelle told Jenna to go on to the cabin to get some rest.

"Boyce is going to drive you to Orchard Hollow," she explained. "It would be hard for you to find Sam's place in the dark, and, besides, Boyce needs a way to get home himself with his jeep still in the shop. My husband Vernon's here to take me on home. So I hope you don't mind if I don't drive on back with the two of you. It's been a long day. I'm ready for some dinner and a little rest." She smiled. "I think our little mother is going to be just fine now. Thanks for all your help tonight, Jenna. Looks like you and I have got ourselves a namesake for all our afternoon's labor."

Shortly afterwards, Jenna found herself heading back down Highway 321 toward Townsend. As the mountain ranges came into sight again, Jenna could see the sunset streaking across the mountain – slashes of pink and blue.

"My mother used to call that a baby sunset," Boyce commented. "A fitting sunset for a night like tonight."

Jenna smiled at him, glad he'd bridged the silence. "It is a pretty sunset," she replied. "I'll have to tell Sam about it."

"How is Sam?" His voice held concern.

"Holding up as well as he can." Her answer was honest. "I wish I could give you a better report. All of us are worried about him."

"Sam's tough," said Boyce. "He might surprise us and turn the corner again."

Jenna laughed softly. "If he did, I think he'd take the first plane down here. He talks about Orchard Hollow and his friends and family here all the time."

"It was good of you to come down. It means a lot to him." He studied her for a minute. "You mean a lot to him, too. He talks about you to all of us. He says you've been like a daughter to him."

"It's easy to like Sam." Jenna dismissed the compliments.

Darkness fell as Boyce drove into Townsend. It was hard to see the landmarks that pointed the way to Orchard Hollow. But when they swung right off the highway onto a small paved side road, Jenna found herself saying, "And turn right on Chestnut Springs Road by the McNally Farm."

Boyce chuckled. "You must be remembering Sam's directions."

They drove up the road a few miles, and then Boyce swung right onto a narrower road in the woods.

"Oh, look, there's the signpost with the carved bird on the top that Sam told me about. The one with everyone's name on it." Jenna craned to see it in the dark.

"Will Bratcher and I made that," Boyce told her. "It's nothing much. Just a signpost with boards tacked on it telling the names of the folks that live on Orchard Hollow Road – the Lansky's, Hester's, Oliver's, and Hart's." He pointed out the window. "There's the Lansky's house on the right there, set back toward the creek. Sarah and Will Lansky are transplanted Yankees; they moved south and opened a little sports store in Townsend called The River Trader. Nice couple."

He pointed in the other direction then. "The lights you can see up on the left in the woods - that's the Hester's place. They're older, Raymond and Wilma. He's a retired ranger, really knows the Smokies, and works part-time at the visitor's center now. Wilma is a great cook. If she feeds you one night, you'll be lucky. She also makes candy apples and sells them down at Raynelle's."

The road angled alongside the creek, climbing up through the woods now. And then it opened out into a loop turnaround as it dead-ended.

"Oh, it's Sam's place!" Jenna's excitement bubbled out spontaneously. "And it's just like he described it."

A rustic, weathered log cabin stood to the right of the loop road set in a cluster of trees. A twining, split rail fence snaked around the yard, and the cabin had a slate grey roof with dormer windows peeking out of the rooftop. A long covered porch spread across the front of the house, with a welcoming barn-red door in the middle. Boyce turned into the driveway that skirted to the left of the house. A shed, with a one-car garage built into it, lay just beyond the cabin at the end of the drive.

It had been a long day, and Jenna felt like crying as she got out of the car and helped Boyce get her luggage out of the trunk. Broad log steps rose up to the porch just like Sam had described. And there was Frances' swing and the rockers the Bratcher boys had made. Everything felt oddly familiar.

"Where do you want these?" Boyce gestured to her bags. "In Sam's room downstairs or in the bedroom upstairs?"

"I think I'll sleep upstairs," Jenna said, remembering Sam thought she'd like that room best – since it was filled with Frances' needlework.

She followed Boyce up the stairs to the bedroom on the left. It was a large, cheerful room decorated in blues and yellow, just as Sam described it. A flower garden quilt covered the high, queen bed and a big, floral rug spread over the hardwood floor. Furnishings included a small dresser with an oval mirror, a chest of drawers, and bedside tables. A stunning oil painting of a field of mountain wildflowers dominated the main wall above the bed and over the chest of drawers hung the small painting of Frances that Sam always talked about. Jenna's eyes welled up with tears when she saw it.

Boyce brushed past her in the door, and said, "I'll just go down and get the rest of your stuff and bring it in. You can put a few things away before you come down if you want. I'll go start a fire for you before I leave."

He left before she could say thanks. Jenna was glad because it gave her a chance to wipe away the tears welling in her eyes before she needed to go down to face him again.

She hung up her clothing bags in the closet and unpacked a few essentials before looking for the upstairs bathroom. It was decorated to have a country look, full of blue and yellow towels and patterned with a floral wallpaper on the inside walls. Jenna washed her face and touched up her makeup before finding her way back down the stairs.

She found Boyce lounged on one of the sofas before the fire, his long legs propped up on a sturdy, wood table between the sofas. He looked up, saw her, and flashed a wide, mischievous grin.

"Son-of-a-Gun, what a day." He shook his head for emphasis. "If I was a woman, I'd just have myself a good cry about right now."

Jenna stopped in her tracks at the bottom of the stairs, upset at first with his implication that she'd been crying. She pulled into herself automatically, readying herself for criticism, trying to arrange her face to be expressionless. But then she saw Boyce still relaxed and sprawled over the couch, continuing to grin at her, and realized he must be teasing her and not criticizing her at all. She relaxed a little then. Perhaps she'd misread the situation.

Chapter 4

*B*oyce watched all the expressions flow over Jenna Howell's face and wondered what sort of life she'd known to be so quick to expect attack. He'd seen her expression go from surprise, to pain, to wariness, and relief - and watched her face change from a wistful, soft expression to a carefully steeled, cool, and collected one.

"The fire looks nice." Jenna attempted a smile and walked over to warm her hands by its warmth. The cabin had been cold and chilly when they arrived, but now the fire was heating up the room quickly.

"I took some liberties," Boyce said. "I brought in some wood and turned up the electric heat for the night. I checked some things around the house, too. You know, made sure the refrigerator was working and stuff like that. I even put the chicken casserole Zita Walker left in the oven."

He sent a big grin her way. "I'm really gonna die if you don't ask me to stay and eat a bite with you. I haven't had anything to eat since early today, and with all that baby delivery business, there wasn't time to think about it before now. I'm about to starve, and Zita Walker makes one fine chicken casserole."

A faint smile played at the edges of her mouth. "Well, of course, you can eat some before you go home," she assured him. "You're as entitled to it as I, since you know all these people here. I can't believe they went to so much trouble over me."

He got up to throw another log on the fire. "It's our way here in the mountains. It's called hospitality. Don't you have that in New York City?"

Boyce watched her prickle up again. Lordy, she was an uptight woman.

He propped his long legs on the battered coffee table in front of the sofa. "Listen, why don't you go do something womanly and see what else is in the kitchen to go with that casserole," he suggested. "Zita and Raynelle left all sorts of containers in there. It'll be good for you to poke around the kitchen and get used to the place. I'm just going to chill out here." He closed his eyes, crossed his arms, and laid his head back on the sofa, sighing audibly.

Out of the corner of his eye, he watched Jenna make her way into the kitchen to see what she could find for dinner.

Boyce grinned to himself, wondering what a city girl like Jenna thought of Sam's old country kitchen. He was sure it wasn't like any Jenna had ever seen - no shiny walls, modern cabinetry, granite countertops, and chrome appliances here. The walls and ceilings were sun-bleached boards with grey chinking showing between them, the kitchen floors wide-plank wood. Dishes, glassware, and cooking supplies sat, in no particular order, on wood shelves above the countertops, and utensils and silverware stood helter-skelter in tall baskets or crockery pots. The only colorful touches appeared in the curtains, towels and potholders, and in a faded, rag rug on the floor.

Yet, surprisingly, it didn't take long for Jenna to find the things she needed to pull a quick meal together. Boyce lazily watched her taking out dishes of green beans and corn and finding plates to put out on the big, plank dining room table. He let his eyes drift lazily shut, enjoying the warmth of the fire and the sounds of Jenna puttering in the kitchen.

A short time later he heard her walk over toward where he lay on the couch with his head back and his eyes closed. He could sense her leaning over him on the couch, trying to see if he was asleep. Playfully, he reached up and grabbed her arms.

"Boo!" he shouted, laughing. "Is dinner ready?"

Jenna was so startled that she burst into tears and literally started to shake.

"Well, double death," he remarked in surprise, getting up to come around the couch toward her. He took one look at her face and simply wrapped her up in his arms. She looked as white as a sheet, and she was trembling all over. He felt like a real oaf.

"I'm sorry, Jenna," he apologized. "I was just fooling around. I didn't mean to scare you like that. I'm really so sorry." He rubbed on her back while he soothed her. She stayed tense at first, and then she leaned into him and finally began to relax.

Lord, she felt wonderful, Boyce thought. Her soft curves fitted up against him in all the right ways, and her head tucked right into his shoulder perfectly. Her hair smelled fresh and lemony and her cologne had a touch of sweet, honeysuckle tones to it. She smelled good enough to eat.

And she's married, he reminded himself.

Boyce pulled her gently away to look at her. "Are you all right now?"

She blushed prettily, and Boyce watched her drop her eyes in confusion. If he didn't know she was a married woman, he'd have thought she was a girl that had never been around men much. She didn't seem to even recognize the reason for the tension in the air between them. And, mercy, there was good tension.

The dark circles he saw under her eyes, and what he knew of her from Sam, caused him to pull away and make a joke to cover the moment.

"Sorry about that, Jenna." He shrugged and grinned at her. "I grew up in a big family and we all teased one another all the time and constantly played jokes on each other. I guess fooling around just comes naturally to me. I didn't mean to scare the dickens out of you."

He cocked his head teasingly to one side. "Are you still going to feed me now or just throw me out?"

She was still shaky, but Boyce watched her struggle to recover herself, to adjust her expression, and then, finally, to lift her eyes to his momentarily.

"No, come eat while the food's still hot." She turned toward the kitchen. "I'm sure I'm overly jumpy in a new and unfamiliar place."

Good recovery, thought Boyce. The lady knew how to be smooth.

They sat down to eat and soon realized how hungry they were. For a little while they both attacked the food and said little.

"You were right about the casserole," said Jenna at last. "It's wonderful. I want to get the recipe for it from Zita."

Boyce noticed with relief that she seemed much calmer now.

"That will make Zita Walker feel proud as a peacock for you to ask her." He forked the last bite of casserole off his plate. "And you might as well get ready for a lot of dinner invitations as a newcomer. Especially because you're thought of as Sam's girl."

She looked up and smiled at that. Gracious, she was so beautiful, Boyce thought. Golden, glowing skin like a gypsy girl, deep brown expressive eyes, and that dark, sleek, black hair swinging down over her shoulders. She was tall and slim, but full and curvy under her clothes. He'd felt those curves when he held her. Right now, he found it hard to keep his eyes off her lips as she licked some bits of casserole off the end of her fork.

And she's married, he reminded himself firmly once again.

"You seem to have your mind far away," Jenna prompted, breaking his thoughts. "Sam calls it wool-gathering."

"Yeah, you caught me lost in a moment," Boyce answered. He was trying to think about what to say to get himself out of this moment when a deep barking erupted from the porch.

Jenna overreacted again - dropped her fork with a clatter and put her hand to her throat in surprise.

Boyce laughed. "Gee whiz, you are jumpy, Jenna. That's just Patrick, my dog. He's picked up on my scent over here and knows I'm home now. I'm going to have to let him in or he'll keep up that barking and drive us both crazy." He went to the door and let in the big red setter, who immediately wove all around Boyce's legs in friendly doggy greeting while Boyce patted him warmly in return.

"Oh, he's a beautiful dog," said Jenna.

Hearing her voice, Patrick pricked up his ears and walked over to sit at Jenna's chair to raise a gentlemanly paw. Jenna shook the proffered paw and stroked the setter's head.

"You know, he looks like Sam's old dog, Dan." She looked up at Boyce with a million dollar smile.

"Patrick is Dan's son." Boyce smiled back at her. "Sam mated his dog Dan to a female Irish setter that a friend of his had in Maryville. The friend gave him pick of the litter, and Sam let me have the pup. He's a lot like Dan in temperament."

Jenna shook her head sadly. "It almost broke Sam's heart when Dan died this year. He loved that dog so much."

"Well, Dan was like Sam and Frances' child. When Dan died, a lot of precious memories went, too." Boyce paused. "Pets are just like people. Some are even better than people." He laughed. "It's hard when they go. Leaves a big void."

Jenna looked thoughtful. "I hope Sam doesn't lose Maizie, too."

"That big yellow cat?" asked Boyce, laughing. "Man, that was one fine cat. Lazy, but fine. And she loved table food, if I remember."

Jenna laughed. "Yes, you know Maizie all right."

"Do you have pets, too?" asked Boyce.

"No," she said, regret in her voice. "Elliott is allergic to them, and he doesn't like animals in the house. My parents didn't care for pets, either, so I've never had any of my own."

Boyce watched Jenna's face totally alter when she mentioned her husband's name. Her smile left her face and she tensed all over. She actually straightened her posture and arranged her face carefully into a calm and poised expression – as if following some set of internal expectations.

When she mentioned her parents she stiffened even more. She reined in and locked up all the life in her to some holding place. It was tragic to watch.

"It's late." She sighed and stood up politely to indicate that Boyce should leave. "I think I need to get some rest."

"I'll help you clean up." Boyce offered this congenially.

"No, I'll do it." She shook her head. "You take Patrick on home. It's been a long day for all of us."

Taking the hint, Boyce started toward the front door.

She walked into the kitchen, and then turned back to smile at him as she saw him pause at the door to let Patrick through first.

"And, thanks, Boyce, for helping me get settled here. I really appreciate it." Her smile then was more genuine and a little more relaxed.

"Don't thank me too quickly," he said, stopping with a foot holding the door. "Raynelle is letting me have you at the gallery two days a week instead of you helping her out at the Apple Barn. She knows I'm short-handed, and Charlotte can't come back to work even part-time for a few weeks, what with the new baby and getting recovered and all. Una Deets works for me Mondays, Wednesdays, and Fridays, but she goes to college on Tuesdays and Thursdays when Charlotte works. We thought we had Leeta, one of Charlotte's cousins, lined up to take Charlotte's place for these weeks. But she ran off last week with a truck driver from Texas. The whole family's upset over it, but it doesn't help me any at the moment."

He spread his hands. "Anyway, I hope you won't mind. Sam said you work volunteer at the gallery in New York, so it will be easy for you to be in a little gallery like mine. You'll have tomorrow to settle in here, but I'll need you at the shop on Thursday. I'll come by tomorrow and talk to you about it more."

At that, Boyce let himself out and shut the door behind him before she could give a response.

Chapter 5

*S*urprisingly, Jenna slept soundly through her first night at Sam's. She thought it was due to the stress of her long road trip and the added adventure of going to the hospital. She imagined she'd be frightened, being alone in the mountains. But, it seemed less frightening to be in the cabin than in New York. And the quiet was amazing.

Usually the cacophony of sounds always played in New York. Here, it was still and soft and quiet. The only noises Jenna heard this morning as she padded around the rustic kitchen, making breakfast, were the songs of birds outside the window. She looked out often to see if she could catch a glimpse of them. Several feeders hung from the trees outside, and Jenna decided she would get some birdseed when she went to the grocery. How wonderful to see and hear birds right outside one's window!

She sighed in pleasure as she looked around the cabin in the light of day. It was so different from Elliott's or her parents' apartments in New York. She noted, with interest, how she immediately thought of both those homes as belonging to someone other than herself just now.

"It's how I feel," she acknowledged to herself. "I never fit in those sleek, smooth, polished decors and I had no input in how either of those places were decorated either."

Of course, the same was true here. Sam and Frances decorated this house. But the cabin felt more comfortable to Jenna, like a real home. Not everything was neat, fashionable, and color-coordinated, and there were bits of individual personality everywhere she looked.

She got a catch in her throat standing in the doorway of Sam's big bedroom downstairs. It was so like him. A dark green spread lay on the bed, much like his spread in New York, with a bear-print blanket draped over the bed rail. The rest of the room echoed Sam's passion for Smoky Mountain black bears – with bear accessories scattered about and photos and paintings of bears on the walls.

The living room sofas were a worn plaid of deep green, maroon, and tan. The two sofas faced each other across a wide, square, rustic coffee table. This was the table Boyce propped his feet on comfortably the night before. Two solid armchairs flanked the other end of the table, across from a huge rock fireplace. From any seat you could see and enjoy the fire. Magazines and books lay scattered over the coffee and end tables – with more piled in a basket near by. It was a friendly, comfortable room.

Jenna let herself out the back door of the kitchen to find a covered porch much like the one on the front of the house. From the back porch, Jenna could hear the babbling sounds of Fall Branch Creek beyond the trees. She promised herself she would explore the creek later on when the day warmed up.

For now, she contented herself to climb back upstairs to finish her unpacking. She loved the upstairs bedroom Sam suggested she'd like best. Funny how Sam knew her so well and he wasn't even her family. The floral designs around the bedroom made her happy just to be among them.

Jenna found herself smiling and forgetting her problems, for once, as she put her things away in the drawers and closets and made herself at home. She carried her laptop computer, printer, and boxes of art supplies over to Sam's study, the other upstairs room she discovered last night. In this room was a big desk that Jenna could work on.

She had stopped by Park Press before she left to assure them she would keep up her commitment for greeting cards while she was away.

"I'm sure I'll be able to continue doing at least the twenty-four card designs a month that are in my contract," she told Jason Bentley, her division manager. "I might be able to do more if you need me to."

She bit her lip nervously. "I'll be making my own way now." Jenna reluctantly told Jason about her personal situation with Elliott and explained why she was leaving the city.

Jason listened, nodding. "Well, good riddance to bad rubbish," he remarked. "I've always thought Elliott was a jerk and I hope you decide to make a clean break from him. You'll get only support from me."

He smiled at Jenna. "I'd be happy for you to branch out and begin creating some other designs for the company if you want – stationery, calendars, recipe cards." He pulled out a folder from his desk file. "Here's some literature you can study about our other lines."

Jenna remembered Jason's kind words as her eyes scanned the big office at Sam's in pleasure. It would be nice to have this large, sunny area to work in and not to have to hide her work away as she did at Elliott's. She knew Elliott thought her whimsical card designs were silly. And he was never interested in seeing any of her work. He delighted in telling her it wasn't the type of art fine artists produced. But it did sell, and she took her own small pleasures in creating it.

She thought of Sam with fondness as she assembled her supplies on his large desk. He always encouraged her art work.

"How did you get started working for Park Press?" he asked her once.

She propped her chin on one hand remembering her answer. "I did a set of greeting cards for an art class assignment in high school," she told Sam. "My teacher entered them in a contest sponsored by Park Press. I won first place and one of my designs got published as a real greeting card. Jason Bentley from Park Press came to visit my parents at our home. He encouraged me to go to college in illustration and told my parents what talent he thought I had."

Jenna frowned, remembering the rest. "But of course, Mother and Daddy insisted I go to Barnard and major in Art History instead of going to a school for illustration."

She hadn't told Sam the words her mother said but she still recalled those, too. "You can't keep playing about and diddling with greeting card designs now that you're grown, Jenna. You need to prepare for your life as a member of New York society, for your future role as a wife to a professional executive." She flipped the pages of a fashion magazine while she talked. "It is unlikely you will work once you marry and with a degree in Art History you can work with the committees and boards of the galleries here in New York. Even the wealthiest women work as volunteers with the galleries."

Her own desires put aside as usual, Jenna dutifully majored in Art History. As a further disappointment, her art teachers at Barnard never viewed her art work as valuable, either. In the few studio classes she took, her professors urged her to paint boldly in surrealistic and modern designs and to avoid painting quaint, detailed works they called "cutsey art."

"It's a wonder I got into my work with Park Press at all," she told Sam.

"How did that happen?" he asked.

Jenna smiled at the memory. "Well, one day when I was volunteering in one of the galleries, Jason Bentley came in. He remembered me and asked what I was doing with my art talent. He convinced me to come down to Park Press to talk with him about doing some freelance work, and that's when I started doing my card designs."

Jenna got up to walk over to the window now, remembering with agitation how she and Elliott quarreled over this when they married.

"You don't need to work now that you're married. I provide well for you." He had paced the apartment with irritation while he talked. "And I don't want your art stuff scattered all over the apartment. I paid a fortune to have this place decorated by one of New York's top designers."

She wept and pleaded and he finally gave in to her and created a little desk area where she could do her designs in a storage closet in their apartment.

"Keep the door shut when you're not working," he told her. "And I'd rather you didn't tell anyone what you do, either." Elliott rolled his eyes. "Since your work is rather trite and embarrassing."

However, sometimes Elliott did tell people what she did when they were entertaining or out at a party. On those occasions, he usually made fun of her for "her little hobby" - providing everyone with a good laugh at her expense. Jenna hated those times.

She sighed over all the painful memories.

"Never mind all that," she told herself, returning to set up her work area.

The birds outside the kitchen window had already given Jenna some new ideas for her cards, but she decided to wait to work on her designs until later. She needed to get to the grocery store for more supplies for the cabin. Zita and Raynelle had left some food, and cleaned the cabin nicely, but Jenna was eager to get fully settled in.

She knew Townsend had a small market for milk and grocery pick-ups, but big grocery shopping had to be done in Maryville. Fortunately, Jenna noticed a big Food City grocery outside of Maryville coming in to Townsend, so she drove back there to load up on all the items she needed. By midday she'd finished unloading her car with Patrick's help. The dog had come bounding over from Boyce's porch when he saw her drive up from the grocery.

In the daylight, Jenna could see Boyce's home tucked back in the trees across the road from Sam's cabin. It was a rustic mountain cabin, also, but the house appeared much larger. The exterior was a mix of stone and logs, its porch angling around two sides of the house. A big rock chimney rose up above the roof and the gables, and a flagstone walk wandered in a pretty curve from the drive back to the front steps. It seemed a nice place, and a big double garage sat behind it with what looked like an apartment over the top.

Patrick seemed so much at home at Sam's place that Jenna didn't have the heart not to let him in the house with her. She petted his head fondly. "My guess is that you lived here with Boyce during the years when he was building his own house across the street. You seem awfully comfortable here."

She smiled at him. "You're a very good dog, too, Patrick – very well-behaved and very intelligent." He wagged his tail.

Patrick raced ahead of Jenna down the woods path when Jenna went to explore the creek behind the house after lunch. He obviously knew the way and waded immediately into the water to sniff out some rocks.

Jenna felt enchanted with the creek. It came tumbling downhill from the mountainside above, rioting around big, smooth rocks and cascading over others in rushing falls. Jenna soon found the rock patio Sam said he and Frances built beside the water. A bench, a rough grill, and an old picnic table stood on the patio. A little trail seemed to wind its way up the side of the creek on the opposite bank, and Jenna promised herself that one day soon she would explore and follow it.

The March day seemed mild compared to what Jenna was used to in New York and she only needed a sweater over her shirt and slacks. She whistled to Patrick. "Let's go walk down Orchard Hollow Road for some more exercise. Sam said it was only three miles to the end of the road."

Patrick led the way happily as Jenna started through the yard toward the street. The road sloped downhill, twining in and out of a pretty open woods, with Fall Branch Creek never far away on the left.

There were no houses along the road until Jenna had walked about two miles. Then she passed the Hester's white country cottage on the left and the Lansky's two-story log cabin on the right. Along the roadside now, she saw purple and yellow crocuses and early daffodils in bloom and noticed that the dogwood and redbud trees were getting ready to bloom in the woods. Spring came earlier here than in New York.

At the road's end, Jenna found the marker she'd seen the night before -with the names of each of the families on Orchard Hollow Road tacked to a post. She smiled fondly, remembering how many times Sam had described this marker to her.

Across the road by the McNally's fence line stood another rustic, art creation - a colorful group of weathered birdhouses crowded together on the top of a chopped off tree trunk. Each faded birdhouse was unique - one blue, another red, one painted like a church with a steeple on the top. Jenna was enchanted with it. She wished she'd brought her sketchbook. This would make a great design for a greeting card. In fact, she had gotten several new ideas on her walk.

Jenna and Patrick were part way up the hill walking back, when a jeep pulled alongside them and slowed down. It was Boyce.

"Wanna ride?" he said. "It's more of a hike going up than walking down."

She accepted the offer, especially at Patrick's whining insistence.

"How far did you walk?" Boyce asked, after they both climbed into the jeep.

"To the creek behind Sam's and then down to the end of the road here."

He whistled appreciatively and grinned at her. "That's about five miles in all. Pretty good for a city girl."

She frowned at him. "I'm used to walking or jogging every day. My friend Carla and I always went to the park - unless the weather was simply awful." She considered this and scowled. "Unfortunately, that's often the case in New York, even at this time of year. I simply can't believe flowers are already blooming down here, that the leaves of the trees are all out, and that the dogwood and redbud trees are budding."

Boyce changed gears as he headed up the hill.

"And look at that!" She gestured with enthusiasm at the hillside. "At those trees there. Their leaves are that yellow green Sam said he only saw in Tennessee in the early spring."

Boyce smiled. "The green that is so hard to capture in paint."

"Sam said that, too." She turned her eyes to his. "It really is so beautiful here, Boyce. Like a fairyland. I almost forgot my troubles today."

Boyce didn't comment on that, but instead slowed to point out some other highlights along the way.

"I see you got your jeep fixed," she said.

"Yep." Boyce pulled into his own driveway now instead of Sam's as they came to the end of the loop road.

He turned to her. "Do you want me to come over to build up the fire for you before it gets dark?" He smiled. "I can show you what to do so you'll know how to handle it on your own another time."

She nodded. "Yes, I'd like that. I love to sit in front of the fire and watch it after it gets dark outside. It's comforting somehow."

"Nothing like a good fire," Boyce remarked, before he went around the house to get more firewood.

Later when he was getting the fire going, Jenna said, "There's still a lot more casserole, beans, and corn if you want to help me finish it up tonight.

And I found an apple pie in the back of the refrigerator that I didn't see last night, too."

Boyce grinned boyishly at her. "You can always twist my arm easily to get me to eat home-cooked food. It's a weakness of mine. Do you cook up in New York City or do you eat out all the time there?"

"I'll have you know that I'm an excellent cook." Jenna planted both hands on her hips. "You just ask Sam. I cook for him all the time. And he loves my food."

Boyce chuckled. "Whoa, woman. I never suggested you couldn't cook; so don't get prickly on me. I just asked if you did, that's all. And with you living across the street it's nice to learn that you *do* cook. You can share some of that excellent home cooking with me now and again, and I will invite you over for my famous homemade chili and maybe even for my Grandma Edith's recipe for beef stew. I'm a fine cook myself for things that fit in one pot and get all cooked up together. You can ask anybody."

Jenna had the grace to laugh.

Dark was falling, and they talked about cooking and mundane things while Jenna heated up their dinner and put it on the table. Boyce pitched in and set the table this time, opened a jar of Zita's homemade pickles, sliced up a tomato, and made coffee. Jenna tried to act like it was an everyday thing for her to have a man working alongside her in the kitchen, even when it wasn't. She had never seen Elliott or her father in a kitchen except to get a snack or mix a drink before dinner.

"Did you stop by the gallery today?" Jenna asked, after she and Boyce had settled down at the table to eat.

"Yeah, and Una's got things under control there." He spooned out casserole onto his plate. "Una's an art student at the college in Maryville. She's been working for me since high school. You'll meet her eventually. Real arty, hippie type. Long braid down her back, peasant clothes, sandals. Does great jewelry and weaves. She sells some of her jewelry at the crafts shops. Not much of a painter, though, but she tries. She's been doing some contemporary scenes of people that show some promise lately. Long bodies, interesting clothes and hats - sort of impressionistic. I've encouraged her with those. They don't fit into the theme of the Hart Gallery, but I think she might get another gallery or shop in town to look at them."

"It's hard to get into the art field." Jenna frowned. "I remember the stories I used to hear in New York about artists who struggled for years before they received any recognition. You're young to be so successful already. How did that happen?"

Boyce shrugged. "I figure Sam has told you that."

"Not really," Jenna answered. "He just always bragged about your art and your talent. He told me he and Frances liked you even when you were a boy, so I assume he's known you and your family for a long time. Sam calls you a local boy that made good."

"Well, that's about the size of it," Boyce said.

Jenna waited a little for Boyce to go on.

"That's all you're going to tell me?" She gave him an irritated look.

"What do you want to know?" He looked surprised.

She leaned forward. "About your life. About how you started painting. About how you became recognized. You know, things like that." She offered him a soft smile.

Boyce studied her face. "Why?" he asked her.

Jenna looked down shyly at her hands, not meeting his eyes now. "I guess because I like you," she said quietly. "Because I'd like to know you better. But only if that's all right," she added, looking up at him questioningly.

Chapter 6

$\mathcal{B}$oyce looked across the table at her. She was sitting there in a soft, pink blouse, her face flushed and uncertain, looking more beautiful than any woman had a right to, and asking him if it was all right that she was interested in him. Lord, have mercy. And she said she liked him, too.

How in the world was he going to deal with this situation when she was a married woman? Boyce knew from Sam that Jenna had experienced trouble with her husband. That's why she came here, to take a space to think about it and decide what she wanted to do. But the woman *was* still married. Boyce held strong moral beliefs about that sort of thing. The woman wasn't available. Furthermore, she was vulnerable right now. She'd been hurt. And Boyce wasn't the kind of man to contribute further to a situation like that. He would have to tread very carefully in this.

"Well, I tell you what, Miss Jenna," he said at last. "I'll tell you a bit about my life, if you'll tell me some about yours. That's fair, isn't it?"

She seemed to consider this. "I guess that would be all right," she said.

He winked at her. "So let's clean up here, and then we'll take our coffee and pie over by the fire and swap tales." Boyce scraped the plates and loaded the dishwasher while she put the food away.

A little later, they lounged around the fire. Boyce had added a few fresh logs before he settled down. Now he sprawled across one of the couches, his feet propped on the coffee table, with Patrick at his feet on the rug. Jenna sat curled up in one of Sam's armchairs with an afghan wrapped around her legs.

"You first," Jenna prompted him.

"Where do you want me to start?" He yawned.

"Right from the beginning, from when you were born." She looked over at him with bright eyes.

He studied her pretty face. "Like I told you, Jenna, there's not a lot to tell. I was born not far from here in a little yellow farmhouse on a back road in Wear's Valley. My mother still lives there; I'll take you to see her one day. I was the youngest of five children, last after Charles, Rena, and the twins, Susan and Shirley."

Her eyes grew wide. "Are the twins identical?"

"Yes, and people got them confused all the time when they were small." He laughed in remembrance. "Twins run in the Hart family. In fact, every generation of Harts, as far back as anybody can remember, counts at least one set of twins somewhere."

"Do your brothers and sisters still live around here?"

"They do. Charles lives in Wear's Valley, not far from Mama. He owns a print and sign shop – prints t-shirts and hats and makes signs. He's married to Vera and has two boys. My older sister, Rena, and her husband live over toward Greenbrier and run a motel. Shirley married Reece Wakefield, one of the finest mandolin players I've ever heard, and Susan, the other twin, married the preacher of the Wildwood Church, Gilbert James. They live on the property behind Mama."

Jenna smiled with pleasure. "How wonderful to have all that family," she said. "And they all sound so interesting. Do you get together often?"

He wolfed down a few more bites of his pie before answering. "Every first Sunday in the month we all get together, go to the family church and have dinner at Mama's place, which is nearby. Everybody brings food and it's a good day with a lot of fine eating, visiting, and catching up for everyone."

"And you're an uncle," she marveled.

Boyce rolled his eyes. "Nine nieces and nephews –it cost me a blessed fortune buying gifts for them all this Christmas."

Jenna reached over to pick up her coffee cup. Boyce studied her hands while she did so. Nice hands with tapered fingers and pretty pink nails.

She looked up to catch his eyes on her and asked another question. "What does your father do?"

He felt a shadow cross over his face. "He's gone," Boyce answered. "Died when most of the kids were nearly grown. I was only twelve. It was the hardest thing I ever faced. I loved him and followed him around everywhere. He was my hero and my role model."

"I'm sorry." She gave him a sympathetic look. "Was he an artist, too?"

Boyce laughed. "No, daddy was a preacher. He preached at the Wildwood Church where Susan's husband preaches today - right behind where my Mama's house is." They sat quietly for a little while, enjoying the silence and the fire. Boyce took the pie dishes and put them in the sink and got both of them some more coffee.

When he came back, he said, "So is it your turn now?"

"No." Her mouth quirked in a smile. "You still haven't told me how you got into art or how you arrived where you are now - as a recognized artist."

"I keep trying to tell you, Jenna, my life history is really not that exciting." He settled back on the sofa and propped his feet up again.

She watched him eagerly.

Resigned to his lot, he continued. "A lot of my art happened early by necessity. When daddy died, mother found herself in a pretty hard place. There was insurance and a little put by - but not much. Charles and Rena had just married and were out on their own, but Susan, Shirley and I still lived at home. Money was tight. We never had a lot, being minister's kids in a small rural community, but we never experienced real hardship either. Now things looked tough. As the only son at home, I felt responsible to help out in some way."

Her mouth dropped open. "But you were only twelve, Boyce. What could you do at so young an age?"

"You'd be surprised," he answered. "I worked well with my hands, just like my daddy and Charles, so I started doing anything I could to make extra money. Charles had started his little print and sign business in a renovated barn on the highway at the back end of our property." He smiled at Jenna. "The best blessing in our family was farmland, that Daddy inherited from his daddy, in Wear's Cove between the Caldwell and Wildwood roads. The south border of our land flanks the highway that cuts through Wear's Cove Valley ."

He dropped a foot off the table to scratch Patrick's back before he continued.

"By the time most of us were nearly grown, the valley started to develop as a tourist route between Townsend and Pigeon Forge. As a teenager, Charles worked for a print and sign shop over in Sevierville. When he graduated from high school, he saved and bought some equipment and fixed up the old barn by the highway as his shop. Daddy, and a couple of uncles and family friends, helped him with the labor and the Hart Print Shop was born."

Jenna draped an afghan over her knees, and Boyce realized the cabin had grown chilly as the night settled in. He got up to add another log to the fire as he talked.

"After daddy died, Charles started paying me to work over at the shop with him so I could help Mama. It was only a half mile from our house. After school every day I got off the school bus and worked at Charles' shop. Charles soon figured out I wasn't strong enough, and didn't stay focused enough, to be much good with the printing equipment – or with cleaning the screens and such - but I was good at painting things. I mainly painted signs at first. I'd always been good at drawing and doodling, and pretty soon my creativity started finding a place for itself there. At first, I painted practical signs for the shop and for stores and buildings around the area. Daddy taught me to carve and whittle, and I used those talents with a knife to cut out designs in the wood and, then later, to shape other things I could paint. Birdhouses were one of the first things I started creating after signs. And my birdhouses started getting more ornate and decorative over time."

Jenna interrupted. "Like those birdhouses out on the stump at the end of Orchard Hollow Road?"

"Just like those." He smiled at her again. "In fact, I made those old birdhouses a long time ago. Sam asked me to create a marker sign for the head of the road and to figure out something to do to decorate the old tree stump that had been cut down across from it."

"I love those birdhouses, Boyce." Her enthusiasm rushed into her voice.

"Well, that's the kind of thing I did as a boy and as a teen for a long time, and then I started experimenting with pictures on board. I gessoed and sealed squares of old board that I either located in the scrap heap, or found discarded by builders around the area, and then I painted scenes on them with my house paints."

He grinned at her. "I didn't have any training, so I just painted what I knew – the mountains around me, the old barns and houses, fields and flowers, birds and creeks. Charles started propping them up in the shop and selling them to tourists. Some art expert that came through called them fine examples of "primitive art." I thought that was a real insult then – the idea that they were primitive. I didn't know beans about art. That art expert also found it amazing that I painted everything with only house paints. It was all I had."

He laughed. "I mixed up my own colors and then kept them in canning jars my Mama gave me. So you see, Jenna, I didn't have any special training. I grew into art by doing it."

She tilted her head thoughtfully. "When did you get into oils and acrylics?"

"When I grew older and took art classes up at Arrowmont. That's a well-known arts and crafts school in Gatlinburg. I won a scholarship one summer and took classes in oils, watercolor, and acrylics."

He took a drink. "I like oils and acrylics the best; they're more like the thicker house paints I learned on. I'm fond of oils because they don't dry so fast; I can keep working around on the design longer, and they produce a rich, deep color and effect. I also like acrylics because they wash up with water and have a fluid look and flexibility I can't always get with oil. However, I was never able to do watercolors well at all. They dry too fast; I can't change my mind with them as I go along. They're unforgiving in that way. I can't work as big as I like to with watercolors, either. Canvas can easily be stretched to any size."

Jenna looked puzzled. "So you didn't go to college and study art?"

He could hear the surprise in her voice. "Well, I know in your world, that's important. I got around to it in time - once I started selling my work and could afford it. Early sales of any importance didn't come for a long time. Then my first major money started coming in from juried craft shows and then from galleries around the area. It was an amazement to me when I got the first check with four digits for my work. As Charles said, 'You can never tell about rich folks and what they'll spend their money on.'"

She looked confused. "He wasn't proud of your success?"

"Sure he was," Boyce assured her, laughing. "He was teasing me. I was still painting birdhouses and signs for him while painting canvas the rest of the time. I wasn't sure the new painting success would last at first and thought I might need my other job to fall back on. I like to paint birdhouses." He chuckled. "You'll see some of them down at the gallery."

She tucked her afghan tighter around her knees. "Where did you study when you went to college?"

"I took about two years at Maryville College, close by, and got all my basics. Then, I transferred over to the University of Tennessee in Knoxville for my last two years and finished my art degree there."

A frown creased her forehead. "Did your professors like your work?"

"Sometimes," he admitted. "Considering I made about as much with my paintings by then as some of them made teaching, it didn't matter much to me what they thought. I tried to pick up what I could. I was open for fresh ideas and novel experiences. Even literature, science, and history opened new doors of thinking for me. I took a lot of classes in different art areas, too, to broaden out and try new things. Art history seemed the greatest revelation to me of all, since I had limited exposure to the works and techniques of other artists. I knew little about art of past ages or about art styles or art periods. That was the best part of the education to me."

He paused. "Sam told me art history was your field so I'm sure you'll relate to that."

"Yes. I majored in Art History at college." She yawned and tried to hide it behind her hand.

Boyce saw it anyway and stopped his story. "You're getting tired, Jenna. I guess we'd better call it a night. But I'm taking a rain check on hearing *your* life story since you made me tell you mine."

He got up from the couch and checked the fire a last time before turning to her with a grin. "Do you want me to drive you down to the gallery tomorrow or do you want to drive on down by yourself? I don't open 'til ten, but you might want to come at 9:30 to start to get familiar with things."

A panicked look came into Jenna's eyes.

"Really, Boyce." She twitched her hands nervously. "I don't think you will find me of much use in the gallery. I told Raynelle I've never really worked before, and I actually thought she was just joking, and being friendly, when she told me she wanted me to work in her store part-time. I didn't take it seriously at all."

"Well, she took it seriously." Boyce frowned down at her. "And it was a godsend for Charlotte and for me when Raynelle said we could borrow you instead." He felt annoyance thread his voice. "I can't paint if I have to work the shop. And Charlotte won't be able to come back for a while. She'll come back when the baby is a little older, and as soon as Charlotte's mama can keep her, but in the meantime I'm in a real bind."

He glared at her. "Are you reneging on your promise?"

"It wasn't exactly a promise, Boyce." She stood up, fiddling with the afghan that had been on her lap. "I've been trying to tell you I didn't take Raynelle seriously when we talked. I didn't really come down here to work, you know." She offered him an apologetic smile. "I came down here to think. I mean, I have some personal problems to try to work out."

Boyce stalked across the room toward the door, really annoyed with her now. "Listen, Jenna. You can do whatever you want. You certainly don't owe me anything."

He turned back to face her at the door. "You know, I personally believe you'd have plenty of time to think - and even time to feel sorry for yourself extensively if you want to - while you worked a little in the gallery for me. It's not that busy a place, and it's only for six hours on two days. You can

60

think all you want between customers, as far as I'm concerned. But, as you well know, if you want to back out of this, you have the right. There's nothing I can do about it. But my daddy always taught me two things you might want to think about here. One, work is good for the soul and idleness is bad for it. Two, the best way to get out of a depression is to do something good for someone else."

"Anything else?" Jenna lifted her chin, a hurt look on her face and tears brimming in her eyes.

"Yeah, one more thing," Boyce said quietly, refusing to feel sorry for her. "I thought you liked me and that we were becoming friends, Jenna. Friends help each other out. I could really use your help for a little while, at least until I can get an ad in the paper or put up a flier over at the college and find someone else to cover for me at the shop. I'd count it a real favor if you'd help me. It's only two days a week."

Jenna stood there quietly, staring at the floor, saying nothing.

"Well, there's that, then," Boyce remarked, turning to go. "You take care. I've got to get home so I can get some sleep. Call Sam and tell him how you're getting along. Raynelle said he's worrying about you. I think it would cheer him to hear your voice." He checked his watch. "It's only about 8:30; it wouldn't be too late to call. It might cheer you, too."

Boyce was out the door and starting across the yard with Patrick when he heard Jenna's voice calling out softly to him through the dark. "Boyce?"

"What?" He knew his voice was curt as he turned around to see her framed by the light in the doorway.

"I'm scared." Her voice was almost a whisper.

"Scared of what?" he asked impatiently.

"Scared that I won't do well; scared I won't know what to do at the shop. Scared that you'll be disappointed in me. Scared about everything right now, and not knowing what I should do about anything." She started to cry.

If it hadn't been so quiet in the still of the mountains, Boyce would hardly have heard her anguished words at all. But what he heard most was the pain in her voice.

He crossed back up to the porch and wrapped her in his arms.

"Beautiful girl," he said into her hair, his voice gentle now. "You need to stop being scared. I think you are capable of doing so much more than you imagine you can do. In some ways, I think you've never had the opportunity to even learn what you can do or what you have to offer. You're like an unawakened princess not knowing the wonder of yourself. It's time you woke up, Jenna - started exploring, imagining, and dreaming about who you really are besides someone's daughter and someone's wife. There's a fine woman in you, and you need to get to know her. She's worthy to know, Jenna. And she's capable of facing her tomorrows with courage."

She was crying even more now.

Dang it, he never understood why some women cried so much. It broke his heart when she cried, and, yet, it made him mad, too. Sometimes he couldn't decide whether to pet Jenna or to try to shake some sense into her. But his daddy always said girls needed a lot more tenderness than men, so he held this girl instead and rubbed her back and petted her hair. Gradually, she stopped crying and then melted into him softly, letting him simply hold her, taking in his strength and kindness. As her body fitted itself warmly up against his, he felt that tension rising again.

Boyce realized that his strokes were changing from soothing to caressing. Parts of him were stirring that had no right to. His senses were heightening again, as they always seemed to do whenever he got too close to this woman. He began to drift into that honeysuckle scent she wore. His mouth pressed up against her hair, and he found himself fighting an urge to move his lips across the soft forehead that was so near his mouth, to lift her face and press his mouth against hers. Just to see what it would be like. Just for a minute.

She sighed a little, softly, as he warred with himself, making the inner battle even harder. He pushed her back from himself gently before he could follow through on any of his thoughts. Before he lost control.

Her eyes were glazed and dilated as she opened them to look up at him, and her mouth softly parted. Mercy, but she was tempting him. And yet Boyce knew instinctively that she had no idea she was tempting him. She was a mystery he'd like to solve. How had this grown woman come to be so incredibly naïve? If he remembered right, she'd been married for two years now. She should know a lot more about men than she seemed to.

He turned away from her abruptly and started down the porch. He had to put some distance between himself and her. He simply had to. As he started out across the lawn away from the cabin, he turned to find her still standing there, slightly dazed, staring after him.

"Be ready at 9:15 am tomorrow," he called to her, trying to sound casual and back to normal again. "I'll honk as I start to leave."

"Everything will be fine at the shop, Jenna. You'll see. Think of it as an adventure. Something you can tell Sam about."

Chapter 7

*J*enna walked back into the cabin in a daze. What just happened out there on the porch? She struggled to think; she tried to remember clearly. She'd been upset. Boyce came up on the porch. He gave her a hug to be nice because she was scared and then he talked to her. Such sweet words. They made her cry more. She always seemed to be crying these days. But he'd been so kind and so tender with her. Not impatient with her like Elliott. Not snapping at her or making fun of her. Just hugging her. Then, suddenly, something else flared up. Some man-woman thing. Or was it really that? Had he felt anything? Or had only she felt it? How embarrassing for that to happen when they were just getting to know each other. He was her neighbor and Sam's friend, and she was still a married woman. She had no right to emotions like that.

She moved over to the mirror, that hung just inside the entry, to look at herself. "What's the matter with you?" she asked herself. "The last thing you need in your life is involvement with another man. In fact, it's almost sick to even feel anything for someone else in that way right now. Especially after what's happened to you."

Jenna shook her head in confusion. "I guess it's because everything in your life is in such a muddle with Elliott's unfaithfulness."

That was the answer. She was on the rebound like in all those novels she always read. Feeling unloved and vulnerable. Imagining feelings where there were none.

She continued talking to herself as she cleaned up the dishes in the kitchen, put the pie away, turned off the coffee pot. "I'm simply an emotional basket case right now. And Boyce was just being nice." She frowned. "After all, he pulled away and then walked toward his house as if nothing of importance really happened."

Jenna curled up in the armchair by the fire for a few minutes to think.

She needed to calm down and regain control before she called Sam. She watched the fire dancing in the fireplace and tried to clear her confused thoughts. But she just kept thinking about Boyce.

"He really is a wonderful person." She hugged a pillow to herself. "So different from Elliott. So easy and comfortable to be with. Such a relaxed man."

She chewed her lip thoughtfully. "And he does seem to like me. After all, he keeps coming over. He keeps staying to eat and to talk."

Jenna sighed. It had been a long time since anyone male, other than Sam, had given her quality time. Made her feel good. Made her feel special.

Was there more to their relationship? She thought about that. Did Boyce find her attractive? Sometimes she caught him looking at her when he thought she seemed busy.

"Maybe he does like me a little as a woman as well as just a friend." She whispered the words. "After all, there was that other hug when he startled me. Things changed that time, too, between us. That's twice now when something physical happened." She sighed. "Or did it?"

Jenna sucked in a shaky breath. Surely a man and a woman could just be friends. For that was all she and Boyce could be, no matter what feelings were floating around. Jenna shook her head. "I need to be careful with Boyce if these kinds of feeling are going to come over me whenever he gets close. I almost melted away in his arms just then on the porch. How embarrassing!"

She swallowed, still thinking about Boyce, picturing him. He was such a good-looking man. Tall, with those broad shoulders, and with those expressive blue eyes. How those eyes could talk. And those capable hands fascinated her. Artist hands. Whenever he put them on her and began to touch her, she had major reactions in all sorts of areas of her body. She laughed at herself for that thought.

"Perhaps it's good to know I'm still very much alive in that way." She shook her head sadly. "I haven't felt anything with Elliott for such a long time. He's so critical and and he's never kind or gentle. I've pretended feelings in order to please him."

She smiled to herself. She certainly hadn't needed to pretend anything with Boyce Hart. "I don't think I've ever had rushes of feelings and sensations like this with any man before. It scares me, but it's sort of exciting, too." She considered this. "And it makes me wonder. Elliott told me so many times I wasn't a passionate woman." She touched her fingers to her mouth thoughtfully. "Maybe he was wrong."

She sighed deeply.

Whatever the situation, Jenna knew she would have to be much more careful around Boyce Hart. She didn't want him to think she was an unfaithful sort of person like Elliott. In fact, she didn't want to be a person like Elliott in any way.

She twisted her hands in her lap. "I truly like Boyce. I want to be friends with him. Surely, we can just be friends?" She bit her lip anxiously. "I can keep any other kinds of feelings I might have to myself. He doesn't have to know. It would be awful if he knew I felt attracted to him when he was just trying to be neighborly and friendly." She paused over the last words.

"Neighborly and friendly." She repeated the words. That was the answer.

Jenna nodded her head. She would just be neighborly, friendly, and nice like Boyce. Like all these people acted around Orchard Hollow. Sam was right about that. The people here really were good and kind.

She smiled, thinking about Sam and some of the stories she had gathered for him from her visits around the area. She glanced at the clock on the wall. It was almost 9:30 - not very late yet. She felt calmer now. It was time to call Sam to share, to tell him all about Orchard Hollow.

Over the coming weeks, Jenna's thoughts slipped back often to that night when Boyce held her so sweetly on the porch. She'd been right to interpret it as only neighborliness on his part. No further romantic episodes had occurred.

"I should be glad about that," she said, feeling foolish as she glanced at a picture of Boyce on a sales brochure at the Hart Gallery.

She straightened the stack of brochures and then looked around for something else to do. Rain poured down in a torrent outside, and business in the Hart Gallery was slow today.

Getting out a feather duster, she began flicking it over the framed prints hanging on the wall. "Boyce was right about work in the gallery being therapeutic," she admitted. "It has been and I really enjoy working here. I like meeting the tourists and I love talking with people about art."

Although she'd fumbled around finding her way the first day on the job, Jenna told Boyce by her second day not to seek a replacement. She even took a smug satisfaction in knowing sales had increased on her work shifts.

The phone rang interrupting her thoughts. Jenna picked it up on the second ring.

"Hart Gallery, this is Jenna," she answered.

"Hi, this is Carla," said a familiar voice. "Is it raining there in Tennessee?"

"Pouring." Jenna smiled, pleased to hear Carla's voice. "And the gallery is slow."

"Same here in New York at the bookstore - so I had time to call." Carla laughed. "I think there's rain all the way up the East Coast today"

"I'm having such a wonderful time here, Carla. I really love the quiet pace of life in Townsend. It's so different from New York."

Jenna sat down on the stool behind the counter. "I've explored the town around my work schedule. I toured all the little arts and crafts shops, the Heritage Center, and the Little River Railroad Museum one day. Another day I rented a bike, rode it on the bike path along the highway and then down the River Road past all the vacation houses along the stream. I even explored an old cemetery behind the Visitor's Center, walked along the Little River and found a swinging bridge. And yesterday when I visited the Townsend Library a local book group was meeting and they were all so nice to me."

Carla cleared her throat. "Listen, Jen. I'm glad you're having a good time and I hate to be the bearer of bad news …"

"Oh, Carla, is it Sam?" Jenna put a hand to her heart.

"No. Sam is fine. He's actually doing better." She paused. "But Elliott called here right before I called you."

"Uh, oh." Alarm raced up Jenna's spine. "Tell me what he said."

Jenna could hear Carla tapping on the desk nervously. "He was still in Paris, of course. He said he tried to phone our place in the Poconos several times and didn't get an answer. He also said he tried calling your apartment. He even called your parents. They told him they thought you were still with us." She giggled then. "He was his usual arrogant self and wanted to know exactly where you were since we were already back."

Jenna clutched the phone anxiously. "What did you tell him?" She bit on a nail. "You didn't tell him where I was, did you Carla?"

Carla swore under her breath. "Don't worry, Jen. It would take torture for me to tell that asshole where you were. I told him just what we planned to tell him - that you decided to stay on in the Poconos for a while. I also explained to him we'd been having trouble with the phone lines up there and that he might have trouble reaching you. I offered to send a message to you through the rental agency we use for the property and have you call him tonight in his hotel room. He assured me that would be unnecessary." She giggled then. "Guess he didn't want to risk Miss Lena answering the phone instead of him."

Jenna felt a wave of anxiety hit her. "Do you think Elliott believed that story about trouble with the telephone lines?" She worried one of her rings anxiously around her finger while she talked. "And do you think Mrs. Bynam is sending those notes to Elliott and my parents?"

"Quit panicking. Everything's going fine. We just had a little snag here today and I thought you needed to be aware of it." Carla's voice held a touch of humor. "The only thing Elliott didn't seem to buy was why you would stay up at our place alone. He said you weren't the type who liked to stay by herself, and he started ranting away about whether you'd be safe there on your own. Geeze, Jenna, he is so bossy."

Jenna didn't like the idea that Elliott was calling and asking questions. "What did you tell him, Carla?"

Carla giggled. "I told him a spur-of-the-moment, bold-faced lie. I told him Mrs. Bynam fell and broke her foot while we were there, and that the real reason you stayed on was to take care of her for a few weeks until she could get around better. He bought that in a heartbeat, Jenna. He said, somewhat disgustingly, that this sounded just like you - always giving your time to strays and allowing yourself to be taken advantage of by old people who were sick."

Jenna sighed. "Well, that sounds like Elliott. And, Carla, it was amazingly clever of you to come up with that story about Mrs. Bynam like that." She paused. "You know, I actually would have stayed to help Mrs. Bynam if she had broken her foot. I like her very much."

"You see? It was a brilliant inspiration." Carla laughed and Jenna found herself laughing back in response.

"Gosh, Jenna. It's good to hear you laugh." Carla heaved a sigh. "I've been so worried about you. This whole thing has been awful."

Jenna twisted the phone cord in her fingers. "We can thank Sam that I am doing better, Carla. Coming down here was a wonderful idea for me. I never realized how oppressive Elliott's apartment felt. Or how unhappy I was. There was so much pressure from Elliott in so many ways every day - and from Mother and Daddy. So many constant expectations. And I never seemed to do anything right."

She paused thoughtfully. "Here, everyone seems to like me just the way I am. I've known peace for the first time in a long time. And I've created some good new art designs, Carla. It's so inspiring here in the mountains, and I have Sam's wonderful big room to work in with a big picture window looking out on the mountains. I sent some of my new designs to Jason at Park Press and he is really thrilled with them. The company wants me to do a great many more. In fact, Jason has been talking to me about coming on full-time when I get back."

Jenna heard Carla clap her hands. "Oh, Jenna, that's wonderful. I am so glad for you. You remember I was the one who used to encourage you to take art classes because I thought your drawings were so good. You always made the most incredible cards for me for my birthdays over the years and I've kept most of them. I used to hate it that Elliott made you do all your work in that cubby-hole office closet. That place was simply dismal. And he never encouraged you, either." She paused. "What do the people there in Tennessee think of your work?"

Jenna hesitated. "Well, I haven't shown any of my work to anyone here. It's not as though it's real art like the paintings we sell in Boyce's gallery, Carla. It's only little greeting card designs. I doubt anyone would be interested. I'm just glad I can be here for a time, and I'm pleased to have some time to begin to learn who I am while I'm here. A new friend told me that's what I needed - to learn who I really am on my own."

Carla interrupted. "Who you are is one terrific person, Jenna. And don't let anyone say you're not."

Jenna smiled. "I'm so glad I have you, Carla. Thanks for being such a support for me through this time and for believing in me."

She heard Carla snort. "Don't be ridiculous, you're my best friend, J. C. And I'm glad you kept using J.C. Martin for your art even after you married Elliott. At least that's one change you won't have to make if you leave Elliott."

Jenna paused and took a deep breath. "Carla, I'm not going to go back to Elliott. I simply can't. I know it's going to cause a big dispute with my parents and probably with Elliott's family - not to mention with Elliott himself - but I've made up my mind."

She sat up straighter. "I got up this morning before coming down to the gallery to work, and I realized I was actually happy. Carla, I haven't been happy in a long time. And I wasn't happy this morning because of things or prestige - I felt happy simply because a ray of sun slipped through the rain clouds, the chickadees came to the feeder even in the morning drizzle, and because the smell of good coffee filled the kitchen. The best thing I've learned here about myself is that simple things make me happy. Some of the silliest, simple things make me happy. I never knew."

"Oh, Jenna." Carla's voice filled with warmth. " I'm really glad you've decided to have your own life without Elliott. I know it's been a hard decision for you, because I know you always wanted to marry and stay married to the same person forever."

Jenna sighed. "I did; I truly did. But I didn't count on the person I married being someone who would betray my trust and be unfaithful to me over and over again. You know, one indiscretion I might have been able to work through, if Elliott had been sorry, but from what Sam and his detective friend learned, unfaithfulness has been a pattern with Elliott for a long time. You know, Carla, the hardest thing, I think, has been learning that Elliott was not who I thought he was at all. He is not a good person in any of the ways that matter to me."

"That's true." Carla agreed with her. "The more Sam's friend Jake investigates Elliott, the more awful things he finds. You won't have any problem gaining a divorce with all that evidence."

"Well, it's taken me almost three weeks to decide I can't go back to him," Jenna confided. "I don't believe I could spend my life with someone like that. I'd rather be like Aunt Lydia and go my own way, even if it means being cut off by my family. That might really happen, Carla. My mother holds very strong views, and Daddy generally goes along with her to keep peace."

Carla made a disagreeable sound. "You'll have John and me, Jenna, no matter what. And John's family and my family. Plus Sam, Henry, and Mary. And Jason Bentley at Park Press and the people there. And all your friends at the art gallery. Plus a lot of other people, too. Just wait and see."

"I'll manage. I know I will. Being here these few weeks has already shown me that, Carla. I've actually been happier here living on my own than I was living with Elliott. That's been a surprise to me."

"Not to me," mumbled Carla.

"By the way, I'm going to need another favor of you, Carla." Jenna cleared her throat. "I hate to ask, but I don't know who else can help me with this. I need you to help me find an apartment. I don't want to go back to Elliott's place. I really hate it there. He can have it and everything in it. It was all his before we married, anyway. There are really only a few things in the whole apartment that are truly mine. I don't want anything of his from that place. I'll just start fresh or get something furnished. Will you look around for me? I want to come back before Elliott returns from Paris and move all my things out. I know it's cowardly, but it's the way I want to do it."

"I don't blame you at all," said Carla. "And you know I'll help you find something. I'll start looking right away. What do you want?"

"Something small and simple, not lavish like what I've had." She thought for a moment. "I just want a one-bedroom or studio-type apartment, Carla, with a good area where I can do my design work. One bath will be enough, along with a small sitting area. Oh - and I really want it to be in the area near you and Sam, if possible. That means a lot to me."

"Hmmm," said Carla. "I do have one idea for a start, but it really is simple, Jen, and it's a third floor walkup with no elevators. It's a one-bedroom apartment, a little roomier than a studio, with a lot of windows on the backside of the apartment; there would be plenty of light for your art. There's a living area, a small kitchen with a dining area, and a bedroom. A plus is that the bedroom is big with a large closet and there's a pretty nice bathroom."

"It sounds fine, Carla." Jenna meant it. "I promise I'm really not fussy. Where is it located?"

Carla giggled. "It's upstairs in our building on the third floor," she said. "It's that little apartment we rent out to grad students sometimes. Since the last student moved out this fall, we've been putting off painting it and have just been using it for extra storage for the bookstore. We could clean it out and fix it up for you. What do you think?"

"I've seen that apartment," said Jenna with excitement. "You and I painted it once. It's on the floor above yours and John's place, isn't it?"

"Yes. If you remember, there's a storage room and that one apartment up there. The back has a lot of windows, but there aren't any views out onto the park like you're used to. It's not a fancy place, but it does have a lot of light."

"It sounds great, really."

Carla made a tut-tutting sound. "You know it's not great, Jenna, and there are two flights of stairs to climb. But it's going to be available at the right time, and it's close to us and to Sam. You and I will still be able to walk in the park every day, and you can live in the apartment until you find something you really like. You won't have to sign a lease, and the rent is reasonable."

She stopped to think. "There is some decent furniture in it, Jenna, but it's not expensive furniture. We'll need to go shopping and get you some new things you'll like more. But to start, there's a bed and some bedroom furniture, a couch and chair in the living room, a table and chairs in the kitchen. Enough so you wouldn't have to sleep or sit on the floor." She laughed.

"I think it might do in a pinch. When is Elliott coming back, Jenna?"

Jenna stopped to think. "Elliott's supposed to come back sometime in the first week in May. I'll have to check my calendar for the exact date, but whatever the date, I'll still have time to move over to the apartment before Elliott returns. And his trip may get extended. They usually do. That would give me more time."

"So when will you come back to New York?"

"Not until the last week in April." Jenna tapped a pencil on the work counter. "I promised Boyce I would work in the gallery until then. Charlotte isn't planning to come back until the first of May. But, truthfully, the other reason I want to stay until then is that I just want another month here. Spring is arriving, and it is incredibly beautiful in the mountains. I want to enjoy it a little longer and get strengthened in myself to face what is ahead for me. "

"John and I will be here to help you, Jenna. Try not to worry too much." Carla's voice dropped with concern. "Are you going to be all right, Jen? You know, deep in your heart."

Jenna thought about this. "Hearts heal, Carla. You read enough romance books to know that. And I am purposed that I am going to heal and be all right. I'm hoping work and staying busy will help, too. A friend here taught me that work has a lot more benefits than I ever realized. So I'm going to try to do more with Park Press when I get back. Jason at the Press thinks I have more potential than I've tapped in to. I hope he's right. I'm going to try not to disappoint him."

Carla giggled. "Your mother will absolutely flip when you tell her that!"

A little trickle of fear caused Jenna to have goose bumps over that comment. "Well, maybe I'll promise Mother I will still volunteer some hours at the gallery for my social image," she replied, trying to cover her disquiet with a joke. "Maybe that will make her feel better."

They both laughed, and Jenna hung up. Small armies of mixed emotions still chased through her mind, but she felt wonderfully better from talking with her best friend. There were so many changes ahead for her.

Jenna walked over to look out the window. Rain still poured down in sheets outside. It looked wet, grey, and dreary. Yet, somehow her heart felt a little lighter despite the day. She had made some important decisions about her life. And it was good having new plans.

Jenna walked around straightening things in the gallery, arranging the prints in the bins, making sure the paintings on the wall were straight, organizing the gift items on the shelves. She stopped and smiled over Boyce's birdhouses.

She and Boyce had shared many good times in the last two weeks. He tagged along to many of the dinners she was invited to, claiming he needed to help her find the way to the different houses - but grinning while he said it. They both knew he just wanted to freeload on the home-cooked meals. They went to Raynelle's, to several of Sam's cousins' homes, and to Charlotte's place. At Charlotte's, Boyce played riotously with Charlotte and Dean's little boy Tyler Dean, both of them having a wonderful time.

Boyce kept finding small toys tucked in his shirt and jacket pockets, and would say, "Ouch, I think there's something poking me in my pocket right here."

Tyler Dean would start jumping all over him, saying, "Look and see, Boyce. Look and see. See if it's something for me."

He'd give Tyler Dean a teasing look. "Well, why would there be something for you in my pocket?"

"Just look." Tyler Dean would insist.

Boyce peeked and felt around in his pocket to prolong the suspense as long as he could. Finally, he would draw out some small toy, which would initiate a whole new game among them all over again.

"He's so good with kids," Charlotte told her that night. She and Jenna sat on the couch with Jennie Rae sleeping in a wooden crib beside them.

Charlotte looked over fondly to check on her. "You know, Dean built this crib for Jennie Rae with his own hands," she said with pride. "And he's fixed up this house real nice for us. He added on that back screened porch just for me so I could sit out there with the children on a nice evening like this." She and Dean exchanged a smile that simply melted Jenna's heart.

Their house, just a simple frame one, sat back of a rural side road outside of Townsend. A lot of the furniture had seen better days, but Charlotte had arranged everything nicely, and the love in the home made up for any lack of grandeur in Jenna's opinion. In addition, Charlotte was a good cook and a sweet hostess. Jenna hated to say goodbye at the end of the evening.

In a surprising way, Charlotte Bratcher had become Jenna's friend. Charlotte called Jenna every day she worked at the gallery, to see how she was getting along. Sometimes she dropped by. She had been a great help to Jenna whenever she ran into trouble at the shop.

Charlotte would say, "You just call me anytime, Jenna. If the kids are hollering, I'll get them quieted and then call you back. But don't call Boyce at work unless you have to. He gets real grumpy when you interrupt his painting. Una and I always call each other and put our heads together until we can figure out what to do about any problem at the shop. If all else fails, we can always go get Raynelle. Running that big store she has, she can usually figure out any little ole problem we have at our gallery. We always let Boyce think we just have everything under control."

Jenna had quickly learned how the store worked. The Hart Gallery stood on one side of the Apple Barn and a little sandwich shop, called The Lemon Tree, sat on the other side. While the tourists shopped at the Apple Barn or the Lemon Tree, they would also come into the Hart Gallery to explore.

Boyce recognized that many people didn't understand the value of fine art and would never pay $500 or more for a painting, or even $100, so he always had lower priced items in the print bins, and on the walls and shelves, that the tourists could buy. His picturesque birdhouses, cute signs, and painted toys always sold well, as did his small framed prints.

Once Boyce told her, "I never want to get to the place that I don't paint and make things all types of people can enjoy. I wouldn't feel right if just well-to-do and rich folks were the only ones who could enjoy my work."

Jenna learned Boyce had a generous heart, too. He took time to entertain a little girl in a wheel chair with a wooden puppet one day, and then he gave it to her to take home. Another time he pretended the price of a painting was wrong, so an older man could afford to buy it for his wife.

Although Jenna and Boyce spent a lot of time in each other's company now, they shared most of that time with others. The mood stayed light and playful between them even when alone. Jenna had become accustomed to Boyce's light-hearted teasing. She often quipped back at him now. Sometimes, she noticed Boyce acted almost careful not to touch her in any way, even to help her into his jeep or over a rock when they went out walking. She'd actually watched him instinctively reach out toward her a few times and, then, purposefully pull back with a frown. Of course, she never let him realize she noticed these instances - because she played many of the same games herself. She carefully avoided sitting too close to Boyce when they were together, and she dropped her eyes when their gazes met unexpectedly.

Una, the art student who worked in the gallery, came by to meet Jenna one day, and whispered to her when Boyce walked out of the room, "That is one dangerously attractive man."

When Jenna looked surprised at the comment, Una laughed. "Don't worry," she told her. "There's nothing secret going on with us that you're not supposed to know about. In fact, there is *nothing* going on with us. Not that I haven't had a few fantasies and flirted. But Boyce just sees me like a little sister." She sighed and shrugged.

Jenna gradually realized that women were very attracted to Boyce. He wasn't sleekly handsome like a magazine ad, but he was good looking in a comfortable, natural way and had a cute boyish charm. He always acted courtly and kind to women who flirted with him, but Jenna never saw him act seriously interested in anyone. Boyce knew many single women. They sometimes dropped by the store looking for him. But Jenna became aware over the weeks that there was no one special in Boyce's life right now.

"When are you going to find you a girl and get married?" Charlotte asked him when they were over at her house. "Every one of your brothers and sisters are married but you. Your mama is starting to wonder if she is ever going to get any grandchildren off of you."

"I keep falling in love with women that are already taken." He pushed out his lower lip in a pout. "Like you, Charlotte." He leaned over to pinch her on the cheek and wink at her.

"Oh, go on with you," she said. "You're just avoiding the subject with your teasing. Besides Dean would punch your eyes out if you made a real pass at me."

They all laughed, but Boyce looked intensely at Jenna when he made that comment about women already taken and it gave Jenna a catch in her throat. Sometimes she wondered if Boyce might be developing some feelings for her, but other times she decided such thoughts were foolish. Admittedly, she often thought about Boyce in ways that were not appropriate for a woman just separated from her husband. Sometimes her thoughts and dreams embarrassed her. But she couldn't seem to stop them.

Of course, going back to New York would put a halt to all those feelings. But, a little part of Jenna didn't want to stop her feelings for Boyce just yet.

"It's one of the things about being in Orchard Hollow that's making me feel more alive," she admitted to herself one night while she was brushing her hair. "Like Una, I enjoy being in the company of that dangerous man."

She paused, brush in hand. "I'm scared sometimes that something will happen and Boyce will realize how I feel." She chewed on her lip. "But I'm even more worried nothing will ever happen again – that he will never know I have any feelings for him. That I'll just go back to New York and always wonder if there was anything between us at all or if it was just my imagination."

She thought about that as she looked out at the continuing rain. A few stray customers came into the shop, braving the wet and shaking out their umbrellas on the porch before they started to browse. But not many.

After cleaning the store, Jenna worked on her designs at the sales desk beside the register. She learned after the first week that she often had plenty of extra time at the gallery in which she could work on her greeting card designs or verses. When anyone came in, she tucked her work quickly under the big, desk calendar beside the register. And at the end of the day, she always tucked her work back down into her tote bag to take home.

She had written a "Thinking of You" verse this afternoon, about taking time to do the things you love, to smell the flowers, to enjoy the sun, to even take a snooze in the middle of the day. For the front of her card, she drew a sunny scene of Boyce's rustic birdhouses clustered on the old stump heading up to Orchard Hollow Road. Snuggled cozily in one of the birdhouses on a nest of twigs, was a fat, snoozing bird. Jenna watched him take shape with satisfaction.

Jenna wrote the verses for her cards and roughed out her sketches by hand on blank greeting cards. "It helps me get a feel for how they will look completed," she told Sam once. "I hand print the verse I've written on the inside. I sketch out the design on the outside of the card, and then I paint in the colors to create a mock up to send in to Park Press. They get it press-ready and turn it into the finished version there."

"What's that little design you always put on the back?" he asked.

She smiled. "It's my martin birdhouse logo with my design name penned underneath, J. C. Martin. I used to hand-letter it on every card but now I have a stamp to use for it."

As Jenna stamped the back of the card design she'd created today, she studied her logo and laughed. It was funny how a birdhouse link existed between her and Boyce. It almost seemed like a quirky little piece of destiny.

Of course, Boyce didn't know about her cards. Nor did Charlotte or anyone else here in Orchard Hollow. The Apple Barn carried some of Jenna's cards in a display rack, but Raynelle hadn't made the connection that the cards were Jenna's. People knew her as Jenna Howell here; they didn't know her maiden name. Jenna sometimes lingered near the card rack so she could hear the comments her buyers made. She used to do the same thing in New York. It helped her know what people liked.

Jenna smiled at the little design she'd created today. For the first time in a long time she was beginning to feel good about her design talents. Here in the mountains, people appreciated crafts more than in the city. She'd watched Zita Walker stitch her quilt designs, Charlotte's mother make apple butter, and Raynelle's husband whittle wooden whistles. Everyone here felt so respectful of even small talents. When she questioned one day whether making apple butter was really an art, Charlotte turned on her in surprise.

"Why, Jenna, I'm surprised at you," she said. "Any God-given talent a person uses with skill and love is an art. I thought you'd know that."

The girl was a natural philosopher sometimes. And she had taught Jenna many simple basics about life.

"You know," Charlotte told her one day, "For a city girl, you sure are dumb about a lot of stuff. Now I don't mean you to take offense, so don't get mad at me. Cause when you first came down her, I was just in awe of you. You had a college education, great clothes, and walked with this smooth gait like a Walking Horse in a show ring - just effortless like, and not even realizing how polished it was. Your haircut looked so nice. And everything about you was just so put together. It made me feel downright frowzy to be around you. But then when I started to get to know you, I found we were really a lot alike in many kinds of ways. I mean, you get all excited about a pretty sunset or a big dandelion in the sidewalk just like me, and you get all emotional and sniffly like me when Jenna Rae does something cute. You hate red nail polish and red lipstick just like me. But you don't always know stuff you should. Like how to read people or to understand things about what makes people tick."

Curiosity and offense did a quick tap dance in Jenna's mind, but curiosity won out quickly. Charlotte's outspokenness was so guileless.

"Give me an example," she said.

"Okay." Charlotte thought for a minute. "Raynelle told me you came down here from New York City to get away because you found your husband had been getting it on with about half the women in your city. But you're not even mad. Instead, you're all unsure about what you ought to do, whether you should go back to him or leave him."

She shook her head in exasperation. "Girl, it was all I could do not to scream at you when I first heard you talking like that. To hear you worrying if your folks were gonna approve if you left this jerk. I mean, who cares what they would think? Parents who won't stand beside you in what's right aren't much to worry over, as far as I'm concerned. Plus, any woman who wouldn't walk out on a jackass who had been cheating on her - as much as we heard Elliott had been cheating on you - would just be plumb stupid. That's what I mean about you being dumb sometimes."

Jenna was speechless for a minute. She felt the color drain out of her face and knew her cheeks must be red with embarrassment. "Does everyone here know everything about my personal life?"

Charlotte looked surprised. "Well, sure. This is a little place, and things get around."

Jenna winced. "That's so embarrassing, Charlotte, thinking everyone is talking about me, that everyone knows."

"Don't be silly, Jenna." Charlotte frowned at her. "And don't let it bother you one minute that people here know about you and what happened. This isn't New York City where everyone has some kind of social image to maintain and where everyone plays all kinds of society games. Here everybody just shares everything, and no one's stories stay on anyone's mind for more than a short time, anyway. Everybody just knows about everybody down here."

She grinned then. "You'll get used to it if you stick around long enough. Actually, it's kind of nice in some ways that you never have to worry about secrets. Everybody always finds out about everything that happens to you, so you finally figure out it's just easier to tell it yourself. At least that way you know the story is right." She laughed at her own joke.

Charlotte studied Jenna carefully then, noticing that she looked a little pale and upset. "You're not going to be mad at me now, are you, Jenna?" Charlotte asked. "I mean you did ask me, and I just told you the honest truth."

Jenna shook her head. "No, I'm not mad, Charlotte. I'm just shocked. I didn't know that anyone knew, except maybe Raynelle."

"Well, you can't fault Raynelle too much." Charlotte shrugged her shoulders. "I guess Sam didn't tell her not to say anything. And besides, everybody agrees that Elliott is just a no good jerk, Jenna. Nobody thinks anything bad about you, except to feel sorry for you and to wonder why you don't see what a creep he is yourself. Sometimes you make excuses for him and for your parents I just don't understand. I mean wrong is wrong, Jenna. It's dumb not to see that."

"I guess you're probably right." Jenna agreed, with a resigned sigh. "And maybe I've needed someone outside my life to simply tell me the honest truth. I've made too many dumb excuses for Elliott for too long, I think."

Charlotte patted her on the hand. "Well, I agree with that, and I'm glad to hear you saying it. He just sounds like an awful person, Jenna. What possessed you to ever marry him anyway?"

"I guess I was just stupid," Jenna answered glumly. "Like you said." She teared up as she acknowledged this, despite her efforts not to. "I don't know why I didn't see more clearly what Elliott was like, Charlotte. I keep beating myself up about this all the time, about why I wasn't more discerning. About how everyone could see what Elliott was like except me."

"Now you go and quit that crying." Charlotte came over to give her a hug. "My Granny Oliver says that there is no shame in making mistakes in this life. It's just a natural thing. But it's what we do after we make them that's really important. You're wiser and smarter now about men, and you'll be more careful about who you choose another time around."

Jenna looked at her in alarm. "Oh. I don't think I'll ever want to be married again, Charlotte."

"Well, look in the mirror and try telling yourself that again." Charlotte gave her an appraising look. "You can't keep bees from buzzing around good honey. And, girl, you are beautiful, sweet, and good. The bees are gonna come a buzzin'. And eventually one will get to you. That's just the way it is. Besides, there are a lot of good men out there. They're not all like Elliott."

"You're becoming a really good friend, Charlotte." Jenna smiled at her.

Charlotte grinned back. "Well, if I am, maybe you'll invite me to come up to New York City to see you one day. I've never been north of Kentucky or west of the Mississippi River, and I'd like to see a big city once in my life."

Jenna laughed, remembering this earlier conversation with Charlotte.

As if on cue, the phone rang and Charlotte's voice greeted Jenna. "Hi, how's your day going?"

"It's going slow, and I was just sitting here thinking about you when you called."

Charlotte laughed. "Well, you see, that's why I called. You messaged me and I caught it. Like a shooting star in the sky. What were you remembering about me?"

"How you wanted to come to New York," she answered tactfully. Then she plunged on. "I'm going to leave Elliott, Charlotte, and I think I've found a little apartment I can rent close to some of my friends in the neighborhood I already know. It won't be a big apartment, but maybe I can fly you up for a visit with me later if you could leave Jennie Rae and Tyler Dean for a few days."

Charlotte paused before answering. "Well, Jenna, that would be real fine if it works out. And I'm proud you've finally decided to divorce Elliott, but I'd be happier if you'd stay here. Maybe a change down here would be good for you. Then you'd never have to see that snake, Elliott Howell, again. Raynelle said you had a bloom in your cheeks now that you've been with us here for a while. It might be that our little area of the world agrees with you."

"I think you're probably right, Charlotte. But I have a lot of things to take care of and clear up in New York. And, besides, there's Sam."

Charlotte's voice brightened. "Raynelle says Sam's a lot better. Maybe you could bring him back with you for a visit soon. He'd love to come down here, and if you traveled with him, maybe he would."

Jenna looked out the window to see the rain increasing. "That's something I might try to do later. I'd love for Sam to be able to come back to his cabin again for a visit."

Charlotte interrupted. "Listen, Jenna, this is really why I called. I need to go over to Maryville to try to get the kids some Easter clothes on Monday. You know, Easter's next Sunday, and I need to get some things for them to wear for Easter church. I was hoping you would go with me, in case I need to get Tyler Dean into the dressing room or something. You could watch Jennie Rae and help me out. I know it's a lot to ask, but it's really hard doing any shopping with two kids all by yourself. The last time I went over to Maryville, I had a time of it. I lost Tyler Dean while I was changing Jennie Rae and I found him up a construction ladder outside the store, trying to help the sign man change the store sign. I thought I'd have a heart attack."

"You don't have to try to convince me any further," said Jenna, laughing. "I'll go with you. I like to go shopping, anyway."

Charlotte giggled. "Well, don't expect to get much done with the kids along with us," she told her. "Plus I have to go thrift shopping since I'm not working for any mad money right now. I really miss my check from the gallery."

Jenna thought about that after she hung up. When she'd gotten her first two-week check here, she'd been shocked. First, she hadn't expected a check for filling in, and second, it wasn't much after taxes and withholding.

Charlotte said, "Boyce pays real good compared to a lot of places around Townsend." However, Jenna knew she got about that same amount for creating only four of her card designs. It gave her a new perspective about her work when comparing it to the wages of people here in the mountains.

It was another of the reasons Jenna had kept her design work quiet. She enjoyed working at the gallery, and she didn't want to let people think she devalued it by comparing it negatively to her other work. Besides, it gave Jenna a confidence boost to think that if people could make it on such small incomes, she might make it on her own with the work she could do. Elliott often ridiculed Jenna for the compensation Park Press paid for her card designs, but in comparison to salaries and compensation here, she was paid well. Jenna knew Charlotte would be in awe that Jenna made as much as she did for a part-time job.

The rain stopped, and shortly after, a steady stream of tourists and locals dropped by the gallery to browse and shop. A couple from Michigan went into raptures over Boyce's paintings and bought two for a room they were redecorating. They took several of Boyce's catalogs so they could order a few more prints after they returned home. Two ladies from West Virginia bought birdhouses, and a young couple in hiking clothes took home a small painting of a waterfall they had just walked to on a hike behind Gatlinburg.

"You can walk right behind this falls and then up the trail behind it." The young girl's voice was bright with enthusiasm.

"Yeah, it is way cool," pronounced the boy. "If you haven't been there, you should go. It's called Grotto Falls. It's a good trail. And it's right behind Gatlinburg."

The girl chimed in. "We went down into Gatlinburg and watched them make homemade taffy right in the window of this store, too. There's this big machine that pulls it and then wraps it and everything. And they gave free samples after they finished. While it was still hot and gooey. Ummmm."

They oozed excitement and talked about what they'd done on vacation the whole time they browsed the store. It made Jenna realize how few places she had visited in the Smokies since she arrived. She needed to get a map and some tourist books and make some plans. After all, she only had a few weeks more to explore.

She smiled, remembering Boyce promised to take her on a hike with him tomorrow. He wanted to go to some trail known for its spring wildflowers to sketch and take some pictures to work from. Also, she was invited over to Boyce's tonight to try his homemade chili recipe. He claimed she'd fed him so often, it was his turn to feed her tonight. This was also his month to host the neighbors on Orchard Hollow Road. Sara and Will Lansky and the Hester's were coming to dinner, too. Boyce told Jenna that every month one of them hosted a get-together at one of their homes. It promised to be a nice weekend.

Una came in the door of the gallery, balancing a load of books across her arm. She was working for Jim tonight, since Jim had an accounting meeting over in Maryville. All the employees were good friends here at the gallery, and they often traded shifts with each other when it was needed.

"I hope it's quiet tonight." She pushed the door shut with her foot. "I need to study for an exam."

Jenna tucked the card design she had been working on quickly under the desk calendar. Una plopped her book bag and books down on top of the calendar, and Jenna realized she'd probably have to retrieve her card design later or risk possible explanations with Una. Not that it mattered. She often left a card design or two she was working on here at the gallery, and she had several others she needed to finish back at the cabin before this one, anyway.

She visited with Una for a little while, ran by the store for milk and eggs, and started home to the cabin at Orchard Hollow. She caught her own thoughts on the word "home." The cabin had begun to seem like home to Jenna. In many ways it seemed more like a home to Jenna than any place she'd ever lived. Here in the quiet of the mountains, she seemed able to really be herself. She knew she would miss this place when she went back to New York.

Chapter 8

*A*fter running a few errands, Boyce stopped by the gallery on his way home. The rain stopped finally, and the sky had cleared. This cheered him, because he was hosting all his Orchard Hollow friends at his house for dinner tonight. His homemade chili simmered in a big crock pot in his kitchen, and he'd picked up a few bottles of good wine and some fresh bread to go with it. He cajoled Myrtle, at the Lemon Tree, into making one of her apple and lemon stack cakes to serve for dessert. Boyce felt eager for some rest and relaxation on a Friday night after a long work week.

He'd enjoyed an exceptionally good day in the studio. He finished a painting he thought he might call *Rafting in the Smokies* - of tubers floating around a turn called the Wye in the Little River above Townsend. It was a popular Smokies spot for summer tubing, picnicking, sunning, and water fun. Last summer, Boyce made extensive preliminary sketches at the Wye. He'd also snapped dozens of pictures of the tourists and locals floating the creek, their rental tubes a riot of color bouncing among the eddies and cascades of the stream. He thought he captured the joy and color of the event in the painting, and the beauty of the spot. It was a happy painting of the pleasures of summertime in the mountains – the tubers' faces wreathed in smiles, their noses and skin touched with red from hours in the sun. It made him think of all the good times he and his brothers and sisters shared tubing and playing at that same spot on a hot summer's day.

Slipping into his work and into old memories helped him keep his mind off Jenna Howell. He reminded himself over and over that she was still officially Mrs. Jenna Howell, a married woman and thus off limits. From what Boyce heard through the grapevine, and from the occasional comments Jenna made to him, she still hadn't made up her mind what she planned to do about the marital situation in her life.

Raynelle told him how Jenna's husband cheated on her time and again.

It made Boyce angry that Jenna had trouble making the decision to leave a man like that. The girl allowed herself to be manipulated and controlled by people in her life who did not have her best interests at heart. He found this aspect of her exasperating. Why did she allow this? Usually, he disliked weakness and indecisiveness in others, but Jenna mowed over all his rational thinking, and his physical response to her was acute.

She bombarded his senses. She bewitched him with her dark, gypsy-like attractiveness and those full lips. Her habit of licking her lips to wet them and her way of putting two fingers up to her mouth while thinking drove him wild. It was tragic how he noticed everything about her, how preoccupied with her he had become. Her deep brown eyes reflected her every emotion and there were little golden flecks in them in the sunlight. He could swim in those eyes. Her hair swung just below her shoulders - rich, thick, and black. He liked the way she wore it bound back in neat chignons or braided most of the time, but one evening when he stopped by to take some firewood in for her, she'd let it down. She'd been dressed in a silk-patterned robe with nothing underneath. He nearly swallowed his tongue. When he accidentally brushed against her coming through the door, and caught her eye afterwards, he'd seen her reaction. She drew a quick intake of breath, her eyes widened and she crossed her arms over her breasts instinctively protecting herself.

Boyce wasn't stupid about women. He knew she was attracted to him and trying to hide it, just as he was. He'd seen her watching him when she thought he wasn't looking over the last weeks, and he had seen hunger and yearning in her eyes. That made it worse, knowing she hid feelings from him. He thought he could probably seduce her. Jenna tried to project a careful, polished image, but Boyce could see that underneath there was a neediness in her. She was a woman hungry for love, and it tempted him to know that about her. With her having that jackass of a husband, she probably hadn't experienced the love and tenderness she deserved.

That was part of the rub in the whole matter. A stubborn part of Boyce didn't want her simply on the rebound - because she was needy and available. And he didn't want to enjoy only a short-term fling with her. He knew she was going back to New York in May. Her husband returned then. Whatever Jenna did, she would have to deal with that situation. He hated to complicate things for her; he didn't want to take advantage of her vulnerability. And Jenna *was* vulnerable. He'd never been around a woman who had all she had going for her and who thought so little of herself. It made him want to head for New York to lash out some harsh words to her husband, her family, and whoever else had caused her to have such low self-esteem.

Boyce found it bittersweet to watch how Jenna blossomed while she stayed here in the mountains. She'd acted so jumpy and defensive when she first came, so quick to pull into some little shell, like a turtle pulling in to protect itself from harm - so used to watching out for predators. She hardly ever laughed when she first arrived and her smiles and facial gestures had often been false and posed. But he'd seen Jenna gradually relaxing here. He watched her realize people weren't always waiting to criticize and judge her. It seemed to truly surprise her when people liked her for just who she was. Watching the changes in her felt like watching a tree bloom out after the cold of winter.

As the weeks passed since her arrival at Sam's place, Jenna even started to laugh and smile with ease. She learned to take teasing without prickling up, or even worse, without starting to cry. She began to tease back a little on her own. Working at the gallery seemed to help her, too. At first, she'd been terrified she might do something wrong, that she might be ridiculed and put down for any mistake. So, Boyce left her on her own after a short instructional time - to figure things out by herself. He thought she could use the confidence she would gain from that, and he was right. Work at the gallery had been good for her, and, she seemed to have an excellent gift for arrangement and design in the store. It made Boyce wonder what else she might be capable of.

He stopped off at the gallery at around five. Una was working in the shop tonight, but Boyce wanted to check the mail that had come in during the day. He was expecting an order from one of his major clients, and, now that he'd finished the big painting he'd been working on, he was ready to think about his next project.

"Hi, Boyce," said Una, as he came in the doorway. She sat intently on the bench by the register, studying a textbook. "That order from the Haldeman Gallery came in today. It's in the back."

Boyce went through the gallery to the back of the shop to sort through the mail and to read Gregor Haldeman's note to him. The gallery owner wanted a new painting or two to display for a late summer showing - on a wildflower them. The gallery continued selling his old works in print reproductions, but Gregor wanted a new original painting or two to hang in the main show if Boyce could make the deadline. Boyce knew anything he sold in Haldeman's would bring in a big price. It was a prestigious gallery in Atlanta, and he was pleased they wanted his work in their new show.

He'd get started on some new ideas right away.

"How's school?" he asked Una conversationally, as he came back out into the store front.

"Fine," she answered, looking up from her book with a smile. "Those new paintings of mine won a place in the art department's spring show. The judges liked them just as you did."

"I told you that style was good," he commented.

She nodded. "Hey, when did you start doing byline work for the greeting card industry under a pseudonym?" she asked him.

He sent her a puzzled look. "What are you talking about?"

"This," Una explained, pulling out a greeting card design from under the desk calendar. "I found it tucked away here when I was cleaning up. It doesn't really look like your work, somehow – really detailed for you and more whimsical than your usual style." She paused thoughtfully. "You know, I've seen some of these cards over at Raynelle's in the Apple Barn, but I didn't know you were doing them. How come you aren't using your own name or letting us carry these over here at the gallery?"

Boyce snatched the card to study it and frowned. "I didn't draw this," he told her. "Where did you say you found this?"

"Under the desk calendar right here." She gestured toward it. "Hey, Boyce, you don't have to deny being a card designer if this is a new side line of yours. It's nothing to be ashamed of in the art field. This work is really good. One of my drawing teachers made all of us bring in card designs we admired for an art class. He showed a card sort of like this and said it was incredible. He raved on and on about the meticulous detail and about all the hidden story meaning imbedded in the designs...."

Boyce interrupted her. "I'm telling you I didn't draw this," he snapped sharply. "It's not my work. I think I'd know my own work when I saw it."

"Well, chill, Boyce." Una answered with a little annoyance of her own. "You don't have to get mad and snap my head off over it. What was I to think? It's not like we have that many artists working in here. And if you didn't draw it, then who did?"

"That's a good question." He scowled.

They both stopped to think about that for a minute.

"Look on the back," Una prompted, with a sudden inspiration. "The other reason I thought it was yours was because of the birdhouse logo. See? That seems like something you would have thought of, doesn't it?"

Boyce flipped the card over to look at the logo on the back. It was a small, tiered birdhouse with the signature J.C. Martin below it. He felt a chill roll up his spine.

"I think I know who did this." He said the words slowly out loud. "Think about it. J.C. Martin – a shortened name, perhaps, for Jenna Chelsea Martin Howell?"

"Wow." Una looked up in surprise. "You think Jenna did this? Our Jenna that's been working here in the gallery for Charlotte?"

Boyce nodded, watching Una's face.

A flash of irritation passed over it. "Well, gee whiz. I wonder why she didn't tell us? She's a pretty well-known designer in the field. I don't know why she wanted to hide that information from us. It's not like it's something to be ashamed of or anything."

"No, it's not," Boyce said with an edge to his voice.

Una shrugged. "I thought she was just some rich, pampered society girl down from New York City having a little get away. She sure had me fooled."

"Me, too." Boyce agreed.

He looked at Jenna's partly finished card again. "Una, I think I'll go over and have a look at some of those other designs you said you saw at Raynelle's Apple Barn. Tell me where to look, okay?"

Thirty minutes later, Boyce drove up Orchard Hollow Road in a simmering rage, his mind filled with unanswered questions about Jenna Howell. He'd studied all the card designs in the rack created by J.C. Martin. They were incredible. At first, Boyce couldn't believe Jenna could possibly have done them. He wondered if one of her relatives worked as a designer. After all, they never finished that follow-up talk about her life. But when he found a J. C. Martin card, picturing Sam's old cat Maizie snoozing on a familiar chair on Sam's porch, the matter quickly resolved. He knew then the cards had to be her work. That she was J. C. Martin as well as Jenna Howell.

Silently fuming, he bought the card with Sam's cat on it before leaving the store. Raynelle's clerk, Irene, babbled away saying this was one of their newest designs from the Park Press and wasn't it cute. Since Irene felt so chatty, Boyce also learned that Park Press was located right downtown in New York City. How convenient.

Boyce felt absolutely humiliated for all the times he'd talked on and on about painting techniques to Jenna like she was completely ignorant on the subject. Studying art history and actually working professionally in the medium were two totally different things. Not once had Jenna stopped to tell him she worked in the art field. Instead, she always listened attentively, like the concepts were completely new to her. He felt like an idiot.

"I love hearing about your art," she said, looking at him with those big brown eyes. Making him feel interesting and important. Why had she done that? He clenched the steering wheel in irritation.

"I don't like being made a fool of," he muttered to himself. "Do I not know this woman at all? Has she been playing some kind of city game with me – pretending to be something she's not? Amusing herself at my expense?"

Boyce ground his teeth just thinking about it. Well, after this company dinner tonight, she was going to have some major explaining to do. He would get some honest answers out of her whether she liked it or not. He didn't like people playing games with him. Not one bit.

That evening, Jenna was the last to arrive. Boyce heard Patrick barking a welcome to her before Raymond Hester let her in the front door. Glancing over from the kitchen, he saw Raymond's wife, Wilma, and Sarah and Will Lansky get up to greet Jenna as she came into the big living area of his house. She looked fantastic.

Boyce ground his teeth that he noticed every detail – that he still felt stirred by her with what he knew about her now. She wore form-fitting black jeans and had a loose, long-sleeved, white shirt knotted at her waist over a skimpy t-shirt. Through its thin, almost transparent material, the overshirt offered a tantalizing glimpse of her shape.

Boyce turned back to stir his chili angrily, annoyed that she had this effect on him.

"Everything looks nice," he heard her say. "I love seeing Boyce's art when I come here. It so suits a mountain home."

Instead of pleasing him, the compliment just further annoyed him.

"Let's eat, folks," he called, rounding everyone up for dinner. He dipped out chili into earthenware bowls to serve. Side dishes lined the counter in informal buffet style and homemade cornbread was just coming out of the oven. Granted, Wilma had come early and made it for him – but it smelled wonderful.

Dinner conversation flowed congenially, but Boyce began to see wariness and confusion in Jenna's eyes as the evening moved on. He told jokes and stories; he engaged the Lanskys and Hesters in numerous discussions, but he skated around conversations with Jenna. And he avoided looking at her. At one point she caught his eye and smiled tentatively. He must have glared at her in return, because she sent him a surprised, hurt look before dropping her eyes.

"Good," Boyce thought maliciously. He wanted her to hurt as he was hurting.

By nine o'clock everyone started leaving for home.

"Shouldn't we stay and help you clean up, dear?" Wilma Hester asked.

"No, don't worry about it." Boyce patted her on the arm affectionately as he helped her into her jacket. "Jenna already volunteered to stay over for a few minutes to help. The two of us will take care of everything in no time. You and Raymond just go on home. And drive safely down the hill after dark."

Jenna sent a questioning look his way, knowing she hadn't volunteered to help him clean up at all. Boyce gave her a cheesy fake smile in return.

They saw the Hester's out and then the Lansky's.

Boyce started for the kitchen then. "I guess we better clean up. I hope you don't mind that I said you'd help."

"Of course not." Her voice whispered softly behind him.

She followed him into the kitchen and started helping him get the dishes ready for the dishwasher. Boyce stayed quiet while they worked - practically seething now with all the unanswered questions in his mind.

He saw Jenna glance at him nervously a few times.

"Your chili tasted delicious," she commented at last, as they finished up the cleaning. She was probably desperate to break the cold silence in the room. "In fact, the whole meal turned out beautifully, and everyone seemed to have a good time."

"Including you, Jenna?" He knew his tone sounded sarcastic, but he couldn't help himself. "Did you have a good time?"

Jenna studied him warily. "Is anything wrong, Boyce?"

"Why do you ask, Jenna?" He gave her a stony look.

Her face flushed. "It's just that you've acted sort of odd all evening. I mean not that anyone else probably noticed, but ..."

"But you did, is that it?" Boyce interrupted, snapping a dish towel against the counter. "You know me so well that you know when something is not right with me when no one else does?" His tone was hateful now.

Jenna stood looking at him in surprise, not knowing what to say.

He glared at her. "Funny, Jenna Chelsea Martin Howell, I find that I don't know you very well at all. And I was actually beginning to think I did."

"Would you tell me what is wrong, Boyce?" She twisted her hands nervously. "I don't like this game you're playing. It's frightening me."

"Well, good." He kicked a cabinet door shut in the kitchen. "I'd like to think I could get you a little upset, since I've been royally upset ever since this afternoon, Ms. J. C. Martin. It took every bit of my self-control to get through this evening - smiling and chatting and making nice with everyone – when I kept wanting to shake you every other second."

Suddenly, it seemed to register to Jenna that he called her J. C. Martin instead of Jenna.

"Why did you call me that, Boyce?" Her voice was cautious.

"Call you what?" he responded sarcastically.

"Call me by my maiden name and my initials?" She bit her lip worriedly.

His eyes narrowed. "The game's up, Jenna. And it's time to talk." He grabbed her arm and practically dragged her over to sit down on one of the couches in the living room.

"You're scaring me, Boyce." Her huge brown eyes looked bewildered.

He ignored her, reaching into a side drawer beside the couch and taking out an envelope. "Here." He tossed the envelope into her lap. "I think these might be yours."

She looked inside the envelope, somewhat reluctantly he noted, to find her new card design that she'd left under the desk calendar at the gallery. Behind it was the card Boyce bought at the Apple Barn of Sam's cat snoozing on his porch.

"Oh, it turned out nice." She held up the finished card of Maizie and smiled brightly. "I haven't seen it, yet. Where did you get it?"

He parroted her words back at her, mimicking her tone. "It turned out nice. Where did you get it?" Boyce glared at her, his anger rising. "What about an explanation for all of this, Ms. Martin? Don't you think you owe me that?"

Boyce could see Jenna studying him in confusion.

"I don't understand why you're angry." She shook her head. "I draw some greeting cards part-time for a little press in New York. I have for years. It's not a big deal. This card of Maizie is one I finished this fall. I didn't realize it was already on the market."

She picked up the hand-drawn card of the weathered birdhouses she'd been working on and smiled tentatively. "This is a new design I'm working on. Don't you recognize the birdhouses, Boyce? I drew my design based on those birdhouses you made on the stump at the beginning of Orchard Hollow Road."

"Obviously, I recognize them, Jenna. That's hardly the point." Boyce's tone cut icily back, and he stalked over to the window to stare outside, turning his back to her.

"Oh." She paused for a moment. "Are you mad that I put your artistic work on my card, Boyce? Is that it? That I used your birdhouses on my card? I guess I didn't think. I should have asked you …"

"I'm not upset about that, Jenna." Boyce jerked around, interrupting her. "I'm upset about you not telling me about your work, about who you are, what you do."

She sent him a puzzled look. "But I have told you about me," she said. "Almost everything about me. You know about me and Sam, about my friend Carla and my life in New York, and about all the mess with Elliott. In fact, I learned today that *everybody* seems to know about my life with Elliott and all he did. It's actually humiliating that everyone here knows *everything* about me while I know so little about them."

Her eyes flashed then. "I can't believe you'd be mad over learning there is *one* little detail about me that you somehow didn't know. Don't I have a right to some privacy?" She planted her hands on her hips. "Is there some unwritten rule around here that a person can't have a single personal thing about their life that not everyone knows?"

She was up and pacing now. "Today I had to listen to Charlotte tell me that I was really dumb about people. That she didn't know why I even had to think twice about divorcing a jerk like Elliott after all he'd done to me. She even asked me why I ever married him."

"What did you tell her?" Boyce asked, watching this new, angry Jenna with fascination, despite himself.

"I told her I probably was dumb to marry him, just like she said." Tears welled in her eyes as she turned to look to him. "But I thought he seemed like a good person when I met him. I really did. He acted sweet to me and I was so young. You'd have to know Elliott really well to recognize the kind of person he is. He can be charming and persuasive when he wants to be. But with him it's phony; it's not sincere. It's a surface, polished charm. He'll say anything, act any way to get what he wants."

"And he wanted you," said Boyce quietly.

"Obviously so." She said this with a touch of bitterness. "Although I certainly fail to see why. He tired of me in less than a month. I think he'd decided it was time to be married and thought I would be an appropriate, biddable wife. I was too stupid to see anything but what he presented to me."

Boyce propped a foot on the fireplace, watching her. "What did your parents think of him?"

She slumped onto the couch again. "They thought he hung the moon," she answered. "He was slick and polished and came from the right family. He knew all the moves to make in a social setting. He charmed my mother and knew all the right things to say to my father. They thought it was wonderful when he proposed to me – an older, successful man like him taking an interest in a little nobody like me."

"And when they learned he cheated on you?" His voice was quiet.

"As my mother said, that's just the way it is in society marriages." She sighed deeply. "She saw no reason why a woman should make a fool of herself and get a divorce over a little indiscretion. She said one's standing in society is more important than infidelity."

A new kind of anger flared in Boyce. "Then she doesn't really love you, if she would say that to you." He clenched his fists by his side. "And your father should beat Elliott to within an inch of his life."

She punched her fist into a sofa pillow. "Well, fine. Then obviously my parents don't love me any more than Elliott." She started to cry. "Welcome to the real world, but no matter what any of them say, I'm getting out. I don't want to live like that or with someone like that. I've found a little place of my own near Carla in New York, and I'm moving out on my own. I talked to Sam about it tonight, and he's getting his attorney to start drawing up the divorce papers. I'm going to have my own life. And I'm tired of everyone criticizing me over every little thing I do, and trying to make me feel guilty just for living my life."

She turned angry eyes on him. "So what if I draw a few little greeting card designs? So what? And so what if they are silly to most people and don't seem like real art? I like them and some people like them, too. And I get paid to do them. That's important to me right now, although it wasn't at first. It's my work, Boyce, and I don't have to apologize for what I do."

Boyce walked over to pick up her card designs to look at them.

Jenna snatched them out of his hand. "And don't you say anything bad about these, do you hear me?" she demanded. "I like them. A lot of people like them. And I'm sorry I didn't tell you I was using your birdhouses for a card idea. I just didn't think about it, that's all."

Boyce studied her troubled face. "What did Elliott think about your work, Jenna?"

She uttered a sound of despair. "He laughed at it. He thought it stupid just like my art professors did at Barnard. But he indulged me and let me keep creating my designs after we married - as long as I kept them out of sight in the apartment and didn't show them to people and embarrass him. I had a little place to work in an office closet. It's all he would give me, and I kept everything there. But I loved my work, even if he made fun of it. It was the only thing that made me happy some days."

She began sobbing now - shaking with her emotions. Boyce sat down on the couch beside her. He reached over to tilt her face up to his.

His voice was gentle now. "How did Elliott take care of your heart, Jenna? How did he love you? How did he make you feel when he held you?"

"Like nothing," she whispered, her eyes sliding away from his. "Like almost nothing. He came and he went and I could have been anybody. When I tried to ask him for more, he told me I wasn't a very passionate person. That it just wasn't something that could happen for me. He told me some women were just that way."

"And you believed that?" he asked softly.

"How would I know what else to believe?" She gave him an anguished look. "He's the only man I've ever known that way. Before that there were only a few kisses at the door or in the car when a date brought me home. I don't know much about these things. Maybe he's right about me, I don't know …"

"No, he's wrong." Boyce shook his head and leaned over to touch his lips to hers. "He's wrong and he's a fool. He has no idea what he had or what he's lost now."

Somewhere along the way, Boyce forgot his anger with Jenna. Now all he could see were her eyes, still swimming with tears, looking at him with wonder.

"You're not mad at me, anymore?" she asked in a whisper.

"No." He touched her face tenderly, wiping her eyes. "And I want to show you just a little how wrong Elliott was about you."

And he proceeded to do so. He kissed her lips, her throat, her neck, her closed eyes. He slipped his hands softly over her face, her hair, her arms and down her back, touching her gently, reverently. A soft sweet sound escaped her, and he wrapped her close in his arms.

Time seemed to stand still while he held her, kissing her, touching her, and breathing in her cologne and fragrances, just as he had longed to do for so many weeks. He took his time to show her just how sweet loving could be. And he took a wonderful pleasure in her responses to his hands and his mouth as they found pleasure with her.

When the sweetness of their loving turned to passion, when her breath and his grew hard and fast and when their hands began to explore each other in magical ways, Boyce thought he might split apart with joy. He had finally gotten his hands and lips on this beautiful woman. And because of what had happened this night, and because of the conversation, he didn't regret it. He wanted to make this wonderful girl feel desirable and passionate and alive. She'd been cruelly denied the most basic joys of marriage.

She was fully arousing him now, but Boyce knew he could contain himself to give her a little pleasure. He slipped his hands under her clothes and touched her in sensitive places to arouse her fully. Her soft hands drifted under his shirt to find his bare skin, and she eagerly pressed her body up against his. It seemed wonderful and heady - touching and loving her, feeling her passion escalate. It was better than he hoped it would be in any of his fantasies. It felt like flying in a swirl of pulsing colors just to be with her. He couldn't even imagine how he would paint it.

He pulled back at last with the self-restraint that only a kind heart knows. It was agonizing to do so. They stared at each other intently with hearts beating wildly.

"Jenna, beautiful Jenna." Boyce whispered her name in a voice rich with passion. "There is nothing missing in you. You are passionate, you are desirable, you are wonderful. I would almost sell my soul just now to be with you all night, to keep touching you, to know you in every way fully. But it is wrong for us right now. You are still a married woman. It is not right. If this is to be for you and me, I want it to be right in every way. I want no shame afterward, no regrets. I want us to both be free. Despite the world's fashion today, I'm not much of a man for casual affairs. I'm the sort who is looking for happily ever after. For someone to share my life with. Not someone to love for just a night or for just a little while."

Her face flushed with embarrassment. "I didn't mean to seem like a loose or an immoral person." She dropped her eyes. "I'm not sure what happened. But I don't want you to think …"

He stopped her words with a kiss on her mouth.

"Don't be sorry." He whispered the words against her lips. "I'm not. And don't apologize, either. I've wanted to touch you, to kiss you and hold you, Jenna, almost from the first day we met."

He leaned back and took her face in his hands. "God's timing isn't always what we want in everything. I tried hard not to reach out to you as I wanted to. I feared I would fall desperately in love with you. And that may have happened despite all my efforts. I may be a terribly unhappy man once you go. But I still want to do what is right with you. I don't want to take advantage of you at this time in your life."

"Thank you." Her voice was a whisper as she put her lips softly against his. "I don't think anyone has ever put me first or thought about what was truly best for me. I just went along with what everyone else wanted."

She paused to look at him. "I would have gone along with you tonight.

I care so much, and my feelings are so strong and new to me. But I would have felt bad later. I'd have felt that I was no better than Elliott." She hung her head.

"I know, and that's why I stopped, but I'm not sorry. And I can't promise I won't kiss you again, Jenna." He smiled roguishly at her. "You're like a drug to my body, calling to me even when you're not near me. I don't know that I have ever been so pulled to any woman as I am to you. You are so beautiful. I can't find words to tell you how you make me feel when you are near me." He pulled her back to him then to hold her curled up against his body, to kiss her hair, her forehead, her face.

They held each other and touched each other in a sort of wonder. But then they drew back when things became too heated. They'd made a decision, and would keep that decision about full intimacy. It wasn't the time.

"Does this mean you're not mad at me any more about being J. C. Martin?" Jenna asked, against the side of his neck.

He laughed, his mouth against her hair. "No, I'm not mad."

He pulled back from her then, and took both her arms in his hands so he could look directly into her eyes.

"I have something to say to you about that, Ms. J. C. Martin." He caught her eyes. "And I want you to hear it well. You are not just some little card design artist, as you say you are, who only does a few little greeting cards. You are a fine artist and illustrator. Don't you realize that if your card designs are here in Tennessee, that they are in racks and store displays all over the southeast and maybe all over the United States? That is not some little thing, Jenna. People buy your cards, love them, and cherish them. That is what art is – creating something from out of yourself that touches other people's lives. I want you to be proud of that gift. And I never want to hear you putting yourself down again for possessing it and for using it. You should revel in it."

"Do you really like my cards?" she asked, softly amazed.

He kissed her forehead. "Yes, I like them very much. I felt so proud they were yours, that you had created them, and that I knew you. But on top of that, I was mad. Mad that you hadn't shared that part of yourself with me. That you'd shut me out. And I imagined all sorts of stupid reasons as to why you hadn't told me about your art."

Jenna looked puzzled then. "How did you find my card at your gallery? I put it down under the desk calendar."

He shrugged. "Una found it, doing one of her gallery clean-ups she does when she gets nervous about an upcoming exam," he answered. "In fact it was Una that knew how well-known J. C. Martin was. She said her art professor at college had raved on and on about your designs, about how wonderfully detailed they were and what hidden messages they had in them."

"You mean a professor of hers thought my work was good?" Jenna asked in wonder. "I'll have to get Una to tell me everything he said."

Boyce laughed. "You'll have to suck up to her first to get her to forgive you for not telling her you were J. C. Martin. She was pretty mad, too."

Jenna crossed her arms in irritation. "Well, I still just can't see why everyone thought I should have told them about a simple part-time job with Park Press," she complained.

"That's because you still haven't figured out how talented you are. Or how well-known your work is in your industry." He paused as a new thought came to him. "What does your boss at your card company say about your work?"

She lifted her shoulders self-consciously. "Oh, well, he likes it. He's actually urging me to do more now that he knows I've left Elliott. They want me to branch out and try some new things."

"Well, you do that." Boyce stood up and held a hand out to her. "And you can start tomorrow getting new ideas when we go hiking. Be ready to go about 9:30, and bring your sketchbook and your camera, because you are going to see some fine Smokies wildflowers on our hike."

She looked up in pleasure as she put her hand in his. "Are you really taking me hiking? I know you said you would, but I thought you might not now."

"Of course, I'm still taking you. In fact, I'd say that you and I are going to spend a lot of time with each other until you leave." He smiled at her. "If I'm lucky, maybe you'll miss me and maybe you'll come back."

She dropped her eyes then, uncomfortable with this thought. "Maybe you'll come to New York to see me," she suggested.

"I don't like the city, Jenna," he said, knowing he needed to be honest. "I don't like any city, but especially not big ones like New York. I can't work there; I tried once for a short time but it wasn't for me."

Seeing her disappointment, he added, "But I might come for a visit to see you in New York. We'll see. For now, let's get you home so you can get some rest."

After he walked her back over to Sam's cabin and turned to start back, he heard her call out to him.

"Boyce," she called out softly through the night. "I didn't tell you mainly because I thought you might not think I was any good."

"Oh, Jenna, you were wrong about that," he called huskily back to her. "I think you were *very good* indeed tonight."

A little giggle floated out over the darkness. "That's not what I meant, Boyce."

"I know, but it's what I meant." He looked back to see her highlighted in the warm light of the doorway and shook his head. "Don't tempt me with more words called out in the darkness, Jenna. Go to bed now, and get some sleep."

Boyce hoped he could get some sleep himself. But he doubted it. She had stirred him up too much. Perhaps he'd sit in front of the fire for an hour and finish out the last of the wine from dinner. It might help. And then again, it might not.

Chapter 9

Saturday dawned clear and fair. By 9:00 am the sun shone brightly and the sky appeared a lovely blue when Jenna glanced out the kitchen window a second time. She was going hiking with Boyce, and she wanted it to be a good day.

Boyce told her what to pack a few days ago and what to wear.

"You don't dress for fashion for a hike in the mountains." He stated this emphatically. "Wear sturdy, comfortable clothes, some thick, cotton lined socks, and well-worn hiking boots, if you have them."

He dug in Sam's storage closet until he found a lightweight backpack Sam once used. He tried it on Jenna's back for size. After adjusting the straps, it was a good fit.

"Put the few things you think you'll need in here, along with a light lunch," he said. "And remember that everything weighs. Don't put a bunch of silly woman's stuff in your pack like it's a pocketbook. Just put in a few practical things like chapstick, band aids, and tissues. Think light so you'll enjoy your hike. For lunch, pack something simple, like a sandwich in foil, some prepackaged peanut butter crackers or a snack bar, and a zip bag of raisins or granola mix. And don't forget to buy a 12 ounce bottle of water to carry with you. Don't get a bigger one thinking that will be better, because water is the heaviest thing you'll be carrying on a day hike."

"Are you always this bossy when you take someone hiking with you?" she asked him teasingly.

He glanced up in annoyance. "Yes, and you'll thank me for it when you've hiked three miles up the trail and your shoulders aren't aching from too heavy a pack and your feet aren't hurting because you have on bad socks or shoes and are starting a blister. You wouldn't believe some of the idiot things novice hikers do on the trails in the Smokies."

Jenna checked her pack again, remembering his instructions. Everything she needed seemed to be there. It would be just like Boyce to look through it before they left. She glanced in the mirror, noting she looked ready for a hike – wearing old jeans, a t-shirt, and a favorite zip-front sweatshirt with a hood.

Glancing at her watch, she realized she had time to spare before Boyce arrived. Time for one more cup of coffee.

She poured it from the pot in the kitchen, and sat down at the kitchen table where she could watch the birds feeding in the back. Chickadees and finches were flitting in and out of the feeders this morning, with a mockingbird fussing in the tree.

Jenna hoped the coffee would give her a little confidence for facing Boyce this morning. She was a little embarrassed about last night and what happened between them. But she felt excited about it, too. He obviously liked her. The mystery over that was gone. However, things had sort of exploded between them and gotten complicated afterwards. She'd snuggled under her comforter for a long time last night remembering the wonderful things Boyce said to her. His kisses had been so sweet, and his hands just as exciting as she'd imagined.

She sighed. Everything had been sweeter than her daydreams. Jenna felt a rush of feelings even now remembering it. She knew she let him touch her in places she shouldn't have. And he'd been the one to pull away. It should have been her that pulled away. She tapped her finger thoughtfully on her coffee cup. It troubled her to remember that. She hadn't shown much restraint.

Still, overall the memories played back positive. "The sweetest memory of all is that Boyce admitted he might be falling in love with me." Jenna said to herself. "I know men just say things like that when they're all stirred up and feeling passionate. But I hope it might really be so."

She considered that idea with a sudden anxiety. "What if it is so? As much as I'm attracted to Boyce, I don't really want another man in my life right now. And I certainly don't want to even think about getting married again." Jenna frowned. "Once you marry a man, everything changes. That's what happened with Elliott. He said romantic things and made me feel special when we were dating too. But he seemed disappointed with me once he got me in bed on our honeymoon."

Jenna hated remembering their first night together. Elliott seemed to think all her efforts of response to him were amusing. He hadn't gone slow with her, even though it was her first time, and he hurt her. Jenna had read enough books now to know he could have been nicer and more gentle that first time - and at other times later.

A part of Jenna wondered what it might have been like with Boyce if things had gone further. But another part of her drew back. She hoped Boyce meant it when he said he didn't want to take advantage of her right now. It was a truly messed up time in her life and no time to be starting a new relationship.

Jenna chewed her lip thinking about this. Boyce said he wanted to see a lot of her before she left to go back to New York. That probably meant he would want to be intimate every time they got together now. He might start pushing to go further. A sliver of alarm slid over her. If that started to happen, she might have to go back to New York early. She didn't want that.

Boyce's knock on the door startled her back to the present. Soon they were loading their packs into the jeep and setting off for the day. Boyce checked her pack, just as she thought he would. He also brought her a small packaged rain poncho to tuck into her backpack, plus a rolled ground seat that could be inflated later to sit on. On the back seat of his jeep were a pile of sketchbooks, pencils, and a camera.

He turned to her conversationally as they started down Orchard Hollow Road. "How many trails have you hiked in the mountains?"

"None, really." She shook her head regretfully. "I've just done some short walks close to the cabin and ventured down a few roadside trails when I took a drive in the mountains. But that's all."

"Well, if you have a good time today, we'll have to do some more hikes before you go back to New York." He stretched his arms out on the steering wheel. "I hike in the mountains year round, but I especially like to hike in the spring when the wildflowers bloom out. They're starting to peak now. I'm going to do a lot of trails in the next weeks to gather photos and sketches for some paintings the Atlanta Haldeman Gallery wants me to do for a late summer show. I just finished the painting I was working on, so the timing is perfect for me to get out and find some new ideas. Besides, I like a change after I've been holed up in the studio for a long time." He turned to smile at her.

Jenna smiled back, and began to relax slightly. Boyce hadn't made a pass at her since he knocked on the door. He hadn't tried to kiss her or given her any smoldering looks or anything. He hadn't even mentioned last night at all. She worried that it would be a factor in the whole day today. Instead, Boyce was acting like it never happened at all. This was just fine with Jenna. In fact, she felt relieved. Boyce was acting just like his old self, and that was going to make the day fun.

They drove from Townsend over the Little River Road to Gatlinburg. The road wound through the lowlands of the Smoky Mountains National Park alongside the tumbling Little River and, later, along Fighting Creek. This meant the road twisted, twined, and snaked in and out along the stream sides with constant views of the tumbling waters and cascades. Boyce pointed out the sights all along the way.

He stopped at the Sinks to let her watch a group of daredevil teenagers, mostly young boys, jump off the high rock bluffs into a wide, deep pool below. They made another stop at the Sugarlands Visitor Center to see the exhibits and to let Jenna browse through the publications for sale. She bought a map Boyce suggested that showed all the hiking trails in the Smokies.

Jenna found the little city of Gatlinburg delightful as they drove through on Highway 441. It was a quaint tourist town filled with shops and attractions. Boyce promised he would bring her back one day just to explore.

Partway through Gatlinburg, they veered to the right to follow Highway 73 as it rose up a hill away from the main part of town. Soon they drove into a more rural community skirting along the edge of the mountains and the park. Boyce said the highway led eventually to another historic town called Cosby, but their destination today was Greenbrier and a trail at the end of the Greenbrier Road called Porters Creek Trail.

"I would have gotten lost if I'd tried to come over here by myself," remarked Jenna.

"Oh, you'd learn your way around the mountains quickly if you stayed here long enough." Boyce flashed a smile at her. "You know, the Greenbrier area was once an old mountain community. Many early settlers lived in theses hills and valleys. They built a school, a mill, churches, and cemeteries. You'll see an old homestead that the park has kept restored off the trail we're hiking on today."

She thought about Boyce's reason for driving all this distance. "Aren't there wildflowers on trails closer to you than this?" It seemed surprising that he would drive so far in search of flowers.

"Don't you like adventures?" He cocked an eyebrow at her. "I travel all over the mountains to hike, depending on my mood. I believe in always being open for a new adventure, even if it means a little drive to have it. Besides, even though there are trails with wildflowers nearer to Townsend, this trail at Greenbrier is known for its wide diversity of wildflowers this time of year. There are some unusual flowers that grow here along this trail that you can't readily see in many other places. Also, it's just a favorite hiking trail of mine in April. You'll find it worth the drive once you see it, Jenna."

She shrugged. "Aren't all the trails about the same?"

Boyce looked shocked at her question. "No, not at all. Every trail possesses its own character and flavor. Each one is unique. What is even better is that the trails are always changing – with the seasons and over time. Even after you've hiked on a trail two or three times, you always see something new the next time."

Jenna sent a smile his way. "You make it sound like fun."

"It is fun." His blue eyes flashed. "The best of fun. And it's free for the taking."

She studied a sweep of purple flowers lining the side of the road. The air smelled sweet and clean, and Jenna could hear the sounds of the mountain stream tumbling by the side of the road.

"I guess a lot of people hike here," she said.

"You would think so." He shook his head. "But, amazingly, most people just drive through the Smokies and hardly ever get out of their cars. The park service did some kind of study once, and they found that eighty percent of people do nothing but drive around when they come to the mountains. They stop at a pullover to look at a view or a stream, but that's about it. If they get curious about a hiking trail, they might walk up it about a half mile or so, but then they'll turn around and go back. You wait. You'll see it's true, even on a gorgeous day like this with the wildflowers out. You'll see people on the first part of the trail, but by the time we've walked two miles, we'll have the mountains pretty much to ourselves. I've hiked beautiful trails where I never saw a single soul the whole day."

Jenna smoothed her windblown hair back. "Do you hike by yourself most of the time?"

"Yes, but that's mainly because I can't usually find anyone to go with me." Boyce slowed the jeep to cross a wooden bridge. "It's better and safer to hike in twos, in case something should happen."

"You mean like bears or snakes or something?" Jenna bit her lip nervously.

Boyce laughed and grinned at her. "Now don't start getting worried about that. You're more likely to see a bear in a campground, or along the road where tourists stop to eat a picnic lunch, than up a trail. And snakes, in general, try to stay away from people about as much as people try to stay away from them. Which means they avoid well-used pathways as much as possible. It's rare to see a bear or a snake if you stay on the main trails. That's what you should always do when hiking in the mountains – stay on the park-maintained trails."

Jenna knew he was teasing her but she still felt annoyed. "Well, you're the one who said you should hike in twos in case something should happen."

"I did. And hiking with a partner means if the unexpected should happen, like tripping and breaking an ankle - or getting injured in some other way - you'd have that partner to bring back help for you."

"Can't you take a cell phone?" This seemed sensible to Jenna.

He grinned at her. "You could, I guess. But it's hard to pick up signals on the trails. The mountains block out usage of cell phones for the most part."

The paved surface of the road ended and they bumped along a more rustic, unpaved roadbed now. The forest shaded the roadway, and the smells of evergreens, earth, and trees filled the air. Rills and little streams bubbled along the roadside and clumps of colorful wildflowers decorated the open spaces.

Jenna pointed toward another sweep of purple flowers along the side of the road. "What are those flowers, Boyce? Do you know?"

Boyce glanced away from the road. "Wild purple phlox," he told her. "And those yellow flowers growing beside them are mountain trillium. I'll show you more trillium varieties up close when we get to our trail. The Smokies are known for trillium this time of year."

They came to the end of the dirt road, and Boyce found a pull-over parking spot for the jeep. He helped Jenna get her pack on, and then put on his own backpack, draping his camera around his shoulder. Then they were off.

They found many people hiking and walking on the earlier part of the trail. Because Boyce verbally shared knowledge with Jenna about the flowers along the trailside, he picked up an entourage. Two older ladies and a young couple soon trooped along with them, asking Boyce a constant stream of questions. He entertained them with stories about the settlers and the region, and he stopped often to acquaint them with aspects of interest on the trail.

Jenna learned to recognize three varieties of trillium, wild geranium, white petaled bloodroot, and ferny wood betony. White and yellow violets danced along the trailside and masses of pale spring beauty spread like a snowy carpet in many places on the forest floor.

"Look," Boyce said, stopping to squat down on the ground beside the trailside. "These plants are called little brown jugs. They have small heart or arrowhead shaped green leaves, and here at the base of the plant are the brown jugs."

The older ladies, like Jenna, leaned over and looked closely. Hard, brown growths shaped like small jugs were clustered at the base of each green plant.

One of the ladies said with amazement, "Well I'd never have seen this unusual plant if you hadn't pointed it out."

"Little brown jugs are hard to find because so many other low plants have leaves that look almost exactly the same," he answered. "Like this one here nearby." He pointed to another group of heart-shaped leaves rising out of the grass below a tree.

"These are wild ginger. And they have a wonderful smell." He picked one and rubbed it between his fingers before handing it around for everyone to sniff. "We're really not supposed to pick anything here in the Smokies, according to park regulations, but I thought we'd make an exception of this one leaf to enjoy a remembrance of the smell of wild ginger."

The rich, sweet aroma delighted Jenna, and she tucked the leaf into her pocket to carry along with her.

Because Porter's Creek Trail was an old mountain roadbed trail, they could walk up its pathway in a group, rather than in single file as on a more narrow trail. The trail offered only a gradual ascent and curled alongside the merry cascades of Porter's Creek.

Boyce pointed out remnants of the old settlements along the way – rock walls, homestead clearings, and steps that led to an old cemetery. The older ladies turned back after a half mile, but the young couple from Indiana continued walking with them. When the trail forked and Boyce wanted to go over to see the old Messer farm buildings, they tagged along. Together, the four explored the old barn, the springhouse, and the rustic, log cabin where the family had once lived. Then they all sat on the cabin porch to rest and have a snack.

Leaning back on an old bench, Boyce looked around the farm site with contentment. "I like to sit here sometimes and imagine what it must have been like to have been a settlement farmer up here."

"It would have been a hard life," the boy said. "And isolated."

"Yes." Boyce agreed. "But peaceful in a way. It's people that bring the most pain and stress into a life. Not nature, even though it can be harsh."

Jenna couldn't help but silently agree with that.

The young couple decided to hike back to their car after their rest. Jenna walked a short way with them. When she returned, Boyce sat with his sketchbook on his lap, making rapid drawings. Along the way up the old settlers' road, Boyce had taken many photographs, but this was the first time he had gotten out his sketchbook. Jenna watched him briefly, and then began to explore around the homestead on her own. She took some pictures herself and collected some ideas for her own designs.

"Uh, Boyce," Jenna said, coming back up to the house. "Where is there a bathroom along this trail?"

"There isn't, Jenna, except the great outdoors." He grinned at her shocked expression. "What did you expect - public restrooms along the trailside?"

"I hadn't really thought about it." She considered her growing discomfort. "But where can you go? There are people around here, you know. It's not as easy for women as men. All you have to do is turn your back; I have to drop my pants!"

"There's no one here but us right now and no one coming," he answered, his attention transferred back to his drawing. "Go behind the cabin where you're out of view and find a quiet spot. I'll keep a watch for you and holler if I see anyone coming."

Jenna started around the house, since there was obviously no other choice in the matter. "Terrific," she muttered.

"Remember to take some tissue." Boyce called after her. "And then bury it under leaves afterwards so it won't litter the area."

Jenna rolled her eyes but followed his instructions.

When Boyce finished his sketches, they continued their hike up Porter's Creek Trail, following alongside the stream and through the woods. The path narrowed as they walked on, and - just as Boyce predicted - they saw fewer and fewer people on the trail as they walked deeper into the woods. Soon it was just the two of them and the quiet and beauty of the mountains.

Boyce reached back to hold Jenna's hand as she followed him over a narrow log bridge over the creek. Then he turned to help her down the bridge steps at the end.

He smiled happily as he looked up at her, but then Jenna saw an angry look cross his face. He turned away and began to stride up the trail away from her.

"What's wrong?" Jenna walked quickly trying to keep up with him.

He glanced back at her with a frown. "I don't like that look you gave me. It makes me feel like dirt. It's the same one you sent me this morning when I came to pick you up. Skittish, anxious, fearful, like I might be some kind of mountain cougar set on doing you harm or having you for dinner."

"I'm sorry." Jenna felt an embarrassed flush steal up her face. "It's just that after last night …."

"Don't even finish that thought," Boyce said, interrupting her. "I don't know what changed your thinking from last night until this morning about something sweet and good, but my guess is it was getting your thoughts on Elliott Howell." He scowled at her before walking on. "I'm *not* Elliott Howell, Jenna. You can't equate me with him in any aspect or in any way. Just because I'm a man doesn't mean I'm like him."

Jenna didn't know what to say. How did Boyce always seem to figure out what she was thinking? It was uncanny. Elliott had seemed oblivious to anything she was *ever* thinking about.

"Look around you here." He gestured broadly with his arm as they walked on. "Everywhere in the forest you see can trees. Right?"

He didn't wait for her to answer. "But none of the trees are the same. There's that tall poplar, reaching high up toward the sky." He pointed in another direction. "And there's a little redbud, short with blossoms all along its branches. Up ahead there is a stand of evergreen trees, mostly white pines, but not a one of those trees is exactly alike. You don't just decide trees are all the same because you've seen one tree, Jenna. They're all different even though they are of the same species. People are like that, too. They're each unique. You can't decide you know about people just because of what you know about one person, and you can't decide you know about all men because of what you've known of one."

He fell into silence then as they walked on. Jenna looked up into the trees and thought about what he'd said.

She was getting ready to apologize again for misjudging him when Boyce slowed his pace and put out a hand to halt her.

"Stop here. Let's go down this side trail," he said, pointing to a narrow path through the grass. "If we're lucky, we'll see a real treat."

Jenna followed him down a short side path, winding away from the main trail and around a cluster of boulders.

"There!" He pointed to some small clumps of flowers by an old tree stump. "Walk carefully. These are fragile and rare. They're called lady's slippers."

He squatted down to show Jenna the wildflowers. "These are pink lady's slippers, but they come in yellow, too. They're in the orchid family."

The stems looked like tulip leaves, but the blossoms looked like dainty little shoes dangling off the ends of the stems.

He smiled up at Jenna, obviously forgetting his earlier annoyance. "These are worth spending a little time drawing and photographing. They're hard to find in the mountains."

"How did you know where to look?" She gazed around. "They were way over here behind the rocks."

"I remembered the place from another time. It's one of the reasons I wanted to come here today. I thought I might do a painting of these." He took his camera out of his backpack and started taking photos from different angles, while Jenna wandered around in the clearings under the nearby trees.

"Here, Boyce," she called. "I've found some more, and some other kind of odd flower, too."

He walked over to join her. "Well done, Jenna. These are in the same wild orchid family as the lady's slippers. They're called showy orchis; they're rare, too. Both plants like these rich, moist woods around Porter's Creek. We'll get some photos and sketches of both."

The whole day was like that for Jenna - full of one discovery and delight after another. It was wonderful to be outdoors and hiking up such a beautiful trail in the mountains. They shared their picnic lunch sitting on a high log bridge over the cascades of the creek. Jenna loved the sound of the rushing water and the feel of cool air; it was so relaxing and their conversation at lunch proved happy and pleasant.

In total, they hiked over six miles on their round-trip walk. Boyce turned them back before they started up the last steep mile of the trail. It was enough of a first hike for Jenna. She pulled off her boots to rub her feet when she got back to the jeep.

Boyce drove them over a different route on their way home, through Pigeon Forge and over Wear's Valley Road back into Townsend. "I thought you'd like to see more of the area," he explained.

Pigeon Forge, a tourist town, was stuffed full of motels, restaurants, attractions, and shops. But it was not as quaint and attractive as Gatlinburg. It looked newer and gaudy, but it had its own fascinations. After the quiet of the mountains, it surprised Jenna to see all the people here - bumper to bumper in their cars, walking up and down the streets in throngs, or enjoying the shopping malls, stores, and amusements.

"Is it always like this?" Jenna gazed out both sides of the jeep window in amazement at all the people thronging the area.

"No, some of the time it's worse." Boyce grinned at her. "When I was a kid there wasn't even a town here, just a scattering of outlying restaurants, shops, and small motels on the route into Gatlinburg. But it sure has changed."

They swung left at a stoplight in Pigeon Forge to start across Wear's Valley Road toward Townsend. Soon they were twining through the foothills of the Smokies and away from the crowds of the town.

"I grew up in this valley." Boyce looked around with obvious pride.

"I remember you telling me that," said Jenna. "Will we pass your brother's shop where you used to work?"

"Sure, after a while." He looked over at her. "You wanna stop and see it?"

She nodded. "If it's okay."

"Will do." He grinned. "Wear's Valley is a special place – secluded but convenient to the attractions of Pigeon Forge as well as the tubing, festivals, and historic sites in and near Townsend. That's why so many people are beginning to discover it."

He pointed to a large log building on the hill to their left. "That's Moonshine Ridge country store – a nice place to explore if you come back one day. And further down in the middle of the valley you'd like the Smoky Mountain Park Store and the Antique and Craft Gallery, filled with consignment booths."

Seeing her glance toward the mountains on either side of the valley, he added, "Cove Mountain and Roundtop Mountain are there on our left and the Chilhowee Mountains are to the right. The Wear's Valley highway weaves right down between them. This was all rich farmland once, and there are still farms here in the valley today."

Jenna looked out the window with pleasure. "I can see what made people want to settle here. It's so peaceful and beautiful."

"My roots are here. It's a comforting feeling to know where your people come from." He glanced over at her. "Do you know where your family came from?"

"The Martins came from the Boston area originally and my Alvarez grandmother from Spain, but my mother's people came from the South, near Staunton, Virginia. That's one reason my Aunt Lydia moved back there when she had her problems."

"What happened with Aunt Lydia?"

Jenna told him and described her visit there on the way to Tennessee. She shared with Boyce about her own upbringing then - how she grew up, where she went to school. She told him how she first got connected with Park Press through her high school designs.

He listened with interest. "Your artistic gift showed up early, too," he commented. "And from what you said, you were drawing even as a girl."

"I suppose. I always loved to draw and to write. When I was little and alone so much, I entertained myself by reading, drawing, and writing."

"While I was busy exploring the outdoors." Boyce laughed and gave her one of those charming grins of his. "I spent very little time indoors as a child."

She smiled at him. "I totally believe that after seeing how comfortable you were in the outdoors today."

"You didn't do so bad yourself for a city girl," he said, kidding her. "The only time you complained was when you had to go to the bathroom outside."

"And I got used to that after a few times." She tossed her head saucily.

Boyce turned his blue eyes to hers thoughtfully. "In case I forget to tell you later, I had a good time with you today, Jenna. I don't say that easily about people I spend my time in the mountains with. I hope you'll go again with me sometime."

Happiness welled up in Jenna's heart. "I would love to," she said. "I want to see a lot of the mountains before I have to go back to New York."

A thought came to her. "By the way, Boyce, do you know where the Smokies trail is that walks behind a waterfall? A couple in the shop talked about it yesterday."

"That's Grotto Falls behind Gatlinburg," Boyce said. "The trail to it is called Trillium Gap and it's a great hike." He told her all about that trail then, and several others, as they drove the rest of the way through the valley to his brother's store.

Chapter 10

*B*oyce always experienced a feeling of going back in time whenever he pulled up at the print and sign shop Charles converted from an old family barn. Over time, as Charles' shop grew more successful, he probably could have torn down the old barn and built a newer, more modern store. But it just wouldn't have been the same. Besides, the rustic character of the old barn always attracted passing tourists.

The cow bell on the door jangled as Boyce opened the door. Looking around, he saw Charles, and his oldest son Chuck, both at work in the shop. With the store always busy on Saturdays, Chuck worked all day with Charles much as Boyce used to do. Chuck looked a lot like his dad, tall and brown-headed like all the Hart men; he had Charles' brown eyes and set, square jaw. Boyce never saw his brother Charles without seeing his father again. The resemblance between the two was strong.

"Boyce, good to see you." Charles came out from behind the counter to give Boyce a clap on the back and a brotherly hug. He studied Jenna with a raised eyebrow.

"Charles, this is Jenna Martin," Boyce said, purposely using Jenna's maiden name in his introduction. "She's Sam Oliver's friend and staying up at his cabin. I was showing her a little of the Smokies today. We went over to Porter's Creek Trail to check out the wildflowers."

"So, you're Sam's girl." Charles gave Jenna a smile and grasped her hand in a warm handshake. "We're all real fond of Sam around here. He and our mama are kin through marriage. So we think of Sam like family. I'm glad to meet you, Jenna."

"I'm glad to meet you, too, Charles," Jenna said, giving Charles one of those soft, radiant smiles of hers that always made Boyce go a little weak in the knees. "Boyce told me a lot about your shop. But it's much more interesting than I imagined it would be." She looked around her at the rustic décor - packed full of signs, crafts, gift items, tourist paraphernalia, paintings, and screen-printed t-shirts, hats, and jackets.

"Well, Boyce may have told you about the shop, but he failed to mention to any of us that you were knock dead gorgeous." Charles gave Boyce a considering look. "I guess that's why he's kept you to himself and gotten you to work in the shop a day or two a week for him. He knew you'd attract more business. For example, my boy Chuck over there has been about to trip over himself looking at you ever since you came in."

"Chuck!" Charles called out. "Come over her and meet a friend of Boyce's."

The boy came over, fumbling his hands in his jeans pockets and grinning. He shook Jenna's hand shyly and gave a bearish hug to Boyce. They all made small talk for a few minutes, and then Chuck went back over to wait on a customer.

"Man, I'm glad you came by," Charles told Boyce, the niceties past. "Mama went over to town with Susan and the girls today and came back with some flats of flowers she wants set out. Do you think you could swing by and put them out for her? I'll be at the store here until close, and Sterling has a baseball game we all want to go to. I told Mama I'd do it tomorrow, but she has some kind of notion that it's going to rain tonight, and she wants them out today before the rain - so they'll get set."

He looked apologetically to Jenna after his request.

"I don't mind if you need to go by your mother's," Jenna said graciously.

"Traitor," Boyce accused her, groaning. "I meant to use you as my excuse to get out of setting out plants again. Mama probably has four flats or more, knowing her."

"Well, too late now." Charles slapped Boyce companionably on the back. "Besides, Mama has been wanting to meet Sam's girl, anyway. It will make her day if you take Jenna by the house."

Boyce gave Jenna a sideways glance, then rolled his eyes and sighed. "You do remember, Jenna, that it was your idea to stop by here on our way home. So this is all your fault," he told her teasingly. "Now, I guess we'll have to run down the road to Mama's before we go on home to Orchard Hollow."

Jenna smiled charmingly and shrugged.

Charles looked apologetically at Jenna again. "Look, I really appreciate you taking time to go with Boyce to do this. Mama gets her mind set on something and she gets stubborn on us. It would be just like her to get out there and start setting those plants out herself if one of us doesn't get over there before dark, and then she might get laid up in her back again."

"Well, you'll owe Jenna for this." Boyce laughed. "And you can pay her back by putting in a display rack of her card designs in here. Jenna is J. C. Martin, Charles, a well-known illustrator. She does a great line of free-hand greeting cards for Park Press out of New York. Raynelle carries her line over at the Apple Barn. I think they would go well here, too."

Jenna protested. "Oh, Boyce, please ... he doesn't have to do that," she said, looking embarrassed as she always did whenever someone praised her art. Boyce wished she'd get over that and realize she was good at what she did. It annoyed him that she thought so little of her artwork.

"You got yourself a deal." Charles smiled at Jenna. "I'll look at your cards when I'm over at the Apple Barn the next time, and I'll get the order information from Raynelle. I could use another card line in here. Do you do any mountain related art – you know, things that make people think of the Smokies? That would sell good here."

Boyce answered for her. "Actually she's been collecting new design ideas and doing some work while she's been down here visiting. She just finished a great design of that old cluster of birdhouses I built for Sam Oliver on the stump where Orchard Hollow Road starts. Do you remember that?"

"Lord, yeah. You made that back when you were just a kid like Chuck – about his same age, I think. Maybe eighteen."

"I can't believe Chuck's eighteen already." Boyce blew out a breath. "He graduates this spring, doesn't he?"

Charles nodded. "Yes, sir. It's something how time flies. And Sterling's just turned fifteen and is driving us crazy wanting to get himself a learner's permit to drive."

Boyce turned to Jenna, grinning mischievously. "Charles is getting ready to hit the big Four-O birthday this year. He and Vera married right after they finished high school, and they started their family before they had the sense to figure out it might have been a good idea to wait a bit. I helped babysit his kids when I was only in elementary school."

"I don't think I'd rub that in too much, little brother," Charles quipped back. "You've got the big Three-O birthday coming up this year yourself, and you haven't even found a woman that will agree to marry your sorry self yet. And you're the only one in the family that hasn't got any kids. Maybe Jenna will have some mercy on you and decide to make an honest man out of you."

"Maybe she'll just do that in time, if I'm lucky," Boyce smarted back, watching the color rise up softly in Jenna's face in embarrassment. "That is if all my sorry family doesn't scare her off first with their bad manners."

There was some good-hearted laughing over this, and then Jenna excused herself to find what she called "a real restroom" before they left.

"She's a fine looking woman, Boyce," Charles said after she was out of earshot. "But are you really going to get anywhere sniffing around a city girl? She's bound to go back. Besides, I heard she's been married before and that she's been down here to get over that. I don't want you getting involved in some kind of problem situation."

Boyce bristled defensively. "Who said I was getting involved?"

"Your face whenever I caught you looking at her," he answered flatly. "I didn't help raise you not to know you pretty well. This is different than just flirting for you. There's something going on here. And she colors up real prettily around you, too."

"Listen, I didn't set out to be taken with her." Boyce knew it was useless to be anything less than honest with Charles. "It was just the time for me to make a fool of myself, I guess. Jenna isn't divorced yet either, so you're right, there are complications. She's been married to an older man that treated her like no man ought to treat a young girl, especially a sweet one like her. And she has scars and fears."

Charles rubbed a hand over his neck. "You always were a one to bring home the wounded animals. And help them heal up."

Boyce picked up a wooden toy from a display bin. "Well, I have my work cut out for me here. This Elliott she married did a number on her. He's made her unsure of herself and scared of men. And, like you said, she's a city girl. I don't know if she'll want to transplant."

Charles leaned against the store counter. "If she's been treated badly, you need to let her get all her problems resolved before you move in on her. Don't forget she's Sam's girl. He's trusting us to take good care of her down here, not to let her get hurt more. Sam won't thank you if you take advantage of this girl while she's down here to heal."

"You're not telling me anything I don't know." Boyce dropped the toy back into the bin crossly. "But knowing all that doesn't make it any easier."

Charles gave him a clap on the back. "Yeah, so smile and make a joke now because the object of our conversation is on her way back across the room."

It took only about five minutes to drive down Caldwell Road to the old Hart place. It was a big, yellow two-storied farmhouse set between spreading oak trees. A long front porch spanned the front of the house, and grey shutters and a grey door were the only adornments except for flowering dogwoods, shrubs, and flower beds full of tulips and daffodils.

"As you can see, Mama is fond of her flowers," said Boyce, swinging into the driveway.

Two little girls came flying out of the house to launch themselves at Boyce as he got out of the car. They were two of his nieces and Boyce hugged and twirled them around while they squealed out their welcomes. On the porch, he could see his mother watching and smiling. She stood shorter than Boyce, a softly rounded woman, with a pleasant, full face and braids wrapped in a coronet around her head. She wore an apron over her dress and was wiping her hands on it as she came down the steps toward them.

She shook a finger at the girls. "Alice, you and Sharon quit climbing all over Boyce and shrieking like that. Mind your manners. We have company."

The girls seemed to notice Jenna for the first time then and quieted down.

"This must be Sam's girl," she continued, coming up to Jenna with a smile.

Boyce made the introductions. "Jenna, this is my mother Ruth Hart. And Mother, this is Jenna Martin."

"I've been wondering when you were going to get around to bringing Sam's girl over to see me," Ruth said chidingly to Boyce. "Jenna, we're delighted to meet you."

She hugged Jenna affectionately. "And these hooligan girls here are two of my granddaughters. Alice Gilbert, the dark-haired one, is eight, and Sharon Gilbert, the little, honey blond, just turned six." She gave them a significant look.

"Pleased to meet you," they said almost in unison, making a renewed effort toward good manners.

"Very nice." His mother nodded at them in satisfaction.

She turned to Boyce and gave him a motherly hug. "Did you go by Charles' store?"

He patted her cheek with affection as she stepped back. "Yes. I took Jenna up in the Smokies on a hike to see the wildflowers today, and I drove her back this way to see the valley. Charles said you had some plants you might want me to put out while I was here."

"That I do." His mother's eyes lit up. "Come on in to the house first, though. I've got fresh lemonade I made for the girls."

Alice tugged on Boyce's arm for attention. "Guess what we're doing?"

He looked down at her. "What?"

Her eyes brightened. "We're dying Easter eggs."

"Lord, yes." His mother rolled her eyes. "The girls got two of those egg dye sets when we went into town today, and I've got two dozen eggs cooling in the kitchen getting ready for them to dye and decorate."

They passed through a worn, comfortable living room and into a yellow and white kitchen. The kitchen opened into a big, sunny dining area dominated by a long wood table and chairs.

"I'd sit you down in the living room proper," Ruth told them. "But I need to get these eggs rinsed off and dried so the girls can dye them. They're about to drive me crazy to get to them. I'm sure you remember how excited you were to dye eggs every Easter about this time, Jenna."

"Actually, I've never dyed eggs," Jenna admitted with obvious regret.

Sharon's mouth dropped open with surprise. "You've never dyed Easter eggs?"

Jenna shook her head.

"Never ever?" Alice echoed, in childish amazement.

"Never ever," Jenna answered, laughing. "They were always bought for me and showed up in an Easter basket. I've always wondered how they were done."

She wandered over to the table to look at the dye sets, tea cups, and paper towels littered over the table top.

Ruth Hart passed Boyce a telling look and shook her head.

"Well, well, Jenna," she said. "This is going to be your lucky day to learn to dye eggs. Alice and Sharon can teach you how, while I go out and show Boyce where I want my plants set out."

Boyce watched Jenna's eyes light up with pleasure. It hurt him to think about the stiff and formal childhood she seemed to have experienced.

After lemonade and a short visit - while the eggs dried - Ruth left Jenna delightfully learning how to dye Easter eggs while she went outside with Boyce.

"That girl was as excited as a child learning to do those eggs," Boyce's mother said to him. "I can't believe a girl could get to be her age and not had anybody show her how to dye an Easter egg."

"You'd be surprised what things no one's shown that girl - or done for her, either," Boyce mumbled.

He turned to see his mother studying him. "You're taken with her," she observed, matter-of-factly.

His jaw clenched. "Now don't you start on me, too, Mama. I've already had a lecture from Charles."

"Well, you seem to have decided what I'm going to say when I've not even opened my mouth." She crossed her arms. "But the truth of it is, my heart goes out to that girl. Raynelle's told me all she's been through, and it makes me real sorry for her. You can tell she is just as sweet and innocent as a rose. Shy, too, for a city girl. And I've been hearing about this girl for two years now from both Raynelle and Zita Walker anyway. I keep up with Sam and his news, too. Probably more than you do - always lost in those paintings of yours. I wanted you to meet this girl when you went up to New York last summer so you could tell me about her, but you didn't get around to it."

He bristled. "She was out at some rich summer home place with her parents on Martha's Vineyard," he explained. "Besides, I was only in New York a few days."

"You never have liked it up there," Ruth said. "Most people would have been excited to have some paintings shown in a big city like that, and would have wanted to see the sights while they were up there."

Boyce shrugged.

His mother laughed a soft laugh and wrapped her arm through his as they walked. "You've always loved it here in the mountains. I can't say I'm sorry, since it keeps you nearer to me." They walked back through the yard toward the barn where Boyce's mother had stored her flats of plants.

"Sit down here a minute on this bench and talk to me," she said, as they passed an old picnic table under a clump of maple trees.

He hesitated. "I need to get your plants out, so I can get Jenna back over to Townsend."

His mother laughed. "She's got two dozen eggs to dye with two excited little girls. She'll be busy for a while."

Boyce gave in with resignation and sat down in the shade.

His mother settled the skirt of her dress over her knees. "How far did you hike today?"

"About six miles or so up Porter's Creek and back." He picked up a stick off the ground to twiddle with it.

"Did Jenna have a good time?" his mother asked.

"Yeah, she did, I think. She'd never been on a hike before in the mountains. I think she took to it. She wants to go again."

Ruth tilted her head. "And you'll take her?"

"Why shouldn't I?" he answered defensively. "Sam told me he wanted me to watch after her while she was down here and to help see that she had a good time."

A faint smile played on her lips. "Sam wasn't figuring on the two of you about near falling in love," she said. "It didn't take me ten minutes to see how it was between you – the way you look at her and she you. The way she about jumped out of her skin when you leaned over her at the table and brushed against her - just trying to show her how to dip an egg in a cup of dye."

He flinched. "Yeah, well, that's a problem. She's about half scared of me," he grumbled.

"Has she cause to be?" His mother glanced up in surprise.

Boyce stood up irritably. "Look, Mama. I'm not going to do anything wrong by Jenna. She's been hurt a lot and I wouldn't add to that. She doesn't trust men much at all right now. Any men, including me." He scowled and snapped the stick in half that he still held in his hand.

His mother shook her head gently. "Give the girl time," she said. "Remember that little vixen fox you brought in from the woods that time? The one that got shot by a hunter? It took that little fox a long time to trust you - or any of us - after what she'd experienced. But she healed after a time."

He sat back down again with a sigh. "I know Jenna will heal, too, Mama. I'm just afraid it will be long after she's gone back to New York and when she's too far away from me."

Her face softened. "If she's the right one, she won't forget. Her heart will bring her back."

Boyce kicked at a pine cone on the ground crossly. "You read too many romance novels. Besides, I thought you'd be upset that I was taken with a divorced woman. You always told us it was best not to marry people that had been divorced. I expected a major lecture from you on just being interested in this girl at all."

She raiser her eyebrows.. "Is that why you haven't brought her by?"

"Maybe, in part," he admitted.

A silence stretched between them while she thought about this. "Oftentimes, people who divorce are people who don't hold commitments or vows before God as important," she said at last. "When the first sign of discomfort comes, the first disillusion, the first fight or two, or the first real problem or challenge to a marriage, they leave. They break their vows. Then they start looking around again. The likelihood is that they will act the same way again with the next partner. But it's different when there's adultery or desertion. Or cruelty or abuse like this girl has faced. Raynelle says she's bloomed like a rose since she's been down here. I'm glad for her.

She's a sweet girl. She deserves a chance at recovery and real happiness. But be careful, Boyce. She's on the rebound right now. She's hurt and confused, just like that little vixen was."

"I know," he said, sighing. "Believe me, I know. That vixen bit me when I was trying to take care of her. Do you remember that? I've still got a little scar here on my second finger from where she nipped me."

"Let me see." His mother took his hand in hers. "Well, well. You surely do, and I remember we bandaged and medicated that bite as best we could."

He stood up then, growing restless. "We'd better get these plants in Mama." He offered her his hand to help her up.

"Yes. It won't take you as long as it would have taken me to do it. I thank you for helping me with it."

Boyce caught her eye. "Thanks for not being too hard on me about Jenna. The situation is difficult enough."

"Love always is." She smiled at him. "And it always seems to come with complications."

An hour later, Boyce had put out four flats of sultana, two in the round flower bed around the birdbath and two more scattered in front of the shrubs on either side of the front porch. He cleaned up at the hose outside and then made his way in the back door. He found Jenna sitting at the kitchen table coloring pictures in a color book with Alice and Sharon.

"Look at our eggs," Sharon cried excitedly. "We made really pretty ones."

Alice jumped up to catch his hand. "Yes, and Jenna learned real fast how to do them. She read the directions in the box and helped us put designs on them and everything!"

"We even wrote our names on some with a wax crayon," Sharon added. "See?'

Boyce looked appreciatively at all the eggs with the girls. He noticed Jenna was as flushed and as excited as they were over the results.

She smiled at him brightly. "We figured out how to make two color eggs by experimenting," she told him. "We put one end into one color and let it dry a little, and then we put the other end in another color, leaving a little ribbon of white between. See? Look how pretty they are – green and yellow here, and this one pink and purple." She turned to look at him, her face a wreath of smiles, and his heart clutched in his chest. "And the little flower and bunny designs that came with the color sets were so cute. We had the best time with those."

"They all look great," he said.

"Jenna's nice," Alice told him. "Will you bring her back to go to Easter church with us next Sunday? Please? Sharon and I have new Easter dresses, and we want Jenna to see them. We'll get Easter baskets, and I told her we might get real baby chickens, and she hasn't ever seen a real baby chicken before."

Sharon jumped into the conversation. "And we're decorating the cross with daffodils in the service. Jenna said it sounded like that would be really beautiful."

Boyce's mother came into the room. "We'd be pleased to have you come and join us at church on Easter," she said graciously. "The girls' father is the minister of the church, as well as being my daughter's husband. Plus, all our family share dinner afterwards."

"It's nice of you to ask." Jenna hesitated. "But I feel that I might be intruding on a family time."

Ruth waved this idea away with one hand. "Nonsense. You're Sam's girl. That makes you a part of our family. He'd be upset if I didn't ask you."

With the girls shouting "Please, Please" Jenna had little chance to give any answer but yes.

"Ours is a persuasive family," Boyce told her teasingly.

"Yes, and now you girls have got to get on home for dinner," said Ruth. "I told your mother I'd send you home after these eggs were done. And, Boyce, you and Jenna are to stay for dinner with me. I've got a crock pot full of homemade vegetable beef soup already cooking, and I've a mind to make some cornbread to go with it. It won't take long to do that. You and Jenna walk the girls over to their house, and I'll have everything done about the time you get back."

Knowing it was useless to argue with his mother about dinner, Boyce conceded gracefully. "What's for dessert?" he asked, leaning over to give her a kiss on the cheek.

She patted his cheek fondly. "An apple butter stack cake. You know you like that with ice cream on it."

"I could die and go to heaven a happy man now," said Boyce, pleasing her.

Jenna cleared her throat, attracting their attention. "I don't want you to go to all that trouble for us, Mrs. Hart."

Boyce's mother sent her a warm smile. "It's no trouble, child. And it keeps me from having to eat alone. Perhaps you don't know how that is."

A pained look crossed Jenna's face. "Actually, I do know what it's like to eat alone. And, you're right, it's so much more fun to share a meal. Thanks for asking us to stay."

"Well, then, you just walk the girls home – and get all these eggs off my kitchen table – and I'll get started warming things up."

The afternoon was still sunny and pleasant as Boyce and Jenna walked Alice and Sharon down the country lane behind his mother's house.

"We call this little road Hart Lane," Boyce told Jenna. "It winds from our place over through the trees - and past the cemetery - to come out at the Wildwood Church. My sister's home is just beyond the church on the road behind us."

Alice's young voice chimed in. "It's 1400 Wildwood Road."

The girls had the four of them holding hands as they walked down the road - Boyce and Jenna in the middle, the girls swinging and skipping on either side. The walk down Hart Road was only a short distance and soon ended at a circular drive between the cemetery and a white country church. Boyce and Jenna stopped and waited at this point while the girls ran across the church grounds and through a field to their own house, a yellow two-story on a little rise past the church.

Boyce smiled at Jenna. "This is tradition. One of us always walks the girls this far to be sure they get back home safely." He noticed with pleasure that he and Jenna were still holding hands and that Jenna hadn't pulled away yet.

"You have such a wonderful life." Jenna sighed wistfully. "Do you know how lucky you are to have a warm, happy family like this?"

"I try to remember to be suitably grateful," he answered with a grin. "Especially when my mother is feeding me her homemade cornbread and apple butter stack cake."

"Oh, you!" She giggled. "All you think about is food!"

"Not all," he said, leaning over to touch his lips to hers in a soft kiss.

She shied back, looking startled and uncertain.

Boyce cupped her face gently. "Don't spoil the moment, Jenna. Affection between friends is a good, sweet thing on a warm April evening after a fine day."

She smiled back at him softly, despite herself.

Sensing her defenses crumbling, Boyce wrapped her in his arms to kiss her more deeply. This time she sighed and nestled against him, slipping her own arms around his neck to draw him nearer, closing her eyes in pleasure.

He pulled away gently then. "There now, wasn't that nice?"

"Yes," she admitted dreamily. "It was nice."

"Well, good," he said, deciding to stop while he was ahead. "Now let's head back to Mama's and have some dinner. I've earned it putting out all those plants of hers."

They walked back down Hart Road, simply holding hands and talking.

Chapter 11

At three a.m. that night, Jenna woke up startled and frightened from a nightmare. The thunder crashed outside as Jenna sat up anxiously in bed, and a big streak of lightning flashed across the dark sky. The rain Boyce's mother predicted had moved in. Jenna tried to calm herself, and settle back under the covers, but the dream kept trying to slip back into her mind. She threw back the covers, got up, and pulled on her robe.

She headed for the kitchen, hunted up cheese and crackers, poured a glass of milk, and then settled down on the big couch in front of the fire. She was glad for the warmth and comfort of the low fire still burning in the hearth. Ever since she'd been small, Jenna found it hard to fall back to sleep right after a bad dream. The dream always tried to continue in her mind, playing on like a bad movie you couldn't turn off. Often the dream seemed more frightening when she woke up and became fully conscious than when she was asleep. She knew if she got up for a short while, had a snack and cleared her mind, she could usually go back to bed and then sleep well again.

Noticing the fire was dying out, Jenna walked over to put on another log like Boyce had taught her. It was quiet and comforting in the cabin, but the bad dream still chased about in her thoughts. Her nightmare had been about Elliott again. Ever since she learned some of the bad things - and the unpleasant details – about Elliott's indiscretions she hadn't known about before, a little sense of fear and foreboding haunted her. Her dreams played out her fears in exaggerated forms.

Jenna knew much of her anxiety continued because she procrastinated instead of confronting her issues with Elliott. Soon, she would have to deal with Elliott Howell, like it or not, and she sensed it would be unpleasant. Frankly, she absolutely dreaded it. Jenna hated confrontations. She knew it was a weakness of hers. She hated anger and quarreling - and the bitter words that always accompanied those scenes, as well. Her parents argued a lot, and Jenna hated hearing the bad things they said to each other when they engaged in their frequent arguments. As a child, she crept upstairs and hid in her room when they started to quarrel. They never hit each other, but their words flew like hurtful, angry darts between them – almost as damaging.

When her mother launched out at Jenna in a tirade, Jenna always retreated and tried to make peace.

"You remind me of your Aunt Lydia when you do that," her mother snapped at her once. "She always tried to be sweet and make peace when a good quarrel was needed to clear the air. You're too much like her and your Grandmother Alvarez. Both spineless when a fight was needed."

But Jenna possessed no fighting spirit. She had a peacemaker spirit. It pleased her when she heard a chaplain at school assembly say once that peacemakers were blessed. Her mother always made it seem like it was a curse to want to live peaceably.

Jenna sighed and snuggled back into the couch, pulling one of the old afghans over her lap. Like it or not, she had to go back to New York soon. She knew moving out before Elliott returned from Paris was cowardly, but she couldn't stand the thought of him standing over her while she packed, picking at her and arguing with her over every little item she might want to take.

Truthfully, there wasn't much she wanted to take from Elliott's apartment. Most everything in the apartment belonged to Elliott before they married anyway. Some wedding gifts that Jenna received from friends and relatives were still packed in boxes in the apartment building's storage room because Elliott didn't think they matched his décor. She would take those. Many of Jenna's own things Elliott simply disliked, so she had packed these things away in storage in her parents' attic. It would be fun to get them out and see them all again. Naturally, she would take her clothes, her art supplies, and her personal things. The rest Elliott could have.

Carla had called her before she went to bed to tell her everything was all set on the new apartment. Her enthusiasm bubbled into her conversation. "I've been up to see the apartment, and everything looks great. It's a little bland in color - that's what you do with rentals so whatever people have will fit in better. So the walls are all painted sandalwood or white, and the sofa, chairs, and ottoman are camel beige. The kitchen and bath are mostly white. But the great thing is that the hardwood floors are a warm, rich brown, there are lots of built-in shelves, and most of the furniture items are decent cherry pieces, even if a little battered."

She laughed then. "The best thing in the apartment are the rugs in the living room and bedroom. They are fantastic old tapestry rugs that came from Berlini's when they had a back room closeout once. They'd been floor samples, and Berlini's let them go for a song. Actually, you helped me pick those out. Do you remember?"

"I do, Carla." Jenna saw a quick picture in her mind of that happy shopping day with Carla. "And they were gorgeous. Don't worry. Everything will be fine. And you and I will have fun fixing the apartment up. You know, I've never gotten to decorate my own place before."

Carla hardly seemed to hear that. "The one thing John and I are doing is ordering a new mattress for the bed and buying a new refrigerator," she said.

"Don't do special things for me, Carla," Jenna responded. "I don't expect that of you."

"We always have to replace a few things after renters leave, Jenna. And it was time for both of these things, anyway." Carla bubbled on. "Oh, and let me tell me you about one thing. The last student we rented to made a worktable over two file cabinets in front of the bedroom window. The light is good, and he did a pretty good job making it. Do you want us to leave it for an art desk or clear it out?"

"Leave it for now, and I'll look at it," Jenna replied. "I'll need a place for my work."

Watching the fire in the dark now, Jenna let her mind drift - thinking how she might fix up her little apartment to make it cozy and nice. It would be simple compared to her parents' and Elliott's places, and even compared to Sam's cabin, but it would be all hers. And the most important thing - it would be away from Elliott. She couldn't bear to think about living with Elliott again, not even for a day. And she cringed to think of him ever touching her again. Getting away and having time to think had taught her that.

"I'm glad I came here," she said to herself as she watched the flames dance in the fire. "It's been a good thing for me. I've met good people and I've learned that I can live by myself and be happy."

And, of course, there had been Boyce. She frowned over that thought. She knew one of the reasons she'd known such happiness here was because Boyce had been so attentive to her and made her feel so special. Loveable.

"I can't remember feeling for anyone what I feel for Boyce." She shook her head as she thought about it. "But my emotions about Boyce are just too complicated to sort out right now. Sometimes I don't know whether my feelings for him are all tied up with how much I simply needed someone to be kind to me right now or if my feelings for him run deeper."

Jenna sighed softly. Boyce had made a lot of allusions to the idea of a long-term relationship recently. "But I don't know if I want that right now. I'm not even out of my last relationship; I'm still married."

A troubling thought slid over her mind. "Probably by the time I sort everything out, Boyce will meet some nice girl and settle down. It's amazing he hasn't already."

It depressed her to consider that, to imagine someone else sitting by the fire with Boyce in the evening, enjoying his warmth and humor, holding his babies. She hated the idea of him being with someone else. But she hated worse the idea she might keep him from the happiness he deserved. He was such a good man. What a contrast that she should meet someone like Boyce Hart after Elliott. With that thought still stirring in her mind, she climbed the stairs back to her bed. Rain poured down outside in a torrent, and the sound of the rain helped Jenna slip back to sleep.

She woke feeling rested and, after breakfast, she settled down to work in Sam's study upstairs. A cocky bluejay on the feeder outside the window had inspired a new design idea. Jenna sketched him on a tree limb and wrote a birthday verse for the inside of the card that seemed to fit the drawing. After making her rough sketch, Jenna worked on the finished card design of the bluejay she would send to Park Press. She had ten designs to mail tomorrow that she'd completed this last week. It was so easy to work here, and ideas came freely from the natural scenes all around her. Jenna pulled out several of her recent photographs to look for more ideas. Soon she got lost in creating and the morning flew by.

At about one o'clock, a knock came on the door. Jenna could hear Patrick barking outside and knew it was Boyce.

She went over to the front window of the upstairs office and knocked to get Boyce's attention below; then she motioned for him to let himself in.

"Can I come up?" he called.

"Sure," she called back.

In a few minutes, he ambled in the doorway looking fantastic in a shirt and tie, his hair tumbled from driving outdoors in the jeep.

"You look good," Jenna told him. She leaned down to pet Patrick, who had followed Boyce up the stairs and was weaving around her chair now, eager for a welcome.

"Been to church." He smiled. "And I decided I'd come see if you'd like to hike up to the Oliver cabin in the Cove with me this afternoon. It's not far from here, and I want to do some sketches of the cabin. A dream for a painting idea came to me last night during the rain with the Oliver cabin in it. Do you ever do that? Just dream an idea and see exactly how you want a piece to turn out when you paint it?"

"Sometimes." She let her eyes rove over him, enjoying seeing how handsome he looked in dress clothes. "But usually it's when I start to work that the ideas start rushing in for me. Like today. I accomplished so much. I'm really pleased."

Boyce loosened his tie. "Are you going to let me see what you've done?"

"Yes, I decided I would when I let you come up." She tidied her desk a little nervously while she talked. "I wanted you to see this design of Patrick especially. I took a photo of him one day sitting on his haunches and looking up at the birds on the bird feeder. He was so intent watching them, that I couldn't resist snapping the picture. I worked from it for my design idea."

Jenna leaned over to pet Patrick again while Boyce looked at her design.

"I like it," he said, studying the finished piece. "The guy's a bird dog, after all, and he's always trying to tree or point a bird. I've seen him do this often, just sit and try to stare down the birds at the feeder." He laughed. "You've really captured it, Jenna. I like the way you got his ears kind of pricked up here – and the way the birds are just going on about their birdy business like he wasn't even there."

Jenna released the breath she hadn't realized she was holding. However, when Boyce opened the card to look at the verse she'd written for the card, she found herself holding her breath once again.

He read through it. "Oh, good idea. You put a get well verse with it. About getting well so you can get out in the sunshine to watch the birds and play with the dog. It's great. So many people will relate to that. It will lift their spirits."

Jenna studied his face carefully. "Are you just being nice, Boyce, or do you really like it?"

He looked at her in surprise. "I may be nice about a lot of things, but with art I'm usually considered to be too candid." He laid the card back down on her desk. "Ask Una if you don't believe me. I tell her flat out the things I like that she does, the things that I think don't work, or the things that are just not my taste. I'll do the same with you if you'll be honest with me about my work, as well."

Jenna considered that. "How would you tell me if you didn't like something?" she asked tentatively.

"I'm not sure." He propped against her desk and gave her a teasing grin. "Let me look at some more of your stuff."

Not waiting for an answer, he started sorting through all the designs she'd made to send up to New York. He studied each one as he looked through them.

"This one," he said, holding out a card to her. "This one with the little girls doing ballet exercises at the barre. I like the idea, but you've made all the little girls look too perfect. I think this design would be better if one or two girls were a little more irregularly shaped – you know, maybe one too thin, one a bit heavy. And I'd put glasses on one or maybe have the ribbons of one of their shoes dragging on the floor or something. It would be better if it were more human."

He opened the card and read the verse. "However, I love the verse about dancing all the way through your birthday. That's great."

Jenna studied her card and frowned. "You might be right," she observed. "All of the girls have the same neat buns tied up with ribbon and they're all the same height and shape. But I've seen little lines of girls just like that in the ballet studios in New York."

"It's your artistic liberty to interpret it however you want," Boyce replied graciously, still studying the card. "But you asked what I'd tell you if I didn't like something or thought it needed improving. This one struck me as a little too perfect."

He grinned at her again. "Of course that's my opinion. You gotta remember, I like the wilted tulip amid the beautiful ones, the leaf with the bug hole among the perfect ones. I like the less than perfect among the perfect. That's life. And everything's beautiful anyway – perfect or not."

His words pleased her. "I'm going to remember that thought for a verse," she told him. "You know, sometimes you are almost a philosopher, Boyce Hart. You say some very profound things."

"Well, right now, my profound thought for you is that I'm starving and I want to get out of this tie." He reached a hand up to jerk at it again. "Do you want to go hiking with me or not? I'm going to stop up at the Last Deli to get lunch to take along this time. I don't want to take time to fix anything. The day is getting away, and everything is green and bright after the rain last night."

"Won't it be muddy?" Jenna frowned.

"Nah, the sun's dried everything out all morning. There won't be more than a few damp spots here and there along the trail. But the creeks will be up and rushing. I always like that."

She gave him a big smile. "Okay, you've talked me into it. How much time do I have to get ready?"

He tossed a teasing reply to her as he started toward the stairs. "Ten minutes from after you hear the front door close, so get a move on it! The sun is calling!"

Fortunately, Jenna was already dressed in jeans and a t-shirt, so she flew through getting her hiking gear together and her boots on. She stood on the porch waiting for Boyce when he walked out his front door.

"You're two minutes late," she called as she started across the street.

"Smart ass." He unlocked his jeep and threw his gear in the back. "I had a phone call that held me up."

They were on their way a few minutes later. Boyce stopped at the deli to buy sandwiches for lunch and caramel apples to eat on the way, then headed up the highway into the mountains.

"You've never lived until you've tasted Nell's caramel apples." He bit into an apple dipped in caramel and rolled in nuts. Ummmm. She soon agreed.

At the Townsend Wye, they turned right on Laurel Creek Road, which snaked its way in and out along the creeksides and under the ridgetops toward Cades Cove.

Boyce gestured out the window. "The Cades Cove area was once a green settler's valley of rich farmland, log cabins, barns, mills, and schools," he told her. "When the park gained possession of the cove lands, some of the old cabins were kept, and they are now maintained by the park service as historic sites. I'd take you back to see others, but I try to avoid driving in the cove on a pretty weekend day like this. The traffic is bumper to bumper, and the tourists literally stop in the road and hold everyone up to gawk at every glimpse of wildlife. It can sometimes take hours just to drive around the eleven mile loop of the cove. It really frazzles my patience, so I avoid it except in the off seasons and weekdays."

This raised a question for Jenna. "I thought you said the John Oliver cabin was inside the cove? And it is Sunday, you know."

"The cabin is in the cove." He gave her a smug smile. "But the trail to it starts before the loop road into the cove begins. We can park and walk in. It's only about two miles to the cabin on the Rich Mountain Trail and it's a nice easy walk through a pretty, open woods. You'll like it."

Soon they had on their packs and were walking down a narrow, single-file woods trail, with Boyce in the lead.

"How come you always get to lead and be first?" Jenna asked teasingly - just to nettle him.

He stopped to gesture that she could walk around him to take the lead, smiling impishly while he made the gesture. "I usually take the lead so I'll be the first to step on a snake or on horse poop in the trail. But I'll be glad for you to be the one to go first, if you want."

She looked down at her feet in alarm. "No, I guess I'll let you lead," she replied primly.

After a few minutes, shuddering at the thought, she asked Boyce, "Have you ever really stepped on a snake?"

"Once." He grinned over his shoulder at her. "A big rattler sunning on a southeast ridge trail. His coloring blended in so cleverly with the dirt path and the dried leaves on the path, that I simply didn't see the old boy until I almost had a foot on him. I hollered so loud in shock, that I think I scared the snake almost half to death. He took off slithering down the hillside as fast as his slithers could carry him. I was sure glad, too. I wasn't keen to get better acquainted."

They both laughed. Boyce knew almost as many mountain stories as Sam, and Jenna loved listening to them.

"I like being with you, Boyce."

He turned his head and winked at her. "Don't sweet talk me out on the trail with no one around, Jenna. I'm likely to get ideas."

"Well, if that happened, all I'd need to do is just wave food around to distract you," she answered flippantly.

He laughed. "And don't mention food, either. I'm likely to get ideas about that, as well. But we need to get on to the Oliver cabin before we dig out our lunch. You know, that deli makes the best club sandwiches – puts them on butter-toasted rolls. And I bought some of their homemade fudge, too. They make it right there in the shop."

"You're making me hungry now." Jenna giggled. "So don't talk about food anymore."

"Want me to sweet talk you instead?" He turned to give her a teasing look. "I've been told I'm good at it. And it would pass the time."

"Better not," she quipped back. "My knees might go weak so I couldn't hike anymore. And you'd have to carry me."

He laughed with pleasure as they hiked on up the trail.

Learning to tease back and forth with Boyce had been new for Jenna.

When she first came to Orchard Hollow, his teasing confused her. Sometimes she had let it hurt her feelings. Now she understood it as just a part of Boyce's fun-loving, comfortable nature. Jenna had always grown up around serious people. None of her family, and few of her friends, told jokes and stories – except for Sam. She wondered sometimes if Boyce was too easy and carefree.

"Don't you even know how to be serious?" she asked him once, provoked with him over a prank he just played on her.

He stopped to study her intently. Then he leaned closer to her to frame her face with his hands, his fingers playing seductively over her lips. "I work hard not to get too serious with you, Jenna Martin," he said huskily. "Very hard. Don't complain or I might just teach you why I try so hard to keep it light with you."

She found herself frozen in place, her whole body alive and tingling from his words and his touch. He ran those magic hands of his over her face and down her arms, and then lifted both her hands to kiss her palms and her fingers. She thought she was simply going to die from all the feelings he caused to run through her body.

Jenna read in books that women could be teases, but she thought Boyce Hart a more subtle and dangerous tease than any woman she ever read about. In fact, she hadn't known men could do some of the things Boyce did that tantalized her so. Most of the little things he did were so subtle she could hardly draw his attention to them to complain. He gave her soft looks across the room that almost melted her. He would catch her eye and hold her glance – and not look away as most people would. Then he'd study her face, her eyes, her mouth with his eyes, until she would get little windmills in her stomach and would wet her lips with nervousness. Then he'd slowly smile at her, knowing she was reacting to him.

"Shhh! Look!" Boyce held up a hand and stopped in the trail in front of her. "Over there in the woods." He pointed as he spoke.

Jenna followed his glance and saw two deer grazing in the forest not far off the trail.

He stood quietly. "Stay still or they'll bolt and run," Boyce said. "That's a buck with the antlers. And look at their white tails. They're pretty, aren't they?"

"I can't believe they're so close to us," Jenna whispered.

"Well, the deer are trusting here in the park." He smiled back at her. "But they're watching us, too. I'm going to try to get a few pictures."

He got in several photos before the glint from the sun on the camera lens startled the deer, making them quickly disappear into the forest.

They continued on up the trail and soon had to rock hop over a couple of streams along their way. The afternoon grew warm, even under the trees, and Jenna took off her light jacket and tied it around her waist.

Eventually, the trail curled up a hill and around a corner to arrive at the Oliver cabin. It was a rustic, hand-hewn cabin sitting at the edge of the forest with a broad, green field spreading out before it. From the cabin's porch, you could see a stunning vista across the Cades Cove valley and up to the high mountain ranges beyond. Jenna and Boyce sat on the front porch steps to enjoy the view while they ate their lunch.

"Mmmmm," Jenna said. "Any food eaten in the mountains always tastes so wonderful. I wonder why that is."

Boyce chuckled. "Because of the walk you took getting here, in part," he answered. "But the rest is a mystery. I can eat a peanut butter sandwich up here and it tastes like a feast."

They laughed and visited companionably over lunch. Then Boyce got out his sketch pad and pencils to make drawings of the cabin. Jenna located her own small sketchbook and walked around the cabin to find mushrooms and plants to draw that took her fancy. She also drew sketches of a swallow-tail butterfly that kept dipping around the porch of the cabin.

"I always have the best time with you," Jenna told Boyce on the hike back to the jeep later. "You're an easy person to be with."

"Good. Maybe you'll miss me and come back to me after you figure out who you are up there in New York." His voice sounded light but the look he sent her was serious.

She took a deep breath. "What if I figure out who I am and it's a city girl?"

Boyce was quiet for a moment. "It's a point that's held me back from doing more than making jokes," he said finally, surprising her.

Before she could make a response back, Boyce shushed her to listen to the sound of a woodpecker far off in the distance. He tried to locate the bird with the small binoculars he carried in his pack, but he never could see it.

After that, there was another creek to rock hop across, and somehow, Jenna never got the nerve to turn the conversation back to that last comment Boyce made.

Back at Jenna's place later, she and Boyce sat on the couch resting. "I enjoyed our hike today, Boyce."

"Me, too." He pulled her hand over to hold it in his and began to trace patterns over her arm with his fingers.

"Guess what I'm drawing?" He grinned at her.

It was all Jenna could do to concentrate or make a guess with his fingers skimming over her arm.

"That's a circle," she said, trying to focus. "And that's a square."

The next shape was a heart and the movements of Boyce's fingers grew more intimate, skimming across the tender skin of her inner arm as he traced the shape again.

To avoid moving in that direction, Jenna shifted the subject. "You know, Carla and I used to play a game like this when we were girls. We wrote words on each other's backs and then tried to guess the words."

"Show me," he said, rolling over on the couch to present his back to her.

Remembering the fun she and Carla had doing this, Jenna climbed up on Boyce's hips like she used to sit on Carla's and started to trace out letters, letting him guess them from the feel of the letters on his back. At first it was fun, just as she remembered, and then odd, strange feelings began to seep up her thighs and legs where she was sitting on him. She became more and more conscious of the feel of him under her body, but she didn't know how to change the situation without saying something personal and inappropriate. Without giving away her own discomfort.

Boyce took care of it for her by suddenly rolling over and pulling her down on top of him. "No more of that game, Jenna." He looked into her eyes with heavy desire. "You're driving me crazy with it." And it was all too obvious that she was. They kissed and cuddled a little then - if you could call cuddling a right word for it, when they were both breathing like two racehorses just out of the gate.

Blowing out a long breath, Boyce stood up. "I need to go now, Jenna. It's getting late. I'll see you tomorrow."

He paced across the room and let himself out the door.

Jenna sat on the couch feeling confused. She wondered if she had done something she shouldn't have.

Walking to the door, she looked out to see him starting across the yard.

"Boyce, did I do something wrong?" she whispered out into the night.

"No, Jenna, you did everything right." His voice sounded husky and soft. "That's why I have to go now."

"But we could just talk," she suggested.

"No, we couldn't just talk." She heard him sigh deeply. "Or at least I couldn't. I can't be with you anymore right now without asking things of you that I shouldn't ask."

Jenna heaved a sigh watching him stride across the yard. Did he mean asking about deeper emotions than either of them were ready to admit yet?

When Boyce was with her and when her emotions were stirred, Jenna often wanted to talk of love and future. But by the morning, she always felt glad things had not gone further or gotten even more complicated.

Later in the evening, she went over to ask Boyce something about art. In all honesty, she just wanted to see him again. She'd felt restless and antsy ever since he left.

He let her in with few words and seemed almost annoyed to see her.

She smiled at him, wanting to soften his mood. "I wanted you to give me your opinion on these designs I've been working on." She laid them out on the table. "I've been trying some new techniques with my paints – trying to infuse more color - but I think it takes away from the initial design."

Boyce walked over to look at them. "I don't know why you came over to show these to me." He frowned. "They're a mess and even you know it. This pouring technique with watercolors doesn't work well with your kind of card designs. It makes them confusing and distorted."

"Yes." She sighed. "Maybe I was just painting out how my life feels now."

He shot her an annoyed look. "Well, maybe you need to do something to fix your life instead of just painting out your feelings."

Hurt now, she turned on Boyce in irritation. "Well, who made you the great authority about me and my life, Boyce Hart?"

He glared at her. "The only way anyone gets to be the authority in your life – because you give your authority up, Jenna. You've been abdicating your rightful authority over your own life for years. You let others dictate who you are, what you like, what you should do, whether your art's good enough, how you should think. Even now, you're down here hiding out in the mountains, letting other people handle getting the details you need for a divorce together for you. Letting other people work out your future. Afraid to go back and face it. Afraid to stand up to your husband or your parents. Afraid to really have your own life. I'd like to see you grow up, Jenna, live on your own, make it on your own, know who and what you really are. Be your own self. And be proud of who you are in the bargain."

His words washed over her painfully. "Well, Boyce Hart, you're going to get your wish. I'll soon be out of your hair and on my own back in New York. And as for you, your life's been so sweet and simple and full of love and kindness that you lack empathy with people who have not had your emotional advantages. That are suffering or hurting or going through some crisis. It's easy to judge and think how a person should act until it's you. Then it's not so simple anymore."

It had been a nasty evening between the two of them in the end. They threw insults and said things they probably should not have said. Jenna wept buckets afterwards when she returned to Sam's. She felt no better than her mother and father who always lost control and screamed at each other in their unpleasant scenes.

She slept fitfully and woke the next day with a splitting headache. She swallowed an aspirin, dressed, and headed for the gallery after a scanty breakfast. Jenna considered calling in sick, but decided it would probably be better to have something to do today to occupy her mind.

At eleven o'clock, Boyce walked in the gallery, looking tired and disheveled. He waited until Jenna's customer left, and then said simply, "I was out of line last night. I came to say I'm sorry. You were right about some of the things you said. I hope you'll forgive me. "

Jenna stood there stunned for a moment. Elliott had never apologized after they had a quarrel. Not ever. Neither had her mother or her father. Elliott's way of handling small disputes was to tell Jenna, "I think we'll go out to dinner tonight, Jenna. It will make you feel so much better for losing control last night." Or acting foolish, or crying, or something. He always turned it around on her so that it seemed like only she had been at fault. When it was her mother, she simply acted as though it never happened at all. It was never mentioned again.

"Is there anything else I can say to make things right?" Boyce asked softly, when Jenna hesitated so long to make a response.

She shook her head. "No. It's all right. I'm sorry, too, for some of the things I said, as well. I hate fighting. I hardly slept at all last night."

"Me, neither. You should have called me." He gave her a teasing look. "I would have come over and we could have kissed and made up so you could have slept better."

"If you'd come over in the night, we probably wouldn't have gotten any sleep at all," Jenna said flippantly.

"Now that you mention it, I think that's probably right." He raised an eyebrow and gave her a long, considering look.

They grinned at each other then, glad to have the argument a thing of the past.

However, as Jenna worked in the gallery through the day, she thought about what Boyce had said the night before. She did need to grow up and get over her timidities and fears. She didn't want to always be a silly, helpless woman someone else had to look after.

Chapter 12

*J*enna rose early the following day to get some household chores done before Charlotte came to pick her up to go shopping. After breakfast, she made sugar cookies for Tyler Dean. She knew they were his favorites, particularly with colored sprinkles on the top. Besides, whatever cookies Tyler Dean didn't eat on their trip, Boyce would make quick work of later.

Charlotte arrived at about nine o'clock and they were soon on their way. "I figured I'd better drive today, since we have the kids," Charlotte told her. "Their seats are already in the back and all their junk. This car here is not as pretty and new as yours, but she sure is a sentimental friend to me and full of memories. Her name is Theda."

"Your car has a name?" Jenna looked at her in surprise.

Charlotte grinned. "Sure, I name all my cars. This one's Theda Thunderbird. I call your car Catalina Cadillac. It seemed like she needed a fancy name."

Jenna's mouth quirked in a smile.

"I got this car back when I was sixteen years old," Charlotte continued. "Daddy has an auto shop and repairs cars, and he found me this black Thunderbird at a car auction, only six years old and not many miles. Whoo-ee, girl. I thought I was hot stuff driving Theda T. to high school after daddy got her fixed up for me. I can remember a lot of fine times with my girlfriends piled into Theda going to the drive-in or to a football game. And then me and Dean dated in Theda. He had a Chevrolet truck, so we often took my car instead. I have some serious memories of young passion in this vehicle, plus all these new memories of carrying my children around in it. I'll probably have myself a good cry when I finally have to trade ole' Theda in."

They drove in silence for a minute, enjoying the spring day.

Charlotte looked over her shoulder to check on three-year old Tyler Dean in the back seat. "Tell Miss Jenna what we're going to do today, Tyler Dean."

His face brightened. "We're goin' to shop for Easter clothes, and if I'm good, I get a new bucket and a shovel and we get to go to the park for a picnic. I get to play in the big sandbox at the park and swing on the swings and climb on the jungle gym."

"That's right," said Charlotte, approvingly. "And what if you're bad?"

A little frown crossed his face. "We don't get to go to the park for a picnic," he said, with a pout in his voice, "and I don't get a new bucket or a new shovel, either. I might even have to take an extra long nap when we get home, too. If I'm real bad, I might even get a spanking."

Charlotte nodded. "I'm glad you remember all that, Tyler Dean. Now, I want you to know that no little boys like to go shopping for clothes, but it's a necessity sometimes. It has to be done. Life is like that. We have to do some things we don't like much in this life, but then there are usually good times to look forward to afterwards. It's good to learn that right off."

Charlotte turned to smile at Jenna. "We always talk ahead about things we are going to do so Tyler Dean knows exactly what to expect and what is expected from him. If I'm clear with him and he knows what his choices are, then he handles it better when things don't work out good. And he sees his responsibility in that. I don't believe in lying to children, like in telling them a shot won't hurt or that it will be fun shopping. Shopping for clothes isn't fun for little boys."

Jenna laughed. "Some men even hate shopping after they are grown. I wonder why that is?"

"Lord, I don't know." Charlotte waved one hand, while keeping the other on the steering wheel. "The ways and differences between men and women is one of life's greatest mysteries. It says in the Bible that it's past understanding. I do know that Tyler Dean's daddy would rather take a beating before going clothes shopping any day. I've promised to get him a new dress shirt for Easter just so he doesn't have to darken the door of a store this week."

Charlotte drove them to a big thrift store over in Maryville first.

As she parked the car, she turned to Jenna. "I want to start here to look for what I need. If I'm lucky, I'll find most everything here and save myself a lot of money."

Jenna followed Charlotte and the children into the store. They were soon weeding through the racks of clothes to see what they could find.

Charlotte told Jenna sizes so she could help her look.

The store had no similarity to the shops and stores in New York Jenna normally patronized. Jenna wrinkled her nose. There was even a slight odor of used clothing in the air.

"They don't have things organized by size in here." Charlotte sorted through a rack of children's clothes while she talked. "You just have to look through. And watch for good brand names and clothes that are almost new. One way you can tell that is by the tag and how crisp it still is."

After searching through the boys' rack for a while, Charlotte found Tyler Dean a pair of navy pants with a little plaid vest. "Isn't this cute?" She held it up with a grin.

Jenna had to agree and was amazed Charlotte had located such a cute outfit in all this disorder. They continued hunting until they found a small white dress shirt to go with it. Charlotte even found a child's red bow tie in a basket of odds and ends. For Jennie Rae, they found a fussy white dress with hand-smocked rosebuds on the front.

"Probably somebody's granny did all this handwork here." Charlotte lovingly examined the little dress she held. "I guess they didn't have another little girl in the family to pass the dress on to."

After locating outfits for the children, Charlotte found Dean a nice blue dress shirt and a tie, but they had more trouble finding something for Charlotte.

"I could just wear a dress I already have." Charlotte told Jenna with a big sigh. "It's vain of me to think I *have* to have a new dress, but everybody at church wears something new for Easter. And I hate to not have a new dress for myself."

Jenna thought for a minute. "We could go over to the mall and buy one," she suggested.

Charlotte gave Jenna a disgusted look. "No, *you* could do that, Miss New York City. I have fifty dollars here for Easter clothes that Dean gave me, and that's it."

Jenna felt ashamed then that she had even mentioned the mall. She busied herself looking through the racks for Charlotte a dress.

"Look here," she said, after a few minutes. She held up a simple skirt and short-sleeved jacket in rose pink for Charlotte to see. "This is your size."

"It's real plain." Charlotte studied it with a frown. "I was sort of wanting a floral dress if I could find one. But that would probably look real good on you, Jenna. You wear real plain-looking things like that."

Jenna considered this. The simple suit did look like her. And the brand name was actually an expensive one. She knew it would cost a lot in a specialty store.

Because she hesitated, Charlotte said, "But maybe you think you're too good to wear a thrift store suit." She raised an eyebrow expressively.

"And maybe I don't think so." Jenna's reply was saucy and she draped the suit over her arm while she kept looking. "You may not know me as well as you think, Miss Townsend Tennessee."

They both laughed at that and kept looking through the clothes' racks. Everything from women's small to plus sizes were all bunched together, and the process of looking proved slow and tedious. But, then, on a side rack, Jenna found a floral princess-style dress in a soft yellow floral in Charlotte's size.

"Ooooo! I just love it!" exclaimed Charlotte. "I hope it fits me."

They went back into the store's dressing room and found both their garments fit perfectly. Jenna had planned to wear a basic black dress she had brought with her to Boyce's church, but this would be a better choice for Easter. She told Charlotte that.

Jenna smiled. "I brought a nice white blouse and some little white sandals with me that will be perfect with this suit, too."

Charlotte tucked their items into her shopping cart behind Jennie Rae's baby carrier. "So, you're going to Boyce's church for Easter and then over to his family's for lunch." She regarded Jenna with interest. "How did all this come about?"

Jenna shrugged. "His mother invited me when we stopped by there after hiking Saturday."

Charlotte studied Jenna thoughtfully and seemed about to make a comment when Tyler Dean began to swing from the clothing rack bar.

"Tyler Dean!" Charlotte's voice was sharp. "Get off that rack right now. Remember our agreement."

He dropped off the rack immediately, looking thoroughly chastised.

"Come on now," she said, taking his hand. "We're going in the back to look for shoes for you and Jennie Rae. You can look at all the toys there while I look at the shoes."

He skipped off excitedly beside her then, as they walked toward the back room of the store. "Can I get a dump truck, too?" he asked.

"Maybe," said Charlotte. "And definitely yes if you can find your bucket and shovel here and save us some money. Why don't you let Jenna help you look, while I try to find some shoes? "

When they left the thrift store, Charlotte had all the things everyone needed for Easter morning. And Tyler Dean, with Jenna's help, had found a big dump truck, and a bucket and shovel among the toys.

"I have sure been blessed today," Charlotte pronounced, as they were putting the children into their car seats. "Plus I have money to spare that I can keep for another day."

"And I have a great new suit," added Jenna.

Charlotte looked up from strapping Tyler Dean into the back seat. "You ever shopped in a thrift shop before?"

"No." Jenna answer was honest. "But I have been to used antique stores in the city and to auctions and flea markets out in the country."

A big grin spread over Charlotte's face. "Well, you can say you've had another fine, new adventure down here in rural Tennessee now. You can tell folks you found yourself a bodaciously beautiful Easter suit in an all American Tennessee thrift store."

Jenna laughed as she climbed into Charlotte's car.

After running a few quick errands, Charlotte drove them through some Maryville side streets to a pretty park set among big, spreading shade trees. Charlotte had fixed all of them a picnic lunch to share and Jenna brought the cookies she made earlier as her contribution. At the park, picnic tables clustered under the shade trees, surrounded by an expansive children's playground filled with grassy play areas.

"I'd have gone out to eat," Charlotte told Jenna. "But it's really a lot easier for me to just picnic with the children. Tyler Dean can run and play after his lunch, and I can just put Jennie Rae to sleep right here in the car where I can watch her."

Jenna pushed Tyler Dean on the swings and played with him while Charlotte fed Jennie Rae and eased her gently into her car seat for her nap. Then they had their lunch of bologna sandwiches, chips, chilled colas from the cooler, and fresh peaches.

Tyler Dean gave Jenna a big grin. "Bawoney sandwiches are my favor-itest kind."

Charlotte winked at Jenna. "I guess you know now why this was the lunch specialty today."

After lunch and cookies, Tyler Dean settled down a few feet away from their table to play in the park's big sandbox.

"He loves that sandbox." Charlotte looked at him fondly. "He's always begging to come here, and he'll just sit and dig and build little roads and drive his cars for an hour if I'll let him. I'm trying to get Dean to build him a sandbox of his own out in the backyard. But I wonder if it will be as exciting after he has his own."

They sat companionably drinking their diet colas and enjoying the sunny April day.

Charlotte broke the silence at last. "You know, my momma says when you can sit quietly and contentedly with someone, and just enjoy being with them without needing to talk, that you're becoming real friends."

"I think that's true," Jenna said, smiling at her. "And we have become real friends. I'll miss you when I go back."

"When are you leaving?" Charlotte frowned at that thought.

"I guess the last weekend in April," Jenna answered. "You'll be ready to come back to work. And I need to start back to New York then."

Jenna told Charlotte about her plans and about the apartment she planned to move into when she got back. "It feels good to have everything resolved in my mind, even if there is so much to do to get it all resolved in reality. My part-time employer said I can work more for him when I get back. So I'll be able to make my way and take care of myself."

"Yeah, I've heard something about that job." Charlotte gave Jenna a disapproving look. "Una told me you were an artist but kept that news all to yourself down here. Hid it from everyone."

Jenna looked up in surprise at Charlotte's tone. "I'm not an artist, not really," she argued. " I just create greeting cards part-time for a press in New York." She shrugged. "I didn't think it was particularly important to tell anyone about it."

Charlotte parroted her words back. "You just create greeting cards. Pooh. Do you know how many people wish they could write out a nice, rhyming verse for a greeting card or draw anything better than a stick man? You need to do some real, serious thinking about the merit of your abilities, Jenna. You ought to be real proud of the work you do. Una showed me some of your cards, and they are really nice. It hurt all our feelings, you know, that you had this glorious gift in you and hadn't even seen fit to share that with any of us."

"I'm sorry, Charlotte." Jenna chewed on her lip regretfully. "It didn't come up right away when I first came and then, somehow, I didn't know how to bring it up later. It's not that I didn't really want you to know."

"That's not true, Jenna. You didn't want to share it for some reason," Charlotte challenged, giving her a pointed look. "It's about as easy for me to see when you're telling a lie as it is for me to see when Tyler Dean is. You give it away with your eyes and the way you twist your hands." She stopped to consider Jenna thoughtfully. "I bet you didn't want to tell Una and me because of how much money you make at that job. Because of you having this fine professional job in the city while me and Una just work in a little country gallery part time. That's it, isn't it?"

Jenna's reply was defensive. "I didn't know what you or Una made until I got my first paycheck."

"But when you did get your paycheck, you particularly avoided bringing it up after that, didn't you?" Her honest eyes probed Jenna's.

She dropped her gaze in embarrassment. "Maybe. I don't know. I have a lot on my mind, Charlotte, and I didn't want you to think I was trying to say I was better than you or something. I like you; I didn't want anything toget in the way of that."

Charlotte shook her head and sighed. "You're still thinking everything's all about money, aren't you?" she demanded. "You were raised to think this is how people rate and value each other. That this is how a person's worth is determined. Well, let me tell you, Jenna - not everyone was raised to think like that. And not everyone does. I wasn't raised that way. I was taught to look on the inside, not the outside. I took to you right off; something drew me to you, even though I knew there were differences between us. And I never held back with you or tried to pretend. It wouldn't have changed anything for me to learn you were rich or poor."

She stopped and laughed at herself. "Shoot, I thought you were rich from the first day with those sleek clothes and that gold Cadillac. I've already told you that. So why did you think knowing about this art job of yours would make a difference?"

"I don't know," admitted Jenna. "Maybe just because so many people have belittled me about my art, made fun of me for it, made me not value it much. I got to where I just didn't want to risk being criticized about it, so I simply stopped mentioning it to anyone. Elliott and his friends used to make fun of me and it hurt. And Mother thought my art was so unimportant. Of so little value, almost something to be ashamed of. So I started thinking so, too."

Charlotte's face softened. "Well, there, that's an honest and true answer," she said. "And it explains a lot. You seem to have so much, but in so many ways, Jenna, I'm richer than you. I've always had people to love me and believe in me and to tell me I'm fine. There were always a pile of relatives and friends to get excited if I even did the least thing of any merit or showed any talent or skill. I guess I was really blessed. I can't think how awful it would have been if I'd married Dean and he'd belittled me and ridiculed me all the time for who and what I am. Maybe I'd have pulled in some, too, and lost confidence and pride in myself." She considered that. "But maybe not. I'm pretty ornery and straight forward."

She laughed and reached over to pat Jenna's knee. "You're going to have to look forward and not back, Jenna. You need to be your own encourager, toot your own horn, and throw your own confetti when you do something good. Give yourself your own party. Tell yourself you're something special and don't wait on somebody else to do it."

Jenna exhaled slowly. "Somebody else told me something like that recently, " she replied. "I guess I need to pay attention to it and think more about doing that."

Charlotte eyed her thoughtfully. "I can just about figure out who that someone was." She paused. "But I'm not ready to get to that subject yet. For now, you tell me about your art, Jenna. I really want to know more about it."

"What do you want to know?" Jenna picked up a cookie to nibble on.

"Well, for a start, despite all my talk about money not mattering, I'm just dying to know what you make doing that kind of work." Charlotte grinned at Jenna. "And then I want to know all about how you got started in it and what your plans are."

So Jenna told Charlotte all about her art and about what she made, too. She even told her about the Press's offer to let her branch out into more design areas when she got back to New York. With Charlotte's enthusiastic interest and encouragement, Jenna even shared some of her ideas for new things. Feeling comfortably accepted, she found herself sharing some of her dreams, too, especially her dream to illustrate children's books. Perhaps to even write one.

"I've never told anyone that." Jenna dropped here eyes. "About wanting to try a book. I don't know if I even could."

Charlotte shrugged casually. "Everything worthwhile starts with a dream or a vision. Then even if it seems impossible or you don't feel qualified, you just try your hardest. Who knows what might happen? Life doesn't have any guarantees. But one thing is for sure, if you never try things, you can be for sure nothing at all will ever happen."

"That's really wise," observed Jenna.

"Well, I'm going to be expecting to get a signed copy of one of your books for my children when your ship comes in." Charlotte smiled warmly at her.

Jenna returned the smile with affection. "And I'm going to expect to be one of the first people you call when you get ready to have that open house for your daycare center you told me you hope to open some day, Charlotte. I know it will be a good one. I've been watching how wonderful you are with your children. If I ever have children, I'm going to call you to get advice."

Charlotte raised her eyebrows. "If you play your cards right, maybe you can run right over and bring them to me to babysit while you do your design work. Then you can get all the free advice you want without a long distance phone call."

She gave Jenna a pointed look and a wink. "I know a pretty good man that, I think, has figured out which honey tree to buzz around. You've been spending a lot of time with him, too. Hikes, dinners, visits to his mama's, invitations to come to Easter church. I haven't seen Boyce Hart pay this much attention to a woman for longer than I can remember. After the two of you were at our house for dinner, Dean and I both said we could generate enough electricity off the tension running between you to save ourselves about one hundred dollars on our next electric bill. If we could figure out how to harness it."

Jenna felt herself flush with embarrassment.

Charlotte laughed. "Well, now I'm making you blush. What did you think, girl, that everyone was blind? This is small town USA. Remember, I told you there are no secrets here."

"I'm still a married woman." Jenna was truly shocked at Charlotte's candor. "And many obstacles lie ahead of me just to resolve this mess I got myself into. I'm not too eager to get involved with another man and to make another mess for myself right away."

An angry look crossed Charlotte's face. "Now, that's a real insulting thing to say about a good person like Boyce," she snapped. "In fact, to even put him in the same category with Mr. No-Good Elliott Howell is neither fair nor nice of you. I'm disappointed you can't see that."

"Men often change after they get married." Jenna crossed her arms stubbornly.

Charlotte got up to check on the baby while she answered. "Some do a little. Sometimes they start leaving their dirty socks on the bathroom floor or forget to bring you flowers. But it's a rare man that turns out to be a Jekyll and Hyde like the one you hooked up with. Jenna, you can't be afraid to think about ever caring for someone fine in the future just because you connected with a low-down, smooth-talking con like Elliott Howell the first time."

Jenna heaved a sigh. "Charlotte, how can I know if someone else won't turn out to be a con, too? No matter how nice I think they are. I thought Elliott was good. I thought he was the right one for me, and look what happened."

Charlotte looked at Jenna thoughtfully. "Let me ask you something. Did you really love Elliott when you married him? Or did you just feel flattered by his attentions and delighted that your parents were so pleased with him for you?"

"I thought I loved him." Jenna searched her memories. "I really thought I did, Charlotte."

"You keep saying 'thought' here, Jenna. That's important." She frowned. "I think you already know that what was between you and Elliott was a poor substitute for the real thing. Making mistakes teaches us. Sometimes we learn what is right by what we do wrong. You're an older and wiser woman now than when you were being courted by Elliott Howell back then. You can't be afraid to love again because you were wronged once. It would be yourself you hurt most if you did that."

Jenna looked away from Charlotte's candid gaze. "Well, the timing is just not good now for me to have feelings for someone and to get involved again."

"Too late." Charlotte wrinkled her nose playfully. "You already have feelings and you already are involved. That's as plain as the nose on your face. And how do you know God wasn't just smiling down on you to bring along a sweet man after you'd been involved with a nasty one? Maybe He wanted you to see right off, before you got too soured and bitter, that all the apples in the bunch aren't rotten just because there's a bad one out there."

"It's confusing, Charlotte." Jenna felt tears welling up behind her eyes. "It's not that simple."

"No, I don't reckon love ever is." She patted Jenna's knee with affection.

Jenna looked up with shock. "I never said I was in love with Boyce, Charlotte, or that he was in love with me."

"No, you didn't." Charlotte eyed her candidly. "And I'm not going to get more pushy than I have been already. But here's what worries me the most. And that's Boyce Hart. I'm as fond of him as a brother. If you hurt him I'm not going to be happy with you at all."

Jenna blinked in surprise.

Charlotte wagged a finger at her. "You see, you've been so focused on you - on your pain and your past hurts and your problems - that you haven't even given much of a thought to Boyce," she said. "How he might be hurting or how he might hurt and have pain and disappointment after you go. How he might suffer. You've wanted the martyr seat all to yourself. I'm just saying love thinks about the other person's heart as much as their own. You need to consider that. Boyce could be hurt, too, in all this. And to be quite frank, I don't want that. I truly love and care for Boyce Hart, and I'm not eager to see his heart broken."

Before Jenna could even think how to answer, Tyler Dean ran over to get them to push him in the swing. And Jennie Rae started to cry.

Charlotte hugged Tyler Dean and gave him a drink from his toddler cup. "Let Jenna push you one more time in the swing, Tyler Dean, and then we've got to start home." She stood up. "I'll take care of Jennie Rae. She's probably wet, and she's probably hungry again, too."

"Come on." Tyler Dean pulled at Jenna's hand. "Push me real high," he ordered. "So my feet can touch the sky."

"I'll push you real high if you'll hold on real tight," Jenna promised him. And while she played with Tyler Dean, she thought about Boyce in the back of her mind. Would he be hurt when she went away? Would she cause his heart pain like Elliott had caused her pain? It was true, in part, what Charlotte said, and it made Jenna ashamed to admit it to herself. She had been thinking almost exclusively about herself and her own problems. She'd only thought about her feelings and her heart. That seemed natural to her with the mess she was in. Boyce seemed so strong and confident that she hadn't really given much thought to his heart at all.

When Charlotte and Jenna pulled up in the driveway of Sam's cabin a little later, Boyce was out in his front yard with Patrick. He wandered over to see Tyler Dean and the baby, and they all stood talking a bit before Charlotte left to take the children home.

"Sounds like you girls had a good time," observed Boyce.

"We did," said Jenna. "Charlotte's become a good friend."

"Wanna have dinner at my place?" Boyce asked her. "I have steaks for the grill, because it's so nice outside tonight, and some sweet potatoes to bake."

"All right. If you'll let me bring the salad."

"Sure thing. Come over later about six." Boyce pulled his keys out of his pocket and headed for his car. "I'm going down to the gallery for a little while to go through the mail. Then I have some prints to take to the post office and a few errands to do. I'll see you later."

Jenna watched Boyce walk back over to his place and decided she would be careful with him tonight. She didn't like to think she might hurt him. What did she know about his heart, anyway? He'd never told her anything about other girlfriends when they talked or even if he'd ever been serious about anyone before - or if he had ever been hurt before. Maybe she would ask him.

She turned back to the cabin and, suddenly, felt a sweep of emotion hit her. She would be going back to New York in less than two weeks. So many problems waited for her there. She hated to think of facing them. And of leaving this peaceful place. Her life here had started to become precious to her.

Chapter 13

$\mathcal{B}$oyce looked, instinctively, toward the calendar hanging on his refrigerator as he put up groceries later in the day.

His face fell as he noted the date. "Jenna goes back to New York in less than two weeks. Lord, I ache to think about her leaving and I'm sure the pain will only get worse as the time draws closer."

He put the last of the perishables away and sat down on the kitchen stool, reaching down to scratch his dog's back. "I stay constantly torn up when I'm with her now, Patrick. One part of me wants to beg her to never leave me, to let me take care of her, to let me go to New York with her to get everything resolved, and to see that no one ever hurts her again. But another part of me believes it's important for her to go back by herself, to face her own problems and to deal with them on her own, to get more personally strong and sure of herself in doing so."

Boyce dug out a dog treat for Patrick from one of the grocery bags. "I stay constantly torn up about how much to commit to Jenna, too. We've both fallen in love with her, haven't we, Boy?"

Patrick swished his tail as if in agreement. Boyce laughed.

"I don't know when I realized I'd fallen in love with her. I think it swept over me almost from the first, like an unexpected rainstorm. I didn't even have enough warning to protect myself from the onslaught." He rubbed a foot against the dog's side. "I hate myself for my feelings sometimes, but there's not much I can do to change them."

Patrick licked his hand in sympathy.

"She's so skittish right now about commitment and marriage. I'm afraid she'll shy away from me if I share my heart fully." Boyce frowned at the thought. "Considering Jenna's track record when faced with tough situations, she might bolt and run straight back to New York. I don't want that. I need all the time I can finagle with her to show her I'm different from Elliott."

He hated the fact that he even needed to prove to her he was different from that man. Sometimes he could almost see her mentally comparing him with Elliott. She'd get a faraway look when she did. It made him want to grind his teeth in frustration.

"I don't want her committing to me because she's looking for a way out of her problems, looking for someone else to take care of her because she's afraid to be on her own. I want her to love me because of who I am and that only." He scowled. "Is it wrong of me to want that?"

He got a cola out of the refrigerator and sat down in a slump on the stool again. "What if I continue to play noble and she goes back to New York and finds out she doesn't need me? That she's just fine on her own? It could happen. She's overdue to learn how fine and capable she really is. How talented and beautiful."

He got up to pace restlessly. "It makes me sick to think that some other man besides me might tell her these things. That another man might kiss her, touch her, or awaken her more. She's my sleeping beauty. I want to be the one to love and awaken her. I don't want anyone else to have her, Patrick." The dog lifted his ears. "But I can't claim her yet. I just can't; it isn't the right time."

Boyce ran his hands through his hair in frustration. He knew that deciding to keep the pressure off and letting Jenna go back to resolve her own problems was the choice he had already made. But his choice terrified him. He didn't want to lose Jenna, and, yet, he had to love her enough to let her go. And hope she might come back.

He whistled to Patrick, and headed outdoors to the studio above the garage. It was too early to think about dinner just yet. Maybe he'd work on some of his sketches or paint a little. He climbed up the stairs and opened the door into his work area.

At his desk, Boyce stopped to look through the stack of preliminary sketches he'd made for the new paintings he planned for the Atlanta gallery. They looked good, and he thought he had some firm ideas in mind of just what he would do for the wildflower show.

Boyce flipped through the sketches of the wildflower close-ups he'd done so far, and then paused and shook his head. A group of sketches of Jenna from their hike in Greenbrier lay mixed in with his flower drawings. He smiled looking through them and remembering that good day.

He stopped to study one in particular of Jenna looking up at the sun with a joyous smile. She stood in a clearing in the forest, a sweep of spring beauties covering the ground as thick as a summer snow beneath her feet.

147

Maybe he could show Gregor Haldeman a painting idea based on these sketches for the Atlanta show.

"Since I can't get the woman out of my mind, I may as well paint her. Maybe it will help alleviate some of the tension I carry all the time." He flipped open a sketchpad and started to work.

Boyce felt more relaxed later when he was back at the house getting ready for his dinner with Jenna. His art always did that for him. He could lose himself in it. It was always so satisfying to see his inward visions take shape on paper and then on canvas. Simply working with color gave him an incredible high; he even liked the smells of paint and pigment. For a long time, his art had been enough for him. Enough, most of the time, to keep him happy and fulfilled. And then Jenna walked into his life.

"I remember the first night we met. She mesmerized me from the first with her gypsy looks. I wanted to paint her even then."

Boyce shook his head, remembering. "I saw her watching me and thought she might flirt with me, but she acted shy, almost awkward. It took me a while to realize she was practically an innocent –even after two years of marriage."

Out the kitchen window, he heard Patrick bark a welcome to Jenna as she walked across the yard. He spied on her through the kitchen window, watching her reach down to pet his dog, to talk to him sweetly. Coming through the yard, she stopped to study and notice things. He loved that about her. They had that in common, that sense of wonder about their world. He walked out on the porch to meet her and found her picking a handful of golden, yellow dandelions.

"Are you picking me a bouquet of weeds?" he asked her teasingly.

"I love dandelions." She gave him one of her dazzling smiles as she came up on the porch. "You can tell if someone loves butter by holding a dandelion under their chin."

She held a dandelion up under his chin, studying the result intently. "Oh, yes, you definitely love butter. There is a yellow glow under your chin that is very distinct."

"Come here, dandelion girl." He drew her in closer with one arm. "I need a welcome before I let you in." He leaned over and kissed her softly. His intent was to be light and informal, but that idea was lost when she leaned sweetly into the kiss and wrapped her arms around his body. Boyce kissed her deeply then, letting his hands roam up her arms and into her hair. Lord, that glorious hair. And she smelled of her lemony fragrance mixed with honeysuckle again.

She pulled away slightly, seeming to regret letting herself go for a moment.

"That's a better welcome than I expected, dandelion girl," he murmured against her hair. "I'll have to ask you over more often."

"Oh, I'll miss you so much, Boyce Hart." She sighed and turned soft brown eyes to seek his. "And I have less than two weeks left to be here."

His heart and ego swelled at her words. She would miss him, and she'd been studying her calendar, too. "Well, we're going to make a lot of memories in that time, Jenna." He smiled at her. "Starting with dinner. I assume that's your salad offering you just sat down on the porch table over there?"

"It is," she answered, smiling. "I planned to bring cookies, too, but Tyler Dean loved them so much, I let him take the rest home."

"It's okay," Boyce said. "I got ice cream, plus two kinds of syrup and chopped nuts for later. I thought we'd be decadent."

"Ummmm." She followed him in with her salad. "I'm hungry. I only ate part of a baloney sandwich and a peach at Charlotte's picnic today. I got distracted talking and forgot to eat much."

"Well, I'll be sure we don't do *too* much talking tonight." He gave her a wicked grin.

"Oh, you." She swatted him on the arm. "Get in there and get my steak ready. I've cooked for you three times this week, and you owe me."

They laughed and talked as Boyce got the rest of the dinner together. While they ate, Boyce caught Jenna up on the local gossip and Jenna told him about her calls to Sam and Carla before she came over.

"Sam says he is much better." Jenna seemed obviously pleased to repeat this. "He said to tell you he is jealous of you for getting so much of my time *and* my cooking."

"Have you told him anything about us becoming rather fond of each other?" he asked Jenna in a teasing tone.

"Absolutely not." She looked upset at the thought. "It would be hard to explain and it wouldn't sound right somehow. Sam is working so hard with Jake Saunders and with the attorney to get so many things done for me in New York. It just wouldn't seem right for me to be ... well, for me to be ..." She paused, searching for the word.

"Involved again so soon?" Boyce offered.

"Yes." Jenna looked at Boyce with a troubled face. "It's not that I feel wrong about being involved. Not really. It's just that it would be hard to explain. Does that make sense? I don't mean for it to hurt you that I haven't shared anything about us with Sam. He knows we've become good friends.

He said he hoped that would happen when he sent me down."

Boyce considered that. "He probably set us up, the old matchmaker."

Jenna looked shocked at that idea. "Oh, I don't think anything like that was in his mind. Sam's not like that. He was just worried about me and wanted me to have a quiet place to get away to think. And to decide what I wanted to do about everything."

"And you've been able to do that here?" Boyce decided to agree with her and keep his reservations to himself. "Are you still sure about the plans you've made? Do you still feel good about your decisions?"

"Yes, I could never go back to Elliott." Her eyes narrowed. "It would be wrong for me." She got up abruptly to carry her empty plate over to the sink, obviously upset just thinking about it.

Relief washed over Boyce as he listened to Jenna. He realized there were moments when he feared she would get cold feet and go back to Elliott after all. In fact, he would probably keep entertaining those fears for a while, despite what she said. Jenna showed him photos from New York and he had seen the man's picture among them. He was a slick, good-looking city man. And he had a powerful personality. That had already been seen.

"Carla told me Elliott called again," Jenna continued, frowning. "He was annoyed because he hadn't been able to talk to me since he left."

Boyce watched her twist her hands nervously.

"He called my mother to complain, and Mother called Carla - upset because Elliott sounded upset." Jenna chewed on a fingernail. "Mother read Carla the riot act about leaving me up there in the Poconos to nurse some neighbor of hers. It worries me that Mother is upset. She's got an intuitive side."

Boyce's jaw clenched. "She never seemed to have much insight about you that I've heard."

Jenna considered this. "Well, no, perhaps not in a kind way," she answered. "But Mother could always sense things. Know when her friends were lying. Know when something was going on that people were trying to keep from her. She often ferreted it out, too. Mother doesn't like not knowing things, you see. When she doesn't know things, she can't be in control. And control is very important for Mother."

"You're more knowledgeable now about your family, I see."

"As Charlotte would say, 'It's about time, isn't it?'" She smiled at Boyce a little sadly. "I had to get away from my life and family to begin to see them as they really are. That's not easy."

"I don't imagine it is. Let's go in the living room. I'll build up the fire and we can sit and talk."

Jenna sighed. "I used to dream night after night that Elliott might say something like that to me, might even want to do something like that with me. Just want to sit and talk and be with me."

"I'm *not* Elliott, Jenna." Boyce announced this crossly through clenched teeth, biting down his rising anger.

"I know." Jenna's answer was soft. "Don't get mad, Boyce. I meant it as a compliment, that you are such a better and nicer person."

"A guy always wants to hear that he's nice." Boyce knew his reply was sarcastic.

Jenna looked amused. "What do you want to hear?" She dropped down into her favorite corner of the sofa near the fire.

He leaned over her on the couch to brush his lips over hers. "That I'm manly, sexy, handsome, talented, and irresistible and that you want to have my babies," he answered smoothly.

"That's a pretty tall order," she quipped back, her voice a little unsteady and breathy. Boyce sat down on the sofa beside her, watching her blush. Probably the idea of having babies was getting to her.

He grinned at her slowly when she looked at him, and she blushed again.

"I'd like to have twins." He tossed that additional comment out at her to see what reaction he could get.

She threw a pillow at him across the space between them.

He tossed it back at her and wrestled her into his arms before she could throw it at him again. She struggled against him, laughing, until Boyce's lips found hers and their wrestling turned to heated passion.

Jenna pulled back this time, her pupils dark, her breathing shallow and ragged. "I don't know if I can bear many more weeks of this," she whispered huskily.

"It gets worse every time." He agreed with her, touching her face gently and wishing he could take the moment further. Instead, he smiled lazily at her in fun. "Or maybe it gets *better* every time, depending on how you look at it."

She giggled then, relaxing. But she pulled further away to settle back over into her side of the sofa.

"I want to know about the other women in your life," she declared out of the blue, surprising him. "You've never told me anything about the women you have loved or even if you've ever loved. If you've ever hurt anyone or if anyone has ever hurt you."

"What brought this sudden interest on?" He sent her a teasing look. "You wondering if I've had twins with some other woman?"

She giggled again. "No, don't be silly. I just think we should both know about each other. After all, you know all about me. You know about my first and only real boyfriend before Elliott, and all about my life with Elliott. I don't know anything about you."

"You couldn't worm this information out of Charlotte?" He raised a brow in question.

"That's not a nice thing to say, Boyce," she answered primly. "And actually, I didn't really try to. I wanted to ask you. I wanted you to tell me."

"Well, let's see." He decided to humor her. "There's not as much a story to tell as you might be thinking."

"You always say that," she complained. "Just tell it anyway."

He propped his feet up on the ottoman to get comfortable. "Okay. My first great love at thirteen was Eleanor Sparks, and, boy, she made me feel sparks whenever I was around her." He grinned. "Then senior year in high school, I fell in love with Julie Blankenship. She was the first girl I ever bought a gift for, one of those dime store heart necklaces. She wore one half and I wore the other."

"Oh, that's sweet." Jenna smiled wistfully. "I always wanted one of those. They're so romantic."

"Well, if I still had it, I'd pass it on to you." He grinned at her. "But Julie took it off to college with her when she left."

"You don't stay in touch?" She looked over at him in question.

"Nope." He shook his head. "Last I heard, she and her husband were in North Carolina somewhere. It was a long time ago, Jenna."

"And what about since you've been grown?" Jenna probed.

He scratched his head. "Well, at twenty-one, I fell hard for Audrey Bierman, an actress making a movie here in Townsend one summer."

He laughed remembering that time. "She was too experienced for a poor, little mountain boy like me, and she had me wrapped around the crook of her finger for quite a while."

"What happened?" Jenna leaned forward eagerly.

"I began to see through the acting eventually. She was just playing a part and entertaining herself while visiting here. She had no intention of staying in a little back mountain place like this and went back to Hollywood where she belonged."

Jenna studied him with her eyes. "Did you ever hear from her again?"

"Only once," he replied. "But we all remember that summer because we've got Jack Teague's twins to remind us of that time."

Jenna looked confused.

"Jack's an older guy, but a good, long time friend. He's been a real Cassanova, a ladies man, for as long as I can remember – good-looking man, big smile, salt and pepper hair, brown eyes. And he's always been attracted to younger women. Ever met him?"

"I think I met him one day in the store." Jenna blushed.

Boyce grinned. "Did he flirt with you?"

"I guess." She looked down at her hands. "He kept suggesting that maybe he could show me around the town sometime."

"That's Jack." Boyce laughed. "Well, anyway, he chased after Audrey's friend that summer - a pretty, little actress named Celine Rosen. It surprised everyone when Celine married Jack as the cast packed up to leave."

He scratched his chin. "Celine was one of those up-and-coming actresses in the movie world, and I thought she'd head straight back to Hollywood for sure. Never met a woman more stuck on herself and her own beauty. Of course, when we saw Celine good and pregnant a few months later, it all made a lot more sense. Jack didn't care about that; he fell hard. After the twins were born, Celine slipped off and left Jack one night while he slept. Took a nice chunk of his bank account and left him a Dear John letter on the table. She also left him heartbroken, embarrassed and humiliated, and with two twin girls to raise on his own."

"That's sad ... but what about Audrey?" Jenna asked him, returning to their original discussion.

"She's the one Celine ran off to in Hollywood. The one time I ever heard from Audrey she sent me a note asking me to tell Jack that Celine arrived safe and was all right. For him not to worry about her."

Boyce paused and studied the fire for a minute.

"I told you about Jack because I always feel a little guilty around Jack and the girls. It could just as easily have been me, I think, that ended up married and dumped with two kids. I was equally stupid and impressed with our Hollywood starlets. It taught me some lessons. It taught me to look deeper than just the physical appearance. And to use a little more of my God-given discernment."

"Do you think all of us have that?" Jenna raised her eyes to his. "God-given discernment?"

"I think we have a lot more of God's nature than we think we do," he answered thoughtfully. "We just don't draw on it. My father used to say the

153

world has a loud, pushy voice, but God has a still, small voice. Most of the time we just don't listen for it."

"That's a nice thought," Jenna said. "A comforting one. To think God wants us to find the right way. That He wants to speak to us."

"The Bible says 'Out of heaven He made us to hear His voice.' Shouldn't be such a surprise to us that He's interested. But it often is." Boyce got up to stir the fire and put another log on.

Jenna smiled at him teasingly as he started back to his seat. "That's the preacher's son talking, I guess."

He frowned. "I'm not ashamed of my father or my faith," he told her, not willing to be teased about this. "Both are two of life's greatest gifts to me."

"You are such a good man, Boyce." Jenna was quiet for a moment. "Do you know I have never had a conversation about God with my husband, my parents, or any of my friends."

"That seems strange, when God is all around us," replied Boyce, shrugging. "To me it would be odder not to talk about God sometimes. Don't you feel Him when you paint or get inspired to do your art? Or feel His love in you with a sweet clutch in your heart when you look at someone you care about?"

She dropped her eyes. "Yes, I do."

Because she seemed embarrassed, Boyce changed the subject. "So, are you satisfied now that you know about the significant women in my past, Jenna?" He sent her a roguish smile. "The others in between have just been women I dated for a short time. I never got very involved."

He paused, studying her. "What are you really wanting to know, Jenna? If I've ever been deeply in love? Or whether I have any secrets stashed away?" He looked at her curiously.

She colored under his gaze, obviously unsure how to answer.

"The truth is best," he said frankly.

She turned her eyes to his. "I mostly wondered if you'd ever really been hurt, and if so how you handled it. How you got through it."

Boyce caught the gist of her thoughts then. "You mean, you wondered if I'd ever been hurt like you?"

"Maybe ..." She hedged.

He shook his head. "Well, I haven't. Audrey was as close to heartless as I've encountered in a woman. She had me fooled for a short time. It hurt some when I realized it. It's easy to be fooled by people, Jenna. We don't walk through life expecting people to be dishonest, manipulative, lying, or betraying. We expect the opposite. We want to believe the best of people."

"And should we believe the best?" Her question was sincere.

"I think so, in general." He considered this. "We get a lot of what we expect in this life. And I'd rather be expecting good and mostly get good, than be always expecting bad and get mostly bad. I'm a pretty upbeat, trusting guy, in general. Optimistic. I think I'd rather risk looking for the good - and get disappointed now and then - than to always be looking for the negative, being wary and suspicious. Don't you think people that are always distrustful and on guard have to be unhappy?"

A furrow touched her brow. "Yes. And I know because I've allowed myself to become locked up, wary and suspicious like that. Unhappy. For me, it was because I had been criticized and hurt so much. I came to expect that from almost everyone. Being down here has helped me gain a better perspective on people than what I had."

"Raynelle says you've bloomed out like a flower down here with us." He smiled at her, watching her blush at the compliment.

She smiled. "Raynelle has been sweet to me."

"Hey, Jenna. Promise me something." He sat forward, catching her gaze.

"What?" A touch of hesitancy came into her voice.

"That if New York starts to take the bloom out of you that you'll come back." Boyce leaned a hand over to touch her face, adding more seriously, "Maybe you belong here, Jenna. Maybe you should stay."

Jenna twisted her hands in confusion, not meeting his eyes.

He watched her. "I'm not putting any pressure on you, Jenna. But think about it when you return to New York. And if your heart calls you back, then come back."

Her answer was evasive. "I might come to bring Sam for a visit if he gets better. I think if I came down here with him, and if we could get someone here to help him get in and out of the bed, that he could manage. It would mean so much to him."

Boyce wished her answer had been different. He tried not to reveal his disappointment as he replied. "If Sam can come, you know I'll help him. And so will Will Lansky down the road if two of us are needed." He paused. "But that's not what I was talking about, Jenna."

She looked at him honestly then. "I have to take one step at a time, Boyce. My life is not in a place that allows me to do anything else right now. I have a lot of hard things ahead for me, and I need to focus on that now. I'm not used to being confrontational, and it is going to take all my energy and all my strength. I have some big life changes coming up, and, to be quite frank, I'm scared."

Boyce reached out to touch her face. "You'll be all right, Jenna. You're stronger and braver than you know."

She bit her lip. "I hope so. It's good to know so many people believe in me. I haven't had that very much before in my life. It really helps."

"You can call me if you need a pep talk." He grinned at her.

"I may, if I think I can without wanting to run back here and hide. Which means if I don't call, it's because I'm having a difficult time and I can't."

He frowned at those words. "That's going to be hard on me, Jenna. It's going to make me want to come up there and get you. To help you."

"Well, don't, Boyce." She crossed her arms with determination. "I've got to do this by myself. It will be hard but I have to do it by myself. It's important in some way."

He shook his head. "Like 'Character is what you are when you are in the dark', that kind of thing?"

"Yes. Like that," she answered, with tears in the corners of her eyes. "So, give me a hug and let me draw in some of your strength to take with me. I'm sorely going to need it when I get back."

Boyce moved across the couch to take her in his arms. "Pull out all the strength you need, dandelion girl. You'll be all right. I know it."

They sat like that for a long time, curled up on the couch and holding each other. Boyce thought he was drawing in as much strength as she was for the tougher days that were to come.

"How long does it take to get a divorce?" he asked her huskily.

"I don't even know, Boyce. But I guess I'll find out soon."

Chapter 14

*O*n Monday, Boyce drove down to Atlanta to see Gregor Haldeman about the summer show. Jenna relished in the freedom of a day all to herself. She drove the short distance to the Townsend Wye - just inside the Great Smoky Mountains National Park. A broad turn in the Little River here had created a popular swimming hole and tubing spot. Across from the Wye parking lot, Chestnut Top Trail rose up from the roadside toward the ridge above. Jenna read in her Smokies guide that a multitude of different wildflowers flourished on the first half mile of the trail. And she wanted to take pictures and make sketches.

The trail climbed steeply in the first half mile, but the books were right about the abundance of wildflowers. Jenna took her wildflower book and identified over twenty-five different species. The trail proved a popular and a public one, so Jenna didn't have to worry about being on her own for this short hike.

The day was summertime warm and the sky an incredible blue. Jenna sang to herself as she walked, feeling more alive and carefree than she had for years. With pleasure, she filled her sketchbook with quick drawings along the way – delicate red columbines, early yellow violets, wild dwarf iris, and white solomon's seal hanging like bells off their green stalks.

On the way back home, she stopped at the Last Deli for a sandwich and sampled the fresh Rocky Road fudge Nell Watson was just cutting up on the counter.

"What are you going to do for the rest of your day?" Nell asked, after Jenna shared her morning adventure.

Jenna sighed. "I'm going to shop for gifts and momentos to take back to New York with me. I'll be leaving soon." The thought depressed her as soon as she voiced it.

Nell reached across to pat her arm. "Well, we'll all miss you around here, Jenna."

"I'll miss everyone, too." She sighed. "I've fallen in love with the mountains and the people here."

"Well, you'll have to come back real soon," Nell added as she turned to another customer.

At Raynelle's store up the street, Jenna bought handmade quilts, pottery, local honey, boxes of taffy, and picture postcards. She'd already bought gifts at Boyce's gallery earlier – favorite prints, whimsical signs, and painted birdhouses.

"After all," she told herself, justifying her purchases as she loaded them into her car. "I'll be decorating a new apartment when I get back to New York."

By late afternoon, Jenna arrived back at Sam's cabin, put up her groceries and filled the outdoor birdfeeders. The towhees and cardinals soon flew in noisily to feast on the fresh seed. Jenna sat at the table watching them while she drank a cola and browsed through the sketches she'd made earlier in the day. She planned to start a chicken casserole in a little while. Boyce wouldn't return from Atlanta until late, but he might want leftovers if he didn't eat on the road.

The phone rang, breaking into Jenna's thoughts. She checked the phone ID before answering. It was Carla.

"Hi!" Jenna's voice was bright with pleasure. "I've had the most wonderful day..."

"Oh, Jenna." Carla interrupted her in a rush, obviously upset. "The most awful thing just happened. Elliott came home today. He learned somehow that you weren't in the Poconos. I don't know how yet. He barreled into our store in a rage. John and I were at a buyer's meeting, and Milton Blake was working the store. Of course, Milton knew nothing about anything. But he said Elliott behaved very aggressively and started making all kinds of unreasonable demands and threats. Poor Milton was just about to press our security button, when Elliott huffed out."

She paused to catch her breath. "He went to Sam's next, Jenna. Sam was alone; Henry had stepped out to do an errand. Elliott got very belligerent and angry with Sam, insisting Sam knew where you were. Evidently, in the course of the quarrel, Sam acknowledged that even if he *did* know where you were he certainly wouldn't tell Elliott."

Jenna clutched the phone, her heart starting to beat furiously.

"Oh, Jenna." She heard Carla's breath catch on a sob. "Elliott completely lost his temper and attacked Sam. He attacked him in his wheelchair!

Can you believe it? He knocked him out onto the floor and threatened him. Fortunately, Henry let himself in the apartment just then. Henry saw Sam sprawled on the floor and Elliott standing over him, and then Henry attacked Elliott."

Jenna's knees went weak and she sat down. "What happened?" she got out.

Carla blew out a breath. "Henry and Elliott had quite a fight. Elliott was literally out of control. But Henry is strong, so Elliott got the worst of it in their struggle – facial bruises, some cracked ribs, and a broken leg from a fall over a stool. Henry called the police and both Sam and Elliott were taken to the hospital. Evidently, Elliott called your mother and father, and they are having a fit to know where you are. Your mother is becoming very accusatory, insisting we are withholding information about you from her and from Elliott. Oh, Jenna, it's just awful."

Jenna's heart was beating up into her throat and her hands started shaking now, too. "How's Sam? Tell me if Sam's all right, Carla."

"I think Henry took him back home shortly after he was examined," she answered. "He was shaken up and bruised, but all right. Henry said he was mad more than anything. But Elliott is still in the hospital, Jenna. He has a big cast on his leg, and I guess he'll be there a while. He's angry, too, but he's also worried now. Henry and Sam have assault charges pending against him. It looks bad for him to have attacked a sick man in a wheel-chair for any reason."

A new fear hit Jenna's mind. "What have you told my mother and father?"

"I made very light of it," she responded. "John and I decided that was the best way to play it. I said you decided to have some quiet vacation time to yourself after you left the Poconos and that I thought I might have a contact number for you. I didn't give it to her, Jenna, although she got hateful about it. But I guess you'll have to call her."

Carla sighed. "I'm sorry, Jenna. I had to come up with some explanation, given the situation. I thought it would be worse if she thought no one knew where you were. She might call the police to start looking for you or something. You know how she is."

"I know." Jenna took a few deep breaths trying to calm herself down. "You did the right thing, Carla. I'm going to pack and start back to New York right now. If I can stay awake to drive straight through, I will. If not, I'll stop somewhere to get a few hours sleep and then hit the road again. I'll call you as soon as I get there – and probably along the way - to see what is happening. Call Mother and tell her I'm on my way back. And call Sam and tell him that I'm on my way home, too."

"I need to tell you this before you hang up," Carla said. "John and I saw Sam at the hospital. Sam's attorney, Maury Berkowitz, was with him. You know he's the one you're working with about your divorce case, too. Maury said to tell you to call him as soon as you could. You should call him before you leave, Jenna. Here's his number and his emergency number – to save you looking them up." Carla stopped to read these off to Jenna. "He said it was really important that you talk to him before you talk to anyone else when you get back."

Jenna shook her head regretfully. "I'm so sorry this happened, Carla. This is all my fault for going off without dealing with this on my own."

"You stop talking like that, Jenna." Carla's voice was sharp. "It's not your fault that Elliott has abusively threatened and attacked Sam. That is Elliott's fault. Sam said to tell you he was fine and for you not to worry about him. He also said to tell you this should help to show you that you are making the right choices."

Tears began to trickle down Jenna's cheeks.

She heard Carla swallow deeply. "Oh, Jenna, I'm almost glad Elliott will be in the hospital when you get back. Otherwise, I would be afraid for you to be alone with him. What a horrid man he is! I can't believe he would attack a kind person like Sam, especially with him in a wheelchair and helpless to fight back."

Jenna sighed heavily. What a mess, she thought. "We'll talk about it more when I get back, Carla. I need to hang up and call Maury now, and then pack and leave as soon as I can. Be sure to let everyone know I am on my way. And thanks, Carla. I've put you and John in a bad spot in the middle of this. It wasn't fair of me."

"Don't be silly," argued Carla. "You needed this time away. It was a good idea; I still believe that. No one knew Elliott would come home early and that all this would happen. None of us knew Elliott was capable of this kind of aggression, either."

Jenna agreed with that. "I'll see you soon, Carla."

"Everything will be okay." Carla's voice sounded soothing now. "Drive carefully and take care."

With shaking hands, Jenna dialed the attorney's number next. Fortunately, Maury Berkowitz was in office and not in court, and his secretary put Jenna right through.

He quickly updated her on the situation and assured her Sam was fine.

"I guess I did everything wrong by leaving." Jenna's voice broke. "But I felt like I needed time to think."

"Stop worrying." Maury reassured her. "Any judge will understand that a woman who just learned of multiple indiscretions on her husband's part would want to get away to consider her future course." Maury paused.

"And any judge will understand a woman in that state wouldn't feel in any way compelled to tell her husband about her plans – or to tell any family members or friends she thought might not be sympathetic about her situation either. You did nothing that can be interpreted as legally wrong, Jenna. However, as soon as you return, we need to get together and write out a complaint and file an action for divorce right away. Sam and I both want to put an order of protection in for you, too, considering Elliott's violent encounter with Sam. I will work on getting a restraining order as well. There are a lot of things you and I need to talk about."

"I know." Jenna sighed. "I guess I should have come to you before I left."

"Did you know exactly what you wanted to do before you left New York?" His question was matter-of-fact and direct.

"No, not really," Jenna answered candidly.

"Do you know now what you want to do?"

"Yes. Absolutely." Her voice was firm.

"Then now is the time to talk. Before, I would have told you to come back when you knew what you wanted to do," he said. "And, Jenna, this business with Sam is not your fault. It is Elliott's fault entirely. And legally, it is to your favor. Sam and I have been talking about several ways in which this situation can be used to your advantage."

Jenna shook her head sadly. "My mind keeps thinking of what I would have done if Sam had been really hurt because of me." She tried hard to keep her emotions in check, but her hands were shaking again.

"But Sam was not hurt," Maury assured her. "And Elliott will not be foolish enough to let something like this happen again. He is a man who enjoys control. He lost his grip when he realized someone he thought to be totally under his control had escaped the noose. It made him furious, and he slipped past reasonable behavior. With criminal charges pending, he's on the defensive versus the offensive now. We have the advantage legally. And considering all that Jake Saunders' report reveals, we have all the advantages in this divorce action. I don't want you to worry. But I also don't want you to do anything wrong here. When you get back, go to your apartment, and then call me right away. I don't care what time it is. I want it documented that you returned to your residence immediately after your trip."

"Do I have to go back to the apartment?" Jenna knew her voice sounded whiney. "I don't want to live there anymore. Plus the place holds very bad memories for me. Carla and John have an apartment that will be ready for me by the weekend. I planned to move there when I returned. I don't want to even stay in Elliott's apartment. I don't want to fight for it or for anything in it except for my personal things."

Maury cleared his throat. "It's good that you've been thinking all these things out," he advised. "But for now, go to the apartment. When the action for divorce is filed, we can write in it that you are choosing to move to a new location. Everything has to be documented now before you do things, Jenna. We'll work together through this process step by step. Don't worry. I will help you. You have strong grounds for a divorce judgment. It may be, with Elliott already knowing this – and wanting to protect his reputation and avoid a trial - that he might even push for a non-court collaborative divorce and a negotiated agreement outside of the court. We'll have to see. I'll explain everything to you when you get back."

"All right." Jenna heaved another sigh. "I'm packing now. I'll probably be on the road by five."

"Jenna." Maury's voice was sharp and authoritarian. "Nothing will be served by you arriving exhausted. Drive about seven or eight hours and then stop around Baltimore and get some sleep. They can give you a wake up call, and you can drive on in to New York to arrive late morning. Time your arrival to miss the morning rush hour coming in. Don't take chances with yourself." He paused. "And, Jenna, the apartment will be easier to face again in the day hours. Plus you can go over to see Sam right away, too."

"Thank you, Mr. Berkowitz," said Jenna quietly. "You're giving me sensible advice at a time when I can't think very sensibly. I'll try to do everything you've suggested. And I will call you when I get in."

"Sam is a good friend of mine." Maury's voice softened with emotion. "He's always talked about you with the warmest regard. It will be a pleasure to help anyone who has been such a good friend to Sam. When you get in tomorrow, I can come to Sam's to meet with you if it will be easier than meeting at your apartment or my office. You might like having Sam there."

"Yes, that might be nice," Jenna agreed. "I know I'll be tired. And since I don't have a parent to assist me in this, Sam's support will be a help to me. It would be hard for him to come with me to your office."

"Then that will be our plan. I'll arrange my schedule and start on the paperwork we'll need tonight," said Maury. "Drive safely, Jenna."

They hung up, and Jenna went upstairs immediately to pack. The tears flowed freely then as she packed and loaded her belongings into the car. There was no way she could reach Boyce. He hated cell phones, and didn't carry anything but a tracfone he could use personally or activate for an emergency. Since she couldn't call him, she sat down and wrote him a quick note and taped it on his front door.

When the car was finally loaded, she calmed down enough to call Charlotte and tell her what had happened.

"Charlotte, I want you to come over and clean out the refrigerator and take all the food home with you," she told her. "And, if you would, clean up Sam's cabin for me. I just don't have time. Give Raynelle the key back when you're done. I'm leaving it under the front mat for you. Tell everyone I'm sorry I didn't have time to say goodbye. Everyone's been so good to me."

She broke down then and started sobbing. "I didn't even get to tell Boyce goodbye, Charlotte. He's in Atlanta. I don't know where and you know he doesn't carry a cell phone. I won't be able to work tomorrow for him, either."

"He'll understand," Charlotte told her, soothingly. "You take deep breaths and get yourself calm now. You have a long drive ahead."

"Someone else told me the same thing," said Jenna, hiccuping on a sob.

"Well, you listen to good advice," Charlotte advised. "And, Jenna, you're going to be all right. God is going to take care of you; do you hear me? We're all going to be praying for you down here. It's powerful when people are praying for you. You know that, don't you? And on the drive back up to New York, you do a lot of praying and laying it all out before God yourself. The Bible says we're supposed to ask for His help, not just assume it's handed down automatically without us asking. So you talk to Him and tell Him how you need Him to help you. And He will, Jenna."

"I will." Jenna croaked out the words between tears. "I don't have much experience praying like that, but I'll try."

"Fortunately, experience isn't a requirement," Charlotte told Jenna in her matter of fact way. "But sincerity is. All you need to do is talk to Him with sincerity like a good friend. Share your heart. There's not always going to be someone to go through everything hard with us in this life, but God is always there. And if things are not okay between you and Him, that is the first thing you need to pray about as you set out on the road. It's good to have a lot of friends and a good attorney and all of that when you're in trouble. But there is nothing that beats having a supernatural friend when things are tough."

"Having a little supernatural help would be really good right now," Jenna admitted, still crying and sniffling around her words.

"Well, remember where you can get that help," Charlotte said.

"I will, and I'll really miss you, Charlotte."

Charlotte's voice grew soft then. "I'll be missing you, too. I love you and am glad and blessed you came into my life, Jenna. You phone me when you can. If you don't call real soon, I'll understand. You have a lot to get through. But you know my love is right here waiting for you."

They hung up, and Jenna walked through the cabin one last time to see if she had left anything. And then she was off.

The trip back north proved long and anxious, and Jenna had plenty of opportunities to try out Charlotte's advice. Praying made the trip less lonely, and talking everything out was calming. Jenna drove almost eight hours before she stopped for the night.

"Well, Lord, I've spent almost the whole trip praying and I have to admit I feel a lot better for talking it all out with you." She paused. "Thanks for listening and I hope You'll help me through all that's to come."

Waking groggily the next morning, Jenna grabbed a muffin, fruit, and coffee at the motel before starting up the road again. Maury was right about it being easier to drive into New York after the morning rush. It was one less stressful event she didn't need right now.

As mid morning arrived, Jenna parked her car in the parking garage in downtown New York and was soon standing in front of her apartment. She took a deep breath before unlocking the door. Walking in, she found everything exactly the same. Everything except for Elliott's suitcases and hang-bags draped over the bed. He evidently hadn't unpacked before he went looking for her. The closet door stood open, and it was obvious Jenna's suitcases were missing and that many of her clothes were gone. She noticed the door to her little work studio flung wide open, too. Elliott must have seen that her laptop and art supplies were also missing.

Jenna shook her head in annoyance with herself. She realized she'd never even considered what Elliott might think if he came back early and found her missing. Or what he would do if he learned she wasn't in the Poconos. She wondered how he found out she wasn't there. Jenna heaved a regretful sigh. Invariably she would learn that soon enough.

She wandered into the kitchen to make some coffee and then, as she'd been advised, called her attorney.

Maury told her he'd be over in an hour and gave her a list of paperwork to look for in Elliott's desk.

164

"Should I call my mother?" she asked with reluctance.

"Will she come right over if you do?"

"Probably," she answered, wincing at the idea.

He chuckled. "Well, then let it wait a little longer. I'd rather you and Sam and I talk together about everything without her. She doesn't have to know when you arrived. And if anyone calls before I get there, don't answer the phone. Okay?"

"Okay." She was glad for his counsel. "I'm glad you know what is right to do."

"Thanks for the flattery, but it's my job, Jenna. Relax. Drink some coffee. Take a shower. Everything's going to be fine. I'll see you in an hour."

As Maury advised, Jenna showered, dressed, and then looked for the financial papers he wanted. After finding what she could, she sat down with a cup of coffee and called Carla.

"Hey, I'm here and all in one piece," she told her.

"Oh, Jen, I'm so glad you're home safe." Carla's voice rushed over the phone. "Do you want me to come right over? I can get John to cover for me at the bookstore ..."

Jenna interrupted her. "No. But thanks, Carla. Maury Berkowitz is on his way over, so I'll be tied up for a while. We're going over to Sam's to talk."

"Well, good," Carla replied. "You'll have some outside support with Sam there. Berkowitz is a good attorney, Jenna. John and I know him, and we've only heard the best things about him. He'll be a great help."

"I hope so." She clenched her hands anxiously, dreading the day.

Jenna heard Carla close the cash register drawer at the store. "Listen, we've moved all the storage boxes and John is painting the apartment today. You can start moving in this weekend. If you don't want to stay at Elliott's until then, you can stay with us. John and I don't want you to stay at your place after Elliott is released from the hospital, Jenna. Even if Elliott is in a cast, we think the man is dangerous. I mean, look what he did to Sam."

"I think Elliott is already regretting that." Jenna rubbed her head where a nagging headache was starting to set up. "It will have dawned on him by now that he overstepped himself, that he lost control. Elliott hates that. He'll still be angry, but he'll be in control now. He won't risk arrest with another attack on someone."

Carla hesitated. "Still, I don't trust him."

"Neither do I," admitted Jenna, with a long sigh. "But for very different reasons."

She walked over to look out the balcony window over Central Park.

"The park's turned green while I've been gone," she commented quietly to Carla.

"You're tired, aren't you, Jen?" Carla asked softly.

"Yes." Jenna rubbed her forehead. "Maury says he's bringing papers to start the divorce action. And you'll be glad to know he's writing in some sort of protective order so that Elliott won't bother me. That seems like a cop out, but I'm glad. I'd prefer to see Elliott more in the company of others. At least for now. He's going to be angry, Carla, and Elliott can be cruel with his words when he is angry. I dread that. He always has a way of making me feel so worthless. He's artful with words."

"He uses his gift in a twisted way." Carla's voice held a touch of anger.

"Yes, that he does. I have been a victim of that gift for a long time, but not for much longer. I plan to move just as soon as Maury says I can, Carla. There are obviously some legal reasons why I need to be here now - until some paperwork is in place. I guess I have to stay until someone says it's okay for me to move out without losing anything of importance in the negotiations."

"Maury probably wants to be sure you can't be accused of desertion or anything."

She shrugged. "Maybe. I don't know much about legal things. I guess I'll learn as I go. But one thing I will not do is take care of Elliott when he comes home to this apartment. I know he will need someone if he is in a cast and recovering, and it would be just like him to expect me to do it despite what has happened. However, I'm determined that will be something I will not do, no matter what I should do legally."

Carla giggled. "I can think of some wonderful malicious tricks we could play on him while he convalesces."

"Well it won't happen," said Jenna, smiling in spite of herself at Carla. "I don't want any vengeance. I just want out. I want my life back. He has stolen enough of it."

"I'm so proud of you," Carla told her. "You're being so brave through all of this."

"No, I've been my usual cowardly self through all of this, avoiding confrontation, running and hiding from any trouble or unpleasantness." She said the words candidly. "But I want to start doing better. I'd like to become someone I can admire."

"You mean kick some butt?" Carla asked with zeal.

"No, be my real self with calm and self-assurance."

"Wow. You've gotten thoughtful while you've been away," declared Carla. "I like that. You know, as an artist, you should be capable of working on a new self very effectively. Judith Viorst said, 'We each are artists of the self', so who better to create a beautiful new self than an artist? And you have such good material to work with." She laughed with warmth. "You know you've always been special to me, Jenna."

"Thanks Carla. And if I turn out even half as nice as you I will count myself happy."

Carla chuckled now. "Shoot, we sound like a mutual admiration society. I think we'd better stop before we get really maudlin here."

The doorbell rang as they started to giggle.

"There's the door." Jenna went over to cautiously check the peephole. "It's Maury, so I've got to go now. Wish me luck. I'll talk to you later."

Maury Berkowitz, a tall, silver-haired man, probably in his late fifties, had an aura of ease and power about him. He shook hands with Jenna firmly and assessed her with kind, but keenly appraising eyes. Jenna liked him right away. They made small talk for a few minutes getting acquainted, and then Maury got right down to business looking over the papers Jenna had gathered and asking her needed questions. They finished with initial business in less than an hour, and called to tell Sam they would soon be over to his place.

Jenna enjoyed a warm reunion with Sam – who looked fit and well. Sam's housekeeper Mary insisted on fixing lunch for all of them while cooking for Sam.

It pleased Jenna to find that she actually understood, more clearly than she thought she would, just what her legal options would be in the divorce action.

Maury gave good explanations. "I have written out all the grounds for initiating a divorce and I've mapped out the requests you should ask for in the divorce, such as expectations about payment of legal fees, who receives possession of the marital residence, and distribution of marital property expected. Because you haven't been working full-time, I've asked for some spousal support for a season, until you can expect to become self-supporting - specifically some monthly income help and insurance coverage. Because you didn't ask for the marital residence or its furnishings, I asked for financial help for you toward a new residence. That should cover your deposit, the first few months rent, and money for some needed furnishings. This is reasonable in a situation like yours and Elliott's."

"What about Elliott's financial assets?" Sam raised a brow. "They are considerable, Maury."

"They are. However, Jenna came to her marriage with some money of her own. From what Jenna told me, that money is still intact and put away. All that needs to be done here is to be sure it is all returned totally to Jenna's maiden name. Jenna made it clear to me that she wants to resume that name after her divorce. I'll help her do that and I'll help her establish new accounts and credit for herself in her own name. Jenna told me she doesn't want to make claim on Elliott's assets, Sam."

"Why not, Jenna?" Sam looked at her in surprise.

"We've only been married two years, Sam. What Elliott has earned and saved should stay his. It is more than fair if he helps me for a short time like Maury laid out. I really didn't even expect that. Park Press is willing to let me work full-time instead of part-time, so I will have employment. The apartment Carla and John are leasing to me is one I will be able to afford. I'm going to be all right. I don't want to try to take more than I feel is fair, even with all the problems and betrayals."

Sam frowned. "You could get more because of emotional damage and trauma. Because of the adulteries."

Jenna shook her head. "Money won't help those hurts, Sam. Getting on with my own life will."

"You see why I love her so much?" Sam said to Maury.

"When can I move out?" Jenna asked on a new note. "That is important to me. I hate to sound neurotic and emotional, but I really don't want to sleep in that place. If possible, I'd like to pack up and get out as soon as I can. It is an oppressive place for me now, filled with bad memories. I would prefer not to stay there even for another day unless I have to."

Sam looked at Maury. "Can she move out without losing any ground? She can come over here and stay with me."

"I'll check." Maury tapped his pen on the table thoughtfully. "If we get this paperwork completed, typed up, and get Jenna's signatures on everything, we should be able to serve Elliott by tomorrow. I don't think we'll have any trouble finding him to serve him in person, since he's in the hospital with his leg strung up in a cast. He's not going anywhere for at least a week."

He stopped, considering his next words. "Once he's served, you can probably start to move out, Jenna. I think I can get legal assent for that since you are not seeking the marital residence in the requests. As for today, go ahead and start your packing. It's something you're going to have to do, anyway, and it'll keep you busy. Tonight, you should probably sleep in the apartment. I'm sorry about that. By tomorrow, I should have an okay for you to stay at Sam's or over at your friend Carla's for the rest of the week - until you can move into your own apartment. However, after Elliott gets out of the hospital, I do not want you staying over here at Sam's too close to Elliott."

Jenna looked up anxiously. "But surely I'll be able to visit Sam?"

"Of course," Maury assured her. "But for a while, we'll have Henry here whenever you come, and we'll try to time your visits when Elliott will be gone. I don't want you running into him in the elevator or the hallway when you are alone. Henry can come down to meet you and escort you in and out of the building."

Jenna sighed audibly and looked disappointed.

Sam smiled. "It will only be for a little while, Jenna girl. Later, once the divorce is final, I'm sure you'll be able to come and go more freely. Right now we just want to protect you in case Elliott has another loss of temper."

Maury cleared his throat. "Speaking of which, Sam and I need to discuss how we're going to proceed with our other matter. Sam, you need to decide whether you want to press formal charges or not against Elliott for assault. It's a serious charge, and even with a good lawyer and some artful defense, Elliott could come out with a criminal record. I don't think he will want that."

Sam looked thoughtful, and then he smiled slyly. "Suppose I was willing to drop charges if Elliott agreed to move out of this apartment building and move a specified distance away from my residence?"

"Well, well." Maury considered this, grinning. "That's an interesting idea."

Sam grinned back. "I'd find it really difficult to continue to see this guy on my floor and in my building any more, considering that he attacked me." He feigned a pitiful tone, smiling all the while. "And I can hardly avoid him with his apartment practically right across from mine. It might be traumatic for me, a sick guy and all." He chuckled.

"You're a clever old dog, Sam Oliver," said Maury, thumping him on the back. "We could try it. Besides, even if you press charges, Elliott probably wouldn't get much legal punishment. His lawyer will find some loophole to make it look as thought he was emotionally distressed or traumatized over finding his wife missing. However, Elliott might not want to take the risk in court, even so. He might prefer moving to having the possibility of an assault charge on his unblemished record. That sort of thing is not good for business."

They all considered this for a minute.

"It just might work," said Maury. "Besides, Elliott might not want to continue living near you any longer, either, Sam. It actually might not bother him to move out – especially to avoid litigation."

Jenna considered this, her eyes brightening. "If Elliott moves, then I won't need protection to come over to see Sam. Right?"

"Another point in favor of trying this." Sam smiled at her. "I want my Jenna to be able to come over to see me whenever she wants to without worrying about running into Elliott Howell."

"Okay." Maury closed his briefcase. "I'll try it. It would be to Elliott's advantage all the way around to agree. He was threatening to sue Henry at first until his attorney straightened him out on that. Hopefully, his attorney will help him see the advantage of this deal."

A new thought came to Jenna. "Will I have to go to court and have a trial to get this divorce?" She chewed on her lip as she considered this.

"Probably not," said Maury. "We are filing action for divorce on grounds of adultery. That's one of the six grounds for divorce in New York. There will be no trial unless Elliott contests. Everything should move along smoothly and the divorce should be processed within about 60 days or so unless Elliott contests or gives an answer to his summons with counter claims. That isn't likely. His attorney will be informed of the evidence we have against him. He would be foolish to contest. Plus, you are asking for only reasonable requests."

They talked a little longer to get all the details for the legal papers in order. Then Mary called them in for lunch. Jenna picked at her food as the men talked, her mind preoccupied with all the changes ahead.

As Maury gathered up his papers to leave after lunch, Jenna thought of another question to ask him.

"When should I go to see Elliott?"

"Why should you even go?" Sam asked this with annoyance.

Jenna gave him a patient look in return. 'You know I have to go and talk to him, Sam. It would be cowardly not to. Plus I need to."

Maury thought about this. "Well, don't go until after the papers are served tomorrow," he said. "I don't want any potential difficulties until then. I'll call you when that is done, and then you can go for a visit if you wish. But I'd like to be present, if you don't mind."

Jenna scowled. "That will make him think that I'm afraid of him. It seems to me that I should see him on my own."

Maury considered this. "Well, I'll slip out of the room for a minute or two if you want. But I won't go far. He's in the hospital. We don't want him to try to come up with stories that you came in and threatened him or that you said anything you didn't. He's going to be looking for opportunities to get back at you. Elliott's the type that doesn't think things are his fault, even when they are. I've been around his kind before."

Jenna squared her shoulders. "I just thought I should go to see him and tell him in person why I went away and why I am seeking a divorce."

Maury cleared his throat. "I think he knows the answers to both. And I'm not too eager, nor is Sam, for him to have a chance to have an abusive field day with you. He won't do that if I'm with you. He'll watch what he says. If he doesn't, I'll caution him legally."

Jenna thought about this. "All right. He probably is still angry right now. Elliott hates sickness and being around hospitals. I'm sure he's found a way to blame me for all of it in his mind. When he gets the divorce papers, he will be angrier. I'm sure he has been planning how he can make me pay for all the inconveniences I've caused him. I don't think, even now, that he has even conceived of the idea that I will divorce him. Certainly Mother has not suggested it to him. I'm sure he truly expects I will take care of him when he gets out of the hospital until he gets well enough to return to work."

Sam gave them a guilty look then. "Actually, he might be a little suspicious that something is up, Jenna. I said a few choice words to Elliott when he came here."

Jenna's eyes flew open. "Sam you didn't tell him I was planning to divorce him, did you?" she asked.

Sam's expression was stubborn. "No, but I told him you *ought* to. I let him know pretty much what I thought of him, and that I knew the kind of man he was. I told him he wasn't worthy to be in the same room with you. He said some pretty foul things to me, and then insisted again that I knew where you were but wasn't telling him."

Anger flared in Sam's eyes. "I was mad, and I as much as admitted that maybe I did know where you were but that I'd never tell him. I guess that's what tipped him over the edge. He flipped out and came at me then. I shouldn't have provoked him, but it really surprised me when he attacked me. It was a good lesson for me that even being disabled doesn't mean I don't have to be careful of people. If Henry hadn't come in, I think Elliott might have really hurt me. He was getting ready to kick me when Henry picked him up from behind and started pounding on him. I was lucky. I gave Henry a raise, too." He chuckled, but Jenna looked worried all over again.

"There, there, girl. You see that I'm okay." Sam soothed. "And it's Mr. Elliott Howell that's laid up in the hospital paying penance for his temper. All of this came to a right and just ending. If it gets the man out of my building and out of my sight, then it will all have been worth it. And that's the truth."

Maury frowned at him. "Sam, I've already given you my legal and personal thoughts on the foolishness of provoking a man like Elliott Howell any time. So I won't go into that more today." He gathered up his coat and briefcase preparing to leave. "Any more questions from you, Jenna, before I go?"

Jenna thought. "I hate to take more of your time," she said. "But perhaps I should ask you what I ought to do about my mother and father. Should I let them know that I am pursuing a divorce before the papers are served or after? I don't want to do the wrong thing."

Sam put in his comments on this. "Jenna's parents are really bad news." He said this with a regretful shake of his head. "I don't think Jenna can trust them to act in her best interest."

Jenna chewed on a nail nervously. "But Mother knows that I came back. She is sure to call or she may even come over. She is going to be very angry, too, that I went away and didn't tell her where I was going."

Maury thought this over briefly. "Don't answer the phone for a while," he advised. "She doesn't know you've arrived yet. Wait and call her late tonight. Tell her you just got in and that you are going to come over to see her right after you go to the hospital to see Elliott tomorrow. If she presses for answers, say you're just exhausted from the trip and that you'll talk to her tomorrow about everything. Tell her you know she deserves an explanation, and that you will give her one then and answer any questions she has. If she presses, find a way to hang up. I don't think she'll come straight over when it's late, even if she's mad."

Sam rolled his chair away from the table. "Maury, why don't you go with her over to her mother's tomorrow," he suggested. "I'll pay you extra legal fees to do so. The girl needs someone to go with her to face that dragon when she tells her she is filing for a divorce. I know that woman. She'll be a terror. But she'll behave herself more if you're there."

Jenna stuck her chin up. "Look, I'm trying to be a grown-up here and deal with my problems by myself. It's hard to do that with you both wanting to insulate me in everything."

"Let me ask you this, Jenna," said Maury. "If you could have been here to be with Sam when you knew he would be facing Elliott, would you have done so?"

"Well, of course, but ..." She stopped in mid sentence, watching Cheshire smiles form on both their faces.

Maury nodded at her. "It's the same thing, Jenna. It's not cowardly to have someone with you when you expect to face an unusually difficult situation. Sometimes, it's wise. Particularly when legal action is under way." He paused. "Sam's right. I'll make time tomorrow to go by with you to break the news to your mother. I'm not in court on Wednesday, and I can rearrange the few appointments I have. There will be a lifetime of opportunities later for you to talk to your mother about this issue on your own if you like. But for now, I think I'd like to go with you. I also know your mother socially. I think it will help if I am there."

Jenna frowned. "A friend told me I needed to learn to face things by myself. It doesn't seem like I'm doing much of that so far."

"Sometimes facing things involves doing things correctly." Maury's eyes met hers. "I actually think you have handled things rather wisely. Most people who are in your situation react, flail out in anger, have fights, say things that are not to their benefit and that they later regret, especially when some of their words and actions are brought up in court. Stopping to think and act before reacting is much wiser. You actually showed good restraint in what you did versus the cowardice you accuse yourself of. You kept yourself to yourself until you could think everything out deliberately. You went away to consider what you wanted to do."

He patted her on the arm. "Putting distance between yourself and a problem often makes it clear how it should be resolved. Then you hired a private investigator before alerting your husband you were wise to his indiscretions. You started legal discussions before alerting Elliott you were going to seek a divorce. Actually, you have kept all the legal advantages in your own court and been very wise. Sometimes restraint is the greatest wisdom, Jenna. I think you are actually to be congratulated in how you have handled every piece of this problem you've found yourself in. I wish all my clients acted so wisely."

"Really?" Jenna looked at him in surprise.

"Really." Maury smiled at her. "Allowing me to go with you to help you present the facts to your husband and to your mother is wise, as well. You're well aware that you will not have their support in your actions so why open yourself to their abuse right now? Handle it officially, with your friend and lawyer tagging along. Let them see that it is official and that you are serious. If necessary, I can affirm that you are totally serious and deliberate in what you are doing. Sam is right. If he could go, or if you had a parent or relative here who would stand up with you as a support, you might not need my presence. They could go with you. But since you do not have anyone else, I am the next best choice."

It was sad to Jenna to realize his words were true. "Carla and John might be able to go," she said.

Maury waved away that idea. "They can be a support afterwards," he said. "You will be living near them, and they might need to buttress you if Elliott or your parents come to your apartment later to threaten you or to try to create difficulties for you. I have not forgotten how your mother acted years ago when Lydia broke her engagement."

Jenna jerked her eyes to his. "You knew Lydia?"

"Lydia and I were school friends." A faint smile played over his lips. "I was in law school when her fiance's scandal hit the gossip columns and began to circulate around society. I gave her free legal advice. I connected her to an attorney friend of mine in the business. She needed some of her money freed to get away and make a new start and my friend helped her get it. Your mother never felt happy about that action of mine. Like I said, I know your mother. I know what she can be like."

"Small world," muttered Sam.

Jenna regarded Maury thoughtfully. "I think I'll be glad to have your company, Maury."

He stood up then. "Good. I'll call you in the morning to tell you when things are in place, and when you should head to the hospital. Plan to be ready about mid morning. If all goes well, our paperwork should be served by then. We'll make our visits, and then I'll take you out to lunch. I don't get an excuse to take a pretty woman to lunch very often. It will be my pleasure."

"I'll tell you all about Lydia then." Jenna smiled. "I visited her on my way down to Tennessee."

Maury raised his eyebrows in interest. "I'll look forward to that very much," he said. "We kept in touch for awhile, but then, you know, life moved on."

After Maury left, Jenna and Sam talked and caught up. Then Jenna excused herself to go start her packing.

"There will be lots of time for visiting later." She reached across the table to pat his cheek. "But now, I want to get as much packed as I can,

Sam. I want to be ready to move by the end of the week, and I need to go find packing boxes so I can get started." She yawned. "Also, I'm tired. I didn't sleep much last night. I probably will go to bed early tonight."

Sam wheeled his chair away from the table. "Mary made you a take home box for supper. She said to tell you it's in the kitchen refrigerator. Take a piece of cake with you, too. I'm sure you don't have much food in the house for tonight."

"Thanks." Jenna leaned down to give Sam a hug.

He gave her a worried look. "Will you be all right over there tonight by yourself? I don't see why you couldn't sneak over here. Who would know?"

"I would," she said, lifting her chin. "At least this is something I can face all on my own. I need to face down some of my fears by myself - just for my self-respect, Sam."

"Hummph." He frowned.

"I'll be fine," she assured him. "Don't worry. And I promise I'll come by and tell you everything that happened after I meet with Elliott and Mother tomorrow. Okay?"

He nodded. "Eventually, when things are settled out, I want you to tell me all about Orchard Hollow."

Her eyes filled with tears then. She couldn't help it. She was sure Sam wondered about it after she was gone.

Chapter 15

Jenna worked on packing her things all afternoon. Although her new apartment, above Tate's Bookstore, was only five or six blocks away, it was on Madison Avenue instead of Fifth, with no park views. Standing on the balcony looking out later, Jenna shivered and hugged her arms against herself. It was still cold in New York, even in April, and nothing here seemed as green and inviting to her as it had before. She smiled, realizing she'd grown used to looking out over the mountain views and green valleys of the foothills of the Smokies.

Jenna arrested her thoughts as they began to drift wistfully southward. Thoughts of Boyce lay always at the edge of her mind - trying to crowd in - but Jenna pushed them back with resolve. It would only lead to crying, and there was too much to do to indulge her emotions right now. She took a deep breath and straightened her shoulders. Time to get back to work, she told herself, as she went back inside to finish the last of her packing.

At the end of the day, Jenna sat down on the sofa, exhausted. Her life from her marriage was all boxed up, and it seemed sad to see how little she was carrying away.

Jenna studied the phone beside her, realizing she couldn't put off calling her mother any longer. It was nearly ten now. When she returned from Sam's earlier, there had been a curt message from her mother on the answering machine.

"You call me as soon as you get in, Jenna Chelsea Howell. Do you hear?" Her voice sounded sharp and brittle.

Gathering her courage, Jenna dialed her home number. Her mother answered almost immediately.

"Hi, Mother, it's Jenna." Jenna tried to keep a calm voice. "I've just gotten in and I wanted to call and let you know."

Her mother's voice snapped back angrily. "You have a great deal of explaining to do, Jenna Chelsea, going off and not telling anyone in your own family where you were. What in the world were you thinking? This whole state of affairs is outrageous. It reminds me of those infantile capers you and Carla used to get into at that girls' school. You're twenty-two years old now, Jenna. I would think you had more sense by now than to do something foolish like this. Where have you been all this time, anyway?"

Jenna took a breath. "Staying at Sam Oliver's cabin in Tennessee. I wanted some time alone to think, Mother. I did tell you I was having marital problems. Space away sometimes helps with that sort of thing."

"Well, I certainly hope so," she said sarcastically. "And I hope your time away has brought you to your senses. You know you may have created more problems for yourself with this idiocy of yours going off on your own as you did. And lying to so many people. Your father and I did not raise you to lie to your own family members. I told Elliott that emphatically, too, after he figured out you were no longer in the Poconos. I apologized for you as well."

Her mother paused to catch a breath. "You owe that man an explanation and an apology yourself, you know. He was very upset when he learned you weren't at Carla and John's place - or at that woman's next door to them. Elliott cut his trip short from Paris to come back because of your childish escapades. He was worried sick, Jenna. And now look at the mess you've caused! The poor man is laid up in the hospital from that distressing incident with that dreadful employee of Sam Oliver's. I don't know what Sam is thinking hiring people as aggressive as that. Do you know what that man did to Elliott? He literally attacked him. Elliott has broken ribs, a broken leg, and his face and arms are covered with bruises. It is just shocking to see. Have you been over to the hospital yet?"

Before Jenna could barely acknowledge she had not been to the hospital yet, her mother set in again.

"This has all happened because of you, Jenna." Her tone was becoming venomous now. "I hope Elliott will forgive you for this. Elliott deserves better, and your father and I both think he has just cause to be upset. Really, Jenna, all of this has just been inexcusable on your part. Simply inexcusable. Elliott's parents are horrified, as well, and there is tittering all through the social parties we've been to these last two days. Your father and I have been deeply disappointed in you."

Jenna listened patiently to her mother's tirade. It was just about what she expected. When a pause occurred in her mother's ranting, Jenna slipped in a question. "How did Elliott find out I wasn't in the Poconos, Mother?"

"A friend of his, Peter something – someone he works with - also has a place near John and Carla's in Pennsylvania. Elliott called that Mrs. Bynam several times and could never find you there. He worried something might have happened to you. She rattled on like a crazy woman, he said, and made no sense. So he asked his friend to check on you when he drove up last weekend. He asked Peter to find you and have you call him. He wanted you to come back to the apartment. Elliott thought that Bynam woman was unstable. He didn't think it safe for you to stay there with her. I have to admit I tried to talk with her myself and she was certainly odd."

Jenna tried not to giggle.

"Were you ever at that Bynam woman's place or at Carla and John's in Pennsylvania at all?" her mother demanded.

Jenna answered honestly. "No. I went directly to Tennessee. Carla and John actually invited me to go to the Poconos with them. Originally, I told Elliott I was going there, too." Jenna embellished the story a little to protect Carla and John at this point. "But then I decided I wanted to get away on my own. I needed to do that, Mother. I asked John and Carla to cover for me so I would have time to think through my situation without anyone trying to influence me."

Jenna's mother paused, trying to make sense of this story. "But I received letters from you and so did Elliott." Jenna heard her intake of breath as the answer suddenly seemed to dawn on her. "You had someone else mail them to us. You purposely deceived us, Jenna – planning all this to the point where you had letters ready to be sent to us. I'm shocked."

"Perhaps it seems deceptive," Jenna admitted. "But my main thought at the time was just to get away on my own for a while. I'd just seen my husband cheating on me with another woman, Mother. I was upset."

"Well, I thought we talked about that earlier," her mother said with obvious annoyance. "I can't believe Elliott's little indiscretion upset you that much. But, of course, you're very young. The young are so idealistic. I hadn't realized you were taking all of this so seriously. However, I'm sure if you just talk to Elliott about everything, Jenna, that the two of you can reach an amicable agreement over this."

Jenna smiled to herself. "I'm going over to see Elliott in the morning, Mother. And I am hoping we can reach an amicable agreement over several things we need to discuss. I'll stop by your place afterwards if you want me to. I'll tell you how things went."

Her mother sounded relieved. "Good, you do that. I don't have anything on my calendar until two."

178

"I'll try to come before that," Jenna assured her.

Jenna heard her mother blow out another irritated breath. "I cannot get over your actions through all this, Jenna. It's just not like you. You are usually much more conscientious and dutiful. Your father and I have both been dreadfully upset. I hope you have not damaged your marriage over this whole impulsive incident. Trust is important in a marriage, Jenna, and you have certainly shown yourself to be untrustworthy to Elliott."

"I do agree that trust is important." Jenna replied quietly. She sighed then. "Mother, I'm really tired. It's been a long day for me. I'll talk to you more tomorrow. I need to rest now."

"Well, then, I'll see you tomorrow," her mother conceded. "I'm glad you are home safe, and I do hope you will be able to smooth things over with Elliott tomorrow. And, Jenna, he will need your help and support at home when they release him from the hospital. I believe the doctors said he can come home early next week after they put him into a different cast that makes him more mobile. He really is suffering and enduring extensive pain, Jenna. You should have been here sooner. He needs you. Your father and I went to the hospital, of course, but it's not the same. I told him you would be coming in today, and I know he is looking forward to seeing you. This has been a very difficult time for him."

"Yes, I'm sure it has." Her jaw clenched. "Good night, Mother."

Jenna hung up with a heavy heart. She felt sad to realize all her mother's concerns were for Elliott – with nothing offered to her but criticism. She would not be happy tomorrow to learn Jenna had filed for divorce.

Jenna lay down on the couch and closed her eyes. Tomorrow, Elliott would be served divorce papers before Jenna arrived at the hospital. He would begin to put the pieces together as to why she had been away, if he hadn't done so already. She was sure he would have questions - and also sure he would try to get her to stay in the marriage. Not because he loved her too much to let her go, but because she was convenient. As her mother voiced - conscientious and dutiful. She kept his house clean, took his shirts to the cleaners, ran his errands, cooked his meals, did his laundry. In addition, Elliott liked the comfortable status that went with being married and being married socially well. He always introduced her: 'This is my wife Jenna Martin Howell.' He liked the prominent Martin name and the standing it lent to his own.

Jenna sighed heavily. She felt tired from the trip, the packing, the strain. She wondered how Elliott would play it tomorrow when she visited the hospital. He would have time to decide on a 'game plan' before she arrived. That's what he called it when he planned how to handle one of his advertising clients.

Once Jenna asked him, "Why don't you just be yourself, Elliott?"

"You are so naïve, Jenna." He answered her dismissively. "You don't get anywhere in this world like that. You have to be whatever is needed to sway the client, to win the account."

She stared at him. "Even if you have to lie?"

He gave her a cool smile. "It's not lying in business, Jenna. It's just smart business. You have to learn how to play people. To figure out how they think and what they want. To figure out the kind of person they desire to do business with. Then that's who you become, exactly who they want you to be. They're happy then - and you're happy. It's a game. An art form."

She could expect a game tomorrow. She was sure of it.

Jenna went back to the bedroom and got ready for bed. Worn out from the emotions of the day, she soon drifted into a deep sleep. Oddly, it wasn't Elliott she dreamed about in the night, but Boyce. The dream woke her in the small hours of the morning. She could almost feel Boyce's presence. Yearning for him, she indulged in a good cry before she fell fitfully back to sleep again.

Chapter 16

*J*enna met Maury Berkowitz the next morning in the coffee shop at the hospital.

She offered him a brave smile as she sat down at the small table with him. "Tell me what has happened since yesterday."

"Elliott was served earlier this morning." Maury said, as he bit into a doughnut. "Everything's in place. I was able to expedite proceedings and got a judge friend of mine to sign some paperwork so you can move out of your apartment. In addition, I attained some orders of protection so Elliott won't come and harass you at your new place."

He finished off his doughnut and drank the last of his coffee. "Are you ready to go up to Elliott's room now? I have the room number."

Jenna watched him gather up his legal papers and stuff them into a briefcase. "Maury, I'd really like to go in and talk to Elliott by myself first." She chose her words carefully. "I want to face him and say a few things I need to say on my own. It's important to me to be able to look back and know I did that."

Maury considered her request. "All right," he said. "You go in, and I'll sit in a chair right outside in the hallway by the door where he can't see me. Leave the door open or ajar. If any difficulty occurs, I'm coming in."

"Thank you." She smiled gratefully.

Elliott seemed to be asleep when Jenna quietly opened his hospital door. He looked pale and drawn, and his leg was hoisted up in a full cast. Flowers and plants from well-wishers crowded his hospital room. For a moment Jenna started to feel guilty that she had not sent flowers and a get-well card of her own, but then she caught herself and remembered why Elliott was here and what he had done to Sam.

"Elliott?" she said, walking over closer to the bed. "Elliott, it's Jenna."

He opened his eyes, and then held out a hand appealingly. "Oh, Jen. It's you. I've been so worried. Are you all right?"

"Yes, I'm fine." She did not move forward to take his hand.

"This has all been a nightmare." He lifted anguished eyes to hers. "When I realized you were not in the Poconos, I panicked. I flew right back from Paris, left the work there for someone else to do. Just told the company I had to get back, that there was an emergency. I was terrified something had happened to you."

He swore under his breath. "It was too long for me to be away from you; I should have known that. I should have taken you to Paris; I should simply have demanded the company work something out. I should never have let you out of my sight. My God, Jenna, if anything had happened to you, I don't know what I would have done."

Jenna smiled. So this was how he was going to play it, she thought.

"Look." He fiddled nervously with the sheets. "I know you're upset because I went away for so long and didn't take you with me. I thought about it later. I know you really wanted to go, and I remembered, too, that you didn't get to take that semester abroad with your school, with Barnard, because of our wedding. But I didn't realize you would get so upset about the situation, Jenna, that you would go off somewhere and then let someone influence you to sign legal papers like this." He motioned to the legal envelope on the bedside table.

"I'm sure that Sam friend of yours did not tell you truthfully what happened at his place, either." Elliott's hand reached towards hers again. "That has probably upset you, too. We can work all this out, Jenna. We can talk everything through. You know I love you, and that I will do anything I can to make you happy. I also promise that we will plan a trip to Paris very soon. I have a long vacation coming up. We'll go as soon as I recover and catch up at work. And while I'm recuperating, we can have some long talks and get close again. You'd like that, wouldn't you? You've always liked those quiet little talks at home." He smiled appealingly at her.

Jenna took a deep breath. "Elliott, I was upset about Paris. I did want to go, and I wanted you to *want* me to go. I hoped you would want to have that special time with me. But then I learned about Lena. Lena went to Paris with you instead of me, Elliott. You seem to be leaving that out. I guess Lena had her trip cut short, too."

If Jenna did not know Elliott so well, she would not have seen the quick mental shift in his face as he realized she knew about Lena.

"The reason for the divorce proceeding is on grounds of adultery, Elliott," Jenna told him. "Not because I didn't get to go to Paris."

He frowned. "But that's silly, Jenna. Lena is my secretary. You have misinterpreted the situation. You have to take your secretary when you are setting up a major office; there is too much work to be done without help in a project of that magnitude. Lena knew the work and she was the obvious choice to help with setting up the new office. Surely you don't think there is something more than a work relationship between Lena Morrow and myself?" Elliott looked cross now. "That's just unfounded. Whoever told you that was lying."

"I saw you, Elliott," Jenna said patiently. "At DaVinci's restaurant where Carla took me for my birthday. I saw you with Lena."

"I often have lunch with my secretary," Elliott said patronizingly. "It's just a part of business."

Jenna shook her head slowly. "Elliott, it is not simply business to have your hands up someone's skirt and your tongue down their throat."

He actually looked stricken for a moment.

"Someone told you that," he declared, trying to bluff and recover. "I didn't see you there. You're going by what someone told you."

"You were very busy then." Jenna went still, watching him. "You didn't see Carla or me there. But I was there, Elliott. There is no point in trying to pretend you have not been having an affair with Lena Morrow. I have evidence to support this, Elliott – from New York and from Paris."

"You've hired a detective." He said this with surprise, the light suddenly dawning. "You had no right to do that, Jenna. I'm your legal husband."

She stepped towards him. "I had every right to do that *because* you're my legal husband. You had no right to cheat on me and betray me."

Elliott straightened the sheets and took a minute to collect himself.

"Look, Jenna, we can work this out," he said softly then, reaching out for her hand once more. She pulled back from his grasp. "Lena doesn't mean anything to me. Sometimes men have small affairs even when they love their wives deeply. It doesn't mean a thing. It doesn't matter."

"It matters to me." Jenna's eyes narrowed.

"You are very young." Elliott smiled smoothly at her. "Sometimes my appetites are more mature than what is right to indulge in with a young bride. That's all it was, Jenna, just appetite. Not love like you and I have. Not sweetness and tenderness. You're the woman I chose to marry. I would never marry someone like Lena. It was just sex with her, not love."

Jenna studied him quietly. It amazed her that Elliott thought she would find reassurance with this type of logic.

"Look," he said, noticing her reticence. "I'll break it off tomorrow. Today, even. I'll fire her and get another secretary. I'll never see her again. We won't ever have to talk about it after this. It will be a little mistake we'll tuck into our past. And when I come home from the hospital, we'll have time to be together. I'll need you to take care of me, to cook for me, to help me get better. We'll get close again. When I am stronger, we'll fly down to the Bahamas for a little vacation. A little second honeymoon. Or go to Paris. You'd like that, wouldn't you, Jenna? It will be okay."

Jenna shook her head. "Elliott, I am not the same naïve young girl you married. You are partly responsible for waking me up from my false idealism. I know Lena was not the only woman you've had affairs with. I know about many of the others now, too. I don't want to be married to someone who is an unfaithful partner, who neglects me and lies to me, who says he is always tied up with business so he can indulge in affairs."

A lump filled her throat. "I don't want a life like that, Elliott. And it will not be all right anymore between us. I don't want to be married to you any longer. I've been unhappy, and you never even saw it. You were too busy with your work and your affairs to see. I was never a vital part of your life. We had no joy and friendship; we had few good times. I always felt lonely and sad. I don't want to live that way anymore. And I will not be there to take care of you when you come home, Elliott. You will need to hire home help or a nurse. I'm moving out today to stay with Carla and John for a few days, and then I'm moving into my new apartment this weekend."

Elliott struggled to sit up in the hospital bed. "You can't just move out and divorce me over a few little affairs and some childish hurt feelings!" Anger tinged his voice now. "I'm your legal husband. We made vows to stay married until death do us part, in sickness and health, in good times and bad. When there are problems in a marriage, you work them out, Jenna. You don't get silly and childish and run away. It's wrong for you to even consider leaving me for such paltry excuses. We can work through these difficulties. You don't want to do an immature thing like this. I take good care of you. I provide very well for you. You haven't even had to work since we've been married. You don't know what it's like to be on your own. How will you take care of yourself?"

"I have my design work," Jenna said this quietly.

"Your little cards," Elliott scoffed. "You can't make a decent living at that. And your useless degree in Art History equips you for absolutely nothing, Jenna. You need to stay with me. I'll take care of you. We'll work all these other little problems out, I promise you. Don't be stupid and make an even bigger mistake here - filing legal actions you will soon regret. If word of this gets out, it will embarrass your parents and all our friends. This is not what you want, Jenna."

"It *is* what I want, Elliott." Her voice was firm. "I went away for over a month to think about it very carefully before I made this decision. This is exactly what I want."

"You can't do this, Jenna." The volume of Elliott's voice rose now in anger. "This is foolish, and I won't have it. Do you hear me? I think that Sam friend of yours put you up to this nonsense."

"Speaking of Sam." Jenna leaned toward him. "I can't believe even you would attack a sick man in a wheelchair. You could have seriously injured Sam. What were you thinking, Elliott? Whatever were you thinking to do such a thing?"

Elliott snapped back his answer. "He wouldn't tell me where you were. And I had a right to know where you were, Jenna. He withheld information from me about my wife, and he enjoyed doing so. He insulted me and he thought he could get away with that because he was in a chair. He said there was nothing I could do to make him tell where you had gone. I lost my temper and I hit him – one man to another. I had a right to know where you were. He'd have told me, too, if that big, black man hadn't come in and sneaked up behind me. I didn't even see him coming. He hit me and threw me across the room. I thought for a minute he was going to kill me. But Sam called him off, told him to stop."

"Sam would do that." Jenna nodded. "He's a kind person."

"Don't you take up for him!" Elliott shouted, pulling up in the bed. "Look at what they did to me! And the bulk of this is *your* fault, Jenna. You're the one who took off and lied and caused all this trouble. Acting silly, emotional, and childish, as usual. I had to come back from Paris early because of you. I left work undone over there that still needs to be completed; I'm missing time from work now. I have a lawsuit pending because of that stupid man threatening to press charges against me, and now you've finally wandered back home where you belong and are trying to threaten divorce like you know what you are doing. It's absurd. Now, I want you to go find this Berkowitz lawyer, Jenna, and tell him you've come to your senses and changed your mind about all of this drivel. And then tell Carla and John Tate the same thing. It figures they would be aiding and abetting you in this. I've never liked either one of them. I'd prefer that you spend less time with them in future."

Elliott paused, trying to check his rising antagonism. "Talk to your mother, Jenna." He tried to grab her wrist. "She says Carla has always been a bad influence on you. You talk to your mother and father about this non-sense of seeking a divorce and imagining you could live on your own. You could never manage that, Jenna. You'd fall flat on your face in a week."

He shook his finger at her. "And don't be so sure that your mother and father will just pick you up and let you come back home, either." He smiled maliciously. "I think you'll find they will be on my side in this."

She listened to him rant on and on. How many times had he worn her down in the past like this – by never listening to her, by ridiculing and subtly threatening her?

Elliott's mouth twisted. "You need to get your head out of fairytales and out of cutesy, little greeting card rhymes and designs and wake up to what the real world is all about. People are not perfect, Jenna. They do the best they can, that's all. You'll see that I've done the best I can as a husband to you after you settle down and stop and think. Divorce is not the answer. My parents have had these little ups and downs and they haven't ever divorced."

"Your father has cheated on your mother?" Jenna asked, picking up on that.

Elliott's answer was flippant. "Here and there over the years of their marriage. But you notice they are still married. My mother was aware that she was the one my father chose to spend his life with; she knew she was the important one to him. She'll tell you that. She's a sensible woman."

Jenna saw now where Elliott had learned his ethical standards about adultery. From his own father and mother.

"I'm sorry, Elliott." Jenna shook her head sadly. "We are just not the same kind of people. I don't see things as you do. I don't want a life where - here and there - over the years you will be unfaithful to me when you want to. What if I was unfaithful to you?"

"Is that what this is all about?" Elliott countered nastily, pushing himself up on his elbow. "Is there someone else? Did you decide to get even with me by having a little affair of your own? I'll tell you right now that in the future if you ever try to get even with me like that at any time, I will find out who the man is and I'll see to it that he is hurt. Badly hurt. In fact, you could be hurt, too. And no one will know, Jenna. Do you understand what I am telling you? You're not going to play around on me. It won't work that way."

She was incredulous. "You mean you can play around on me but I can't play around on you?"

He looked down his nose at her. "It's different for men than for women.

Everyone knows that. I'm not having everyone talking about my wife and calling her a slut. You keep that in mind."

Jenna sighed patiently. "I'm not having an affair with another man, Elliott. Calm down. As you've said yourself I'm the idealistic type who believes in faithfulness. I don't believe in cheating."

"Well, good." Elliott seemed relieved, as if that settled something.

There was an awkward silence for a minute.

Then Elliott said, "Look, I'll get to come home by Monday, Jenna. I'd appreciate it if you'd go home and bring me a few things I need from the apartment. And then stay here with me. The staff can set up a cot or something. If you're here, the doctor might even let me go home earlier. He'll see that I have someone who will take care of me." He tried to reach toward the bedside table. "I can make a little list of the things I need if you'll hand me a piece of paper from out of that drawer and find me a pen."

Jenna was appalled. Did he never listen to her? "Elliott, no. Haven't you heard a thing I've said to you? I am moving out and I will not be there when you come home. And I will not come sit with you here in the hospital. Our life together is over, Elliott. I don't want to be married to you anymore. And, speaking of lists, I brought you a list of the things I'm taking with me when I move. Here...." She offered him the list from out of her purse.

Elliott snatched it from her hand and ripped it in half.

"I'm not looking at any list of what you're taking," he replied nastily. "I told you we're not getting a divorce, and I meant it. Whoever has told you that you can do this is lying to you. You don't have any grounds that will hold up in court. You need to spare yourself some embarrassment and back out now before you appear even more foolish than you already do. I think you will find that you will be very sorry if you proceed any further with this business, Jenna. You have more to lose than you can possibly imagine, and you cannot live on your own without me. You need me, and I need you. I want you to come to your senses and remember who you are, Mrs. Elliott Howell. We are man and wife and will continue to be so, do you hear me?"

"I think this is where I need to come in," said Maury Berkowitz, breezing into the room with an almost merry smile. He held out his hand to Elliott. "I'm Maury Berkowitz, Jenna's attorney. I'm the one who told her that she does have grounds for a divorce, more grounds than I'm usually privileged to have with most of my clients."

He handed Elliott one of his cards from his coat pocket. "Now, I would suggest you talk to your lawyer, Mr. Howell, as I already have done, and you may find that he, also, agrees with me that Jenna has a very sound case. In fact, Mr. Howell, it would be to your distinct advantage for you and your attorney to agree to all my client's modest demands and avoid any futile counter claims and a court trial. I believe it is you that is the one who needs to come to his senses. You have been an exceedingly foolish man and have ruined what could have been a fine marriage with an exceedingly fine woman."

Maury walked over to take Jenna's arm. "Now Jenna is going to move out of your apartment today. She graciously decided you could keep your place of residence, which was generous of her. She also agreed to leave you the bulk of the furnishings, which was also generous of her. In fact, she has asked for only modest requests for which you should be grateful. What I would like to point out to you now is that the court has put an order of protection over Jenna. You should be *very* careful about any future threats you make to her, and if you wish to see her, for any reason, you should contact me to set up a meeting. Do not go near her residence or call her on your own. I hope I have made that perfectly clear."

"You have no right to say these things to me." Irritation thinned his voice. "Do you know who I am?"

Maury grinned. "Well, I'd love to answer that last question in my own way, but it wouldn't be professional of me, Mr. Howell. And, as to the first statement, I have every right to tell you about my client's legal actions and to protect her legal rights."

"You'll be hearing from my lawyer about this," he shot back.

Elliott turned to look at Jenna, trying to appeal to her once more. "It's still not too late for you to back out of this foolishness, Jenna. Think about this carefully."

"I already have, Elliott." She calmly studied him. "I am very sure about what I am doing, and I expect to get along very well on my own, so don't worry about me." She smiled. "I hope you feel better soon, Elliott. Maybe you should reconsider breaking up with Lena right now. She might be willing to come take care of you when you come home. It would be nice for you to have someone you know with you while you recover."

She left then with Maury - Elliott sputtering behind her.

"Good final remarks," said Maury, as they walked down the hall.

Jenna sighed heavily. "That was just terrible." Tears trickled down her cheeks.

"He was rough on you, but you held your own pretty well." He patted her arm. "Don't pay any attention to those threats Elliott made, Jenna. Nothing will come of them. It was all bluster. Bullies always threaten when they think they might not be winning. He was just trying to scare you, trying to hold control."

"I saw that this time." Jenna turned her eyes to Maury. "But I still didn't like it. You know, Maury, he said things like that to me before and I'd cave in. I thought he knew better than I did. And he scared me."

Maury punched the elevator button. "Well, if you can see that, you're getting healthier by the minute, young lady. You could also see a counselor because of the verbal abuse. I can recommend one that does good work."

"Actually, I already had some good wholesome counseling while I was away." Jenna smiled slightly at the memory. "I met some good people where I stayed in the mountains. They were honest and plain spoken, called a spade a spade. They helped me a lot. But thanks for the offer, anyway."

Maury looked at his watch. "It's eleven now. You ready for a go at your mother before we call it a day? I'd like to be with you for this one. You've already had a run with her last night, and you've had Elliott to beat on you this morning. I don't think you need much more today."

"Do you think Elliott will call Mother before we get there?" Jenna asked this nervously.

"No," he answered. "I think he'll call his attorney first. He didn't call him earlier because he thought he'd dissuade you. Now, he'll call him. He'll also remember I said I already spoke to his lawyer and that will make him mad as he begins to think about it. He'll let off some steam on his attorney now. Later on, he'll think about your mother. Or maybe your dad. He may try to get one of them to talk to you since the court order will keep him away personally. If that happens, you just contact me."

"How long will all of this last?" Jenna asked, dreading the answer.

"The worst will be this first week," Maury said. "You're seeing that already. You'll have to deal with the reactions of all the significant people you have to tell. Some will be shocked and try to change your mind. Some will support you and encourage you in what you are doing. Some will just feel awkward, not knowing what to say. You'll continue to face those mixed responses off and on for a while, and then eventually, most everyone you know will have heard. It will get to be old news. Life will go on, yours and everyone else's. It's late April now. In late June or by early July, if all goes as I expect, you should see the legal end of this completed."

"Who is Elliott's attorney?" Jenna thought to ask.

"Stan Oldham, a sound, sensible man and a rather good friend of mine outside the courtroom." He chuckled at his own joke. "Oldham and Old-ham is an old family firm, and Stan Oldham is not some foolish upstart looking for a quick day in court. He'll talk some sense into Elliott. He knows what strong grounds we have. He understands we're asking for only modest requests, and he knows the extensive evidence we have. He also realizes Elliott has nothing to counter or contest. Before it's done, I expect Stan Oldham to ask us to keep this out of the courts and the news media for Elliott's career. Maybe even offer concessions to hush it up."

"I hope you're right," said Jenna, wishing everything was over now.

"Well, we're at the dragon's lair now," said Maury jovially, as their cab pulled up at the curb of Jenna's mother's and father's apartment building. "Are you ready?"

Jenna took a deep breath. "As ready as I'll ever be, I guess."

They headed into the building for round two with Jenna's mother.

Chapter 17

*T*he visit with Jenna's mother was a nightmare, even worse than the phone call the night before. Jenna had been grateful for Maury's support. Her mother in a rage was never pleasant, and this particular event proved spectacular.

"Whew! That woman can really put out some fireworks," Maury commented dryly when they left. "But I don't want you to worry about all her threats. She obviously believes you're making a mistake, but she'll come around in time."

Jenna seriously wondered about that. She felt weary and battered.

"The only threat she can really put in place is if she and your father cut you out of their will over this. You have some money in trust from your grandparents that they can't keep from you, but they could fulfill the threat to disinherit you. It's within their legal rights to do that. There is some big money involved there, as well as property, like the Howell summer home at the Vineyard. I wouldn't be a good attorney if I didn't advise you to count the cost."

Jenna looked pointedly at Maury.

"Yeah, yeah." He scratched at his chin. "Right now money doesn't seem important to you. But it could later."

She lost her patience. "I would like to think my parents loved me, Mr. Berkowitz, that they wanted me to be happy and loved in a marriage, not used and betrayed. If they will disinherit me because I am getting out of such a marriage, then so be it."

Maury shrugged. "I have to say these things, Jenna, as your attorney. As a friend I can tell you that I have a daughter a few years younger than you. Eighteen now. If this had happened to her, there would be no question of whose side I would be on. In fact, I'd be hard pressed not to beat the stuffing out of the man who had hurt her, even knowing the legal ramifications if I did."

Jenna smiled at him. "Someone else told me that, too. It's nice to hear it again."

Maury shook his head thoughtfully. "Maybe your father will feel differently, Jenna. You haven't talked to him. He may have a different take on this. You are an only child, after all. That will make a difference once your parents have a chance to think this over more rationally."

Jenna thought about this for a minute. "I was close to my father when I was young," she said. "But after I began to grow up, he seemed to pull away from me. Left me to my mother to deal with. I hardly even talk with him any more. I don't know how he will feel about me leaving Elliott. Mother made it clear that both of them heartily disapprove, that their support is with Elliott. As you heard, she thinks I am acting emotionally and foolishly. Their feelings may not change. After all, they have never changed their attitude about Aunt Lydia even after all these years."

Maury chuckled at that memory. "Your mother remembered that Lydia and I were friends. She said I hadn't changed my ways in giving bad advice to young women."

They rode along in the cab in silence for a few minutes. Jenna had declined Maury's offer to take her to lunch. She doubted she could eat after all this.

Maury cleared his throat. "If at any time you change your mind about the divorce, Jenna, you have only to call me."

She slanted him a sharp glance. "I will not be changing my mind," she said emphatically. "Even if I lose the favor and support of everyone I know."

"You won't lose my support." Maury patted Jenna on her arm in a fatherly manner as the cab drew up to Jenna's apartment building. "You won't lose Sam's or Carla and John's love and support, either. Try not to worry too much. This will all work itself out in time. Soon you'll have a new beginning to enjoy. You deserve it. You're a fine young woman. I'm just sorry your own parents don't see that and haven't been willing to stand by you."

"Me, too, and thanks, Maury, for all you're doing for me. I really do appreciate it."

She let herself into her apartment, dropped onto the sofa for a short rest, and then called Carla. By late afternoon, John Tate and Henry Aiken came to move Jenna's boxes, bags, and belongings into the storage room above Tates' and Jenna moved temporarily into Carla and John's guest-room. She wasn't eager for Elliott or her mother to be able to find her for another call or visit any time soon. A subtle fear lurked in Jenna's heart that Elliott might find a way to get out of the hospital and let himself into their apartment while she slept. She knew fears like these were irrational, but, nevertheless, she felt safer at Carla and John's right now.

That night, Carla and John worked hard to make Jenna laugh and forget her troubles for a time. They cooked together and played games afterwards. Still, when Jenna was alone in her own room later, the stress of the day crowded in on her. She cried herself to sleep and tossed and turned fitfully with bad dreams all night.

Thursday, Jenna took care of needed business. She visited her bank to open her own individual account in her work name, J.C. Martin. She made calls to give her address to needed business contacts. She changed her cell phone number. She visited the post office to have her personal mail routed to her new residence. Then, after lunch she went to Park Press for her appointment with Jason Brantley.

"Welcome back," Jason said, getting up from his desk to reach out a handshake to her as she came in. "Have a seat." He gestured at a chair. "Can I get you some coffee or something to drink?"

"No, thanks." She twisted her hands nervously in her lap. "I just finished lunch. I'm fine."

"I see a portfolio under your arm." He gestured toward it. "I hope that means you've got some more designs for me."

"Yes." She eyed him warily. "I have all the new ones I did before I returned to New York Monday."

She took a deep breath then and told Jason briefly why she had come back earlier than she had originally planned. Jason knew Sam Oliver well, and he interrupted her story to be assured that Sam was all right after his attack.

"This is my new address and phone." She handed him a note she had printed out for him. "I should be settled in by the weekend. Then I'll get back to work. I have so many new design ideas and I wanted to talk with you about doing more work for the press. You suggested I might do that before I left. I hope the offer is still good."

"Absolutely." Jason's face brightened. "We've wanted you to do more work for us for a long time. Your designs sell well, Jenna. As I told you, I think you could branch out into some new lines for us. We'll talk more about that after you get settled in your new place." He eyed her portfolio. "For now, how about letting me see what you've done. The designs you sent me – based on scenes from around the mountains - sold very well. I hope you brought me more like that."

"Yes, I have." Jenna smiled, feeling more relaxed now. "I have photos and a sketchbook full of drawings from my visit in Tennessee to work from. I can do more designs with that theme, if you'd like."

"That's great, Jenna." He began to leaf through the stack of designs she had given him from her portfolio case.

She waited while he studied them, trying to read his response.

"These are wonderful," he exclaimed, looking up at last. "I have always liked your work, but these ideas have a new dimension. It's almost like an entirely new line for you. I like them. I really do."

He began to talk animatedly then about each individual design, stopping to ask questions and to offer ideas for future work. Jenna responded with her own ideas and questions, and the time flew quickly by.

Jason stopped to glance at the clock reluctantly.

"Can you come back next Friday to talk some more?" He picked up a pen to make a note on his desk calendar. "I have another appointment coming in now."

Jenna agreed and they set a firm time to meet again.

He stood up to see her out. "Work if you have time this week and bring me what you have when you come back," he requested. 'I know you're moving and going through a lot of personal change right now. Just do what you can for this week. When things straighten out a little, I'd like to write a new contract with you. Put you on salary and benefits. That should be a help to you right now. We've wanted you full-time for a long time, so this is a boon for us. I don't think I'll have any trouble running it all through the brass. I've already probed and gotten a thumbs up."

He paused and looked at Jenna steadily for a few minutes. "I can't tell you how happy I am that you're getting away from that jerk Elliott Howell. Perhaps I never told you, but he came by here once and tried to bribe me to fire you. Danged arrogant and disagreeable man. He had no appreciation for your talent, and I didn't care for the way he talked about you, either. He made insulting, demeaning comments about our business when he was here. I never told you – because the man was your husband, after all. I wanted to be respectful about that. But, quite frankly, I'm glad he won't be your husband much longer."

Jenna paled and put her hand over her mouth in shock while Jason talked.

"Oh, Jason, I am so sorry," she responded, when he finally finished. "I

194

knew Elliott didn't like me working here, but I had no idea he would come here and approach you. He had no right to do that. I really don't know what to say."

"Say you won't change your mind about getting rid of him." Jason grinned broadly at Jenna. "You deserve better. I'll take you out to dinner to celebrate when the divorce is final. Park Press will even pick up the tab for the meal."

Jenna smiled in spite of herself. "I'll look forward to that," she said. "And thanks, Jason, for your encouragement. It's been especially helpful right now."

"It's genuine," stated Jason, getting up to see her out.

Jenna turned to go.

"Oh, wait a minute." Jason stopped her. "I forgot to give you my gift. We'll call it a moving present." He went over to a cabinet and dug through a box.

"Here," he said, at last, bringing out four framed art works. "These are four of your prints we blew up for a promotional and then put in some simple black frames. See if you can find a spot for them in your new place. Celebrate yourself, Jenna. Put your own art up on the walls."

She looked at them with pleasure. "Thanks, Jason. I'll do that."

Jenna left in better humor and with a lighter heart. For the first time in a long time, she began to look forward to the future.

Chapter 18

*B*ack in Townsend, Boyce felt less enthusiastic about his future. He missed Jenna. He worried about her daily. His life felt flat without her. Even Patrick missed her. He ran over to Sam's place every time they went out, looking for her. When Boyce went to check the cabin, Patrick nosed through the house searching for Jenna, only to come back disappointed, his tail no longer wagging with eagerness. Boyce knew just how he felt.

"Have you talked to her?" Una asked him. "Did she make it up to New York safely? Is she all right?"

Boyce frowned. "Sam says she's all right."

Una crossed her arms. "And why haven't you talked to her, Boyce Hart? Charlotte said Jenna was real upset not to get to say goodbye to you."

She paused with the feather duster she was using to dust the pictures in the gallery. "It looked pretty obvious to anybody with eyes that you and Jenna had a thing going for each other."

Boyce looked at her in annoyance. "Jenna is still a married woman, Una. Or have you forgotten that?"

She raised her eyebrows. "Well, excuse me! It seems like the story I heard was that she was going to get a divorce."

"Yeah, well she hasn't gotten it yet." Boyce snapped out his reply crossly.

Una studied him. "You know, my sister Louise got a divorce. It was a really hard time for her. It seems to me like Jenna could use all the friends she can get right now."

Boyce slammed a bird house he'd picked up onto the counter in irritation. "Fine, Una. Then you call Jenna and have a nice chat with her. You and she were friends, too. I wasn't her only friend down here."

Una rolled her eyes dramatically. "Chill out, Boyce. Gee." She turned her back on him and walked into the back room.

Boyce repeated almost the same conversation with Raynelle that afternoon. It gave him a pain around the heart.

"Look, Raynelle. Jenna told me she didn't want me calling her in New York while she sorted everything out. It doesn't mean I'm not thinking about her."

Raynelle tilted her head to one side. "You know, Sam doesn't even seem to know there was anything going on between you two."

"Jenna didn't want him to know, Raynelle. She didn't think he would understand." He ran his hand through his hair. "After all, she'd come down here to try to get over a failed relationship. It wasn't exactly the time to start up another one."

Raynelle put an arm around his waist affectionately. "Love ain't always nice about when she shows up, is she?"

"No." Boyce sighed.

She looked thoughtful then. "Do you think Jenna will come back when all this is past?"

"I don't know." He shook his head. "She had a whole other life in New York before she came here. And Townsend's a far cry from New York City in every way. This might have just been a healing place for her."

"That's a possibility." Raynelle straightened a few items on a store shelf. "I guess only time will tell."

Boyce caught Raynelle's eyes. "Don't tell Sam anything about this, okay? It's Jenna's place to do that if she wants to. I don't think she told any of her friends up there about us. She thought they wouldn't understand."

"I see." She gave him a sympathetic look.

Boyce started out of the Apple Barn, certainly not feeling any better for his talk with Raynelle.

"I've probably just made a dang fool of myself again," he said, slamming a cabinet door shut in the shop. "Maybe it's just not in the cards for me to ever find happiness in love."

Boyce painted moodily in his studio for the next several days, trying not to think too much about Jenna. He promised her he wouldn't call and he meant to keep that promise. But that didn't mean he could stop thinking about her. Or wondering how she was getting along.

At night he physically ached for her. Sometimes he got up and sat in front of the fire for hours, warring with his emotions.

He completed the painting of Jenna that he started. It had almost been a relief to take it to Haldeman's with his other paintings for the show. It hurt him to look at it.

His saving balms in this bad time were his weekly talks with Sam. He'd always called Sam to check on him - and he continued to do so. Through Sam he kept up – in part - with what was going on with Jenna. She wasn't having an easy time of it, and Boyce hated that he couldn't be there for her – to be a strength and comfort to her.

"How are you doing, Son?" his mother asked when he was over at her house for dinner one night.

There was no point in lying to his mother. "Not so good. But I reckon I'll heal in time."

"She'll come back if she's supposed to," his mother said. "Her heart will call her back. I told you that."

He gave her an anguished look. "And what if it doesn't? What if it's 'Out of sight, out of mind' with her?"

She studied him. "You said she made you promise not to call her, right?"

He nodded sullenly.

Her face brightened. "But did she say you couldn't write, Son?"

"What's the difference?" He gave her a cross look.

"You're not thinking smart, Boyce. There's a lot of difference." She smiled at him. "If she didn't make you promise not to write, then you can write to her. Keep yourself in her thoughts."

She patted his arm fondly. "You write a nice letter. I've gotten a few from you over the years when you were traveling." She paused remembering. "You always drew me little pictures, tucked in special items you thought would please me. I liked that. Women like that sort of thing, Son."

A flash of hope surged up in Boyce's middle. "You don't think she'll be angry if I write to her?"

"No." She shook her head. "I think it might make her heart right glad. The poor thing is probably going through a real rough time. She could use a friend."

Boyce thought about this. "I could send the letter to Sam. He'd give it to her."

"I'd say he would." His mother's eyes twinkled.

"I'll think on it," he told her. But he already knew he would try it. He'd promised her he wouldn't call. There was sense in that, he guessed. But he'd never promised her he wouldn't write.

Boyce thought on the letter and worked on it off and on for a couple of days. He drew pictures for Jenna. He found pressed wildflowers from their hike at Porter's Creek and decided she might enjoy having a few to re-member that day. While hiking another trail on Rich Mountain he found a small, white quartz rock on the trail – an almost perfect one. He tucked it in his pocket, thinking Jenna might enjoy it. He chose some other small gifts to send her – mostly things he found outdoors.

And he prayed a lot about what he should say to her. If ever he needed help from a higher power, it was certainly now.

Chapter 19

*J*enna moved into her new apartment on the weekend. It was small but she made it homey by bringing in favorite things and hanging her own pictures on the wall. The reds, blues, and tans of the old oriental rugs inspired a nice color scheme, and it was fun for Jenna to give her own creativity free reign in decorating her new place.

By Monday, Jenna finished the last of her unpacking and treated herself by going to Sam's for lunch. Elliott was not being released from the hospital until Tuesday, so Jenna knew she had one more day to come and go in the old apartment building with no risk of running into him.

Lunch consisted of one of Mary's casseroles with homemade rolls and a fresh fruit salad. Everything tasted delicious, as always, and Jenna enjoyed catching up with Sam on all the news in his life. She gave him updates about herself, too.

"Everything is going to work out all right, Jenna. You'll see." He patted her hand. "You're going to find that 'all things are going to work for good for you,' just like the Bible scripture."

"You sound like Boyce." This popped out before Jenna thought.

Sam turned his eyes to hers. "Boyce's daddy was a good preacher, you know. Frances and I went to his church for many a year before he passed. I was always sorry C. J. Hart died so young."

He paused and snapped his fingers. "Speaking of Boyce, he sent me something to give to you. I think it's your last paycheck. I forgot to mention it to you when we talked this morning. Sorry about that." He rolled his chair over to a side table to fumble in a drawer. "Looks like Boyce might have sent you something else with your check. It's a right big envelope."

Jenna felt her heart beating so hard in her chest that she thought she might have an anxiety attack. She tried to paste a casual smile on her face so Sam wouldn't notice.

"I caught him up on your news, too," Sam said, watching her. "Actually, I offered to give him the phone number over at Carla's so he could call you. I didn't think you would mind that. But he said he didn't think he ought to call. Said you told him it would be best if you were just on your own for a while with all you had to sort out." He stopped, studying the package from Boyce while he thought.

Then he looked at her with a small frown. "We can never have enough friends in this life. Especially good friends. Those folks in Townsend have come to think of you as a friend, Jenna. It surprises me that you wouldn't want to keep in touch with them."

Jenna found herself twisting her fingers in her lap, wondering how to answer. Finally, she said, "I'm hoping to keep up with everyone, Sam. I loved it there. It was one of the happiest times of my life. I think about everyone there all the time."

"Well," Sam replied, smiling now. "That sounds a bit more like you. So maybe you'll give Boyce a call, tell him you got his package, give him your new phone number. Stay in touch."

Jenna dropped her eyes to study her hands again. How could she answer him?

Sam watched her. "You know," he said, thoughtfully. "Boyce talked in a different sort of way than I can ever remember him talking to me before. A little strained. Tiptoeing all around normal questions and comments. Acting oddish just like you are. Got me to wondering." He scratched his chin. "Now with you acting the same way, it's got me to wondering even more. Anything you want to talk about to me?"

Jenna looked up at Sam with anguish in her eyes. "Not just now, Sam. It's confusing." A couple of tears threatened in the corners of her eyes, and she knew Sam could see that she was trying to hold them back.

"There, there, girl," he said soothingly, patting her arm in a comforting way. "You don't need to tell me a thing you don't want to. You've had about all a body can take emotionally in this last week with Elliott and your mother going at you. And you had to move and change everything in your life. There's time enough to sort out anything else later on. You know I'll always be around if you need an ear to bend."

"Thanks, Sam," she answered him quietly, still studying her hands in her lap instead of looking at him directly.

"I guess I'm too much of a nosy old man sometimes," he muttered. "I ought to mind my own business more."

She looked up, upset at his words. "Oh, no, Sam. You're not nosy and you're not old, either. I love you caring about me the way you do and even wanting to know my business. It's just that this time it's hard to share."

Sam laughed. "I've not forgotten about young things and young ways, Jenna. Boyce grumbled at me, too, when I asked him too many questions, and he called me a devious old matchmaker."

"Surely he didn't say that to you!" Jenna exclaimed without thinking. She felt a deep blush creep over her face. "I told him he was all wrong about that."

"Well, well, well," said Sam smugly. "I admit I thought the two of you might make good friends, you having a lot in common, but I never thought things would go this well. I'm absolutely delighted. Two of my most favorite people in this world."

Jenna sat forward. "Now, listen, Sam. I don't want you building this into one of your little stories. It's just that a few feelings got stirred up. There was some attraction, I admit, but that's all it was. I don't want you thinking more."

"Oh, not me." Sam waved a hand with a grin of insincerity. "I'm sure you know more about all of this than me, anyway. And if there's any telling to be done about you and Boyce, I'll leave that story to you."

Jenna eyed him warily.

"So, are you gonna call him?" Sam grinned.

"No," she said emphatically. "I don't think that's wise right now. And that's my choice to make, Sam." She took the envelope out of his hand.

"You gonna open it?" He eyed it curiously.

"No. I think I'll just wait until later." She tried to sound nonchalant. "Right now I'd rather visit with you." She gave him a big smile.

He laughed. "Girl, if there was a contest for trying to lie, you'd lose big every time. So I think you'd be better off just telling the truth to me."

Jenna studied the package in her hands.

"I might cry when I open it," she told him, honestly. "And I'd rather be by myself if that was to happen."

"I can understand that." He nodded, patting her arm again.

Jenna got up and put the package with her purse and coat by the door, hoping she wouldn't think about it so much if she weren't holding it.

When she got up, Sam wheeled his chair away from the table and into the living room. After cleaning up their dishes from lunch, Jenna came over to sit in her favorite chair beside him.

"You know what Boyce told me?" Sam said, picking up their conversation again.

"What?" Jenna sighed inwardly, hoping he wasn't going to quiz her about her feelings about Boyce again.

He gave her a pleased grin. "Boyce told me if I keep improving that you might drive me down to see the old place again. Said you and he talked about it. He suggested you could cook for me and do the home chores while he and Will Lanksy helped me manage around the cabin. He said everyone there would kick in to help and that they would all be real glad to see me again. "

"That's true, you know. Everyone would love to see you again." She smiled at Sam, relieved the conversation had shifted away from her personal life. "Would you like to go, Sam?"

"Can't think of much I'd like better." He grinned at her. "Maybe we'll think about it some more when all of this trouble is past with you."

"Yes, that would be a better time." A lump filled her throat.

"You know," Sam confided thoughtfully. "I've been wondering why you've avoided telling me tales about Orchard Hollow since you got back. Do you suppose now that we've had this little talk and cleared the air – that you might feel better about catching me up on things? I promise I'll not probe into any places you don't want to go right now. Or at least I'll try." He gave her a devilish look.

Jenna gave him an exasperated glance.

"I already told you what I did at Orchard Hollow, Sam. I called you nearly every day on the phone," she reminded him.

"Yeah, but like you've told me many a time, it's always good to hear the stories about Orchard Hollow again."

She laughed. "That's the truth. It always is."

He eyed her speculatively. "And I'm sure you've got some more stories you missed telling me on the phone."

She stopped to think for a minute. "Have I told you the story about how Raynelle accidentally locked Vernon out of the house one night – and how he had to sleep on the porch swing? He said he was afraid to go knocking on the door in the middle of the night because Raynelle might get her gun out and shoot first and ask questions later. She did that once when there was a possom on the porch, and Vernon said if that possom hadn't outrun her with that gun then he wouldn't have a chance of doing so either. He figured the porch was safer."

Sam laughed and slapped his leg. "No, you haven't told me that one," he said, grinning with delight already. "Tell me another story, Jenna; tell me all the things everybody said and did. All the little details."

"Okay. If you want." Jenna settled back in her chair. "I know a few more stories I haven't told you - including a cute one about Tyler Dean trying to trade out Jennie Rae to the boy next door for a tricycle he wanted. The trade worked out pretty good until Charlotte started looking for Jennie Rae. She'd left her out on the porch in her stroller while she went in the house to start supper, but when she came back, there was no sign of the baby or the stroller. Tyler Dean braved it out, saying he didn't know what could have happened to her until Charlotte started to get almost hysterical. Then Tyler Dean suggested that the stroller just *might* have rolled on over to the Greeley's next door."

She had Sam laughing now.

"Of course, the truth came out then." She gave him a smug smile. "I'm getting a pretty good collection of Orchard Hollow stories of my own now, aren't I?"

"That you are." He nodded. "That you are."

The two talked and laughed together for an hour or so, and then Jenna said her goodbyes and gathered up her things to leave. It had seemed almost like old times tonight with Sam.

"Next time you come, don't forget to call and work something out ahead with me and Henry," Sam reminded her. "Don't come alone. At least not until Elliott can be convinced to move. Maury and I are working on that. I've got a real good case for assault if I want to press it, and the police have been pushing me to do so. They don't take well to people who knock crippled folks around." He grinned. "I never thought this little infirmity of mine would come in so handy."

She sighed. Despite the jokes, it would be hard for Sam having Elliott across the hall when he came home.

"You know, Sam, you could move yourself if it bothers you so much to live near Elliott," she said. "I really don't like the idea that he could hurt you again."

"He's not likely to do that." Sam dismissed this idea with a shake of his head. "Besides, I've lived here in this apartment a long time now, and I'm not interested in trying to move again. It's easier for you young ones to move about."

Jenna turned to give him a fond look. "I would have liked to stay here at The Carlton near you, Sam, but I can't afford the rent here on my own. You know that."

Sam studied her. "Are you going to be all right where you are with your finances?" he asked. "I have more money than is good for me, you know.

You're welcome to some if you need it."

"No, Sam, I'm going to be fine, but thank you. And it means so much to me that you would offer." She leaned over to kiss his cheek.

"What would you do if you had a whole lot of money, Jenna? You know, won the power ball or something?"

She laughed. "Well, now that you've sent me down to the mountains and given me a taste for it, I'd probably buy myself a vacation place near Orchard Hollow."

"Would you now?" Sam's eyes lit up. "The old place got to you just like I said it would, didn't it? Don't you wish you'd gone before? I was always trying to get you to."

"No, I think I went at just the right time." She smiled to herself. "And maybe if you keep getting better, we'll go down together soon."

He gave her a thumbs up sign. "Well that's as good a get-well incentive as any man needs - to look forward to a trip to a pretty place with a pretty woman."

Jenna hugged him goodbye. "You take care of yourself, Sam," she said. "I'll see you again real soon, I'm sure."

He gave her a teasing look. "Maybe you'll tell me what was in that envelope when you come back."

She shook her head at him chidingly and closed the door.

When she got back to her apartment, Jenna sat down at the kitchen table with a glass of tea and studied Boyce's envelope thoughtfully. She looked at the familiarity of Boyce's handwriting and studied the postmark, calling up the scenes from the place it came from. When she opened it at last, she found her paycheck in a familiar Hart Gallery envelope. She also found a folded letter, some drawings, and a tiny box with a rubber band around it. Jenna smiled to see a small quartz rock and an arrowhead taped inside a folded piece of bubble wrap and her eyes misted over when she found a pressed flower inside a small plastic sleeve. She remembered finding that flower on one of their hikes.

She folded out the letter to read. *Dear Jenna*, it said.

I know you told me not to call you while you sorted things through in New York on your own, but you didn't tell me not to write to you. Now don't ask me not to write again, Jenna, because I really need some way to feel in touch with you. If you have a kind heart for an old friend in Tennessee, you'll write me back. Patrick is fond of letters, and I'll let him smell yours so he'll feel better. I'll read them to him, too, because he is lonesome for you. He walks all around the rooms of Sam's cabin with me looking for you in every corner. Almost as bad as me.

The pressed flower in the plastic is one I saved from the wildflower hike we took at Porter's Creek. I thought you might like it to stir a memory of a nice day. The arrowhead is one I found up the mountain this week. You always said you liked the one I wore around my neck, so I thought you'd like one of your own to keep. In the Smokies, there is a lot of quartz rock to be found for those who are looking. Somehow this little rock I found looked like a small star and it made me think of you and all the times we sat out on the porch looking for constellations in the night sky and making wishes. Wish on this little star, whenever you can't see the stars in the city, and always remember what the sky looks like in Orchard Hollow on a clear night.

Jenna stopped to hunt for a Kleenex. She was already crying like a ninny. She'd expected it. Why did she have to be such an emotional sort of person these days? She had never been particularly prone to crying before in her life. Nor had she gotten weepy over a man before. She sighed. How could she be so homesick for a man or a place she had known such a short time? She read on, sniffling.

The sketches I enclosed are some I started doodling on sitting up in Sam's office where you used to work. Don't laugh at them. You'll see they are card design ideas. You'll also see that illustration is not my forte in the art world. However, you were so much on my mind that these are what came out. Creating rhyming verse was beyond my talents, too. You'll note my little designs just have inspirational scriptures with them instead of verse. I guess, as you would say, that's the preacher's son in me. The designs I've sent you here are mostly of things we shared, and they made me both happy and sad to put them down. I decided it was only fair that you shared equally with me in these mixed emotions. It would hurt my heart a lot to think I was sitting down here missing you and that you weren't sitting up there being a little miserable missing me too. I get grumpy suffering alone. Maybe if we send things back and forth to each other, it will help both of us a little. Artists like us have to find a means of expression. So draw and write for me, too. I will watch the mail next week.

Boyce went on to tell her a few bits of news, and then there was a final paragraph before the letter closed.

Whoops. Almost forgot. The little box is a special present. I got it in Atlanta for you, but when I got home to give it to you, you had left to go back to New York. I'm not going to give you an explanation for this little gift. I think you'll figure it out. And when you open it, you'll know where the other one is.

From my heart to yours, … Boyce

206

In the taped up little box, was a gold half-heart on a long, serpentine chain. The crying started again in earnest then. Jenna remembered clearly the night Boyce had told her how he gave a half heart necklace to a long-ago high school sweetheart. Jenna remarked that she'd always wanted someone to give her one of those. And he remembered her words. Only this heart wasn't a dime-store one; it was 14K gold. She knew, instinctively, he was wearing the other one - silly or not for a guy. And all to please her. She put the necklace around her neck and held it up tightly against her heart.

Oh, but she would rather have him here with her instead of just a heart necklace, to feel and hear his own heart beating when she held him close. She sighed deeply, her emotions surfaced.

She turned to study the phone hanging on the kitchen wall. Should she call? Part of her said yes and part of her said no. Jenna's heart and emotions cried out to call, but a new, surprisingly stubborn streak in her resisted. She realized that she really wanted to get through this life problem – all of it – on her own. To get strong, to know she could handle things, that she could make it. She wanted to be someone she could like and be proud of, not just someone people needed to feel sorry for. Someone competent, someone independent, someone she would like to know and love. When she met Boyce again, when she talked to him again, she didn't want to be a pitiful and needy person. She wanted to be a strong person in her own right. She wanted to be an equal.

She wiped her tears and squared her shoulders with resolution.

"You can do this, Jenna," she told herself. "Remember what Boyce used to tell you - that you didn't know what a fine, capable person you were. Well, let's find out. Let's become someone that's not just someone's daughter or someone's wife. Let's become someone that's her own person."

Her little pep talk helped her in some way. She felt better.

"I'll write to him." She lifted her chin. "We can write each other. And we can come to know each other better that way. The absence will either strengthen our friendship or make us both realize it was just a fleeting thing. Like Boyce's actress friend, Audrey, that came and went."

Jenna went to her desk, took out paper and pen, and began to write. She wrote Boyce about what she had been doing since she got back. She sketched him a casual blueprint of her apartment layout as she talked about it. She drew pictures for him; she wrote snatches of verse. She found some copies of photos she wanted to send him. She thanked him for his gifts. She signed her letter as he did *From my heart to yours*, and then she packed everything into an envelope and addressed it to go out in tomorrow's mail.

She looked through Boyce's card designs then, realizing she forgot to really study them before. She found herself laughing and hugging them to herself. The little sketches were charming - Boyce's usual dash-it-off-in-black-ink style. And the scriptures he put with many of his sketches were wonderful ones, thoughts of joy and blessing, words about friendship and nature. Funny, she had never noticed those types of verses in her Bible. She felt a sudden convicting moment then - probably because she spent so little time ever reading her Bible. It was just something she mostly kept on the shelf. A just-in-case sort of book. Now, she found herself a little intrigued about it. Perhaps she'd read it more carefully.

Jenna once asked Boyce how he read his Bible, whether he had a plan for a few verses a day or a help book to aid him in studying different parts. He had looked at her kind of oddly before he answered.

"I read it mostly like any other book, Jenna, from beginning to end, from front to back." He gave her a teasing grin. "It's a story. Stories work better like that. Start from the first. Read to the finish. Like any book, if it's really a good story, you read it again and maybe even again. This book is one I've read a lot. It's a *good* book." He winked at her at his own little joke at the last.

She frowned. "Well, of course, it's good, but isn't it hard to understand? I mean, the Bible is a complicated book."

He raised an eyebrow at her. "Spoken like a true person who has never read it, my daddy would say." He laughed in remembrance. "Or like a person whose heart isn't close to God," he added more seriously. "The Spirit brings the understanding, Jenna. The less of God in you, the harder the reading, Daddy used to say. You'll have to figure out where the problem is, whether it's just in not having ever read the Bible or in not being right inside. Either one is easy to fix with a little time and sincere effort."

Jenna thought about that now. That was something else she would fix before she saw Boyce again. She wanted to be more of an equal there, too. Before she met and talked with Boyce, she hadn't realized people could even get close to God like that. But Boyce talked to God. She'd heard him do it even while they were walking up the hiking trail. Once she found him sitting out on the porch - praying with his head in his hands and with all his thoughts focused above.

She got up and rummaged through her bookshelves for her Bible. She knew it was here somewhere. She found it at last and brought it over to the sofa with her. It was a pretty, maroon leather Bible with gold leaf pages. Guiltily, she realized that most of the pages were still stuck together from where they'd never been turned.

She'd picked up Boyce's Bible one day and noticed how worn it was and how much he had marked and scribbled in it.

He saw her studying it. "My daddy used to say he could tell the depth of a Christian by how used, loved, and marked up their Bible was."

"Well, by this Bible, that makes you pretty deep, huh?" she teased.

He surprised her with a serious answer. "I truly hope so, Jenna. I'm working for that."

Thinking back, Jenna recalled the advice she received from Charlotte about praying before she left for New York. Charlotte said to talk to God like a friend. Jenna tried it in the car over the many miles on the way home. It felt odd at first, but then became easier. She felt more calm and peaceful after a while, found her thoughts were clearer. She decided she'd work on that, too. Have some prayer and Bible time every day.

"I'd like to have a deeper faith," she acknowledged, thinking out loud. "Too much of my life has simply been a surface sort of thing. I want everything in my life now to be real. I want everything to be sincere and to be my own, to be something genuine and not just what other people tell me and what other people say is right for me. A strong person knows her own way." She sat up straighter with the words. "Strong people know who they are, what they are, and where they are going. I want to know all of those things. I want to be strong inside, too." She looked down at the Bible on her lap. "And, I think I've figured out where a lot of my answers might be."

She opened up her Bible to read, deciding to start like Boyce suggested, right at the beginning. Then she realized she didn't have a pen or a marker to highlight anything she might want to mark or remember, so she jumped up to find one. While she was up, she got a note pad so she could write out any especially meaningful scriptures she might find as she read. Perhaps she would try working some inspirational verses into some of her card designs. She had never done that before. And Jason wanted her to expand and consider some new card line ideas. This might work well.

Jenna looked around her apartment with a small smile. She was on her way. And as Sam said, everything was going to be all right. She had to believe that. And she hoped, with all of her being, that it was true.

Chapter 20

*O*n a warm evening in late June, Boyce Hart sat out on the screened porch at Charlotte and Dean's house. After a nice dinner and evening with his friends, he relaxed now, with his feet propped up on the porch rail, while Charlotte and Dean put the children to bed.

The summer evening spread quietly around him like a dark quilt. Boyce watched the night fireflies, listened to the June bugs, and thought about Jenna.

Would there ever be a time when he wouldn't think about Jenna at odd times throughout every day? Or a time when she wouldn't wander in and out of his mind at will?

"It's been two months now," he said softly to Patrick, who lay curled up at his feet. "And I haven't seen her or talked to her since she left in April." He sighed heavily. "But at least she writes to me. That's something."

The dog thumped his tail in reply, glad to have come with Boyce tonight.

"Yeah, she stays in touch, and sends us pictures, keepsakes, and rough drawings of the greeting card designs she's working on." Boyce scratched the dog's head absently.

"I know she still thinks about the mountains because of the familiar scenes in the new Country Roads Series she's been working on." He paused, listening to a screech owl in the woods nearby. "I can tell from her letters, too, that she's been growing spiritually. She's put that aspect of herself into her Hope Series – the inspirational line she's started. Jenna said creating those cards had done a lot to keep her cheerful in a hard time. She also said I'd helped inspire the Hope Series with those cards I'd sent in my first letter."

He smiled, remembering that. There was little comparison between those old, rough ink sketches he sent Jenna in late April and the soft, dreamy watercolor cards she sent to him. The detail of her work always impressed him. She still continued the pattern, too, of hiding little surprises in her designs you only noticed after studying them for a while – a shadowy fish just below the surface of a pond, an inchworm on the stem of a flower, a kitten's head peeping out of a pile of birthday bags.

"It takes patience and a special gift to do such small and intricate work." Boyce shook his head. "It's certainly not my gifting. I like to work big, to spread paint on lavishly." Many times he left the details of a face or a flower blurred and incomplete, trusting them to the imagination of the viewer.

Patrick pricked his ears, hearing the owl again.

Boyce calmed him and then listened for Dean and Charlotte. He could still hear their soft voices settling the children through the open window.

He picked up a twig off the porch, turning it in his hand. "Jenna says I help her with her work, but she helps me with mine, too. I've gotten to where I send her my sketch ideas and she sends back her comments. Sometimes I incorporate them, Patrick, sometimes I don't. But it's interesting to get an outside view."

Boyce enjoyed the ongoing critiques they mailed back and forth. People who didn't do art always tended to think everything he did looked wonderful, so it provided little help to get their opinions. It pleased Boyce that Jenna no longer feared giving Boyce her own views – or flinched at receiving his. He thought this a great sign of increasing confidence and growth on her part.

"I like the road bending back into the woods in your new sketch," she wrote him last week. "But I find myself wanting to glimpse something at the end of the road, something to look forward to."

Sometimes rather than just making suggestions, she would also get tough. The week before she wrote, "That scene you drew of all the children playing in the stream was really sexist. All the boys were active - swimming, tubing, running on the bank, jumping in the water - and all the girls were passive, lying in the sun, watching the boys, wading only in the edges of the water. Carla and I would have been jumping off the rocks with the boys into the pond when we were that age. You need to be more sensitive about stereotypes."

After her letter, he changed the activities of the children before he completed the final painting. She made a good point. Still, he razzed her back in a letter by saying she'd better examine her own drawings with the same critical lens.

"Your little dancers are always ballerinas and your fairies are always girls," he told her. "Boys dance, too, and there are male fairies, as well as male elves and gnomes."

She accepted his criticism with good grace and soon sent him back some designs with boys at the barre in a dance studio and with male fairy folk peeping out of a hole in the base of a giant poplar tree.

"We saw a tree just like this when we were hiking this spring," she wrote him. "It made me think fairies might live there. Do you remember?"

Yes, he remembered. He remembered everything, God help him. And being away from her like this was tearing him apart.

Charlotte came out on the porch with Dean. "What are you thinking about looking so pensive?" she asked. "As if I couldn't guess. Lord, Boyce, why don't you just go up there to New York City and get her. Her divorce is going to be final next week on July 7th. I know she misses you, too. Whenever I talk to her about you, and push at her with some questions a little, her voice gets all misty and choked up sounding. I can tell she's unhappy deep down."

She settled into the porch swing beside her husband. "Dean, don't you think Boyce just ought to go up there and get her?"

"Might be a good idea," drawled Dean, in his laid back way. "Just go bundle her up in a gunny sack, throw her in the car, and bring her on back down here. The old timey way."

"Oh, thanks a lot." Charlotte punched his arm. "I meant to do it romantic, Dean. Go up there and take flowers and say sweet things and sweep her off her feet."

Boyce shook his head at them in amusement.

"Well how come you're waiting like you are?" pressed Charlotte. "I don't understand why you couldn't have gone up to see her, called her, kept yourself more before her face all this time. 'Absence doesn't always make the heart grow fonder,' you know. Sometimes it's 'out of sight, out of mind'!"

"It's what she wanted right now." Boyce winced at the thought that Charlotte's words might well be the truth.

Dean scratched his head. "Women don't always know what they want," he observed lazily. "With all that's happened to that girl, maybe she don't know what she needs most. Maybe she's just confused. It always struck me as odd that you haven't talked to her, that you haven't been up there. She's a pretty woman, Boyce. Somebody else might come along and snatch her up."

Boyce felt an agonizing wrench in his heart at Dean's words. That was his own ongoing fear and nightmare being voiced.

"You know, Jenna's been going out to lunch a lot with this Jason Brantley she works for." Charlotte plunged the knife in deeper. "Once they went to an art show, too. She talks about him all the time and I found out he's *single*." She emphasized the last word. "She says they're just friends, but it seems to me a man seeing a woman right often outside of the office is being a little bit more than friendly."

"That don't sound good." Dean agreed. He glanced over to catch Boyce's eyes and then amended his words kindly. "Of course, it might not mean nothing, either."

"It's been a risk," Boyce said at last. "To let her do this the way she wanted to. I agreed because I believed, and I still do, that she needed some time to come into her own. To realize who she was, to get strong and confident. To establish some independence. She'd been almost like what those books describe as co-dependent. I thought she needed a space to see who she was on her own. I didn't want to rush her back into another relationship just to have a relationship."

"I don't think that's how it would have been," Charlotte argued, still stubbornly holding to her stance.

"Well, Boyce has gotta do what he thinks is right," Dean said, trying to play the middleman. "We've gotta respect that, Charlotte."

Dean sat up suddenly, dropping his feet to the porch floor and stopping the movement of the swing. It startled Patrick. "You know, I just thought of something. It might not have helped Jenna's divorce any if Boyce had been up there buzzing around. Right now, all the wrong has been on Elliott's side. If anyone had seen Boyce at Jenna's, or seen them out and about, they might have tried to make something out of it, tried to make Jenna look bad. What's that legal term they use?"

"Grounds, I think. It might have given Elliott grounds for a counter suit or worse," Boyce answered him. "Actually, I'd thought of that, too, all along. Elliott Howell is probably the type that would have looked for something he could trump up against Jenna if he could find it. He'd like to play himself into the role of the victim if he could. I didn't want to give him any ammunition for that, even a bullet to try to shoot at her. Right now, it's all on him. Jenna is clean and innocent going into court."

"Lord, I didn't even think of that." Charlotte put a hand up to her mouth. "And that snake Elliott would be just the type to have her followed and would probably be looking at every little thing she does. In fact, once I teased Jenna about whether she was going out on any dates yet, and she said there would be no dating for her until after she divorced. She has probably been thinking about that, too."

Charlotte paused, thoughtfully, another idea passing through her mind now. "You know, Jenna mentioned that Jason asked to take her out to dinner to celebrate after the divorce is finalized. I bet that's why she hasn't gone out with him yet."

Dean shoved at her playfully. "Aw, Charlotte," he drawled. "That was a right insensitive thing of you to say in front of Boyce. There's no cause for you to put more worried thoughts into the man's mind than are probably already there right now." He shook his head. "Why, I'd have been about half crazy if you'd been up in New York with all those slick, city men back before we married. This whole thing is hard enough for Boyce without you adding fuel to the fire. We ought to be trying to cheer Boyce up through this." He sent an encouraging smile Boyce's way.

Boyce made an effort to smile back. He thought to himself that if they tried to cheer him up much more tonight, he'd just go shoot himself!

He artfully changed the subject to talk about the gallery. Charlotte had returned to work two days a week now. Her mother and Dean's mother traded keeping the children those days. They liked having the little ones for a day each week, and Charlotte liked making a little money of her own and getting out in the public.

"I heard Sam Oliver is much better now," Dean put in a little later. "And that he's coming down to the mountains to stay at his place for a while this summer."

Charlotte smiled at that. "Yeah, Jenna's bringing him down in late July for a whole week. She just told me yesterday it's all final. She said that guy Henry – the one who takes care of Sam - is coming with them to help make it easier for Sam. Jenna talked him into coming along. Told him he'd love Tennessee."

She leaned over to pick a honeysuckle bloom off the bush by the porch. "Won't that be nice for Sam to see everyone again and to see his place?"

Dean slapped his knee. "Well, shoot fire. Won't that be nice for Boyce? He'll get to be with Jenna again if they don't work out something sooner. And she'll be legally split up by that time. Boyce can stake a real claim then." He grinned at Boyce encouragingly.

Charlotte glared at him. "Well I'm sure Jenna would love to hear herself talked about like a claim to be staked out," she snapped. "You men! Women don't like to be talked about like that. And Boyce, don't you dare say anything like that around Jenna, you hear? It'll tick her off real bad."

"I'll be careful," promised Boyce, laughing inwardly to even think of

214

what Jenna would say if he dared to try a line like that with her. However, his heart did leap to learn she planned to come soon. Late July was only a month away. She'd written that she planned to bring Sam later in the summer if he would agree to the trip, but it felt good to know the trip was firmly scheduled now.

Of course, it wouldn't be the same with Sam and Henry staying at the cabin with Jenna. She would be cooking and tending to Sam while she visited. And she would be seeing that Sam got around to the family, friends, and old sights he wanted to see again. Boyce might get precious little time with her alone.

As he drove home from Charlotte and Dean's, he wondered if it would be better - or worse for him - after she came to visit with Sam and then went back to New York again. He would have to start aching and missing her all over again. The more he thought about it, the more he wondered if it might only make it worse for him to see her.

Boyce sat morosely in front of the fireplace later and considered the situation again. Maybe he should just play it light and friendly with her when she came back? If he touched her and held her it would only make it harder on him when she left again. Dadgumit, it was awful to dread and want something at the same time. He yearned and feared to see her face. He ached and feared to touch her again. The thought of more love and passion was a torment to dream of. But Boyce did dream, as he sat in front of the small fire he'd built to take the chill off the night air. His thoughts, like the fire, were not chilly at all.

Chapter 21

*I*n New York, a week later, Jenna and Carla sprawled comfortably in Jenna's living room - celebrating Jenna's divorce. John had been up earlier, too, after the three friends shared dinner together, and now Carla lingered a little longer to talk.

"Do you want some more wine?" Carla got up to pour a small portion of wine into her glass and then held the bottle up in question to Jenna.

"Maybe a bit." Jenna pushed her glass closer for Carla to reach. They were finishing out the last of a sweet, white Riesling left over from dinner.

Carla lifted her glass toward Jenna after she poured. "Well, here's to J. C. Martin." She grinned. " And to the last of *Mrs*. Jenna Howell. And, thank goodness, to the last of Elliott Howell, too."

Jenna sighed, frowning at her wine glass moodily. "It seems awful to toast to something like this."

"Why?" countered Carla. "People toast to the end of a bad event or a war, and they toast to the beginning of a new era or a new year. What's the difference?"

"Nothing, I guess," answered Jenna quietly.

"I hope you're not getting maudlin about this," Carla said to her, settling back into the sofa. "You know this is a good thing for you. I realize no one ever really likes to get divorced, but, in your case, honey, it was the right thing to do. And the court session proved a brief one since there wasn't a trial - and since the attorneys had already agreed on everything ahead of time. It wasn't really unpleasant or anything."

She paused, slanting Jenna a thoughtful look. "You're not upset about this, are you?"

"I don't know." Jenna looked down at her hands. " Not really. I know it was the right thing. It's just such an anticlimactic moment in a way. It's been the first thing in my mind for months, my biggest worry and fear, and now it's finally over. It doesn't seem real yet."

"It's real." Carla tucked a sofa cushion behind her back. "It's genuine and you've got the papers. That steely look on Elliott's face told me he knew it was real." She laughed. "He hated to think he lost. I really think he believed you'd change your mind before it got to the last minute. He certainly had your mother call you often enough."

Carla sat her wine glass down on the table. "I still can't believe how often Elliott kept conveniently running into you when you were out – working on you all this time to change your mind. New York is supposed to be a big place where you never see anyone twice. But I think you ran into Elliott once too often for it to be a total coincidence. It began to feel like a stalker movie." She giggled over that.

Jenna's mouth quirked in a smile. "Actually, he hired a detective and had me followed, Carla. That's how he knew how to find me. The detective discovered the consistent routines in my week and Elliott zeroed in on those as a way to see me."

"You're kidding?" Carla exclaimed, her mouth popping open in surprise. "How did you find that out?"

Jenna shivered. "Elliott let it slip the last time I saw him two days ago," she answered. "He showed up at Paludi's, the little café where I eat lunch every week before I meet Jason Brantley at Park Press."

"What happened?" demanded Carla.

"Elliott wandered over to my table, like it was a pleasant coincidence, and asked if he could join me for lunch."

"And you said yes?" Carla's voice was incredulous.

"It was a public place." Jenna bristled. "I felt safe. Also, Frank Paludi, the owner of the shop, likes me. I'm a regular customer. He was keeping an eye on things."

"So tell," Carla prompted. "What happened?"

Jenna toyed with her wine glass. "The usual. Elliott played nice, working hard to charm me, giving me compliments. I almost started to relax."

She shook her head. "Then he leaned forward and asked, 'Are you sure we're doing the right thing, Jenna – going through with this divorce? We've both changed and matured while we've been apart. Our marriage would be different if we got back together now. Don't you think we should give it another try so we'll never look back and regret we acted in haste?'"

"That snake. What did you say?" Carla made a face.

"I said no, of course. I agreed it might be true we both had changed. I told him I certainly had changed – become a stronger person, felt good about myself and my life now." She paused a minute before continuing.

"Elliott suggested I might be lonely and struggle with finances as a *divorcee*." Jenna rolled her eyes. "He really enjoyed emphasizing that last word, Carla. It irritated him when I told him I actually enjoyed living on my own and wasn't having trouble with finances. He didn't like it one bit, either, when I explained Park Press had put me on salary and given me the opportunity to expand my design work into several new areas."

Carla snorted. "That hardly surprises me."

Jenna stopped to take a breath. "Amazingly, I felt rather calm. I chatted on about how satisfying my work was, how much I enjoyed it and what it meant to me. I didn't care whether he liked hearing it or not, Carla."

"How did Elliott handle this new and improved Jenna?" Carla giggled.

"The more I talked, the angrier Elliott became. I could see that flush of red begin to rise up his neck." She frowned. "It was obvious he resented me being happy, disliked me being productive. Finally, he interrupted me and got ugly. He said sarcastically he was certainly glad *my* work was going well, because I had made so many problems for him that *his* work at Abercrombie had suffered."

Carla interrupted, grinning. "Yeah, I heard word seeped into Elliott's company about what he did to Sam. He dumped Lena, too, and she decided to talk. A lot. John said Abercrombie's president, Dean Harkness, did not like the negative press." She paused. "Do you think they'll fire him?"

Jenna shook her head. "No. But Elliott said Harkness is sending him over to Paris for a year until things cool down here. Naturally, Elliott blamed me for this, and he claimed it was my fault that he's having to move out of his apartment. He had a few choice words to say about Sam, too. Stuff about Sam blackmailing him and about Henry being an animal that needed to be put down. It started to get unpleasant."

"You should have gotten up and walked out, Jenna," Carla crossed her arms in irritation. "You shouldn't have listened to that!"

"No, I wanted to listen, Carla." Jenna took a breath. "It didn't hurt me, anymore, and it sort of fascinated me in a way to see that. It used to be so painful when Elliott blamed me for things in his life or when he tried to belittle me. I'd feel guilty. This time I just felt sorry for him. Isn't that great?"

She looked over at Carla with a small smile. "I actually interrupted him and said, 'Listen, Elliott - all of these things that happened are *your* fault and not mine.'"

Carla gave a little whoop and patted Jenna on the back. "Good for you!

How did Elliott handle that?"

Jenna winced. "He reached across the table and grabbed my arm. He said, 'Don't get uppity with me, Jenna. You're nothing, do you hear? I've had a detective following you. I know things about you. I know where you go and what you do. I can find ways to hurt you. I can end your silly little job if I want to. You'd better wake up before this divorce goes through and find a way to stop these proceedings. You belong to me and I want it to stay that way.'"

"That creep! How dare he!" Carla exclaimed. "What did you do then?"

"Frank Paludi came over to our table. He said, 'Anything wrong here?' and just looked pointedly at Elliott and at his grip on my arm. Elliott finally let me go then and left. But I still have the bruises." She pulled up her sleeve and showed Carla her arm.

"That man should really be arrested for the things he does." Carla scowled in anger. "And you should have showed the judge your arm in court, Jenna."

Jenna disagreed. "No, I was getting what I wanted in court. This doesn't matter." She looked at the fading bruises on her arm. "In fact, this just helped me to see what kind of man Elliott is. I'm truly amazed I was so lacking in discernment before. I guess I just saw what I wanted to see."

"I don't think so," said Carla. "As you've said yourself so often, Elliott is a master at falseness and deception. You didn't realize he was playing a part; you thought he was genuine."

"But you weren't fooled, were you, Carla?" Jenna looked directly into her eyes.

Carla twisted in her seat uncomfortably. "Admittedly, I never really liked Elliott much. I wasn't sure why. I talked to Mother about it, and she said my instincts were probably right. She knew the Howells and said it troubled her for you to marry into their family. She called them a synthetic family. I've remembered those words as you've had these problems with Elliott."

Jenna sighed. "Your upbringing was a blessing to you, Carla. I hope you appreciate that. Your mother, dad, and your brothers were all such comfortable, normal people. I used to love to go over to your house."

She smiled at her friend. "That was your lucky difference, Carla. Your parents encouraged you to think for yourself, to develop your own interests and goals, to be yourself, and to follow your own star. That has made you stronger. That made you more discerning, too, as you walked your way.

While you were growing and developing, I was held back. My confidence fell off because the important people in my life didn't have confidence in me. My mother always criticized me and tried to subtly, and not so subtly, control me. Eventually, I kind of lost myself in the struggle. It was often easier to conform than to try to fight. Compromising led to mistakes."

"I guess I'd better thank my mother the next time I see her," Carla quipped.

"Yes, you'd better," Jenna told her, giving her a friendly punch.

"Well, you don't act confused and unconfident now." Carla pushed her hair back behind her ear. "You're plucky and spunky again like you were when we were girls."

"I am, aren't I?" said Jenna, smiling. "I'd like to think that."

"John and I have both noticed that you've changed a lot." Carla gave her an appraising look.

"What specifically have you noticed?" Jenna asked her curiously.

Carla seemed a little uncomfortable for a moment. "Well, you walk differently for one thing – more confidently, without kind of hanging your head like you used to. You look people in the eyes and say what you think more often, instead of apologizing that you have an opinion and a brain." Carla grinned.

"Also, you've become more disciplined in your life, Jen. You seemed to drift around before, kind of wispy, and always busy about nothing. Now you have a work schedule and you're really accomplishing things. I admire that. Your work with Park Press these last months has been astonishing. John and I are thrilled with every new product you produce, and everything of yours we put in the bookstore sells tremendously. I enjoy telling people my friend created those things."

She gave Jenna a wide smile. "I've always loved you Jenna, but I've been really proud of you lately. You've been through a hard time, but you've gone through it sort of triumphantly where most people would have just fallen apart and wallowed in themselves. You've really been great. And, despite being betrayed by Elliott, harangued by your mother on a continual basis, and practically stalked by Elliott, you've become a more kind and loving person, too, which is kind of amazing."

Carla wrinkled her nose. "I sort of expected you to become a little hard and brittle, Jenna, from being hurt so deeply, to cut yourself off from people. But you seem to have reached out more. You talk to people on the street, in the grocery store, in the library. You've always been what everyone would call nice, but now there's a new caring in you. John says maybe part of it is the faith thing - since we find you holed up in your Bible so often. Honestly, that book is marked up like a college textbook now, and you're doing those inspirational cards." She shrugged. "Anyway, whatever it is, Jenna, the changes are terrific."

"Would you say I'm someone better to know?" Jenna asked the question - knowing she was fishing a little.

Carla hesitated. "Well, sure, but I hope that's not a trick question and that I'm not going to get in trouble now for answering it honestly."

"No, it's a wonderful answer." Jenna leaned over to give her a hug. "You don't know how hard I've been working to become a better and stronger person. And it really has not been easy. I am so glad you noticed. I wanted to come out of this whole mess better and not worse. I wanted to become someone I could like and admire more. Does that sound stupid?"

"No, you big nut," Carla hugged her back. "It sounds kind of touching. I might have to cry or something if you keep this up much longer."

"Okay, I'll stop." Jenna grinned.

Carla gave her a teasing look. "What are you going to do with this new and wonderful person you've been working on next?"

"I haven't fully decided yet," she answered primly. "But I'll let you know when I do. Now, tell me something wonderful and touching about you so I won't feel so sappy."

"Okay." Carla looked at her and smiled mischievously. "Get ready. This is about as sappy and touching as you can get. I'm going to have a baby. What do you think?"

"Oh, Carla! I can't believe it!" Jenna clapped her hands. "It's wonderful! When did you find out?"

She flushed. "I think I've been suspicious for a couple of weeks, but one of those little tests finally told the tale just yesterday. It's one of the reasons I wanted to stay up here to talk with you. I wanted you to be the first to know after John and my family."

Jenna threw her arms around Carla to hug her.

"I'm so excited. I'm going to be an aunt!" she explained. "I've always thought of you as a sister, you know. So that sort of makes me an aunt, doesn't it? When is the baby due, Carla? What did John say?"

Carla put a hand to her midriff thoughtfully. "It's due in mid January. John is thrilled and he's already looking through baby name books in the store. He's been following me around reading out "name the baby" ideas and asking me all the time if I need to sit down and rest." She blew out a breath. "The baby isn't due for seven months now and the man is already driving me crazy."

They laughed together.

Jenna sighed with pleasure. "This is so wonderful, Carla. I'm so happy for you and John."

Carla leaned over to put a hand on Jenna's knee. "Listen, Jenna, instead of remembering this as the day you got a divorce, maybe you can always remember this as the day you learned you were going to be an auntie. It would be a good memory to counter any negatives." She grinned at Jenna. "And I'm going to teach the baby to call you Auntie Jenna, so get ready!"

"I can't wait," Jenna said, sighing. "I'm going to paint Mother Goose prints for the nursery. You've always loved those."

The rest of the evening was taken up with talking about the baby and plans for a nursery.

Chapter 22

*A*s promised, Jenna stopped by Sam's two weeks later before she went to the Park Press awards dinner. Sam wanted to see how she looked "all gussied up", as he called it. When Jenna arrived, he gave her a long, low wolf whistle.

"Don't you look fine indeed?" Sam whistled and insisted she turn around for a full examination.

For the occasion, Jenna had chosen a sleek, mid-calf black dress and a sheer, matching black jacket trimmed with iridescent crystal beads. Around her neck hung a diamond solitaire pendant and in her ears sparkled matching stud earrings. Her hair was wound up in a simple chignon.

She stopped pivoting and turned her eyes to Sam's. "I wanted an elegant, classic look. I thought it would help me feel confident. This is the first awards dinner I've ever been able to go to."

"Well, all the eyes will be on you," Sam assured her. "You'll be the belle of the ball, a regular Cinderella."

"Thanks, Sam." Jenna leaned over to give him a hug. "I wish you could go with me. It's supposed to be a nice dinner, with speakers and entertainment. And Jason says I'm going to get some kind of little award."

She settled down carefully in a chair to visit with Sam for a few minutes before she went to the dinner.

Sam rolled his chair close to her. "Your art has really bloomed, Jenna. I've had Mary collecting things for me from your new lines." He smiled at her. "Of course, you know my favorite designs are those based on scenes from the Smokies and around Orchard Hollow."

"Why does that not surprise me?" She teased. "Which do you like best?"

"The one of my cabin, of course." He grinned.

"Are you looking forward to going down for our trip?" Jenna asked him.

"Yes, I surely am," Sam assured her. "We're going to have us a fine time."

He paused thoughtfully. "However, that makes me think of a little item of news I need to talk to you about. I've done something in relation to Elliott's attack on me that you might not totally approve of."

"You mean making Elliott leave his apartment in order to have those assault charges dropped?" she asked. "I already know about that. You told me, and Elliott mentioned it, too. His real estate agent is showing the apartment while he's in Paris. I guess he'll move when the lease is up - or sooner if he can work out the arrangements."

"Well, yes, there's that business." Sam scratched his chin. "Maury worked that one out as slickly as we both hoped. I'm glad to have Elliott leaving, too. I'm not sorry for doing that. But we did do a little more finagling through some other legal dealings I figure it's about time I spoke to you about."

Jenna raised an eyebrow in question and Sam shared what he had done.

"I'm not sure you should have done that." Jenna told him as she checked her watch and stood up to leave.

"It was my choice to do it." Sam gave her a stubborn look as he rolled his chair toward the door to see her out. "You run on to the ball now, Cinderella. We'll talk more the next time we get together. And we'll make our plans about going to Orchard Hollow. Boy oh boy, I'll get to make a whole new set of stories to tell while I'm down there."

Jenna laughed. "Take care, Sam. I'll see you later."

"Make some memories tonight!" Sam called after her.

A short time later, Jenna was doing exactly that. Park Press had rented a glamorous ballroom in one of New York's old hotels, and Jenna felt pleased at how many people she knew from the design and publications company. She enjoyed networking around the room before Jason escorted her to the table they were sharing with six others from their division.

"You look beautiful." Jason's eyes moved over her appreciatively. "I hope you'll remember you promised to let me take you out to dinner to celebrate after your divorce." A little cloud slipped over Jenna's festivities. She wished Jason hadn't brought up her divorce right now. However, others at the table were involved in animated conversations of their own, and no one paid much attention to their words.

"I haven't forgotten," she answered quietly. "We'll plan that sometime soon. It was nice of you to remember."

He looked at her more intently and slipped a hand across the table to lay it over hers. "It wasn't just nice of me to remember, Jenna," he confided. "I've been looking forward to it. In fact, I've been hoping we might enjoy some other times together. You know you've always been one of my favorite people. I'd like to get to know you better."

Jenna caught her breath for a minute, and then pulled her hand away discreetly. Jason was making a pass at her! She scrambled to think how to handle it. He seemed a wonderful man, and he had always been such an encouragement to her.

She smiled at him at last, deciding to just be honest. "You are one of my best friends," she told him. "It will always be my pleasure to spend time with you."

He grinned. "I didn't really expect more than that right now, Jenna. Besides, like a nightingale, you've flown a pretty rigid cage and only just now tasted freedom and started to sing again."

Jenna looked at him, pleased. "What a truly beautiful thought."

"Well, your new joy has overflowed into your art, too," he told her. "Everyone in the company has been simply stunned with your new work."

"Thank you." She smiled again. "I'm hoping to get more new ideas when I go back to Orchard Hollow soon. You do remember I'll be taking Sam Oliver down to his place in the mountains next Friday on the 28th?"

"Yes, and you know that's fine with me and with the Press." He studied the plate of food that had just been brought to him with pleasure. "If going on location helps your art and productivity, Jenna, you are welcome to go away anytime you'd like. Just keep sending me designs from wherever you are!"

They both laughed then, which attracted the attention of others at their table. Soon they were all engaged in entertaining conversation, enjoying their dinner, a rich merlot, and the excitement of the evening.

After dinner the president of Park Press, Mark Graham, talked about his vision for growth of their company and a motivational speaker shared inspirational words about the art of creativity. Park Press had several publication and design branches and the speeches and awards continued for over an hour afterwards.

Their own card and gift design branch was one of the latter parts of the company to receive awards. Jason received one for growth and productivity of his unit, and one of the design artists, Bradley Chapman, received an award for greatest volume of sales. In addition, Grace Merryman received recognition for creating a new line of gift items. And then Jenna heard her name.

"Park Press would also like to give special recognition to our best rising young artist of the year, Ms. Jenna Martin, who most of you may know better as J.C. Martin," President Mark Graham said. "She has contributed designs to us part-time for a few years, but this spring she joined us on full-time staff and has already initiated two successful new design lines – the Country Roads series, a collection of rural scenes, and the Hope series, a line of inspirational cards. Both of these lines have been received with an unprecedented success and are already being incorporated into note card and calendar designs, due to their wide popularity. Her work is crisp, fresh, and utterly delightful, and we hope she will continue to work with us for many years to come. Please join me in congratulating J.C. Martin, Best New Artist of the Year for Park Press."

With flushed cheeks and an excited smile, Jenna stood and walked up to the stage to receive her award. Applause followed behind her, quieted, and then erupted enthusiastically again as she accepted her awards plaque from President Graham. When she stepped to the microphone, Jenna felt absolutely wonderful. Her fellow employees were still applauding, and some of her friends from her own design unit were whistling and calling out encouragement.

"I don't know how to express how pleased I am to receive this honor," Jenna said, looking out over the room. "In fact, I'm not sure what could make this moment more perfect!" Everyone laughed, and she paused to smile out over the audience again. Then, suddenly, out of the corner of her eye, she saw him. Boyce Hart stood in the back of the room.

For a moment Jenna couldn't speak. Boyce was leaning casually back against a pillar at the back of the ballroom, stunning in a black tuxedo. Jenna's knees went weak just to look at him. Standing beside him, unbelievably, was her father. He wore a black tux, too, and he was smiling at her.

As she struggled to collect herself, Boyce gave her one of those wonderful nods of confidence of his and then tapped his mouth as a reminder to her that she needed to finish her speech.

Jenna pulled her eyes away from Boyce and back to the task at hand. "I just realized some people I care about have slipped in to see me get this award," she told everyone honestly. "What a wonderful evening. It means so much to me that they, and that each of you, are here. I want everyone to know how much I appreciate this honor. It is a wonderful encouragement to me. Thank you all so much again."

She worked her way back toward her seat on unsteady legs. She wanted to run to the back of the room immediately to find Boyce, but of course she couldn't. There were a few more divisions yet to receive awards. She would have to wait. She sat down, no longer able to see the back of the room.

The rest of the awards presentations were a blur to Jenna. As the presentations closed and the evening finally ended, Jenna made her way through the well-wishers as quickly as she could toward the back of the ballroom. She looked for Boyce, but she didn't see him. Slipping out into the lobby, she scanned the crowded room. And then she saw her father coming toward her.

"I was really proud of you tonight." He embraced her a little awkwardly and kissed her cheek. Jenna struggled with the tears that tried to well up. She couldn't remember the last time her father had hugged or kissed her.

Her eyes slipped over him. He was still so handsome with only a peppering of gray in his dark hair. "How did you know to be here?"

"Boyce Hart brought me," he answered.

Watching her search the area for him again, he added, "He's already left, Jenna."

"Left?" She was stunned and felt the color wash out of her face.

"He said you had an agreement and that you would understand." His eyes watched her carefully. "But he also told me to tell you he chose to break his agreement just a little to see you get your award. He asked me to tell you he was proud of you. That you looked brave and strong up there."

Jenna blinked back the tears that threatened to spill over.

Seeming to sense her emotions, her father pointed to the café across the lobby in the hotel. "Let's go in that little coffee shop, Jenna. We can get a cup of coffee and visit for a minute."

He took her arm and led her into the shop to a seat, ordering two coffees for them after they sat down.

Jenna raised questioning eyes to her father. "How did Boyce find you? I'm confused."

"He's quite a man, your friend Boyce." He took a sip of his hot coffee. "This morning he showed up at my office and demanded to see me. He told my secretary that it was urgent, that it was about my daughter. I had him shown in."

Her father smiled at her. "Oh course, at first I thought maybe you had been hurt. When I found out you were okay, I felt relieved. But that didn't last long. Because then your friend Boyce laid in to me something fierce. He gave me a fine, long, tongue-lashing lecture about what a no-account father I was, how I didn't deserve a daughter like you, and how I'd failed you when you needed me most."

Jenna caught her breath. "Oh, Daddy, I'm sorry," she began.

Her father waved away her apologies and stopped her from saying more. "Don't apologize, Daughter." He frowned. "I'm the one who needs to apologize to you. The man was right. I guess it took another man lay-ing-in to me for me to realize it. I admit I've always liked Elliott, but that shouldn't have blinded me to the wrongs he's done to you. And as Boyce so flatly told me, any real man who was a real father to his only daughter, would have done some major damage to Elliott for what he did to you – or at least would have sincerely wanted to."

He scowled. "He told me only a weak and spineless man would care more about social reputation than his own daughter's welfare. He said I ought to be ashamed for suggesting you stay married to a man like Elliott Howell - who would cheat on his wife and dishonor countless women in careless adultery. He wouldn't even shake my hand when we met. He said it shamed him to meet me."

Jenna winced at Boyce's stark honesty. "Well, then … how did you end up here with him tonight?"

"Eventually, your friend Boyce settled down a bit, but not much. I thought for a time he might hit me, and I didn't look forward to that much." He chuckled, much to Jenna's surprise.

Noticing Jenna's shocked expression, he added, "I don't think I've met a real man like that in a long time. And he was right about everything he told me, even though it made me as mad as a hornet at the time."

He stopped and drank a little more of the coffee the waitress had brought. "After all the anger boiled off of our discussion, we got to talking. About our work. About the New York Yankees' last season. About you. And about your mother."

"About Mother?" Jenna almost choked on her own coffee.

He nodded. "Yes. He said I was out of line to let Evelyn 'have at you' the way she did and to never step up to bat about it. Actually, he used some other terminology to describe my manhood at this point, but the explana-tion I gave you will do." He chuckled again.

Jenna wondered if she would wake up from this moment if she pinched herself. She hadn't heard her father laugh in years! He had just been a seri-ous presence away at work or in the background of her life since she was a young girl.

"Is Mother here?" Jenna suddenly asked, wondering if she, too, would suddenly come wandering in.

"No, and she doesn't know I'm here, either," he told her, shaking his head. "That scene will come along later."

Jenna struggled to make sense of everything. "But how did you end up here with Boyce tonight? I still don't understand that."

He leaned back in the booth. "Well, after we finished our talk, Boyce said I could start making up some of the wrong I'd done to you by coming with him to see you get this award tonight. He said you wrote him you might get an award, and that he'd flown up to see you receive it."

Jenna's father's eyes caught hers. "Boyce said when you cared about people you made sure you got to their significant events if you possibly could. He said, pointedly, there was no reason why I couldn't get myself here if he could."

She felt a flush steal up her face.

Jenna's father smiled at her before he continued his story. "Your friend Boyce stood up about that time and told me he'd pick me up in front of my office building at seven o'clock. He said he expected me to be there waiting."

He laughed. "Before he left, he turned around and said, 'Oh, and be sure to wear a tux; it's a dress event.' Then he added, 'Don't bring your wife. I'm not ready to deal with her yet, and I want this to be a nice night for Jenna.' And that was that."

Jenna was incredulous. "How did you get your tux and get ready in time?"

"I rented one," he admitted, laughing again. "I knew if I went home, Evelyn might get wind of my plans."

Looking at Jenna across the table, he reached over and took one of her hands. "I wanted to come, Jenna. At first my anger at your friend's insults clouded my decision. I was mad at your friend for all he said. I had no intention of coming with him tonight, of letting him tell me what to do. But as the day wore on, I thought more and more about it and decided I really wanted to be here."

He sighed then. "In addition, I called Maury Berkowitz and talked with him. He referred me to your detective, Jake Saunders, and I had a talk with him, as well."

He shook his head. "Truly, Jenna, I wasn't aware of all Elliott had done to hurt you. I admit to being truly shocked by what I learned today. Elliott convinced Evelyn and me he only had one minor indiscretion and that he deeply regretted it. He said he wanted to try to make it up to you and that it would never happen again. He seemed so sincere, and I believed him." He looked down repentantly then.

Jenna leaned forward to put a hand over his on the table. "Elliott is a very artful liar, Daddy. No one should know that more than me. He is easy to believe, and he can be very charming. I believed in him for a long time, as well. It was hard for me at first to accept the truth about him."

"Thank you for that kindness," her father replied. "But as your friend Boyce Hart told me, it was my job as a father to find out what sort of man you were marrying, to have him checked out. And then when there was trouble later, I should have been more willing to support you than to condemn you."

Jenna grew thoughtful. "Boyce shouldn't have spoken to you like that. I mean, it's not as though...." She stopped in mid thought and caught herself before she said more.

Her father laughed. "Mr. Hart made it perfectly clear to me, Jenna, that there was only friendship and affection between you."

"He offered kindness to me when I badly needed kindness and friendship when I needed a good friend," Jenna told her father honestly.

Her father ran a hand through his dark hair. "Well, I'm glad he was there for you - since I wasn't and should have been." His eyes met hers. "I admit I questioned Boyce about your relationship, but I didn't get much out of him. I'll be honest in saying, though, that in my opinion, a man that flies off at another man on behalf of a woman must care deeply for her."

Seeing Jenna's blush and confusion, he added, "But that's your own business, Jenna. All I can say is that he seems a fine man." He cleared his throat. "However, if you should ever get further involved or committed with him - or with any man again - I'm going to have him thoroughly investigated before I give my approval to a serious commitment."

Jenna felt appalled. "You wouldn't really do that, would you?"

His eyes narrowed. "Absolutely, and I should have done it before. It might have saved you hurt and heartache. I'm going to be a lot more careful in future about accepting many things on face value alone. Your friend Boyce gave me a lot to think about."

"Will Mother be angry that you came tonight?" Jenna bit her lip in worry.

He lifted her chin with one finger. "You leave that to me, Jenna. I was proud to be here. I took pictures, too. I'll send you some copies when I get them developed. While I did my shooting, I sneaked a few of Boyce Hart. That seemed a memory I wanted to capture, too. Even if I never see him again, I'll sure never forget him."

Jenna murmured, "Yes, he has that way about him."

They visited at length, she and her father. Afterwards, he hailed a cab for them and took her home. She shyly invited him up to see her apartment, and, to her surprise, he said yes.

After climbing the stairs, they found a note from Carla stuck on the door. It read:

Dear J.C. ...

Come down when you get home and tell me about everything! And come get your beautiful roses, too. They arrived at the bookstore for you right before we closed. I'll enjoy them until you come to claim them.

John and I are so proud of you. Congratulations, ... Carla

"You sent me roses?" Jenna asked her father, smiling at him.

He shook his head regretfully. "No, but I wish I'd thought of it."

Later, as he prepared to leave, he turned to tweak her on the cheek. "Do you need anything, Little Daughter?"

Hearing her pet name from childhood touched her. "No. I'm fine, really." She smiled at him. "You being here tonight means everything, though. Thank you."

He took her hand in his. "I'd like to be around more," he confided to her. "Come have lunch with me one day soon, will you?"

"I will." She walked with him to the door.

"And, listen," he added, regarding her steadily. "Regarding that business about our disinheriting you; don't pay any attention to it. I told your mother I would never agree to that. If you need money for anything, you contact me. Will you do that? I don't want you going without. You've had enough problems already. I don't want you having more. Your friend Boyce told me, 'family is everything.'"

He hesitated, evidently thinking of something else.

Jenna was curious. "What else did Boyce tell you?"

"That loving is our obligation before God. He's right about that, too, you know," he answered thoughtfully. "Did you know his father was a preacher before he died?"

"Yes, he told me."

"I think the man taught that boy well," her father commented. He leaned over then to give her a light kiss on the cheek. "Take care, Daughter. And lock up after I'm gone."

She watched him leave in a daze, then closed the door and started to lock up before she remembered Carla's note and headed downstairs.

A short time later Jenna walked back into her apartment with her roses. They were from Boyce. He'd signed them 'from one heart to another,' the way they always signed their letters. They were a mixed bouquet of colors -

pink, yellow, red, white, and peach. Boyce wrote, 'I figured an artist needed more than one color.'

She loved them. From a cabinet in the living room, she retrieved a cut crystal vase to put them in and kept burying her nose in them while she arranged them.

Then, of course, she sat down at last and wept. Her day had just been too filled with raw emotions not to. Her eyes moved from the roses to her award plaque, still lying on the entry table. What a wonderful thing to be recognized for her art!

She paused, thoughtfully. Jason had noticed her too, not only as a colleague, but as a woman. That had been unexpected - but a nice compliment. To be pursued as a woman in her own right.

"However, everything paled when I saw Boyce and Daddy there." Jenna spoke her thoughts out loud as she often did. "Daddy acted so kind. I still can hardly believe that. And Boyce was responsible for him coming. He stood up to Daddy. That's incredible. He even rebuked my father. I can't believe someone would do that for me, care that much about me."

Tears dribbled down her cheeks now. "If I entertained even a thought about exploring a further relationship with Jason Brantley, it flew right out the window the moment I saw Boyce tonight. He still has a hold on my heart. Even after all this distance between us. How can that be?" She sniffed and reached for a tissue to blow her nose.

"I wish he'd stayed." She hugged a sofa cushion to her as she said the words. "It tore at my heart to see him tonight and not talk to him, touch him or hold him." This last admission brought on a new sweep of tears.

"But he did come." Jenna marveled. "All the way from Townsend, Tennessee. And he honored his promise to me by not even staying to speak to me."

She wept then for that wretched promise she made him agree to. And she cried bitterly that she had kept Boyce away from her all this time. For at this moment, Jenna knew she would give every rose in the world, every award she could gain, to just have him here with her.

Jenna considered calling him, but realized she didn't know where to find him. He might be in a hotel in the city or on a plane flying home. Knowing Boyce, he probably headed right back to the mountains. He didn't like New York. But he had come for her. She would remember that forever, that moment of looking up and seeing him standing at the back of the room.

Later, her dress clothes put carefully away, Jenna curled up in the middle of her bed and wondered how she would ever sleep. She hugged her pillow to her, thinking of Boyce as she used to think of youthful boyfriends - embracing her pillow and imagining it to be him. But the fantasies she indulged in were not girlish ones.

She bit her lip. "I wish I knew how Boyce felt. He never told me he loved me. He hinted at a future relationship a few times, but he never actually said he wanted to marry me, either."

She punched the pillow, frowning now. "I've been gone a long time. Maybe he doesn't feel the same about me. Maybe he doesn't want to be more deeply involved with a divorced woman. Maybe that's really why he didn't stay." She sighed. "He only signed the roses 'from one heart to another.' He didn't even sign them 'Love, Boyce.' That's not a good sign."

Doubts crowded her mind in the dark, depressing her. "I guess I won't know until I get to Orchard Hollow and see him again. I certainly don't want to be foolish and say anything to him until he says something to me."

After tossing and turning for an hour, Jenna decided to get up and call Boyce's house. Maybe he would be home. His answering machine spoke to her after the fourth ring. With a sigh of regret, she gathered her courage and left a short message: *Thanks for the roses. Thanks for touching my father's heart. Thanks for being there for me tonight, Boyce. I wish I could have seen you, but I will see you soon. Sam and Henry and I will be there on the 28th.*

She could have said more, but she didn't. She would be in Orchard Hollow in a week. She would know then - from how Boyce acted - how he felt.

Jenna climbed back into bed and, with a sigh, decided to try the game she and Sam so often played together – the game that always calmed her and helped her forget her problems. Only this time she wove herself stories about Orchard Hollow.

"The mountains never look the same in the Smokies," she murmured. "There are all shades of blue and purple on the far horizon, and closer up is every shade imaginable in the spring time. There's a sort of yellow green color at the first hint of spring ..."

She told stories to herself until she finally fell asleep. And in her dreams, she lived them.

Chapter 23

$\mathcal{B}$oyce realized he had reread the same order sheet several times and still didn't have a clue as to what he'd read. He pushed the papers on his desk back with distraction and ran his fingers through his hair in a gesture of pure frustration. He looked at the clock. It was late. He needed to go home.

Here it was Saturday night, and he was still down at the office in the gallery trying to catch up on his correspondence and accounts. Or so he told himself.

"What a lie." He admitted out loud. "The truth is I've been avoiding Jenna Martin all day."

She, Sam, and Henry had left to go back to New York this afternoon, and he just wasn't up to the goodbyes. He fabricated excuses about the need to go to Knoxville today for unavoidable meetings – just to avoid telling her goodbye in person. He actually drove into downtown Knoxville and met with some contacts of his at several of the galleries so he wouldn't be caught out a liar.

Jenna arrived in Townsend last Friday, and Boyce had been miserable the whole time. She, on the other hand, had been cheerful, loving, and kind - to him and to everyone. A whirl of activity commenced from the moment she arrived. Sam, of course, wanted to go everywhere and do everything. They took sightseeing trips, visited relatives and old friends of Sam's, and entertained an endless stream of guests at the cabin.

Boyce popped a pencil in half. "I think every danged person in Townsend and the surrounding area heard Sam Oliver would be in town and headed this way. Even strangers called asking if they could come by to have Sam sign a copy of one of his books."

It didn't help that Sam's newest adventure book had just come out. Everyone wanted to bring one over and have Sam sign it.

The cabin buzzed with people - a constant zoo. Jenna, with an easy, gracious charm, cooked and entertained for everyone like a pro. Raynelle, Zita, and some of Sam's other relatives and friends drizzled in and out of Sam's place in streams, bringing pies, casseroles, salads, cakes, and home-canned pickles, jellies, and vegetables.

"I never saw so much food," Boyce grumbled, remembering it. The presence of ongoing, home-cooked food actually drew more people in.

Boyce stood up and slammed a closet door shut in the shop. "There wasn't a danged time I dropped over that someone wasn't there - visiting, picking and singing, eating, and enjoying themselves."

At any other time, Boyce would have been delighted with all this activity, but this time was different. He wanted to have Jenna all to himself after all their time apart. To steal sweet times alone with her. And it just hadn't happened.

He looked out the gallery window toward the half moon hanging in the darkened sky. "Part of the reason I didn't have any time with her was my own danged fault."

Boyce kicked at a cabinet in frustration. "I wasn't sure where I stood with her after all this time. That message she left me on the answering machine after I'd been in New York sounded pretty casual."

He mimicked it. "'Thanks for being there for me … I wish I could have seen you.' It was pretty informal. I hated to make a fool of myself professing my love like some lovesick swain and have her look at me like I was crazy. So I made a bargain with myself to keep a little distance from her when she came down." He snorted. "As though I needed to make an effort."

Boyce raked his hands through his hair again. "I knew she was only going to be here for a week before going back to New York." He walked over to the window to look out at the moon. "And why shouldn't she go back? Her illustration work is taking off now. She has her own place and her own friends there, like Carla and John. She's thrilled about Carla expecting a baby - all excited about being an aunt."

Jenna carried on about this upcoming event until Boyce could have screamed. All he could think about when she chatted away about being an auntie was how much he'd like her to be carrying his child. The pictures in his mind simply tormented him, and he despised himself for his thoughts. He wanted to grab her up and carry her off and away from everyone - and hated himself because he knew he couldn't.

"She changed while she was away, too." Boyce paced the room, talking to himself. "In all honesty, I'm proud of the changes in her. She walks and talks with more confidence now. She's more at ease with herself and with others. That timid girl always trying so hard to please, trying so hard to be what she thought everyone wanted her to be, is gone."

Gone, too, were the quick tears and the downcast eyes. "She's even more comfortable with her talent." He smiled at that memory. "She actually talked to people about her art, not belittling it any more."

Despite his grief, Boyce had to admit he liked this new stronger version of Jenna. But, at the same time, he missed the more timid and unsure Jenna, too. She had needed him more. This new Jenna seemed able to take him or leave him. It was what he had always feared.

He prowled the room restlessly. What was he going to do with himself now that she was gone?

"Maybe Dean was right," he told himself. "Maybe I should just go up there to New York and get her, make her come back here with me." He heaved a deep sigh, trying to think about his options. Wondering if he really had any at all.

When Jenna first came last Friday, the two of them had a brief time to sit out on the front porch to talk. Granted a houseful of people milled around in the cabin behind them and kept coming in and out to interrupt, but they did enjoy a short space of private time. She told him how much she appreciated him coming up to New York for the awards ceremony. He tried to diminish that by saying he needed to come up to New York anyway to see a dealer at one of the galleries. Then he mentally berated himself for not just telling her he had come solely to see her.

"You looked incredibly beautiful that night," he said. "I was so proud when you walked up on that stage smiling. You looked out over the audience and spoke to them with such poise, just like getting up in that way was an every day thing for you. I really felt like giving a war whoop."

She laughed. "I think I was too pleased and surprised to be nervous. And then I looked back and saw you - and my father beside you. I thought my knees would fall out from under me. Didn't you think how it might affect me to just look back there and see the two of you? To have no warning that you would be there? That both of you would be there?"

He leaned toward her. "I wanted to surprise you. Seeing your father was something I hadn't planned. The idea just came to me when I got to New York. I wanted to have a few words with the man. And then our conversation led to a little more."

Her dark eyes found his. "Yes, I heard about that." She gave him a chastising look. "I'm not sure it was really your place to lecture my father in that way."

Boyce leaned back in his rocking chair. "Somebody needed to, Jenna. I won't apologize that it was me. He needed to hear what he heard."

She glanced sideways at him. "Actually, he said the same thing, which surprised me," she admitted. "But don't start getting overly smug over that fact."

He grinned at her. It seemed like old times with her just then - until Raynelle came out on the porch and wanted to know where to find the can opener in the kitchen. And, of course, Jenna got up to go help her find it.

She smiled at him as she let herself in the front door. "You know I'll never forget you doing that for me, Boyce." And then she was gone.

Their times panned out like that all week – in just bits and spurts. He couldn't get enough sense of how Jenna felt to know if it was safe to move in closer. And her cheerfulness confused him.

They all went to Gatlinburg and played tourist. Jenna had never been before, and Sam wanted Henry to see the colorful town at the base of the mountains. The four of them poked in and out of the shops, laughing over the novelties and the endless array of gift items for sale. Boyce had wanted to take Jenna to Gatlinburg on his own someday but now he had to share the time with Sam and Henry. It had been like that the entire week. Everything they did had been as a foursome.

Before the week was out, Boyce's friends and family began giving him looks of sympathy. They saw Jenna acting bright, gay, and happy, while they all knew he had been grumpy and moody for months. He knew they hoped to see he and Jenna deepening their relationship – not running around like casual friends. The week reminded Boyce of high school when your friends felt sorry for you when your steady broke up with you. Everyone was just a little too nice to him. It ticked him off. He hated for people to feel sorry for him.

Of course, not everyone acted tactful and discreet about what they thought. When he stopped by the store Thursday to get the mail, Charlotte was working in the gallery. As soon as the last customer left, she cornered him.

"Well, Boyce Hart." She put her hands on her hips with annoyance. "Are you just going to let Jenna come and go and never make a move to change things between you? She's been so blithe and happy down here; it's been downright confusing to me to watch it. I think she's just settled her mind to you going your way and she going hers and has decided to make the best of it."

She glared at him. "You know, she's not the kind of woman that's going to come and beg you to take her. A woman doesn't much respect a man that won't say what's on his mind. I thought you had a little more gumption, Boyce. You know we all want Jenna to stay."

"Look, Charlotte," he countered sullenly. "I haven't had a moment with Jenna since she's been down here. All her time has been taken up with Sam and Henry and with all the people coming in and out of the house all the time."

"Pooh." Charlotte smarted her reply back. "Those are just excuses. I've watched you around her. You've been holding back. You haven't acted around her like a man in love. You've acted like a nice, good friend. If you're not careful, that's exactly what you're going to end up being."

She gave him an irritated look. " I've personally managed to have some nice long talks with Jenna. And I haven't had any trouble getting her alone, so I don't know what your problem is. But I can tell you that she is beginning to get her confidence. That Jason Brantley has been making moves on her, too, just like I told you he would. And he won't be the only one for very long. You're about to make yourself a big, foolish mistake by fiddling about here."

Even Boyce's mother had words with him. She had them all over to the house for lunch one day, and took Boyce quietly aside before everyone left.

"Son, what's going on here?" she asked. "I thought you and this girl were developing feelings for each other. The last time you had her here - still a married woman then - the two of you could hardly keep your eyes off each other. Now, you're acting awkward and moody, not at all like yourself. And she's acting like she has just dipped into the elixir of life. I've never seen a girl so merry and happy. I don't understand it. Is she just happy to have her divorce behind her?"

"Maybe," Boyce grumbled in response. "I don't know. I can't figure it out either."

His mother studied him. "Have you talked to her about it?"

He kicked at a rock in the driveway. "No, but I guess I'm going to have to."

Yet, somehow another day slipped away in a flurry of activity and suddenly Friday night arrived – and Boyce found himself at a goodbye party.

A big crowd spilled out of Sam's cabin and into the front yard tonight and music and laughter filled the air. Boyce's brother-in-law, Reece Wakefield, and his band entertained everyone out on the front porch - picking and singing all of Sam's favorite songs - and a crowd of folks sat in lawn chairs all over the front yard enjoying the warm summer evening and the good music. Food sat piled on tables inside the cabin, left over from a potluck earlier. All the neighbors from Orchard Hollow had been invited, as well as what looked like about half of Townsend and Wear's Valley's population.

Boyce felt ashamed that he couldn't enjoy the pleasure of such a fine evening. These were the best of times in the mountains, one of the reasons he loved to live here. But his discontent overshadowed everything else tonight. Jenna would be leaving tomorrow, and he'd had no time with her at all.

They had corresponded for months. She had poured out her heart in her letters, told him everything in her life. He expected a greater degree of intimacy when she got here. Granted, he hadn't expected her to come down here and throw herself in his arms and declare her undying love. Though that would certainly have been nice. But he had expected more. He expected her to watch him as he did her, to let him know by her ways that she was thinking of him, that she was aware of him. Instead, her attention stayed focused on Sam. It was Sam she watched, Sam she tried so hard to please, Sam she worried over. Boyce loved the man almost as much as a father himself, but over the last week he almost resented him.

Sam even seemed to be somewhat aware of his feelings. He actually winked at Boyce one day when he found him scowling at him.

Plus, Sam and Jenna passed frequent conspiratorial looks, like they shared some private secret together. Perhaps no one else noticed that. But Boyce did. It made him feel like an outsider. And it annoyed the heck out of him, too.

He leaned against a tree trunk as darkness fell, listening to the music and enjoying the evening as much as he could. Jenna flitted in and out of the house for a while, bringing different people drinks, taking some of the children in for the bathroom. Now, she leaned over Sam's chair talking to him softly. Sam reached up and patted her face sweetly. Boyce felt another of those stabs of jealousy. He shook his head at himself. It was a wretched shame when a man found himself jealous of an old man in a wheelchair where his girl was concerned.

Jenna started to mill around in the crowd then, talking to people. She seemed to be enjoying herself. It irked Boyce just to watch her. Why wasn't she as broken up as he was? Wasn't she thinking at all that she would be leaving here tomorrow? Didn't she care?

Jenna had worked her way over to where Boyce stood now. After speaking to the Lansky's, she turned to listen to the band as they played an old mountain tune called *Down in the Valley*. He slipped over and took her hand.

"Let's go for a walk," he whispered.

Her eyes widened. "But I'm the hostess. I need to be here."

"You won't be missed that much for a few minutes," he told her insistently. He practically dragged her around toward the back path that led away from the cabin and down toward the creek.

Even in the night air a thread of her honeysuckle scent drifted over to him, swamping his senses. He tucked his arm into hers. "I've hardly seen anything of you this week, Jenna."

"Don't be silly." She gave his arm a friendly squeeze. "You've seen me every day I've been here."

"That's not what I mean," he answered huskily.

They'd left behind the lights and voices of the party now, and they could hear the faint sounds of the music to their backs and the sounds of the creek ahead. Boyce stopped to turn Jenna toward him and let his hands drift down her arms and around her back.

He pulled her into him, and with a deep sigh she leaned softly up against his chest. The feel of her was wonderful. And when they began to kiss, Boyce's blood began to pound in his veins.

She acted bolder now, which surprised him and excited him. She nibbled at his lips and slipped her hands up under the back of his shirt. His own hands wandered over her and soon their breath quickened, their heartbeat accelerated, and their knees weakened from the needs surging through them.

"I've missed you, Jenna," he whispered against her mouth. "Say you missed me, too. This whole week has been an agony seeing you, being around you, but not being able to be alone with you."

She pulled away a little to look up at him in the moonlight. "I sort of got the impression you were holding yourself at arm's length. Weren't you, Boyce?"

The dark brought out his honesty. "I had thought to keep it light while you were here. I thought it might be easier on us both when you had to leave again."

"You thought that, did you?" There was a touch of humor behind her voice.

He felt annoyed. "All right, I thought that for me." His voice sounded more gruff than he intended. "I had a hard enough time the last time you left, Jenna. I was trying to make it easier on myself."

"And has it been easier?" She gave him a soft look. "Has it made it easier for you by keeping your distance?"

"No, it's been a misery," he muttered, gathering her back in his arms. "It's been torture all week seeing you, wanting you. And it will be an even worse agony when you leave tomorrow, Jenna."

"Is there something you need to tell me, Boyce?" She nuzzled her lips up against his neck. His skin and senses came alive with pleasure.

"You know how I feel," he answered her huskily, taking her lips with his again to show her.

"No, I don't." She pulled away again to look up at him. "I'm not sure I do know how you feel, Boyce. I've been hoping all week you would tell me."

"You want me to say it, don't you?" His voice sounded cross, even to him. "You want me to tell you that I love you. Surely you know that by now, Jenna."

"No." She looked sad. "How can I know what you've never put into words?"

He took her hands in his, feeling regretful now. "I've loved you almost since I first met you, Jenna. How could you not know that? Haven't I shown you in a million ways?"

"Ways are not as good as words sometimes, Boyce." She smiled at him. "Words are magic, like paint to paper. They supply the color and the wonder. I like the words."

He looked down into her gypsy-brown eyes and was lost. "Well, then Ms. Martin, let me say the words again. I love you deeply and sincerely with all my heart. You fill my mind and senses when you are with me and when you are away. I have few moments when you are not in my thoughts. You haunt my steps. I imagine you when you are not with me. When you are with me, you are like a drug. I find I only want more and more of you."

He swept her back into his arms then, to show her in other ways how he felt.

"And can you say the same, Jenna?" he asked, putting his heart all the way out on the limb now.

She looked thoughtful. "I have fought loving you," she told him candidly. "At first because I had no right to and later because I was afraid. Then I hesitated again because I wanted to become stronger. I wanted to be more worthy of being loved."

He kissed her nose.

"You're a ninny," he told her. "You were always worthy of being loved."

She dropped her eyes from his. "Maybe, but I didn't feel so. I was like a little ship all battered and bruised from a cruel storm."

He smiled at the picture she painted with her words. "And so are you fixed now?"

"Yes, I think I am." She smiled up at him sweetly.

His hands came up to cup her face. "You still haven't answered my question," he prompted her, rubbing his fingers softly over her lips.

He heard her breathing quicken and her answer came out in a whisper. "It's hard to think rationally when you do that."

"Good. I don't want you to think rationally." Boyce threaded his fingers through her hair, catching the scent of her shampoo on the night air. "I want you to think with your heart."

"Heart to heart?" She sent a soft smile his way.

He caught her eyes with his. "I'd like it to be Boyce Hart to Jenna Hart." There, he'd said it.

She touched his face with wonder. "I do love you, Boyce Hart. Surely you know I do. I knew it for certain and sure at the awards dinner when I looked out over the audience and saw you there. I hadn't had a chance to prepare my defenses, you see. And my heart just cried out over all my logic. That's when I knew."

"So, what's next?" He stroked her back.

"Sam has to go back to New York," she told him.

His voice tightened. "And what about you?"

She turned her brown eyes to his. "What do you want me to do, Boyce? I haven't been sure."

Her question annoyed him. "I want you to stay. I'll pay for plane fare for Sam and Henry to fly back. Heck, I'll pay for someone to drive them back. But I want you to stay, Jenna."

She stroked her hand down his face. "You mean you want the 'happily ever after'?" she asked him teasingly.

He wrapped her up in his arms again. "Yes, the happily ever after and the happily right *now*."

She pulled away, frowning slightly. "I'll have to see to Sam first, Boyce. I have to see Sam back to New York. When that's all done, I'll talk to you about the happily ever after. Tomorrow is an important day for Sam. He'll have a lot of goodbyes to say. He may not be able to come back for a long time. If ever. I need to be with him."

Anger sliced through Sam and that green edge of jealousy again.

"Fine," he said with an edge. "You just take Sam back to New York. You be with him tomorrow and on the trip back. You finish out things the way you and Sam planned so it will be special. And you give me a call back in New York when you think you can spare the time."

Her eyebrows jerked up in surprise, but Boyce paid no attention to it. He'd been put neatly in his place. He turned and started to stride back up the path toward the cabin.

"Boyce?" she called. "I think you've misunderstood ..."

"I think your hostess duties are calling you, Jenna," he remarked coldly, interrupting her.

She didn't answer, and he didn't look back.

Resentment slashing through him, Boyce stalked through the side of the woods and cut across the road below the festivities at Sam's to his own place. When he got there, he whistled for Patrick and then slipped out his back door. He started up a familiar mountain trail behind his cabin, needing to walk off some of his frustrations. It didn't matter that it was dark. He and Patrick knew the way. And he just needed to be alone.

Boyce shook his head as he walked through the night. He'd laid out his heart to Jenna, even proposed, and she told him it all would have to wait for Sam. She had to see to Sam; she had to go back to New York. She hadn't even said if she would marry him.

"So fine." He ground the words out. "I guess I'll wait again. And maybe she'll call after a while. Maybe she'll write me some more letters." He kicked at a stone in the path. "But it's not what I wanted, and I can't pretend that it is."

The whole week had been one long, exasperating experience, and at the end, when it looked like things were going to work out like he wanted, everything had gone sour. She had conditions. She still insisted she had to go back to New York. She wanted to put Sam first. It rankled him. And it ruined everything.

The next morning, when he went over to say his polite goodbyes and learned Jenna was in the shower, he felt a sense of relief. He knew he could avoid seeing her.

He told Sam and Henry his fib about needing to go into Knoxville.

"Jenna will be down in a minute," Sam said to him, wheeling his chair over closer to Boyce. "If you can wait a few minutes, you can see her."

Boyce made a point of studying his watch as though considering it.

"No, I'd better get on off." He avoided Sam's eyes. "You tell her I stopped by and why I had to leave. She said she'd call me when she got back to New York."

"She said that, did she?" Sam looked amused. "Just in that way she said she'd call you when she got back to New York?"

Boyce, confused, wasn't sure how he was supposed to answer that. He found his annoyance rising again.

"She said she had to see you back to New York." His response sounded too curt. He knew it as soon as it was out. "You are going back to New York, aren't you, Sam?"

"That I am," he said, smiling as though at some secret joke.

Boyce scowled. He wasn't in the mood for any of Sam's jokes today.

Sam patted Boyce on the arm then and grinned at him widely. "You have a good day, Boyce. You have a good day. And when you get back, stop over here at the cabin and check on things for me. Be sure I didn't leave any lights on - or leave anything behind. Would you do that?"

Boyce's anger softened. "You know I will take care of things for you, Sam." He shook Sam's hand with warmth. "Don't worry. I'll take care of everything. I always do. You know that."

"I'm counting on that attribute in you." Sam reached out to shake Boyce's hand firmly. "You're a good man, Boyce Hart. I've always thought you deserved life's best."

Boyce felt churlish now as he remembered that warm goodbye from Sam. He felt the first twang of guilt. It had been wrong of him to be jealous of Sam. And it was kind of Jenna to care that Sam had a good time down here. As she'd explained, with Sam's poor health, who knew when he might be strong enough to make the trip again.

Boyce sighed heavily. He might have over-reacted a little through all of this. "I just didn't want to let her go again," he said out loud. "I just didn't want to let her go."

He closed up the gallery with a heavy heart and started for home.

When he pulled up at his house at the end of Orchard Hollow Road and looked over to Sam's place, he saw a small shaft of light coming through the front window.

He shook his head. "I guess Sam left a light on at his place. I'd better go over and turn it off and check on things."

He got his key out as he started across the lawn and soon let himself in Sam's front door. On the couch, stretched out asleep in front of a small fire, lay Jenna.

Boyce stopped dead in his tracks for a minute, thinking he might be having a fantasy. Then he slipped over to the sofa, and got down on his knees beside her.

Her shiny, dark hair was down, lying about her shoulders, and the firelight played over her gypsy gold skin. Merciful heavens, she looked so beautiful. What was she doing here? Had something happened to Sam?

"Jenna?" he said to her softly. "Jenna, wake up. It's Boyce." He watched her eyes open sleepily, and then watched her mouth curve in a sweet smile.

"Is everything all right, Jenna?" His voice was anxious now. "Has anything happened to Sam?"

"No, Sam is fine." She reached up to touch his face softly. "I saw to Sam just like I told you I needed to. We made it a special last day, and then I put him and Henry on the 3:00 pm flight straight back to New York."

"You decided to stay for me?" Boyce asked, touched and incredulous.

"I'd always planned to stay." Jenna yawned slightly. "I meant to tell you but I never seemed to have a chance. And you kept acting so stand-offish. I wasn't sure how you felt. I started to think maybe you wouldn't want me to stay."

She sighed. "I was getting ready to tell you last night when you got mad about Sam."

A spurt of annoyance shot through Boyce. He jumped up to put space between he and Jenna and then turned angry eyes on her. "You knew this whole week you would be staying on here for a while longer and you didn't see fit to tell me?"

Boyce paced across the room. "Do you know the agonizing week I've been through – thinking you were only here for a short week and then leaving? Do you know how awful it was for me - as the week drifted by full of people and events without any private time for us? Do you have any idea how I felt? I was hurting, Jenna. If you'd told me you were staying a little longer after Sam left it would have really helped."

She bit her lip. "Don't be angry, Boyce." She sat up on the couch and pushed her hair out of her face. "I meant to tell you."

"Did Sam know all this week that you were staying on after he left?"
She nodded.

"Well, great. You both knew and neither one of you bothered to tell me. And both of you knew I was hurting and having a hard week."

She wrinkled her brow. "You're seeing this like a conspiracy, but it wasn't. In fact, I came looking for you last night – after you got mad - to tell you but I couldn't find you. I even told Sam last night that I was going to tell you first thing this morning – and then you left."

Boyce frowned. "And Sam didn't bother to fill me in?"

She looked puzzled. "He said you had to go to Knoxville but that he'd asked you to come by here on your way home tonight." She smiled then. "He said our story would be a good one we'd all enjoy telling someday."

Boyce snapped his answer back. "Well don't expect me to jump up and down because I got to have a part in a cute and amusing story I knew nothing about."

He kicked at the woodpile beside the fireplace in frustration. "Especially when apparently I was the *only* actor that didn't know he was in a play at all."

Boyce heard Jenna sigh deeply. "I'm sorry, Boyce. But if you had told me earlier in the week that you cared, I would have shared with you sooner. And last night, when it was finally the right time … you got so upset about me needing to see to Sam that I didn't get to tell you everything I wanted to."

"There's more?" His reply sounded sarcastic, even to him.

She crossed her arms, giving him an irritated look. "Are you even going to let me tell you the rest, Boyce Hart?"

"Maybe," he answered, poking at the ashes in the fireplace. "If you'll tell me how long you're going to stay before you go back. I'd like to have the truth in front of me this time. And no more games."

"I'm not going back at all."

He turned to her, stunned, and searched her face. "What about your job? What about your apartment and your friends?"

She smiled at him. "I'll still have my job and my friends. And I'm keeping my apartment for times I need to be in New York. My company is still there, and my family, and there will be times I will want to go back."

She twisted her hair up and secured it with a clip. "Park Press has said I can do my work from here. They just want me to keep on working!" She smiled.

Boyce frowned, trying to understand. "So, Sam is just going to let you stay here at his place indefinitely? Isn't that rather an imposition on your part?"

"Oh, stop being so cross." She stood up to face him. "I won't be imposing on Sam at all. This is my place now, Boyce. I bought it."

Boyce knew his mouth dropped open. "Sam Oliver let you buy the place he and Frances built?" His eyes narrowed. "I find that hard to believe."

"Well, there are some conditions." She crossed the room toward Boyce. "We're sort of partners in the cabin for now, meaning that Sam gets to come down whenever he can and that he'll still have a stake here for as long as he lives. But after that, the cabin is mine."

"How can you afford it?" asked Boyce. "A place like this in the mountains doesn't come cheap."

Jenna sighed then. "Actually Elliott bought it for me," she announced with a giggle. "Of course, he doesn't exactly know that. But, indirectly, it's true."

Boyce crossed his arms, scowling now. "I think you'd better explain," he demanded.

She leaned against an arm chair. "You see, Sam agreed to drop assault charges against Elliott if he agreed to two stipulations. First – that Elliot move out of the apartment building where he and Sam live. And second - that Elliott pay a settlement award if Sam would drop the charges."

"He blackmailed Elliott?" Boyce was shocked.

"Well, now, that's not exactly the way Sam and Maury put it." Jenna lowered her lashes. "You see, Sam wanted Elliott out of the apartment. But Sam and Maury also wanted me to sue for more damages in the divorce, and I didn't want to. So they decided that Elliott would pay a little settlement money through Sam. That seemed fair to them."

"And this seemed fair to you?" He was surprised.

A little frown creased her forehead. "I didn't know anything about it until Sam told me the night of the awards banquet. Sam said he knew I wouldn't take the money, so he said he was giving me the cabin and he was taking the money. He's leaving it in a special fund for Henry and Mary for all the care they've given them. He worries they won't have enough retirement saved up to live comfortably after he's gone."

"Good Lord," Boyce marveled. "That man just never stops being an amazement to me."

Jenna gave him an appealing look and started toward him. "So you're not mad now, Boyce?"

"No, I'm still mad, Jenna," Boyce said, backing away from her. "And I'm going to go home to sleep on all of this now. You and Sam played a dirty trick on me. You both kept things from me that I think you should have told me much earlier. It would have saved me a lot of grief and anxiety."

She dropped her lower lip in disappointment. "Will I see you tomorrow?" she asked tentatively.

"I'll think about it." He let himself out of the door, emotions warring.

He was halfway across the yard when he heard her voice calling out to him. "Boyce?"

He paused, a little in exasperation and a little in delight at all the memories her calling out to him in the dark brought back to mind. This had always been the pattern with them since the first.

"What do you want, Jenna?" he called back quietly.

"I want the happily ever after, Boyce. Do you think we could do something about that Hart and Hart suggestion you made *soon*?" Her voice slipped into a whisper. "I don't like sleeping alone any more."

He groaned. Mercy, she had a way of getting to him like no other woman.

"Yeah, we'll think about that and try to plan something real soon," he answered her. "I don't like to sleep alone any more, either."

Her soft laugh in response tantalized his senses.

He paused. "What will you do with your new mountain cabin after we hang up one shingle over here at my place?"

She laughed. "Let Sam come whenever he wants and let my friends come here to visit. I want them to see Orchard Hollow. I know they'll love it. It will be nice for us to always have a guest house."

He looked toward where she stood – framed in the light of the doorway. So beautiful. "Sounds like you've been thinking this all out."

"Yes, I have." Her voice was silky and seductive. "I've been thinking it all out on those long nights when I couldn't sleep. When I was thinking of you."

He shook his head. "You're asking for trouble talking like that to me, Jenna. It's very late, and we haven't had a proper wedding ceremony yet."

"Well, we could practice around the edges a little," she suggested. "I made a nice fire just like you taught me. We could sit on the couch together and watch it and talk."

"That we could." He let the last of his anger go and turned around to walk back toward the house, grinning now. "We can talk heart to heart."

Her soft giggle floated out over the night air as he started across the lawn toward her. Oddly, Boyce's last thought before he reached her porch was that his life was unlikely to ever be uneventful again.

Epilogue

On a fine Sunday afternoon in late September, two months later, Boyce Hart and Jenna Martin were married in the Wildwood Church in Wear's Valley. A few folks might have said it was too soon after Jenna's divorce, while others said it wasn't soon enough.

Boyce wore a black tux, and Jenna wore a long, simple white lawn dress, trimmed in old lace. On her hair, she wore a garland of multi-colored roses with a swath of veil trailing down behind it, and in her arms, she carried a mixed bouquet of roses.

The little church was packed with friends and family. Boyce's brother Charles was the best man and Jenna's friend Carla was the matron of honor. Tyler Dean served as the ring bearer, and one of Boyce's little nieces, Rita, was the flower girl. Rita and Tyler Dean almost got into a skirmish coming down the aisle because Tyler Dean wanted to help her throw down the petals before the bride, but other than that the wedding went smoothly. Jenna's father proudly gave her away. Sam, Henry, Mary, and Carla's husband, John, attended from New York, but Jenna's mother didn't make it down - reportedly due to ill health.

The reception was held on the lawn behind Boyce's mother's house. Charles and Boyce built a brush arbor for a covered setting for the tables - soon loaded with food and refreshments brought by all - and Reece Wakefield's band provided entertainment well into the night. The women of the family draped the arbor and many of the trees with white lights, and the whole backyard looked like it was filled with stars. At least that's what Alice and Sharon said. They wore their new Easter dresses, since Jenna hadn't gotten to see them in the spring.

Loreen and Betty Jo McFee were determined that they were going to catch the bouquet this time. Alice Graham, visiting the wedding with Scott and Vivian Jamison, sat on a bench well back from the festivities. She had been spotlighted for inadvertently catching a bouquet at the last wedding she attended in the valley and didn't want to repeat the experience. However, the bouquet sailed across the air and plopped into her lap, anyway, only to be snatched up immediately by the McFee girls.

They claimed Alice catching the bouquet wasn't legitimate, and they tussled over the bouquet while many of the guests gasped. Alice remained totally unperturbed through it all.

When Doris McFee broke up her daughters' squabble and tried to give Alice back the bouquet, Alice refused to take it. She agreed with Loreen and Betty Jo that she hadn't been standing with the young girls to catch the bouquet and that it wasn't right that she caught it. She sweetly suggested the McFee girls should split the bouquet so they could both enjoy the flowers and share the memory.

Ruth Hart whispered to her daughter, Susan, that a generous heart like Alice's was a blessing to see. "Blessings will come back to Alice Graham for all the love she gives away," Ruth said. "You mark my word, Susan. Something good is going to come that girl's way."

———————————————

To find out if blessings do come Alice Graham's way, watch for the next book in the Smoky Mountain series, entitled *For Six Good Reasons,* set in the Greenbrier area. After that, plan to take a trip to Gatlinburg to meet Delia Walker and Tanner Cross in the fourth novel, *Delia's Place.*

ABOUT THE AUTHOR

Dr. Lin Stepp is a native Tennessean, a business woman, and an educator. She is on faculty at Tusculum College where she teaches a Research writing sequel and several Psychology courses, including Developmental and Educational Psychology. Her business background includes over 20 years in marketing, sales, production art, and regional publishing. She and her husband began their own sales and publications business, S & S Communications, in 1989. The company publishes a regional fishing and hunting guide magazine and has a sports sales subsidiary handling sports products and media sales in East Tennessee. She has editorial and writing experience in regional magazines and in the academic field. *Tell Me About Orchard Hollow* is the second of twelve contemporary Southern romances in a series of linked novels set in the Smoky Mountains of East Tennessee and North Carolina.

AUTHOR'S WEBSITE

Special thanks go to my talented daughter, Katherine Stepp,who created my author's website. Visit me there to read more about my life and interests and to keep up with signings, events, and future publication dates for the continuing books in The Smoky Mountain series.WEBSITE ADDRESS: http://www.linstepp.com

CPSIA information can be obtained
at www.ICGtesting.com
Printed in the USA
BVOW09s1153210517
484765BV00001B/24/P